Praise for *A Proposal They Can't Refuse*

the first of Natalie Caña's Vega Family Love Stories

Oprah Daily—"The 28 Most Anticipated Romance Books of 2022"

Latinx in Publishing—"2022 Latinx Romance & Women's Fiction to Add to Your TBR"

Entertainment Weekly—"Romance Authors Share Red-Hot Book Recommendations"

HipLatina—"10 Latinx Romance Authors to Keep on Your Radar"

Parade—"Parade Picks—Summertime Hits"

"Caña has cooked up a romance that succeeds from Page 1…. A sizzling, emotional romance with a generous helping of family and culture."
—*Kirkus Reviews* (starred)

"The well-written storyline, fast-paced plot, deft characterizations, and delectable descriptions will keep readers turning the pages long into the night."
—*Library Journal* (starred, Debut of the Month)

"Flawless… [Caña delivers] diverse true-to-life characters that leap off the page with originality and heart."
—*Booklist* (starred)

"This delightful mix of food, familia, and culture will leave readers hungry for more."
—*Publishers Weekly* (starred)

"An utterly charming romance that pays homage to the importance of culture, family, and friendship, *A Proposal They Can't Refuse* is a surefire winner!"
—Mia Sosa, *USA TODAY* bestselling author of *The Worst Best Man*

"Natalie Caña's debut will leave you smiling, hungry, and eager to read her next book!"
—Denise Williams, bestselling author of *How to Fail at Flirting*

"¡Wepa! Familia meddling, swoony friends-to-lovers angst, and quick-witted banter combine for a deliciously delightful debut!"
—Priscilla Oliveras, *USA TODAY* bestselling author of *Island Affair*

NATALIE CAÑA

A DISH BEST SERVED HOT

mira

mira™

ISBN-13: 978-0-7783-3350-0

A Dish Best Served Hot

Recycling programs
for this product may
not exist in your area.

For questions and comments about the quality of this book, please contact us at
CustomerService@Harlequin.com.

Mira
22 Adelaide St. West, 41st Floor
Toronto, Ontario M5H 4E3, Canada
BookClubbish.com

Printed in U.S.A.

"There can be no love without justice."
—bell hooks

This book is for those who fight to add both justice and love to our world.

PROLOGUE

Santiago Vega II—known to family and friends as Junior, much to his annoyance—took his time getting back to the front office after dropping off paperwork for Miss Wallis, the school secretary. He loved it when the halls of his high school were empty and mostly silent. It gave him a sense of calm he never got otherwise. Not when he was the oldest of a five-child family who lived in a tiny apartment directly above the restaurant his family ran. The restaurant where his grandpa's band loved to play music at all hours of the day, because it was always filled to the gills with people from the neighborhood. Junior was surrounded by people all the time—loud, demanding people—so he enjoyed moments of quiet stillness whenever he could.

That made it all the more annoying when he heard raised voices down the hallway.

"You better stay away from her!"

"You two aren't even together anymore."

"She's mine!"

Oh great. Two idiots were about to fight over a girl and Junior had to go that way to get back to his work-study.

Junior turned the corner to one of the side hallways and stopped dead in his tracks. It was worse than two idiot guys. It was Jose Mendez, one of the largest offensive linemen on their high school football team, and Lola León, the biggest trouble-maker in the school.

Lola was constantly in the office when he was there, but when Junior was there helping out during his free period, she was al-ways there to talk to the principal after getting kicked out of one class or another. Sure, he didn't know her well, she was a junior to his senior, but it wasn't hard for Junior to tell why she was constantly pissing everyone off. She had a terrible attitude and a mouth to accompany it. She said what she wanted and did what she wanted without a care for anyone around her.

As if to prove his point she opened her mouth and said, "Aww, is your fragile male ego hurt because she liked my kiss more than yours?"

Junior's eyebrows rose. He'd heard that Lola liked girls, but he'd assumed those were ignorant rumors based on how she dressed—in baggy clothes that looked like she'd taken them from a large man's closet. At least, he'd hoped that was the case after seeing her for the first time in the office a few weeks ago. It didn't matter that he had no intention of actually talking to the pretty girl. A part of him was selfish enough to be hopeful.

Her taunt seemed to be the last straw for Jose. "Bitch. I'll give you something to do with that smart mouth of yours." He rushed her and crowded her into a corner before she could dodge. His hand tangled into her long dark hair and pulled it hard.

Junior jumped into action without thinking. There was no way he was going to sit back and let someone be hurt. Especially not a young woman who didn't even reach Jose's shoulder. He charged forward, trying to remember everything his abuelo had taught him about taking down someone bigger than you.

He wrapped his forearm around Jose's neck and locked it into place with the crook of his other arm. He moved his head to one side just in case Jose decided to try to headbutt him. He looked down at Lola, whose head was pulled back exposing her neck and a pair of wide brown eyes.

Junior didn't think he'd ever seen her look scared. Pissed off and scowling yes, but not afraid. For some reason her fear released a new level of anger in him. Junior was quiet and serious, but not usually angry. Except at that moment he was livid.

"Let. Her. Go." He growled in a voice he'd only ever let out when someone was messing with one of his younger siblings. When Jose didn't immediately do as he said, Junior tightened his grip.

Jose let go of Lola's hair to grab Junior's arm with both hands and attempt to pull him off. Somehow he couldn't. Instead he wheezed.

"Get behind me," Junior barked to Lola, who was rubbing her no-doubt tender head.

It took her a second, but eventually she did.

As soon as she was behind him, Junior started to loosen his grip around Jose's neck. However, he knew the impulsive hothead would do something in retaliation, so, at the same time he released his neck, he kicked Jose in the back of the knee.

He jumped out of the way as Jose went down coughing and rubbing his throat. Then he spun on his heel, grabbed Lola's hand, and began running in the opposite direction. He wanted to put as much distance as possible between them and Jose.

His head swiveled back and forth, trying to find a place for them to lie low, before he grabbed the handle to a door and swung it open. He herded Lola through the empty classroom door, pulling it closed behind them, and backed them both away from the narrow glass window. A second later Junior heard uneven pounding footprints rush past the door. He stayed silent and still until the footsteps faded.

Finally, he turned his attention to the girl next to him. He took a deep breath and told himself to ignore how pretty she was, but wasn't prepared for the way her eyes would snare him as soon as they met his. Her eyes were a reddish brown that made him think of lava the moment it hit air and began to cool—dark around the edges and still burning bright in the middle. Junior lost his ability to breathe. He couldn't do anything but stare.

She was the one to break the silence. "I think he's gone," she whispered.

"He'll double back," Junior murmured.

"How do you know?"

"Because he's not one to let things go."

That caused her to make a face and a sound almost like a snort.

Junior noticed a dusting of freckles across the bridge of her screwed-up nose and pale cheeks. He blinked in confusion. It was just so incongruous for Lola León, whose entire family was known for being dangerous hard-asses, to have something as sweet and innocent as freckles.

When he realized how long he'd been staring at her face, and was no doubt making her feel uncomfortable, he cleared his throat. "So what'd you do to piss off Jose?" he asked.

Lola looked like she contemplated lying, but must've decided against it because she replied, "I kissed his ex-girlfriend." She looked away from him and the air around her seemed to still. It was like she was waiting for him to say something messed up.

"Why?" he asked. He knew Jose's ex, Yesenia. Part of the dance squad and daughter of everyone's favorite gym teacher, she was one of the most popular girls in the school. Sure, she was beautiful, but she was also dumb as a bag of rocks and selfish to boot.

"'Why' what?" Lola asked.

"Why'd you kiss her? I've known Yesenia since we were kids and she's awful."

Lola just stared at him.

Junior rubbed the back of his neck. "I'm just saying. I don't think there's a whole lot going on in that girl's head. You could do better. Not to mention, she's a very traditional girl from a very traditional family. So just, you know, be careful…"

Lola's voice was full of incredulity when she asked, "Are you trying to protect my feelings?"

He blushed. "It's just that…" He paused. "I mean. It can't be easy for you to be, you know." He paused, unsure if it would be okay for him to say the word. He didn't want to offend her.

"Bisexual?"

So she did like guys. The warmth on his cheeks deepened for some reason. "I just wouldn't want you to fall for someone who would just make things harder. That's all. You can love whoever you want, but I just think it should be someone who loves you back." He shrugged awkwardly.

She tilted her head and looked at him like he was a brand-new species of animal. "You know, I think you might be one of the first people in this school to tell me that."

"Tell you what?"

"That I can love anyone I want. Most people I know tell me it's just a phase or that I like being difficult."

Junior didn't know how to respond, so he stayed quiet.

"What's your name?" she asked.

"Junior," he replied. Then he shook his head as if to clear the cobwebs. "I mean, no. That's not right."

Her smile was wry. "Do you not know your own name?"

He gave her a look. "My name is Santiago Vega. Like my dad, so everyone calls me Junior which really makes no sense because no one even calls my dad Santiago."

"Santiago, huh? Like the city in Chile?"

"Right, but the city is actually named for Saint James."

"I'm sure whatever he did to get that title was something super cool and not at all colonialist."

Junior was so nervous that he totally missed her ironic tone. He just started talking.

"He was one of Jesus's first disciples. He eventually traveled to

Spain while spreading the word and ended up becoming Spain's patron saint. You can actually follow his path from France through Spain if you want. It takes like a month to walk and leads to a huge church." He shut his mouth abruptly, highly aware that he was babbling. The daughter of Humboldt Park's most notorious gang leader didn't give a shit about the religious origins of his name.

"You're a bit of a nerd, huh?" Lola asked with a curl to her lips. "Makes sense you'd be named after a saint."

He didn't hear any derision in her tone, but he felt defensive anyway. "Why do you say that?"

"Because look at you." She gestured to him. "You jump into the middle of fights to save the underdog. You dish out words of wisdom to protect people. Don't you volunteer in the office for fun? Shit. I bet you have straight As and help little old ladies cross the street. You basically are a saint."

His brow creased. "I don't think that's how it works." Besides, it wasn't like he was perfect. He had plenty of flaws. Junior was no doubt about to embarrass himself more by enumerating said flaws, but he was quite literally saved by the bell, which blared through the room and caused them both to startle.

Lola recovered first. "Well, to answer your earlier question, I kissed Yesenia because she asked me to. I'm not in love with her or anything." She slipped around him and made her way to the door. At the last moment she turned back to him. "Thanks for saving me...Saint." Then she closed the door behind her and rushed to her next class.

The next morning when they saw each other down the hallway she shouted, "What up, Saint?" in her loudest voice, making sure everyone heard her, and that was it. The nickname spread around the school and then the neighborhood like a forest fire. He was no longer Junior or even Santiago. He was Saint. And Lola was no longer the troublemaker from the office. She was everything he wanted and everything he eventually lost.

1

A chorus of hisses, grunts, and rough exhales drowned out the El Alfa song playing from the community center multipurpose room's stereo system. Lola León smiled to herself as she watched the adults in the room, mostly women in their forties and above, go through the move she'd demonstrated moments earlier. She loved having a full class. Her hope was to one day have multiple classes at different times to allow anyone interested to join.

"Stop!" she called.

Immediately the sounds stopped, leaving only the bass-heavy dembow music from the famous Dominican artist that had gone viral thanks to a social media dance challenge.

Before she could congratulate her students on a job well done, a voice called out, "When do we get to ball squeezing?"

She knew that voice well. It belonged to her youngest and most gung-ho student. A student who should technically be at the high school right now.

Lola met Ruby's eyes in the mirror in front of them and raised a brow. "Ball squeezing?"

Ruby nodded, causing the sweat beading on her dark brown

skin to run down her face to her neck. "Yeah. You know, the shit that will really take a motherfucker out. Like 'oh, you thought you could just keep grabbing my ass whenever I walked to my desk in chemistry? How do you like it when I grab these?'" She made a grab-and-squeeze motion with her hand. "And then you just crush them like an egg until yolk and whites are all over the place."

Another voice chimed in. This one from the oldest member of the class, Gladys, who must have been in her early seventies. "That makes me wonder, which is more effective, Lola, squeezing the balls or kicking them?"

Lola bit a lip to keep from smiling at the question and gave it some serious thought before answering. She also made a mental note to check in with Ruby after class, the specifics of her scenario were a bit too detailed. "We know Krav Maga is about attacking the most sensitive parts of your assailant for self-defense, right?"

Nods all around.

"But what else do I always tell you?"

"Keep as much distance between yourself and your assailant as possible," the group said in unison.

"Exactly." Lola held up a finger. "If you have the space to kick, you kick. If you can't kick, use your knee. If the angle is wrong or you won't be able to put the right amount of force behind your strike, then by all means grab those nuts and crack them. I like to do a grab, twist, and push motion." Lola demonstrated the motion slowly so everyone could see and then more quickly. "But remember that your goal isn't to completely annihilate your opponent. This isn't an MMA fight you're trying to win. You want to incapacitate them in order to get away."

Lola liked to give the reminder frequently because some of her students thought they were going to use their Krav Maga knowledge to become neighborhood vigilantes going around kicking everyone's ass. She didn't blame them. When her mother had first made her begin classes at age seventeen, she'd been the same way. She'd even gotten into some trouble for going around hammer punching dudes. Through time and continued practice she'd learned just how much damage the moves she'd mastered could do, so she was now more conscious of how she used them. Honest self-defense only. Being obnoxious wasn't enough of a reason to take someone out. Sadly.

Her students would learn that eventually. They were less than two months into the course, so they were still learning the very basics. Which reminded her. "Let's practice how to plant our feet when someone is trying to push us. Partner up."

Lola led her students through more and more practice moves until both she and they were pouring sweat and time was up. As everyone filed out she called Ruby over to talk.

Ruby didn't even let Lola open her mouth before she was defending herself. "Look I already know what you're going to ask and yes I am still supposed to be at school. But honestly it's not even that big of a deal because I only skipped my last two periods and one of them is study hall. I don't even need a study hall because I'm getting As in all my classes so I wouldn't even really be studying. I'd just be messing around and distracting other people who do need to study because they are stupid and not acing their classes. So basically, isn't it better for me to be here learning something useful and letting others learn at school?" The girl finally paused to take a breath and Lola jumped in before she started again.

"What's the other class?"

"Huh?" Ruby screwed up her face like she was confused, but Lola knew better.

"What other class did you skip to come here, Ruby?"

She stayed quiet.

"I'm going to take a wild guess here and say that it's chemistry."

A shrug, which meant "yes" in teenager.

"Do you want to talk about it?"

"Why? It's not like you can do anything about it."

"I can help you figure out a solution that won't get you in trouble with the truancy officers."

Ruby scoffed. "I've already done everything we're told to do. I told him to stop, I told the teacher, I talked to the guidance counselor, I reported it to the principal. They did nothing because he's the highest scorer on the basketball team and I'm just the quiet nerdy girl who lives in a homeless shelter with her gay little brother."

Lola, who operated on a simmer at all times, felt her blood begin to boil. "That's not okay."

Another shrug. This one to convey, "it is what it is."

"I'm going to talk to Yara. She'll have some thoughts on what to do." Yaraliz Vasquez was the director of El Hogar, the shelter Ruby and Marcus currently lived in with about ten other unhoused teens, most of whom had been kicked out of their homes because their self-righteous parents couldn't tolerate their gender identity or sexual orientation.

El Hogar was one of the buildings that made up the three-block-long community center named El Vecindario because its plethora of buildings created its own little neighborhood while also serving the community at large. El Centro, the main multipurpose building that opened in the '70s, had everything from a small art gallery to a pool for swimming classes and a large mirrored room for dance, as well as the Krav Maga class Lola had just finished teaching. Over the years they had added El Hogar, a bilingual charter school, an old folks' home, and a health clinic. El Vecindario really did its very best to find a way to fulfill every one of the community's needs and Lola was proud to be back in Humboldt Park working there.

Her favorite of the many tasks she did was spending time in

El Hogar with kids like Ruby. While Lola had never been un-housed, she knew what it was like to feel unwanted by the people who were responsible for raising you and looking out for your well-being. "I can call your school if you want. Talk to the principal on your behalf."

"He won't care. He only cares when parents are there causing a scene."

Of course, Ruby and Marcus's mother wouldn't do that since she'd washed her hands of her kids. When Ruby wouldn't let her bully Marcus into attending classes at their church designed to get "confused" kids back on track, she'd sent them both packing.

"Listen, I'm going to take care of this. Until then, I need you to go to school every day and stay all day, so that these idiots have no legs to stand on when I go light their asses up. Can you do that?"

"I guess."

Lola figured that was as much enthusiasm as she could ask for. "Until then, let me show you a move to use when someone attacks you from behind. I'll focus on someone reaching for your butt."

Lola spent the next twenty minutes going over the move repeatedly with Ruby until they were interrupted by the teacher of the next class, a beginners' salsa class. Lola and Ruby quickly wiped down and put away the mats, gathered all their things, and left. Lola had every intention of walking Ruby back to El Hogar, but as soon as she reached the main lobby a voice called to her. "Lola!"

She turned and saw head secretary Mrs. Lopez waving her down. She turned quickly to Ruby. "Go straight back to El Hogar and wait for me before you talk to Yara. Got it?"

The teen nodded and left.

Lola stepped into the main office and up to the front desk that spanned the length of the room. "Yes?"

She couldn't help but notice that the woman seemed to be buzzing with energy, poised to explode, but it wasn't possible to tell if it was in a negative or positive way. "She's just finishing up a meeting, but Mrs. Fonseca would like to talk to you."

Before Lola could ask why, the door to the director's office swung open and a petite blonde woman strode out. She had a large tote bag stuffed with what looked like colorful classroom supplies and an equally large box of stuff in her hands. Her light eyes were red-rimmed and her face streaked with tears, but she didn't seem sad. She looked pissed. "You two are the ones getting paid the big bucks, so you can find someone to take over my position," she was saying to the people in the office. "The expectations, the students, the *parents*, and you do nothing to support us. It's impossible to work here. It's toxic and I won't do it another minute." She used her hip to push the door open and brushed past Lola.

Lola finally placed the blonde's face, usually coming in and out of the school connected to El Centro. Wide-eyed, Lola looked at Mrs. Lopez, who stared back at her equally wide-eyed. Their expressions holding a silent conversation.

Oh shit. Did you see that?

Yes, girl. That was crazy.

Yeah, it was.

The conversation would've continued, but a voice called out from the office. "Mrs. Lopez, did you get a hold of Lola yet?"

"She's right here, señora."

"Send her in, please."

Lola was already making her way to the door, but she took her time about it because she had a sneaking suspicion what the director of the community center wanted to discuss with her.

When she'd come back to El Centro three months ago, the place Lola had spent the majority of her childhood, it had been a shock to see Mrs. Fonseca still in the director's office. Lola was very familiar with the woman who'd been running the organization for at least twenty-six years. She was the reason Lola had gotten into community service in the first place.

As an unusually young director, Mrs. Fonseca had always been inspiring and exacting while also being pragmatic. Even though she didn't have decades of experience before taking on the role, she knew how to get people to act, and understood the struggle. She had high expectations for her staff, but she was right there in the trenches with them trying to make progress.

Now the decades of battle showed clearly in the deep lines in her forehead, but there were also plenty of laugh lines around her sparkling brown eyes. She was waiting for Lola behind her desk, a calm but pleasant look on her face. It was so similar to every other time Lola had walked into her office that she actually had to look down at herself to make sure she wasn't a silent child or surly teenager anymore.

With her was Dolores Galván, the principal of the school La Escuela Estrellita.

Lola hadn't done much collaboration with the woman yet, beyond some volunteering for school functions, but she got a good vibe from the woman. Although considering the way that teacher had just stormed out, Lola wondered if she'd been wrong.

"You asked to see me?" Lola said into the silence.

"Yes, please have a seat." Mrs. Fonseca motioned Lola to the open chair in front of her desk.

She still couldn't get over how calm they were after what had just happened. Lola would've been freaking out.

"As I'm sure you can guess," Dolores began, "I'm now short a teacher."

Lola nodded, because really what could she say to that?

Mrs. Fonseca jumped in. "I remember you had mentioned having some academic teaching experience during your interview."

Oh shit.

"Yes…" Lola had originally wanted to become a teacher, like the second grade teacher who'd changed her life. It had only taken a few years in the stifling environment of the classroom, however, for Lola to realize that she could do much more for kids by working to improve the community surrounding their schools. She'd gone back to school for public administration and nonprofit management with a focus on human services.

"Well, I have a long-term subbing position for you, if you're interested," Dolores said. "It's our four-year-old kindergarten classroom."

Lola's eyebrows went up. That lady had been a preschool teacher? That was…unexpected. Usually when teachers quit in the middle of the year they were in charge of older students whose behaviors tended to be more intense. But for any teacher to up and quit once the school year had started—something was seriously wrong. "I haven't taught preschool since my student teaching," Lola hedged. "I'm more familiar with fourth and fifth grades. Although I haven't been in the classroom for almost five years now."

"It's just until the end of the year," she said.

Mrs. Fonseca chimed in again. "Lola, I know you want a full-time position here, and one that's not in a classroom. While I don't have that at the moment, there is a good chance something will be opening up soon. I want to be able to offer that to you, but I'd want to see you interact with all aspects of El Vecindario. Our focus has always been on the youth of the community and the school is a large part of that."

Damn. Lola had been planning to politely decline, but she couldn't now. Not if it could lead to a full-time position at El Vecindario. She'd been working part-time teaching her Krav Maga classes and volunteering at different buildings since she moved back to Humboldt Park, but she wanted something more permanent. "Can I be real with you?"

Mrs. Fonseca smiled. "Lola, I don't think you are capable of being anything else."

True enough. "You know I'm back because of Benny. He's a lot and I don't really need added stress, you know what I mean. And this class *seems* like it's going to be added stress." Lola gestured vaguely to the door the teacher had stormed out of.

"Look, I know you're probably apprehensive given what you heard and saw, but let me assure you that the situation is hardly as severe as Ms. Kirkland made it seem. She's upset about an incident with a parent that didn't go the way she expected," Dolores explained.

Lola sat back. "I need more than that. I can't just be expected to jump into a potentially hostile environment without any information."

Mrs. Fonseca sighed but nodded. "You know how these things go, Lola. These young people come here from their middle-class, suburban experiences expecting to make a huge impact and save these poor Brown kids from their terrible lives, like some Michelle Pfeiffer movie, and when reality hits they either sink or swim."

Ah. The white savior complex. Yes. Lola was very familiar with it. "So that's what happened with her?" She directed her question at Dolores.

Dolores nodded. "She thought that going above my head to Fonseca would change the outcome of her situation."

Lola snorted. "She demanded to speak to the manager."

Mrs. Fonseca huffed. "Basically."

Dolores continued. "I'm sad to see her go. She's a good teacher and she's passionate. She just needs to learn that she doesn't always know better than the families we serve."

Lola laughed. "That's a nice way of saying that she needs to sit down and be humble."

Mrs. Fonseca just shook her head and gave Lola the same amused but exasperated look she used to give her. "It's not really about her at this point. It's about the fact that there is now a room of twenty-five four-year-olds who still need to receive a solid foundation to build on, so we stop seeing these academic gaps that only widen as these kids get older."

Lola had always respected that about Mrs. Fonseca. She knew her community inside and out and she was determined to see every single kid that roamed the halls of the center succeed. Lola strived to be like her. "I'll do it," she told Mrs. Fonseca.

"Great. I'd like to have you go there this afternoon to get a feel for it."

Lola was about to say that she needed to go home to change out of her workout clothes first when her phone trilled from her pocket. Lola had every number set to vibrate during the day except the number of her grandfather's senior living facility. "I'm sorry. I have to take this. It's Casa del Sol."

Mrs. Fonseca nodded and stood up. Dolores followed. "Take it here. We'll step out to make some plans." She moved around her desk and headed out the door before Lola could say anything.

"Hi, Lola, it's Tanisha," the voice on the other end said as soon as Lola answered.

"Hey, Tanisha, what's up? Is Benny okay?"

Her grandfather, whom she'd called Benny since she first met him at age seven, had been diagnosed with diabetes a few years ago and had initially done a great job caring for himself. Then Lola started getting calls from the nursing staff multiple times a week complaining that regulating his medication was getting more and more complicated because of his refusal to eat normally. She'd tried to talk to him about it, but in typical Benny fashion he'd told her that she could mind her own damn business if she was going to be living it up on the other side of the country. So Lola moved back home from San Diego in hopes that being close by would help the situation. Except Benny still told her to mind her own damn business.

"Well, he's actually not feeling so great. He's been having a lot of stomach issues today. I think he caught a stomach bug and I don't want him getting dehydrated."

Lola's heart started to race. "Does he need to go to the hospital?" Tanisha was one of a few very capable nurse practitioners who worked at the neighboring clinic, Clínica Luna Nueva, and volunteered their services at Casa del Sol, so Lola knew Benny was in good hands. Still, dehydration was dangerous for someone of Benny's age and with his health issues.

"For now, I'd like to start giving him some fluids here, but he's being difficult about getting an IV. I was hoping you could come talk to him, maybe help calm him down a bit."

"I'm in a meeting with Fonseca over at The Center right now. Could I just talk to him on the phone?"

"Give me a second. I'll see if I can get him on, but he was adamant that he wasn't going to talk to anyone."

The sounds of Latin jazz came on the line and Lola took the time to lower her phone and massage her temples, but she had to pick it up again quickly when the song cut off and Benny's voice irritably asked, "¿Que tú quieres?"

"I want you to let Tanisha take care of you," Lola responded. "If you have the stomach flu, you can very easily get dehydrated and you can end up in the hospital."

"I'm trying to tell her that I don't have a stomach flu," he growled. "Papo Vega poisoned me!"

Since she wasn't in the room with him Lola allowed herself to roll her eyes. Her abuelo was apt to blame everything on Papo Vega, the man he called his nemesis. He once blamed the guy for eating his butterscotch pudding at the table they shared in the cafeteria only to find out later that Papo hadn't even been at lunch that day. Benny hadn't backed down. He'd been adamant that he'd seen Papo sneak his dessert. That was Benicio "Benny" León for you, all bullheaded opinions and adamant action.

Lola had inherited that from him along with her social justice warrior tendencies. Her grandfather had been a member of the Puerto Rican Nationalist Party since his late teens. He'd proudly taken part in the revolts of the '50s protesting the United States' continued control over the island. He and those like him wanted out from under the US's colonial regime. The regime that kept them poor, undereducated, and without recourse. The same hypocritical regime that made it illegal to speak of freedom, sing or whistle their national anthem, "La Borinqueña," or own a Puerto Rican flag. Benny had fought tooth and nail toward the independence of Puerto Rico even after his new wife had convinced him to move to Humboldt Park where her brothers had found good jobs. His persistence sparked that same fire in Lola. So from the age of twelve, Lola spoke out, she fought, and she remained stubbornly dedicated to her cause—to champion the underdog at whatever cost. Meanwhile, Benny stayed dedicated to his new cause—to hate Papo Vega.

"Benny," she sighed.

"No, no," he interrupted, shutting her down before she could launch into her we-can't-blame-Papo-for-everything-just-because-we-don't-like-him speech. "This time he really did it. He poisoned me! He put that caca medicine in my juice. Como se llama? Es-lax?"

Okay. That didn't sound like Benny's usual paranoid delusions. She could feel the ever-present flame inside her growing, threatening to become an all-out fire. "He put Ex-Lax in your juice?"

"Sí."

"How do you know that? Maybe you just have a stomach flu,"

she said in an attempt to calm herself before she lit shit up like the Great Chicago Fire.

"He told me!" Benny burst out, offended. "He laughed about it!"

Oh hell no. Lola felt her body heat. She felt like the Human Torch, completely engulfed and ready to burn the bad guys to a crisp. "I'm on my way," she told her grandfather.

2

The old-school salsa music blared out of the even more old-school boom box, causing the one wonky speaker to rattle and buzz. Saint didn't know how that wasn't driving everyone else crazy. Maybe it was because the whirling sounds of the electric drills and the hum of the circular saws that echoed through the worksite—a Tudor-style lakefront home they'd taken down to the studs—camouflaged the sound for everyone else. However, Saint had always been sensitive to sounds. For him the rattle and buzz was distinctly out of place and therefore extremely irritating.

He wished he'd remembered to grab his noise-canceling headphones from his bedside table that morning, but his four-year-old daughter had decided to play sick. She'd mixed mustard and pickle juice—two things she absolutely hated—into her morning OJ before chugging it, which caused her to gag and eventually vomit all over the kitchen island, herself, and him. By the time he'd gotten everything cleaned up and the two of them ready to go, he'd been rushing out the door. All while Rosie hung on his leg, begging and crying to not go to school. He knew that there was an adjustment process to the whole going-to-school-for-the-first-time thing and he couldn't wait until they finally finished it, because dropping off a sobbing four-year-old at his sister's place every morning was exhausting.

"Junior, have you listened to literally anything I've said in the past four minutes?"

"Don't call me that," he commanded as he shook off his thoughts and turned back into the very one-sided conversation his cousin Alex was having with him.

"Ha. I knew that would work," Alex said in triumph. She knew, much like everyone in his family, that he'd hated being called Junior since he was a kid. "I said your name about fifteen times and you weren't answering, so I had to get creative."

"What were you saying, Alexandra?" he asked, purposefully using her full first name.

Her light green eyes narrowed with menace. "Call me Alexandra again and I'll have all the guys calling you Junior for the rest of your life."

Not only would she do it, but it would actually work. Her father, his tío Luís, owned the construction company they both worked for, but it was Alex who held the real power. At twenty-two she had better command of her crew than some of the officers he'd seen when he was a Green Beret. Whatever she said was what they did, not just because she was Tío Luís's daughter, but because she was smart, she knew what she was talking about, and she was almost always the first one ready to jump in and do whatever needed to get done.

"Seriously? You still aren't listening to me!"

"What are you doing here anyway? Shouldn't you be in class or something?"

Alex was a senior at the University of Chicago. She should've been graduating at the end of the spring semester, but thanks to some bad advice from her counselor she was stuck there for another semester, which she'd been complaining to him about for the hundredth time right before he'd gotten distracted by the boom box speaker.

She just shrugged her small shoulders and Saint marveled once again that such a tiny person worked construction. She was barely over five feet tall and if she weighed more than one hundred and twenty pounds he'd eat her tiny work boots. She seemed to constantly be drowning in her loose-fitting jeans and flannel shirts and yet he'd seen her lift concrete slabs and carry loads of lumber. Like the other women in their family, she was a force to be reckoned with and Saint appreciated that about her.

The damn speaker let out another buzzing rattle and Saint was just about to ask Alex if she heard that, but she started talking again first.

"Anyway, as I was saying before you started ignoring me. My dad is up to something."

Saint looked over to the empty space that would eventually become their client's new state-of-the-art kitchen, where his uncle was consulting with the plumber about moving some lines to accommodate an island sink. Technically, Tío Luís wasn't Saint's uncle, at least not anymore. Tío Luís had been married to Saint's aunt Carmen, otherwise known as Flaca to family, for a little over fifteen years. Oddly enough he was more a part of the Vega clan now—after twelve years of separation—than Tía Flaca was. Probably because she'd moved to New York with their oldest daughter and left Luís in Chicago with Alex and her big sister, Gabi. It was still a touchy subject everyone tended to avoid.

"He looks like he's working," Saint said to his cousin.

She rolled her eyes and flipped her long brown ponytail over her shoulder. "What did you expect? To see him twirling the ends of his mustache while chuckling sinisterly? Obviously he's not up to it right now, but he's been acting weird lately. Cagey and secretive."

Saint thought back to the last few weeks. Nothing stuck out

to him and he was usually pretty observant. It was something others assumed he got from being a soldier, but he knew came from being the oldest of eighteen rambunctious cousins (just on his father's side) who spent inordinate amounts of time together. Years of trying to keep them all safe, out of trouble, and relatively happy at family events had honed his observational skills long before Uncle Sam ever did.

"I think he's dating," Alex burst out, completely breaking Saint's concentration again.

Saint stared at her blankly. Tío Luís dating? There was no way. That was harder to picture than Saint dating, and dating was the absolutely last thing Saint planned to ever do. Shit, Saint would reenlist before he dated.

Alex continued, "The other day I walked into his office when he was on the phone and he stopped talking. He looked all panicked. Then he said that he had to go and hung up right away. When I asked him who it was he mumbled something about a client and asked me about class." She paused dramatically, waiting for Saint's reaction. When he didn't react at all she threw up her hands. "About class, Saint. He never asks me about my classes. He just assumes that I'm doing what I'm supposed to do and am getting good grades."

"Well, maybe now that he's paying for an extra semester, he realized that he should've been asking you about your classes."

"Hey! You already know that isn't my fault and don't try to derail the conversation. We're talking about my dad's secret girlfriend."

"He doesn't have a secret girlfriend."

She gave him an alert look. "You know what's going on?"

Saint shook his head. He didn't really think there was anything going on besides his cousin's overactive imagination.

"It's not just me," she said as if reading his mind. "Gabi said that the other day he left the office on some errand and when she said she'd go with him so they could get lunch after, he said no." She stared at Saint in horror, like she'd just told him her father had unzipped his face and a lizard creature had emerged. "That's it. Just no."

Saint's eyebrows almost went up. That was surprising. Tío Luís never said no to his daughters. It was a joke amongst the family how you could tell Gabi and Alex were Cruzes, because they were spoiled, unlike the cousins with the Vega last name who were frequently told no, even as adults in control of their own lives.

"You should talk to him," Alex said suddenly. "I bet he'd tell you what's going on. You're his favorite."

Saint made a sound of dissent. He wasn't Tío's favorite. It was just that they were the same in a lot of ways. Mostly in that they were both fathers who'd unexpectedly become the sole caretakers of their daughters. They'd both had to learn very quickly how to not only be a girl dad, but to be the only parent. Of course, he realized single moms experienced the same exact thing with even more pressure to perform their roles to perfection, but that didn't negate that he and his uncle understood a part of each other that no one else they knew could relate to personally.

Alex pointed at him. "Don't scoff at me. It's true. You're like the son he never had." There was something in her voice when she said that. It wasn't quite anger or resentment, but whatever it was she brushed it off quickly. "Anyway. You can find out what's going on and then tell me."

She wanted him to go undercover and snoop out some imaginary situation to report back to her? Saint stared at her.

"Don't give me that look," she said. "I *need* to know what's going on."

"So you want me to spy on your dad and betray his trust because you're curious."

She shrugged again, completely unconcerned with the invasion of her dad's privacy. He was family and, to the Vegas, that meant nothing was private. Technically, Alex was a Cruz, but the personality was all Vega. Meaning she was intrusive and opinionated, but always well-meaning and loyal.

"What if something is wrong?" she said.

"One second ago you thought he had a girlfriend, now you think there is something wrong? Pick a dilemma."

Alex actually growled at him. "Fine. If you won't help, I'll do it myself." She looked to her dad. "Papi," she shouted.

Everyone stopped working.

Saint winced. Seriously? How did such a tiny person create that much noise? She was like a blow horn.

"Saint thinks there is something going on with you. Like you have a girlfriend or something."

The little shit. Saint's mouth fell open.

"So what is it?" she continued. "Do I have a new stepmom or am I going to have to kick someone's ass or what?"

Tío Luís's eyes darted around the space, noting all the interested and entertained eyes on him. He flushed red under his deep tan skin. "Alex," he admonished walking up to them. "¿Has perdido tu mente? ¿Cómo dices esas cosas en frente de todos?"

At least it was clear he knew that Saint had nothing to do with his cousin's outburst.

"What? Aren't you always saying that we're one big family? Don't you think they want to know this stuff too?" She motioned to the crew, who really was like one big nosy family.

Tío Luís rubbed the back of his neck. "I have no idea what you're talking about," he grumbled. "You just embarrassed me for no reason."

Poor Tío Luís.

As the single father of a spirited daughter, Saint felt for him. He really did. He lived in fear of the day Rosie truly understood her power over him. He already knew he'd be wearing the same look Tío Luís did whenever he dealt with Alex, a sort of frustrated adoration.

Saint's phone vibrated in his pocket, saving him from having to continue to take part in this unbelievably uncomfortable scene. Saint stepped away and pulled his phone out of his pocket. The words World's Greatest Sister flashed across his screen along with a picture of said sister making that weird pouty face girls made in selfies. He didn't know how many times he'd changed her contact information to a normal name and picture, just for Kamilah to change it right back.

"Stop messing with my phone," he told her upon answering.

"Stop having easily guessable passcodes," she replied. "I don't know why you keep changing it. It's like you're challenging me."

God save him from these women. Weren't little sisters supposed to get less obnoxious with age? "You're too old to be this annoying." He walked past the table saw and out the front door so he could hear.

"Well, that's a fine way to talk to your favorite sister. I should tell Mami. She was just telling Madrina Marisela how great you are, her precious baby boy. If only she knew how rude you actually are."

He loved his little sister and she was his favorite. Simply because she was his only sister. Although, lord knew Alex usually felt like another one. He knew better than to continue down this route though. "Mila, why are you calling me?"

"What?" She sounded distracted.

"Why are you calling me?"

"Oh right. I need you to go to the senior center. They called, but I can't leave. The lunch rush is insane today." The loud hum of many conversations happening in the background floated through the phone as if to underscore her claim.

His baby sister was now the sole owner of their family restaurant, El Coquí, and he was incredibly proud of everything she'd accomplished there in only a few short months. Where they had once had empty tables and the threat of closure, they now saw a packed house from open to close and big-name regulars like the mayor of Chicago.

"Is Abuelo okay?" Saint asked. His grandfather had heart issues, so his health was always at the forefront of their minds.

"He's okay physically, but he's in trouble."

"Again?" Saint asked even though he knew the answer. Of course, his abuelo was in trouble again. He was like fucking Dennis the Menace, constantly coming up with pranks and schemes to entertain himself, and since Kamilah took over the restaurant, Saint had found himself dealing with the consequences of said pranks more and more often.

"I don't know what he did this time, but it's bad. When Maria called, she didn't say we needed to talk. She said that I need to come get him. I think they are really going to kick him out this time, Saint." His sister had always been high-strung, but this time the anxiety in her voice could easily be well-founded.

Just last month Saint had been forced to go plead for his grandfather, who was being threatened with expulsion from an art therapy class. Saint had sat there for forty-five minutes listening to the director yammer on and on about Abuelo's painting being alarmingly disrespectful. Something about a sacrilegious depiction of the Last Supper featuring her and other staff members except, instead of Jesus and his disciples feasting on bread and wine, they were painted as Lucifer and his demons eating the food from the cafeteria. Eventually they'd settled on an apology to those depicted and temporary suspension, but Saint had known it was only a matter of time before his abuelo did something else.

A loud bang sounded over the phone and Kamilah cursed. "The new guy I hired just dropped a whole caldero of rice on the floor. I gotta go."

"Yeah me too. I better hurry up."

"I'm sorry. If I could get away—"

"Don't worry about it. I'll talk to you later."

"Okay, te quiero mucho. Cuídate." She always ended their conversations the same way. She ended just about every conversation she had with "I love you," but he was the only one she told to take care of himself. It had started when he was serving and still continued even though he'd been discharged. He sometimes wondered if it was simply habit or if his sister was more observant than he gave her credit for.

After he hung up, he rushed back inside to tell his uncle that he had to go, but he'd be back as soon as possible. Then he hopped in his truck and raced to the center. He'd just got stuck at a red light when his phone whistled signifying an incoming text. It was from Abuelo.

Avanza. Me quieren hacer esto: Below that was a GIF of an older Latina taking off her leather sandal and throwing it at her kid. The word *Chancletazo* popped up like the old school comic book "Boom, Pow, Bam."

Who the hell had not only taught his eighty-year-old abuelo how to text, but to send GIFs? Saint sighed and rushed to the center. The minute he walked in, he knew that Kamilah had been right. Abuelo was in some serious trouble.

Maria Lopez-Hermann, the director of Casa del Sol Senior Living, stood at the door to her office. Usually Saint sensed a sort of fond exasperation from her, like the parent of a particularly naughty kid. That was gone. She was more stern-faced than he'd ever seen her and the muscle ticking at the side of her jaw showed how upset she was about whatever had happened. But that wasn't what set all of Saint's warning instincts flaring. It was that behind her he could see Abuelo Papo sitting in the chair in front of Maria's desk, head tilted down while he stared at the interlocked fingers of his hands. It was the posture of someone who knew they'd fucked up, that they were in deep shit, and they deserved every bit of it.

"What happened?" Saint asked.

"Mr. Vega had an altercation with another one of our residents and decided to get revenge by poisoning him. The other resident has fragile health and his family member is demanding your grandfather be kicked out."

Fuck.

3

Lola looked Benny over again. He was sitting next to her at the conference table with one of his hands gripping the IV pole next to him. He was on his second bag of fluids. She couldn't be sure if it was her imagination, but he looked even more skinny and wrinkly than he had when she'd visited him yesterday. Her poor abuelo looked like a damn raisin. Her anger sparked all over again, but it was quickly tempered by concern. "Are you sure you're okay?" Lola asked Benny for the fiftieth time since she'd arrived.

He waved her off. "I'm fine. I'm just mad."

"That makes two of us."

The door to the small conference room opened and the director of the facility entered followed by an old man, presumably Papo Vega, and then... "Oh fuck!"

Lola popped up out of her chair with so much force that it slid back a foot before it tipped over.

The last person to enter the room froze in the doorway. He stared at her as if he'd just seen a ghost. "Lola?"

Ugh. That voice. From the moment she first heard it, it had done things to her. That voice saying her name had caused her to do things. Dumb things. Unfortunately for her that pattern seemed to continue, because before she could stop herself she blurted out, "There are approximately a hundred of you Vegas strutting around Humboldt Park. Why did it have to be you?"

"You know him?" Benny asked in Spanish at the same time Papo said, "I see your granddaughter is as rude as you are."

"Abuelo," his voice said.

This time Lola was able to note the differences. It was deeper. Way deeper. And rough, as if he were unused to using it. It prickled over her skin, causing bumps to rise along her arms. She was grateful she was wearing long sleeves, so no one could witness her shame.

His voice should not still affect her like this. Not after seventeen years. She was supposed to have left all that stupidity behind the same way she'd left Saint Vega behind.

That's right. She had left him behind. She was the one in control. Not him.

Lola took a deep breath. She channeled her yoga instructor back in San Diego and she centered herself. Reclaimed her energy. "We went to high school together," she told Benny. To Papo Vega she said, "You have no idea just how rude I can be when someone hurts my family."

"I need to talk to you," Saint said to her. "Privately."

Oh hell no. There was no way that was going to happen. If his voice made her do stupid things, being alone with him was ten times worse. "There is no need to speak privately. Your YouTube prankster here poisoned my diabetic abuelo and almost caused him to be hospitalized. That's all there is to talk about."

"It wasn't poison," Papo Vega grumbled. "It was just prune juice."

"Benny said that you told him it was Ex-Lax," Lola shot back.

"Well, then he's a fool *and* a liar, because all I said was that he was full of shit and I could prove it."

Maria let loose something that could only be described as a groan of dismay and covered her face with both hands.

"Lola." Saint's voice came again, tinged with some sort of emotion she couldn't place. "Talk to me privately."

She tried to ignore him, but he dominated the space in the room. He'd definitely grown a few inches since high school and filled out. He wore a faded black T-shirt under a sawdust-covered flannel, an equally covered pair of dark jeans, and well-worn work boots. Apparently he was a construction worker now. His rich brown hair was cut in a close fade on the sides and only long enough on the top to get a wavy impression of what she knew were gorgeous curls. He was so close that she could smell the sawdust and sweat on him. Something that shouldn't have made her mouth water, but did.

He leaned in close and said the one word that would break her resolve. "Please."

Lola growled in frustration. "Fine. We'll talk privately for two minutes, then I'm coming back here to handle this." With that she pushed past him and strode out into the hallway. She was about to make her way out the front door when a hand wrapped around her wrist and pulled her in the opposite direction.

Saint opened a door to his left and pulled her in behind him. It was some sort of storage closet. Surrounding her were file boxes, clear totes of office supplies, and even some cleaning products. The door shut and Lola swung to face Saint in the dark.

He hit a light switch somewhere then stood in front of the door staring at her. His gaze traveled from her head to her toes.

Lola knew exactly what he was seeing. An older version of her old self. She still had freckles on her face, thick dark hair with just a hint of a wave, and enough pounds on her five-six frame to have her old doctor constantly bitching about her size and throwing around bullshit terms like *BMI* and *obese*.

Well, fuck that guy and fuck this noise, because although she may not look it, Lola was very different from her teenage self. She now embraced everything about herself including her face and her body. She was a strong, independent, beautiful, badass bitch and she wasn't taking shit from anyone.

"Are you actually going to say anything or do you plan to spend your two minutes staring at me?"

She expected the attitude to elicit an equally antagonistic response from Saint. What she did not expect was for him to reach out and pull her into his arms. The smell of freshly cut wood and sweat got even stronger, and Lola felt like she was wrapped up in the coils of an anaconda, surrounded by solid muscle.

"Oh my god, Lola," he whispered. He tightened his hold on her to the point that she felt like a stress toy in the hand of a bodybuilder. He gave a tiny shiver and for some odd reason Lola felt her eyes begin to water.

She didn't know what was going on, but Saint's obvious emotion over seeing her was affecting her too. "Saint," she breathed.

At the sound of her voice he pulled back, but only far enough to take her face in his hands. His deep brown eyes bounced around her face like they couldn't decide what to focus on. "I never thought. I didn't believe. You're safe. You're here."

Before Lola could inquire about that "safe" bit, Saint lowered his head and fused their mouths together.

And just like that, Lola was seventeen again. She was standing in the arms of the boy she loved, and he was kissing her with a desperation that reflected her own. As much as she wanted to deny it, as much as they both pretended it wasn't, their love was ending and they were saying goodbye.

At the thought, Lola wrenched herself away, pushing against Saint's chest. "What the hell? Have you never heard of asking for consent before kissing someone?"

"I'm sorry," Saint panted. He scrubbed his palms over his face. "I saw you and I just couldn't believe you were here." He froze for a second then dropped his hands. The shocked disbelief was gone from his face and in its place was anger.

Lola frowned. What did he have to be angry about?

"What the fuck, Lola?" he asked.

"What?"

"You disappeared and no one knew where you were. With everything going on with your dad and brother…" He trailed off, but quickly found more to say. "Everyone thought the worst, and now you show up as if it's nothing? As if you just went to run a quick errand."

Lola blinked at him because she honestly had no words.

Lola was the daughter of Rafael León, the ruthless ex-leader of Los Insurrectos. When he'd finally gone to prison, along with her brother, it had meant that she was no longer protected by his name or her brother's infamous fists. She'd become a target. The situation had been dire enough for her mother to come out of hiding, sneak into Benny's house in the middle of the night, and spirit Lola out of Chicago. They'd bounced around the country for a week before finally feeling like it was safe enough to make their way to her mother's safe haven in San Diego.

"Do you have any idea what I went through, trying to complete basic training while thinking you could've been hurt… or gone?"

Was he serious with this shit? "I didn't leave for fun, Saint. I was in danger."

"I know that. But how could you just leave without telling anyone?"

Lola crossed her arms over her chest. "Benny knew where I was."

"Well, I didn't. For the last seventeen years all I've had are rumors."

"But the letter," she said.

"What letter?"

"The one I sent you."

"Oh right. Now you sent me a letter."

Lola felt her temper rising. "Don't you dare call me a liar. I sent you a letter. I told you that my mom had come for me and—" She stopped. The letter had also said that she wouldn't contact him anymore, that she needed to move on and start a new life, but she didn't think this was the moment to bring that up.

Saint looked dumbfounded and Lola felt the same. Could it be that he really hadn't gotten her letter? How was that even possible? It had been 2005 not 1805. It wasn't like letters were being delivered via mail coach. Then again, her Amazon package had gotten lost in transit just two days ago.

They stared at each other in silence as the ramifications of their discovery settled between them. So much damage caused by the disappearance of one fucking letter.

The door to the closet swung open and Papo Vega stood there. "¿Qué demonios hacen encerrados aquí?"

What were they doing locked in the closet? Oh nothing. Just having their freaking minds blown.

"Abuelo, we need a minute," Saint said.

"Sorry, but I can't give you one. Ese pendejo, Benny, is telling Maria that if she doesn't call the police on me, he will. He's saying it's attempted murder and calling her my accomplice."

Oh right. She was here because this guy had poisoned her grandfather. "Don't call my grandpa an asshole."

"I meant it more like 'idiot,' but yeah he's an asshole too."

"Abuelo," Saint said in warning.

"What? I'm agreeing with her."

Saint gave a world-weary sigh and grabbed his grandpa's upper arm. With one last look at her over his shoulder, he led his grandpa back into the conference room.

Lola followed and found Benny in his seat, but she could tell by the stubborn tilt of his head and the red flush over his cheeks and neck that he'd just finished ranting about something. "We're back," Lola announced unnecessarily.

"Great," Maria said. "Now we can begin. The fact of the matter is that this is just the last in a series of incidents involving these two." She motioned between the two older men. "And we need to put a stop to them, before they get any worse, so let's all have a seat and discuss this like the rational adults we are."

Lola knew that voice. She'd adopted it many times while dealing with hormonal fifth graders and angry teens. It was the "I can see you are one step away from meltdown, but I'm still in charge of the situation" voice.

Maria waited until everyone had been seated before taking her place at the head. Lola lifted her chair and took her previous spot next to Benny, who now sat directly in front of Papo. Lola was annoyed to find herself facing Saint. She didn't want to have to look at him right now. Looking at him caused her thoughts to go pinging around her head like a pinball machine and she couldn't afford that at the moment. She'd just have to ignore him. She turned her attention back to Maria and firmly directed herself to keep it there.

"I want him gone." Lola pointed at Papo Vega.

"Miss León, I know you are upset and rightfully so," the director started.

Lola cut her off before she could voice the "but" that was clearly about to appear next. "My grandfather is hooked up to an IV pole receiving his second bag of fluids right now." She pointed to the offending object as if they couldn't see it. "He's dehydrated, which at his age and considering his health issues could be fatal. All because that man thought it would be funny to give him diarrhea as if this were some childish summer camp movie instead of an assisted living facility."

"Yes, but—"

"There is no but," Lola interrupted again. She crossed her

arms and leaned forward. "He put my grandpa's life in danger in the name of a cruel prank."

"I am not going to excuse this horrendous act by Mr. Vega," Maria assured her. "However, in the last few months there have been multiple incidents involving Mr. Vega and Mr. León and they have both played active roles in initiating them."

"Abuelo, why didn't you tell me about any of this?" Saint asked his grandfather, who simply stared at the table and shrugged. The brash and confident man who'd sauntered in the door was now uncommonly subdued. The Papo Vega she and the rest of the neighborhood knew was as loud and vibrant as the salsa sound he was famous for. He blazed like a shooting star. This old man was decidedly dull, like a light with the dimmer turned to its lowest setting.

Lola hardened her heart against the pathetic picture he made. "In any of these run-ins has my grandfather done anything physical to Mr. Vega?" she asked Maria.

"Well, no—"

"Then I fail to see why that's relevant to this situation in which my grandpa was physically harmed."

"What Mr. Vega did was really stupid and wrong," Maria said. "However, I think we need to take into account his state of mind. It's only been a few months since his best friend passed, which explains a lot of his recent recklessness. He's hurting and acting out because of it."

Lola sucked her teeth at that. "What you're basically saying is that because he's hurt, he gets to hurt others and we—" she motioned to herself and Benny "—are supposed to be understanding and forgiving. But by that logic my grandfather should be excused for anything he does in retaliation, because of the pain that he's currently in, and y'all will have to be okay with that." She chanced a look at Benny, who seemed a little too enthused by the idea of retaliation.

"That's not what I meant," Maria said to her.

"Isn't it though?" Lola asked. "Otherwise, why bring it up? Either his behavior is excusable or it's not."

"You're right," Saint cut in.

Lola's eyes shot to him in time to catch him rising from his chair.

"What Abuelo did was dangerous and cruel," Saint continued in that deep, even voice that was just gruff enough to suggest that he didn't use it often. "He needs to face the consequences of his actions."

"Saint," Papo exclaimed, shock and betrayal in his voice.

Saint turned to his grandfather. "In the last two months I have had to come down here to bail you out of trouble five times," he told him in a stern voice. "Todo el mimando se acabó. Punto y final."

It was clear that Saint was putting his foot down and his grandpa was going to have to fall in line.

It gave Lola a brief glance at the commanding officer he'd become in the military. She wasn't sure how she felt about that.

Saint maintained his focus on Papo. "You went too far and you know it. Otherwise you'd be here trying to defend yourself."

"I would never put someone in danger on purpose," Papo exclaimed. "I thought he would get churra and then he'd leave me alone."

"Leave you alone?" Saint asked.

"¡Sí! He's a bully and he's always messing with me. One time, in front of everyone, he told me that my dentures make me look like a horse and everyone started calling me Mr. Ed! He looks for ways to mess with me all the time. ¡No me deja en paz!"

That was news to Lola. She looked at Benny, who was very purposefully not meeting her gaze. She guessed it wasn't totally out of the realm of possibility given Benny's antipathy toward Papo, but that still didn't make what he did okay.

As if to echo her thoughts Saint said, "¿Y qué? That means you get to poison him?"

"I told you already that it wasn't Ex-Lax. I kept adding prune juice to his grape juice." He paused briefly. "And I sprinkled some fiber powder on his Caesar salad like parmesan cheese. But that was only one time."

"Abuelo…"

"Okay, fine, two maybe three times, but he barely even ate it."

Saint closed his eyes and rubbed a hand over his face as if completely at a loss. "Don't even try to be cute. You need to face what you did."

Lola felt her own righteous fury slowly extinguishing. It was hard to be mad when someone was agreeing with her and saying exactly what she would say. But then he started talking again.

"I don't think kicking him out is the answer," he told Maria.

"Yes, it is," Lola stated, she kept her attention on Maria. "I don't want him around Benny."

"I don't blame you," Saint said, "but he wants to get kicked out. He doesn't want to be here without Killian, so he's actively trying to get himself kicked out."

Papo's jaw was on the floor, clearly surprised that his grandson so clearly saw through his motives. He snapped his mouth closed and glared at the wall.

"That's not my problem," Lola said, still refusing to meet his eyes.

"True, but him getting kicked out isn't really justice. It's an easy fix. He needs to face the consequences of his actions and make reparations for all of his recent recklessness."

Lola considered his point. If he was kicked out, Papo would just go live with one of his many family members and be coddled and spoiled. Which was clearly what the old man wanted. Well, he shouldn't get what he wanted, at least not before justice was truly served.

"What are you suggesting?" she asked Saint.

"I think Abuelo should be grounded and forced to make it up to everyone he's inconvenienced with his childish actions."

"What does that mean exactly?"

"On top of personal apologies to everyone, he can no longer just come and go as he pleases. He is not allowed out of this building unless he has a doctor's appointment or it's an emergency." He looked at his grandfather as he emphasized the last word.

Papo glared back at him. "You're going to abandon me here so I can get even more depressed."

"I didn't say no visits. I said no field trips."

Papo crossed his arms and looked away.

"While we are discussing his mental health, he should be required to see the in-house therapist."

"We cannot force him to receive therapy," Maria interjected.

"Fine, if he agrees to see the therapist, then he can have one outing a week in which he will be escorted by me and *only* me."

Papo gasped. "That's blackmail!"

Saint shrugged. "I learned from the best."

Papo scowled and mumbled something about his past biting him in the ass.

"Also," Saint continued, "since he will no longer be going anywhere without me, he has the time to volunteer where extra help is needed. It will be good for him to see all the work that goes into caring for people like him. Maybe that way he will learn that he's not the most important person in this facility and his actions affect everyone around him."

Well, damn. So far this was a pretty good punishment.

"That's not enough," Benny yelled in Spanish. He pounded a fist on the table. "I want him to be kicked out. I don't want to see his stupid traitor face *more*. I want to see it less."

"Who are you calling a traitor?" Papa tossed right back at Benny.

"You. I'm calling *you* a traitor."

Now both men were standing and yelling at each other across the table.

"I don't even know you like that! What is your problem with me?"

"I don't like you. I don't like anything about you!"

"That. Is. Enough," Maria said loudly and firmly. She stood. "You will both sit down and you will stop acting like children."

Benny and Papo plopped into their seats, but continued to slaughter each other with looks.

"As you can see, this is not as black-and-white as it appears. Both men are guilty of being the aggressors in this situation and as such, both will receive a warning and consequences."

Lola was ready to open her mouth, but Maria raised her hand. "Please, let me finish before you unleash your fire, Lola."

They'd come to know each other better ever since Lola returned and had been stopping by to check on Benny daily while volunteering a few hours a week. They'd built mutual respect, so Lola closed her mouth and ceded the floor. For now.

"Because what Mr. Vega did was far beyond anything Mr. León has done. His consequences will be far more severe. Not only will he do everything Saint has suggested, but this is also his last warning. Any other incidences of this nature will result in an immediate expulsion from the center regardless of intent or his state of mind. I will not budge on this. Have I made myself perfectly clear?"

Both Vegas nodded their heads.

"As for Mr. León, as soon as he is fully recovered, he will also volunteer during our community activities. I think it is imperative for him to learn that while no one can or will force him to be friends with the other residents, he cannot and will not antagonize someone else, especially not because they just happen to be someone he doesn't like.

"Lola, if this resolution does not meet with your approval and you're still concerned about your grandfather's safety, we will cover all contract termination and relocation fees so your grandfather may move to another facility. Of course, you are also welcome to submit a formal complaint with El Vecindario."

She stood and brushed down her wrinkled skirt. "Now. I ask that if you would like to continue to visit with your grand-fathers you do so in their respective lodgings." She motioned to the door. Clearly, they were all dismissed.

Papo Vega was the first one to leave the room. Saint hung back. He stared at her, the look on his face saying he wanted to talk.

Too bad. Lola had done all of the talking to him that she was going to do. Instead, she turned to Benny. "Do you want to stay, or do you want to go?" she asked him. "I'll get you out of here right now if you want."

"Oh. Now you ask me what I want? After you disappeared with the enemy for twenty minutes then did nothing to help me?" The sarcasm was thicker than his accent.

Out of the corner of her eye she watched Saint engage Maria in conversation in front of the door.

"I was trying to defend you," she said. "Although lord knows why since you did a great job of making yourself look like the instigator and him like the victim."

"Don't start," Benny told her in Spanish. "And you can forget about whatever plans you have to complain to the city or who-ever, because I'm not leaving."

Lola sighed. "Benny, don't you want to be safe and happy? There are plenty of other places."

"I'm telling you that I'm not leaving."

"What if you moved in with me?"

He snorted. "Where? You live in a closet. You don't even have a bedroom."

"It's a studio not a closet." And she did have a bedroom. Sort of.

"Same thing. Besides, I lived here first. Let him leave."

She could tell by his tone that that was all he was going to say on the matter. Benny was nothing if not stubborn.

"Fine," she said. "Then you'll stay and do your volunteering with Papo Vega. Whatever you want." She reached for his hand and put it on her arm. "Let me walk you back to your room so you can rest."

Considering his mood, she thought for sure that Benny was going to tell her to go away. Imagine her surprise when he patted her hand and said, "Okay."

They slid past Maria and Saint through the door. Lola kept her attention on Benny even though she could feel Saint's eyes on her.

As soon as they rounded the corner her grandfather said, "While we walk you can tell me why that boy was looking at you like he'd seen a resurrected Jesus."

Lola snorted and took a page out of Benny's book. "Mind your business."

4

Saint trudged through the construction office in a fog. It was the state he'd been in since he'd first entered the conference room and saw Lola freaking León standing there. She'd been the last person on earth he'd expected to see. With her dark eyes igniting sparks of fire in him it was almost as if they'd stepped right back in time.

Except nothing else about her resembled the girl who'd simply disappeared from his life. Gone was the choppy haircut with chunky blond highlights and a thick curtain of bangs that she'd used to distract from the freckles on her face. A cut and color job he'd watched her do herself after sneaking into her bedroom window while her grandfather slept in his recliner in the living room a few feet down the hall. The baggy cargo pants and T-shirts she'd used to hide what she called her "Buddha belly and badonkadonk" had also been completely absent.

In place of that girl desperately wanting to be taken seriously was a confident woman with her wavy dark hair pulled back away from her freckled face and her bombshell curves on prominent display in formfitting workout clothes.

And just like that sixteen-year-old girl had, the thirty-four-year-old woman absolutely knocked Saint on his ass. Because with Lola León it wasn't just about her looks. It was about her "Fuck you. I'll do what I want" energy. From the moment he saw her sitting in the office waiting to talk to the principal after getting kicked out of class again, he'd been absolutely fascinated. He'd never met someone so wholly themselves but also completely hidden. He'd wanted to get to know all about her. The real her. Then he'd wanted everything with her, but life had other plans in store for them both.

A letter. She'd sent him a letter.

He still didn't know how he felt about that. A part of him was relieved that she'd thought about him and had wanted him to know she was safe, but then he thought about the torture he went through when his brother Cristian had told him she was gone and no one knew where. He'd wanted to leave basic training and go home to find her, but he couldn't and that had made everything all the worse.

By the time he'd finished training and had been given two weeks of leave, there had already been rumors that she'd gone into hiding or witness protection or something. Saint had even visited Benny with his brothers to offer their help in looking for her. Benny hadn't said one damn thing about Lola being safe, but neither had he seemed distraught. Saint had let that give him some hope. He'd gone on to Afghanistan and did his duty, but in the darkest moments of the night, when he'd been the most terrified, he'd thought about her and wondered if he was being just as naively hopeful about her as he had been about war.

"Saint," Tío Luís called from his office, shaking Saint out of his fog. "Come in here for a moment."

Saint walked into his uncle's office and was about to make his way to the chair in front of the desk when his Tío added, "Close the door."

Saint's eyebrow went up. That certainly was not like Tío Luís, whose entire leadership style began with having an open door policy. He thought briefly back to Alex's suspicions from earlier in the day, but quickly dismissed them. He was close to Tío Luís, but they weren't in the habit of talking about their personal lives. Probably because neither of them had one, but still. If by some miracle Tío Luís was seeing someone, he wouldn't be calling Saint into his office to chat about it.

Once the door was closed and Saint was settled in the chair in front of him, Tío Luís began. "I just got off the phone with our new client."

Saint stayed quiet because that was hardly news. Cruz and Sons (an ironic name if ever there was one) was constantly getting new clients.

His tío continued, "This is a high paying job. But I need the team we have to keep our other projects going, so we'll have to hire on a new crew for this." He paused. "I want you to lead it."

Saint blinked. "Me?" Tío Luís was always the lead on their bigger jobs. "What about Alex? Or Gabi?" But Gabi, like Saint, preferred to stay in the background. She was an amazing engineer and capable of creating beautiful designs, but she wasn't the type to rally a bunch of rowdy men.

"As much as I would love to put one of my girls in charge, it wouldn't work for this job."

"Alex is young, but she's capable."

"She won't do it," Tío stated.

"You asked her already?"

"No, but I know she won't."

That had all of Saint's red flags waving. "Why not?"

Tío used his thumb and index finger to squeeze and massage the bridge of his nose. Then he opened his eyes and looked Saint right in his. "I'm not going to lie to you. This is not the kind of job we usually go for. It's a full renovation of the old building on Evergreen Avenue. The homeless shelter. We are going to turn it into studios and condos."

"What?" Saint was shocked. Not only was this not the type of job they usually did, but it went against everything they stood for. For years Tío Luís had been turning down jobs and meetings with developers because he refused to contribute to the gentrification happening in Humboldt Park. In fact, after helping Kamilah revamp El Coquí, he, Saint, Gabi, and Alex began taking on some pro bono work to help neighborhood businesses update using leftover materials from other jobs. They wanted to lift up their neighbors, not tear them down.

"See that's why I can't tell my girls," Tío Luís said with a shake of his head. "I couldn't stand it if they looked at me like you are right now."

"I'm not giving you a look."

"You are. You're looking at me like I'm a sellout and I don't blame you because I am."

"I don't think you're a sellout. I'm just confused. You've never accepted this kind of job before, so why now? Is the company struggling?" Saint doubted it. Sometimes they had more jobs than they had hours in the day.

"Saint, before we go on I need you to promise me that everything we've talked about here today will stay between us."

Saint didn't like that. Not one bit. He wasn't the most talkative guy and he enjoyed his privacy so he was very much of the "but that's not my business" mindset. However, people tended to tell him things. He hated it because usually when they did it was something bad. Saint had enough of his own demons. He didn't want to add other people's too. But Saint would do anything in his power to keep his loved ones safe even if that meant being their unwilling confidant. "I won't say anything," he promised, although it felt like he was making a huge mistake.

"I have rheumatoid arthritis," his Tío confessed. "I thought I was just getting older, you know. I'm fifty-five and I've been doing this kind of work since I was fifteen, so it made sense for my joints to hurt. But the doctors suspected it was more and it is.

I don't really know much, most of what they said went over my head, but I know I'm at stage two which is when the swelling starts causing damage to the cartilage. I need to start treatment right away to help slow everything down or I will start losing mobility."

Saint quickly started trying to remember anything and everything he knew about rheumatoid arthritis. "It's an autoimmune disease, right?"

Tío Luís nodded. "It makes my immune system attack the healthy tissues."

"So how do they treat it? With pills? Physical therapy?"

"My doctor wants to do a mix of things: a pill, injections, and physical therapy. He said the earlier we start, the better chances of a remission of symptoms."

That all sounded expensive and with his Tío being a small business owner it wasn't like he had the best health insurance. Knowing his uncle the way he did, Saint and the workers probably had better plans than his tío. "That's why you accepted this job. It will help pay for treatment."

He nodded sadly, "The injections alone are almost six thousand dollars per dose until I can get some sort of assistance. I've tried a few different ones, but have been rejected because my insurance wants me to try other brands first."

"I'm guessing these brands are cheaper?"

"A tiny bit, but the doctor says they don't work as good."

Saint shook his head. "Bullshit."

"I know, but now you see why I have to do this. The job isn't complicated and it's paying almost triple our other jobs combined because the developers want it done quickly. I couldn't turn them down. As much as it hurt me, I just couldn't."

"I get it," Saint told him and he did. As a soldier, Saint knew better than anyone that sometimes we had to do things even when we knew they were wrong. Even when it meant we sold pieces of our souls until we weren't sure there was even any left. "I'll do it. I'll lead this project and I won't tell anyone anything."

Tío Luís sagged in relief. "Thank you, mijo. You have no idea how much I appreciate this."

"Don't mention it," Saint said. "Besides, I owe you for everything you've done for me."

Tío scoffed. "You owe me nothing. You know that. This is what family does. We help each other when we need it. Now go. It's getting late and I know you have to pick up Rosie. We'll discuss more details tomorrow."

Saint nodded and left the office. He quickly made his way to his truck, praying he wouldn't bump into nosey Alex, and hopped in. On his way to El Coquí, he contemplated everything he'd just agreed to do, completing a huge project while keeping a secret from everyone he knew. Exactly what his sister had done a few months ago. Something that had blown up in her face spectacularly and almost got her ostracized from the family. The red flags were piling up, and like a bull he was charging right at them instead of away.

He pulled around to the back of the building that housed the family restaurant along with the apartment he'd grown up in and backed his truck into a tiny space between the building and the dumpster enclosure. He used to be able to find parking on the street or in the small lot on the side, but not anymore. El Coquí was now constantly packed and so was Kane Distillery, the business that shared the building. Now if Saint wanted to park on the street he'd have to go a few blocks away. He didn't complain about that though. It actually made him happy. His sister was killing this restaurant owner game and her fiancé was the most sought-after craft whiskey distiller in Chicago.

Saint pulled the door to El Coquí open, releasing a wave of salsa music, and slid inside. Even over the noise he heard Rosie shout, "Papi!" His reason for living jumped off a barstool, nearly falling on her face, before running past the tables full of customers to take a flying leap at him.

Saint caught her midflight, scooped her up, and planted a kiss on her cheek. "Mi amor, I missed you today."

She wrapped her little arms around his neck and squeezed. It was the best feeling in the world. "I missed you too."

"How was school?" he asked, already knowing the answer.

She leaned back and shrugged. It was her way of saying, *The same as yesterday and the day before and every day since the first day.*

In short, not good.

"Did you at least talk to your teacher?"

"No." This was said in the same tone as one would say, *Have you lost your damn mind?*

"Why not?"

Rosie decided a change of subject was in order. "Guess what." She didn't wait. "Tío Leo made me a cocktail!"

Saint noticed a ring of something sticky around her lips and her breath smelled like cherries. He looked to the bar where his youngest brother was making a drink for a customer. Leo thought it was hilarious to pump Rosie full of Shirley Temples and then send her home with a sugar high that Saint had to deal with. He looked back at his daughter and saw there was already a familiar manic light in her green-blue eyes. Rosie loved to feel like a grown-up as she sat at the bar chugging her *cocktails.* "You're cut off now," he told her as he started to carry her back to the bar. "And hand over the keys to your car."

Rosie giggled. "I don't have a car."

"Oh good. Then I don't have to worry about you driving under the influence." He plopped her back onto her stool and her high ponytail of light brown ringlets bounced while the large leopard-print bow he'd put in her hair that morning flopped. He looked up at his brother. "No more kiddie cocktails."

"But why? She handles her ginger ale like a champ. She can drink us all under the table when it comes to shots of grenadine." Leo's pale green eyes—the ones he'd inherited from Abuelo Papo, were full of his ever-present mirth. Saint sometimes wondered if there was anything his little brother didn't find humor in. It seemed like the only thing he took seriously was his day job as a firefighter, but Saint had his suspicions about that too.

"Then you can try to put her to bed later," he told him.

"Ooh." Leo made a faux grimace and sucked his teeth. "I would, but unfortunately I'm here till close."

Saint's look let his brother know exactly what he thought about that. "At least get something to wipe her face."

The swinging doors that led to the kitchen flew open and his sister stepped out of the kitchen followed closely by their parents. It was clear that they were all annoyed.

Kamilah made a straight beeline to him. "Can you kindly remind your parents that they don't run El Coquí anymore?"

His father looked to him too. "Tell your sister that we know that, but we do know things about running a restaurant, and she could benefit from listening to us."

Mami shook her head, her light brown hair with blond highlights brushing against Papi's shoulder. "Déjala, Santos. Ya sabes que no hay peor sordo que el que no quiere oír."

"That's ableist," Kamilah said to their mother even though it was a waste of breath.

Saint doubted his mother knew what *ableist* meant much less how a saying comparing not listening to being deaf would be offensive. She certainly wouldn't listen to any criticism at the moment. He would bring it up later. "Bendiciones, Mami," he said instead. He leaned down to give his mother a kiss on the cheek.

As expected, she was immediately distracted from the argument. "Hola, mi vida." She gave him a kiss on the cheek and then lifted her hands to cup his face in between her palms. She eyed him carefully with her light brown eyes. "You look tired. Are you still not sleeping? You need to stop stressing out so much. El estrés mata."

Unlike his sister, Saint knew better than to argue with his mother. "Sí, Mami." Then he turned to his dad, Santiago Vega Senior. "Hola, Papi." They embraced briefly and gave each other a pound on the back.

His dad also eyed him, but unlike Mami he said nothing. Everyone always said how alike Saint and his father were in looks and temperament, but Saint thought his dad had way more patience than he did. Sure, Saint had led soldiers in war, but his father had raised five rowdy kids, expertly cared for his easily excitable wife, and ran a successful business for over thirty years. That was bravery and competency on a whole other level.

"Wela, Welo," Rosie called, effectively distracting both of them from their argument with Kamilah and their examination of Saint. "Look what Tío Leo got me." She held up a *Beauty and the Beast* coloring book and a pack of colored pencils.

"Que lindo," Mami said, making her way over to see.

Papi followed.

"Welo, help me color the one of Belle and the Beast dancing." She passed him a brown-colored pencil and tapped on the Beast. Then she patted the empty stool next to her with her little hand.

His father sat. Because much like her father and grandfather, Rosie's commands were typically followed without question.

Saint frowned at the coloring book in suspicion. His brother was not one to think ahead so he doubted he'd already had it with him when he'd picked Rosie up from school. "When did Tío get you that?"

Without looking up from the close eye she kept on Papi's progress, she answered, "When we went to the store."

"You went to the store?"

"Uh-huh. After we went to Starbucks."

"You went to Starbucks?"

Rosie's eyes rounded. "Oops. I wasn't supposed to tell anyone about that."

Four dark heads turned in Leo's direction.

"About what?" Kamilah asked in that, "well, well, well," voice that only siblings could use to maximum effect.

"That we saw—"

A wet rag was slapped onto Rosie's face, cutting her off.

"You have cherry goo all over you," Leo said as he scrubbed at her face and used his palm to cover her mouth.

"Taking your four-year-old niece with you to stalk one of your girlfriends." Kamilah shook her head in mock reprove. "I am appalled. At the very least you should've gotten her the coloring book first so she wouldn't know what was going on." She turned to Rosie and leaned in like one comadre getting gossip from another. "Who did you see?"

Rosie couldn't answer because she was busy trying to pry Leo's hand away from her mouth.

"Say one word, you little traitor, and I will never take you to get ice cream at our special place again," Leo whispered loudly.

Rosie nodded and he let go.

"Guess what else happened today! Ms. Kirkland left during nap time and never came back. Then Mrs. Galván, the principal, came at the end of the day and told us that tomorrow we're getting a new teacher!"

Exclamations of shock and disbelief arose from all around.

Then Rosie's face fell and her shoulders slumped. "I think she left because of me. Because I wouldn't talk to her."

It was a mind-boggling situation. Saint's chatterbox daughter would not talk at school. As soon as they hit the school grounds she clammed up completely and would not say a word until she was back with her family. Saint didn't understand it. No one did. But one thing he knew for sure was that this was one hundred percent not Rosie's fault.

He scooped her off the chair and held her close. "No, mi amor. She didn't leave because of you."

The truth was that Ms. Kirkland had probably left because of him. She'd been after him all year about Rosie's silence and even though he'd done everything she suggested, she still treated him like a deadbeat dad. Never mind that Saint frequently worked overtime to keep a roof over his daughter's head and food in her stomach. Never mind that his immediate family had been integral parts of Rosie's upbringing since the moment he'd brought her home to Chicago just shy of her first birthday. Because Saint wasn't there dropping Rosie off and picking her up every day, because he couldn't abandon everything and spend his days in class with his daughter, because he couldn't force her to engage in lessons, he was a shitty parent who couldn't be bothered to care about his daughter's education.

Her disdain for him had been clear in every interaction. After she'd tried to get his daughter evaluated for a bunch of learning disorders without his agreement, Saint had finally had enough. He'd gone to the director of the community center in charge of the charter school and filed a complaint. Ms. Kirkland would've been informed of it in the last few days. It was probably the straw that broke the camel's back.

"I don't know what that teacher's problem is," Leo said. "When I was in school, my teachers would've paid good money for me to sit nicely and not talk."

"I'll pay you money to not talk," Kamilah offered.

Leo used his middle finger to rub an imaginary stain off the bar while making eye contact with their sister.

"Leo," Saint warned.

"Come on, Rosie," Kamilah said, holding a hand out to his daughter. "Let's go show Tío Liam how you learned to do cartwheels in gym."

Rosie wiggled to get out of Saint's grip. "We gotta go outside because I still bump into stuff inside."

"I bet I can do more cartwheels than you can," Kamilah challenged her niece as they walked away, their voices slowly fading the farther they got.

"No way," Rosie exclaimed. "You're too big. You gotta be little like me to do 'em right."

"I bet you ten dollars."

"Okay," she agreed readily. A beat later she said, "Hey, Tití?"

"What?"

"Can I borrow ten dollars?"

Kamilah barked out a laugh. "How are you going to try to give me back my own money?"

They passed through the doorway that led to Kane Distillery and Saint could no longer hear their conversation.

"That girl is a trip," Leo said.

"She's smart," Saint countered.

"She is," Papi assured him. "And she's too curious to hate school for long."

"Y ahora esa bruja se fue," Mami added. "Maybe she'll like her new teacher more and will talk to her."

"God, I hope so," Saint sighed. There was one thing for sure. He was going to have to go make sure this new teacher knew from the get-go that neither he nor his daughter were going to be pushed around anymore. "But I was actually talking about Kamilah." He gave his parents a serious look. "You two need to stop ganging up on her. She's doing a great job and she doesn't need you both in here nitpicking everything she does."

"We aren't picking on her!" Mami said, immediately offended. "We are trying to give her advice so she doesn't get overwhelmed like we did."

Papi nodded. "There were two of us and it was still a lot. Running a restaurant is like trying to run an obstacle course blindfolded."

Leo chimed in from behind the bar. "I don't think she finds any of this overwhelming. The other day I walked in and she was in back prepping while also reading one of Liam's business books. You should've seen her. She was giving her watch voice memos and everything. She thrives on this and the tips I make every shift prove it." He moved off to help a patron.

"She's doing well now," Papi agreed. "Because she's still riding the wave from the media exposure she got from the contest, but people are fickle. They'll forget about it soon and she'll have to figure out another way to bring them in."

"And she will," Saint said. "If there is anything Kamilah never lacks, it's ideas and determination."

"That's true," Papi said.

"Look," Leo added, coming back. "You two wanted out of the restaurant running business, so be out of it. Enjoy your retirement and let Kamilah do what she's going to do. This place isn't your responsibility anymore. Go on vacation or something. Be free, my little birdies." Then he moved off again to go help more patrons.

Their parents were quiet for a moment, absorbing everything they'd just heard.

Mami spoke first. "Tienen razón, Santos. It's clear she doesn't want us here looking over her shoulder all the time and it doesn't really seem like she needs it. She has Liam to help her now and the boys."

Papi sighed. "I know, mi amor. It's just hard."

Finally, Saint understood. It wasn't that their parents didn't believe in Kamilah, it was that they were struggling with letting go of their life's work even though they didn't want it anymore. They didn't know what to do now.

Saint would figure out something to give his parents purpose and set them on a new path that included a more positive and healthy relationship with his little sister. He'd do it because Saint had been taking charge of his family and watching over them since he was a kid. He wasn't going to stop now.

5

Lola took another look around the room. The new positions of the tables gave clearer pathways to aid with transitions, she'd taken down some of the posters and charts to make the procedural graphics stand out more, and there was a brand-new calming area that had cost her a hundred dollars at Target—along with a chunk of change she'd spent on other things she wanted for the classroom. She hoped she'd made enough changes to make it clear that there was a fresh start happening, but not enough to cause the kids to spiral.

She'd gone back to the building after the school day had let out and spent hours in what was now her classroom. She'd gone through Ms. Kirkland's previous lesson plans, dug into the curriculum, and tried to envision what a typical day was like in that room. Thankfully the paraprofessional assigned to the class worked the after school program and was available to answer questions about the usual routine.

Afterward she'd sent frantic texts to her mother in San Diego, begging her to dig through all of her teaching stuff to find her old preschool plans from when she was student teaching. Her mom had come through and had sent Lola at least two hundred pictures of old lesson plans, instructional theory, activities, etc. Then Lola had stayed up to the wee hours of the morning making a plan for the rest of the week, which basically went like this: set up expectations, get to know students, and survive—in no specific order.

She was exhausted and the day hadn't even started yet.

The door opened and Mrs. Fonseca walked in with Dolores.

Dolores paused and took a look around the room, quickly cataloging the changes and giving Lola a nod before pointing them out to Mrs. Fonseca.

"I knew you could do this," Mrs. Fonseca said with a nod of her own.

Lola almost laughed. "I haven't even done anything yet."

Mrs. Fonseca shook her head. "You could've just showed up and tried to fit yourself into Ms. Kirkland's place. It's clear that you have a plan to make this room yours." She smiled. "Besides, you forget that I know you. You never back down even when something seems impossible. If anything, you dig in."

"I have yet to figure out if that's a good thing or not," Lola confessed.

"We need people like you, who won't stop until the job is done."

"Yeah, but imagine how much less stressed I'd be and how much more sleep I'd get."

Dolores laughed. "Well, I definitely don't want you getting no sleep. To that end, I have asked our instructional coach to support you with this transition. She should be stopping by at some point today. Of course, I'm here for anything you need too."

"Thank you."

"Also, we wanted to talk to you a bit more about the situation I mentioned yesterday."

"The pissed off parent?"

"Yes." Mrs. Fonseca nodded. "He emailed us both last night and requested a brief meeting today."

"Today?"

"This morning. In a few minutes actually."

What? Lola was still trying to get stuff together for her first day. "I have things to get done before the day starts. Could we maybe do this after school or another day this week?"

Mrs. Fonseca grimaced apologetically. "I'm sorry, but he requested we do it before his daughter comes to school today to make sure we are all on the same page."

"On the same page? I don't even know his daughter yet."

"I get it. It seems backward, but I also think we need to have this discussion ASAP."

There was really nothing else to say about it, then. "Okay. Can you give me more information before we head in?" she asked Dolores since she figured the principal would have the most information.

"Basically, this student, Rosalyn, doesn't talk," Dolores said.

"She's nonverbal?"

"Well, she has the ability to speak, and does so at home, but she hasn't spoken at school. She barely participates and it's been nearly impossible to assess her proficiency in any academics. Ms. Kirkland was concerned, so she requested an evaluation without first discussing it with this parent. You can see why he'd be upset."

Lola nodded. "So the parent isn't concerned about her silence at school or he doesn't think it's a red flag for a potential learning disorder?"

"He's worried about her not talking, but he does not think this is a learning disorder and refuses to have her evaluated."

Lola was about to ask for more information when Dolores lifted a finger. She pressed the earpiece that was attached to her radio. "Go for Galván." She listened. "Send them to the class. We'll meet here."

Lola gave a frantic look around. They were going to meet here? Her table was a mess still.

"It's okay," Dolores told her, guessing her thoughts. "We can sit at this table." She pointed to the large kidney table by the door.

Lola grabbed one of her brand-new notebooks and a pen. She sat herself at one of the tiny chairs at the table. Before she could get a bigger chair the door opened and Saint Fucking Vega walked in. "Are you kidding me?"

The other women gave her a sharp look. Oops. She hadn't meant to say that out loud. But what the hell? Saint had a daughter? That meant he probably had a wife or girlfriend. What the fuck was he doing kissing her in closets?

"We have to stop meeting like this," he said, then he bent over and Lola finally got a good look at the little person currently sliding out of his arms.

She was wearing olive green overalls with a beige shirt underneath and a pair of leopard print canvas shoes that matched the huge bow in her hair. With her light brown skin, and a riot of tight reddish brown ringlets, she was just a whole package of absolute adorableness.

"Oh, you are the cutest little thing I've seen in the longest time," Lola told her as she stood up.

Rosalyn was practically hiding behind her dad's jean-clad leg, but Lola didn't let that stop her.

She motioned to her own olive green trousers and beige blouse. "Look, we even match. Although, your leopard print is way cooler than my boring tan." She held out a foot to show off her ankle boots and was gratified to see that Rosalyn was at least looking at her.

Lola moved a little closer, but stopped when Rosalyn moved back. She took a step back and sank to her haunches. "I don't know about you, Rosalyn, but I'm going to take this as a good sign. I think you and I are going to get along."

The little girl frowned at her as if to say, *That's what you think.*

"Of course, we'll have to get to know each other first and it will take some work, but it will be worth it. You'll see."

Rosalyn looked up at her dad, which unfortunately meant that Lola had to look at him too. She'd tried not to at the seniors' home. She'd been careful to keep her gaze averted and to never look at him head-on because she knew the effect he had on her, but there was no hope for it now.

Saint had certainly grown into all the physical promise of his youth. He wasn't much taller than the six feet he'd been as a teen, but he had filled out. He seemed almost twice as wide as he had been. There were cords of muscle straining against the shoulders and chest of his sweater. Even his neck was thicker. It was as if he'd inflated like one of those huge pool floats that you can ride on. And great. Now she was thinking about riding him. There was no doubt in her mind that it would be good. Really good, but very intense. It was clear from his energy.

It was difficult to reconcile the differences between the fresh-faced and doe-eyed seventeen-year-old boy she'd loved and this dark and almost menacing man with a cynical look in his eye even as he smiled down at his daughter. The Saint she'd known had been all lightness and hope despite his serious nature. This man. It was clear that this man had those rose-colored glasses ripped right off his face. He'd seen the darkness of the world, battled it, and was now a part of it. It made her sad for the boy she'd known. He'd really had no idea what he was getting himself into, but Lola had known. Even then she'd known that they'd take that naive boy who saw everything through rose-colored glasses and they'd destroy him. She hadn't wanted that for him, but he'd made it clear that she had no say in the matter, despite the love they shared.

"Guess what, mi amor."

His deep voice washed over her and again all her nerves prickled. It was like dipping your fingers and toes into hot water after they'd been freezing and numb. It wasn't exactly painful, but it wasn't pleasurable either. Lola was so caught up in the feeling that she answered, "What?" as if he were talking to her and not his daughter.

There was a beat of silence in which Lola realized what she'd just done. Her eyes flew to Mrs. Fonseca and Dolores first, who were wearing matching blank expressions. Good. Maybe they hadn't heard. She slowly turned her eyes to Saint. Her hopes were dashed.

Partially hidden in the scruff of his short beard, his full bottom lip was quirked to the side in a smirk. His deep brown eyes were crinkled a bit at the corners. He'd heard.

Lola cleared her throat and looked back at the little girl at his hip. "*What* a great time we are going to have together, Rosalyn."

He ignored that ridiculous attempt to correct her egregious error. "Rosie, I know your new teacher from a long time ago."

The little girl's eyes widened and she looked at Lola with a speculative light in her eyes.

Lola jumped at the chance to gain any ground with the kid. "In fact, your dad used to be my friend."

"Friend." His tone of voice made it clear to the adults in the room that what they had was much more than mere friendship.

Rosie tilted her head and stared at Lola as if trying to solve a puzzle. There was a wealth of intelligence and comprehension behind the look, which made it clear that the little girl also understood the message behind her father's words.

Of course, Lola wouldn't make any decisions until she had more information and had observed the little girl herself, but so far she wasn't seeing much evidence of a learning disorder.

"Rosie, I hope it's okay that I call you that too." There was no response. Not that Lola expected one. "Mrs. Galván, Mrs. Fonseca, your dad, and I want to talk about how to make sure you have a great rest of the school year. I want you to know that I would love for you to be a part of our talk. It doesn't seem nice to talk about you like you aren't here and you don't understand when I bet you do. But if you don't want to, I completely understand that too. I added some new things to the room that you might like to check out."

Rosie looked back to her dad for direction, but he didn't tell her what to do. Instead he just said, "Whatever you want to do, mamita."

After a moment, she let her dad's hand go and went directly to the new calming area.

"Great," Mrs. Fonseca said. "Why don't we get started." She motioned them both to the table.

This time Lola grabbed a large chair from the neighboring table and sat. She would not be forced to look up at the man the whole meeting.

She bit her lip as she watched Saint perch precariously on one of the tiny chairs at the table. His legs were spread wide as he planted his feet solidly on the ground and tried to prevent his knees from disappearing into his armpits. Lola almost offered to get him another large chair, but decided against it. Let him be at a disadvantage for once.

"Mr. Vega, I know you're concerned about how this change will affect Rosie specifically," Dolores began.

He nodded, but he didn't take his eyes off Lola. She felt like a bug under a magnifying glass.

"I want to assure you that Rosie's well-being is our priority."

He spared the principal a brief glance. "You've told me that before," he said. "Then your staff tried to have my daughter evaluated without my permission." His gaze went back to Lola.

Mrs. Fonseca jumped in. "Saint, as the mother of a child who required special education services, I completely understand what you're feeling right now." It was clear to Lola that Mrs. Fonseca was using his nickname to remind him of the years he'd spent under her care in the same community center they were in now. It didn't seem to have the effect she was hoping for—Saint remained as stern faced as before.

"I'm sorry, Mrs. Fonseca, but it's not the same thing at all, because Rosie doesn't require those services and Ms. Kirkland went behind my back after I expressly told her that I wasn't in agreement with her suspicions. It's hard to put my trust in what you say after that."

"Well, as you know, I don't do anything behind someone's back," Lola told him. "I will tell you what I think flat out."

"And what do you think, Lola? Do you think I'm wrong for wanting to make sure my four-year-old isn't labeled with a learning disorder I don't think she has?"

"Of course not," she said. "She's your daughter and you know her best. I do just want to make it clear that the school cannot actually diagnose her with anything. An evaluation is to see if she qualifies for educational services under that label, but only a qualified medical professional can make a diagnosis."

"I know that," he said. "But this label would follow her all through school and will affect how she's treated by staff and other students. I don't want that for her if it's not a necessity and I don't think it is."

"You have every right as a parent to decline an evaluation just as you'd have every right to request one," Lola said. "Sadly, we do know that Black, Latine, and Indigenous students are disproportionately labeled with disabilities over students of other races. I don't blame you one bit for advocating for Rosie."

Saint smiled and shook his head.

"What?" she asked.

"You haven't changed at all," he said.

She didn't know what to say that wouldn't derail the conversation at hand, so instead she kept it as professional as possible. "I've heard that she doesn't demonstrate the same behaviors at home, so I'd like to ask what you think is happening to cause this swing from one extreme to the other."

"I don't know," he said. "Rosie has never liked change and I know she can be stubborn."

Lola almost asked him, sarcastically, where he thought Rosie got it from, but then she remembered Mrs. Fonseca sitting there observing her every word and determining her capability to work for El Vecindario in a permanent role.

"However, she's never done anything like this. I figured she'd stop once she got used to coming to school, but she hasn't. She still cries almost every day no matter who brings her. When I ask her if she hates school she says no, but when I ask her why she won't talk she says she doesn't know. She denies that anyone is messing with her. I tried to incentivize her with the rewards chart, but she couldn't care less about it."

Lola could hear the worry and frustration in his voice. She didn't understand how anyone could think he didn't care or was unconcerned. This was clearly a parent who cared about his child and was deeply upset about the situation. "Let's take her silence off the table completely," Lola said. "Are there any other concerns?"

"Like what?"

"When she's at home, does she talk to you and others in complete sentences?"

He scoffed. "En casa ella habla hasta por los codos."

Lola laughed. Benny would say the same thing about her constant stream of conversation.

"Does she show you any hint that she's learning things at school and practicing those skills at home?"

"If I ask her what she did at school she will shrug and say she doesn't remember. She fights me when it's time to do her home-work, but when we are playing around or we aren't talking about school at all, she'll do stuff." He dug in his pocket and pulled out his phone. "Like the other day I told her that I needed help making a grocery list." He scrolled through what looked like endless pictures of Rosie. "She did this." He handed Lola his phone, which held a picture of Rosie holding up a small whiteboard. On the board, written in uneven and sometimes backward letters were the words "egz," "mlk," "brd," and "fut."

Lola smiled. "Eggs, milk, bread, and fruit." She handed the phone to Dolores to look at.

Saint nodded. "I didn't help her. She did that by sounding out the words herself."

"She's obviously learning letter sound correspondence," Dolores commented before handing the phone to Mrs. Fonseca.

Lola nodded. "It's been a while since I was in a preschool classroom," she confessed to Saint. "But this is very normal for a child her age."

He looked relieved.

She felt a softening toward him that she really shouldn't. "Look, I'm not here to tell you what to do about Rosie." That garnered a frown. "I haven't been in the classroom for a few years and special education was never my area of expertise." The frown deepened. He probably wondered what the hell she was doing taking over the classroom, then. Lola had to get things back on track. "But I do know some things about early childhood development and while I can't speak to anything until I spend time with her, know that when I do I will be one hundred percent up-front with you. I take my job very seriously. From the moment your child passes the doorway, they become mine too and I'm a momma bear."

He didn't seem too impressed with her claim, so she tried to explain it in a way that she knew this former solider would understand. "My job is to teach them the curriculum, but my duty is to make sure my students feel safe, accepted, and free to grow as humans. I will do my duty to your daughter, Saint. That I promise you."

He stared at her in silence for a few moments. "I'd like to believe you, Lola, but we both know you don't always keep your promises."

Lola sucked in a breath. She knew exactly what promise he was referring to. She'd promised to wait for him to come back from basic training. Instead, she'd disappeared in the middle of the night and left everything behind. Including him.

"I'm going to trust you, Lola. But she already feels responsible for her teacher leaving and thinks she's bad because she can't make herself talk. That's not okay with me. I will not let my daughter continue to be hurt." There was a definite threat in his words and somehow instead of getting mad, Lola was relieved. This was the Saint she knew. The one who put his family before all else and would go to any length to defend them even if it put him at odds with her.

"I get it," she said. She liked knowing exactly where they stood, which was at opposite ends of the field.

Hours later Lola hobbled up the short stairs that led to the front doors of El Hogar and stifled a yawn. She'd forgotten how much energy it took to teach preschoolers. She taught Krav Maga multiple times a week and did yoga almost every day and she still felt like she'd been through a grueling workout. During her first day she'd given more hugs, calmed more breakdowns, done more squatting/kneeling, and danced more than she had in years. She made a mental note to wear shoes with tons of support from now on. Her heels were cute, but not practical for all the things a preschool teacher had to do.

If she had her way she would've headed straight home, had a hot shower, and finished off one of the hard ciders she'd gotten from a local brewery during a tour she'd taken with some coworkers a few days ago. However, Lola had promised Ruby she'd talk to Yara and she already felt terrible about not doing it the night before. She tried her best to always keep her word, especially when she gave it to one of the kids she helped. It was hard enough to earn their trust, so she would move mountains to keep it.

She pushed the buzzer and waited until she heard a matching buzz. She stepped through the door and gave Mariana, one of the overnight staff, a tired smile.

They smiled back and then paused and gave her a thorough once-over. They tipped their head and a lock of bright teal hair fell over a deep brown eye. "What's up with you? You look like you just met up with a vampire in the back alley and they almost sucked you dry?"

Lola chuckled. "Close. I just spent the day with twenty-five four-year-old energy vampires."

Mariana tossed their head back and laughed. "I forgot. Brittany mentioned you taking over the preschool class." Brittany was another volunteer at El Hogar who taught fifth grade at the school. She was also Mariana's live-in girlfriend. Lola wondered how they made it work when Brittany was at work all day and Mariana at work most nights. Mariana gave her a commiserating look. "More power to you. I can't work with kids with ages in the single digits. I tried and started molting like a bird."

"I'd forgotten just how hard they are to keep up with." Lola rubbed a hand over her face. "I'm going to have to start slamming energy drinks or something."

Mariana gave her a wry look. "I see those kids playing outside. You'd need to start using coke to reach that level of energy."

Lola snorted. "Probably just as healthy as an energy drink."

They laughed again. "Facts."

"Is Yara still here?" Lola asked even though she knew there

was a ninety-nine percent chance she was. Yara usually had to be dragged out by her hunky husband or kicked out by the rest of the staff before she went home.

Mariana's face changed from slightly amused to serious. "She's in her office," they said. "She stormed in there an hour or so ago and hasn't come out since."

Lola raised her eyebrows.

"Enter at your own risk," Mariana said.

Lola wasn't exactly worried. She'd known Yaraliz back when her name had been Yariel Martinez, a hero at the center since the time he'd dunked on Michael Nicholson while wearing his mom's five-inch heels. She and Yara were not the only two who were still around from back then, but it was close as a majority of the staff at El Vecindario were either much younger or much older than them. Yara had been visibly ecstatic when Lola had walked into her office three months ago and inquired about volunteering.

Her face, as Lola walked in now, was the exact opposite. Despite the deep V between her eyes, Yara was a beautiful Afro-Latina with brown skin and the kind of cheekbones people would kill for. She had a tiny hook at the end of her nose and generous lips, which were currently tipped down. Her eyes, a gorgeous mix of browns and tilted at the ends giving her an almost feline look, were red-rimmed as if she'd been crying.

"Is everything okay?" Lola asked.

Yara shook her head. "I just got out of an emergency meeting Fonseca called. The owners of El Hogar's building sold it to some condo developers." The absolute disgust in her tone was clear.

"But. But. They can't," Lola sputtered. Thanks to the Latine community's lingering conservative mindsets, El Hogar was one of the only LGBTQIA+ friendly shelters in Humboldt Park. It was definitely the longest running and the most well-known. Lola had spent a lot of time there with friends in her youth.

The workers of El Hogar had been the first ones to tell her that it was okay for her to be attracted to whomever she was attracted to. For a long time, they'd been the only people to tell her that. "How is this possible? What about the contract with El Vecindario? Who owns the building?"

"The Long Grove–based grandkids of some couple that bought the building back when Humboldt Park was still mostly Polish."

Lola shook her head. "Of course." Any residents of the wealthy Chicago suburb would be largely unconcerned with preserving a poor neighborhood's community center. They probably would've sold a long time ago if it weren't for the fact that the buildings in the neighborhood hadn't been worth much of anything until recently. "So the sale is final?" Lola asked, her brain already whirling with next steps.

"Unfortunately, yes. The family did everything quietly and as quickly as possible to make sure none of us found out until it was done."

"Those assholes!" Lola exclaimed.

"I know, right?"

"Did you guys get in contact with the new owners, make sure that they know you want to keep the space?"

"Girl, did you not hear me say 'condo developer'? They aren't letting us keep the space. They want to gut it and turn it into expensive condos."

Lola felt her blood pressure rising. Fucking gentrifiers coming into the neighborhood people like she and Yaraliz had spent their entire lives trying to help, just to kick out the residents, slap a new coat of paint on it, and act like they really did some shit. It was bad enough that local places were being closed to make way for some bullshit craftsman candlemakers or some high-end boutique gyms, but now they were coming for the community center. The one that had been a home to so many displaced and lost queer youths like herself. She couldn't let it happen.

Yara massaged her temples. "It's so bad. Fonseca told me that they informed her we need to be out of here by the end of next week."

"That's bullshit! How can they expect us to find a new place by the end of next week?"

Yara just shook her head. "I don't think they give a shit about the logistics of relocating a bunch of unhoused youth."

"What did Fonseca say? I know she can't be okay with this."

"She's definitely not. When I met with her, I could tell she'd just gone through a few rounds in the ring with them." She shook her head. "I never thought I'd hear that woman cuss. Let me tell you, it's terrifying."

"No," Lola said. "What's about to be terrifying is how quickly we are going to round everyone up and make these mother-fuckers regret ever messing with El Hogar."

For the first time since Lola walked in, Yara cracked a smile. She reached over and laid her hand on top of Lola's. "There's the Lola I remember from before she disappeared overnight."

That comment, or some version of it, was getting old fast. "Yara, you know I couldn't say goodbye before I left. I couldn't let anyone know where I was going."

Yara nodded. "I know." She gave Lola's hand a squeeze.

With a smile, Yara squeezed her hand again. "Well, all that matters is that you're home now and I'm happy you're here with us."

Lola squeezed back. "Yes. I'm home and no one is closing the doors to El Hogar on my watch." It was time Humboldt Park remembered exactly who Lola León was.

6

Saint sat in his truck, staring at the building in front of him and trying to convince himself that he was still a good person despite the sucky thing he was about to do. It had only been two weeks since his uncle had informed him of their new job and his shitty promotion to lead contractor, yet El Hogar was already empty and ready for their first walk through.

He gulped down the horrible taste in his mouth and closed his eyes. He tried to focus on anything other than what he was there for. Unfortunately, his mind decided to conjure up something even worse. It reminded him that the last time he'd been there, it had been to pick up Lola for a very special date. A date that had changed him completely.

Saint had never been so nervous in his life. He also had never told a girl he loved her, at least not a girl he wasn't related to. He'd said it to his mom, sister, and abuelas many times, but this was a different kind of love. He looked over at Lola sitting beside him. She was staring out the bus window, so he couldn't see much of her face, but he could tell she was smiling by the plump apple of her cheek. She'd obviously guessed where he was taking her. It was a bit alarming how well she knew him.

The rest of the people in his life treated him like he was this deep mystery that no one understood, but Lola had seemed to know the real him from the moment Saint had pulled her into that empty classroom six months earlier.

The bus pulled into the Navy Pier Terminal and Lola turned to him, her deep brown eyes peeking out from her thick fringe of bangs. "I haven't been to Navy Pier in years."

Saint stood up and stepped into the aisle. "Why not?"

"Last time, my brother came with some of the guys and I begged him to let me go along." She paused and looked at her feet. "We didn't stay long though."

"Why not?"

"They ran into some dudes they had beef with and started a fight. We got kicked out and had to go home."

Saint did his best not to shake his head like he wanted to. Her home was only a few blocks away from his, but sometimes the things she said made him think she'd been raised in a war zone. While his home was loud and busy, it was always safe. His parents were honest, hardworking, law-abiding citizens who went to church every Sunday and taught their children to be good people. Everyone in his family was like that. It boggled his mind that seemingly no one in Lola's family was, except for her. They did whatever they wanted without thinking about how it affected others, even their own family members. It left Lola mostly alone and fending for herself. Sure, she had her abuelo, but even he did the bare minimum, which left Lola to take care of herself.

"Bueno, we're here now and we're going to have more fun than you ever had before," he promised.

Lola smiled at him and his world lit up. He loved making her smile. She didn't do it enough.

"I'm holding you to that," she said, picking up the pace until she was practically dragging him.

They decided to get food first, so they stopped at America's Dog & Burger for hot dogs, fries, and two sodas. Lola badgered him until *he agreed to try a Chicago-style hot dog. Growing up in a family who seldom ate anything but Puerto Rican food prepared at home, Saint was skeptical about hot dogs in general but especially hot dogs with yellow mustard, bright green relish, fresh chopped onions, juicy red tomato wedges, a kosher-style pickle spear, a couple of spicy sport peppers, and finally, a dash of celery salt all on a poppy seed bun.*

Saint stared at the hot dog in his hand. "I should've gotten a cheeseburger," he grumbled.

"Take a bite," Lola said. "I know it sounds weird, but you'll like it. I promise."

Saint made a face. "Why does it need relish and a pickle? That seems like overkill."

She rolled her eyes. "If you are going to be such a big baby about it then go get a burger."

"I'll do it," he shot back. "Just give me a second." He took a deep breath and blew it out. Then he shoved one end of the loaded hot dog in his mouth and bit off a piece that included a bit of everything.

"So? What do you think?"

Saint took his time chewing. He was sure that his sister would be able to perfectly describe the taste. She was an aspiring chef who spent her time watching cooking shows and using her small allowance to buy ingredients for the recipes they featured. But Saint wasn't Kamilah, so he did his best to distinguish the different flavors before he swallowed. "It's a hot dog with a bunch of tangy stuff on it."

"Care to elaborate on that?"

He shrugged and took another bite. "I don't know. It's salty, but there is like a vinegar taste too. It has a bit of pica from the peppers. I can't really taste the things separately."

"Do you like it?"

Saint shrugged again. "Se deja comer."

Lola laughed. "What a glowing review."

He didn't know what else to say. He couldn't say he liked it, but it wasn't horrible. It was okay—edible.

"You don't have to finish it. I'll eat that and you can get something else."

He really couldn't though. He was already spending the little bit of money he had to pay for their trip. He couldn't splurge on extra food for himself. But he didn't want Lola to know that. She'd try to pay for herself and he knew that she had even less money than he did. "This is fine." He took another bite of the hot dog and shoved some fries in his mouth at the same time.

She eyed him skeptically. "If you're sure."

He nodded and finished off the hot dog in two more bites. "When we're done we should go get our tickets for the Ferris wheel."

Lola froze for a second before finishing the bite in her mouth. She took a long drink from her straw. "I'm not going on the Ferris wheel."

"Why not?" Saint asked.

"I don't trust that rickety death trap."

"Lola, it was made in 1995. It's barely ten years old."

"If humans were supposed to be that high in the air, we'd have wings." She took another drink of her soda as if unconcerned, but he could tell she was just pretending.

"You told me you want to travel the world?"

"Your point?"

"If you don't like heights, how are you going to get on a plane?"

"Why do I need to get on a plane?"

"Uh. To get to other continents."

"I'm sure there are still passenger ships that cross the oceans."

Saint had to laugh. Lola needed to be a lawyer, because she had an argument for everything. "Now I see why your teachers are always kicking you out of class."

"Hey," she scolded. "Most of my teachers actually like me. It's only my history and English teachers who kick me out and that's because I challenge their white-washed, Westernized, and misogynist curriculum. They'd rather maintain control of the class than be actual educators or engage in truthful discussions. But that's America for you—"

Saint cut her off before she could really get going. "Okay. We won't go on the Ferris wheel. Let's go on the carousel instead."

"Okay." Lola hopped up and collected their trash.

"I want to ride the zebra," Lola told him.

"I'll take the horse next to it."

"Okay. What's the plan if one of these kids gets to it first?"

"Wait until the next ride?"

"Nah, we take 'em out."

Saint paused but then he saw the sparkle in her eye. "You want us to take out a bunch of kids?"

"Of course, look at them. They look like a bunch of little punks. Especially that one at the front hiding behind his mommy's leg."

"You mean the toddler in the overalls and those soft shoes babies wear when they first learn to walk?"

"Yeah. Him. He's the worst of the bunch. You can tell. It's always the quiet ones."

Saint laughed and wrapped his arms around her. "Loca Lola," he said fondly.

She leaned into him. The front of her luscious body pressed all along the front of his, but he felt her suck in her stomach at the last minute.

He didn't get why she felt the need to do that. She never just let herself completely be with him. He hated it when she hated on her own body, saying that she was too fat to date a guy as fit as him. He loved every single inch of Lola. She was soft and warm and her skin constantly smelled like the cinnamon bun lotion he'd gotten her for Christmas because it reminded him of the dusting of freckles across the bridge of her nose and cheeks. It made him hungry. It was getting really difficult for him not to put his hands all over her like he wanted, but Lola had made it clear that she wasn't ready for anything more than kissing. He respected her feelings and did his best to keep everything light and affectionate instead of hot and heavy.

Saint stifled a groan when she nuzzled into his shoulder. Luckily the carousel came to a stop and they were in the next group to board. They handed over their tickets and Lola made a beeline to the zebra, brushing past people and ducking in between the animals like she was playing laser tag. She even mean-mugged a trio of middle schoolers until they chose a different row of animals.

Once he settled on his horse next to her, Saint shook his head with a smile. "You know we have more tickets, right? It didn't need to be that intense."

"They were behind us in line and heard me say I wanted the zebra. They were just being jerks and I don't put up with that nonsense."

Saint laughed. "Ay, mi Lola. I love you."

Her eyes grew so big he worried they'd fall out. "What?"

He cleared his throat. While his plan had been to tell her today, he hadn't exactly meant to tell her like this, but what was done was done. He didn't regret it at all. Saint turned on his horse and looked her in the eye, so she'd know that he wasn't joking. "I love you," he said clearly.

The longer Lola stared at him wide-eyed and silent, the harder his heart pounded. Right when he was about to begin panicking her face lit up with the biggest smile he'd ever gotten from her and her cheeks flushed. "I love you too," she whispered so quietly that he read her lips more than heard her words.

He didn't care that she hadn't proclaimed it as loudly as he had. He didn't care that they were sitting on plastic animals instead of at the top of the Ferris wheel like he'd planned. Saint was still on top of the world because the girl he loved just told him that she loved him back.

A hard knock pulled Saint out of his journey to the past. He turned and saw Tío Luís standing by the driver's side window of his truck dressed in an expensive-looking shirt and tie. Saint looked down at his black slacks and white button-down and wondered if he should've put in more effort. "I look like a damn cater waiter," he mumbled to himself while turning off his truck and sliding out.

"Are you ready?" his tío asked. "You were able to look over everything I sent you?"

Saint nodded and followed his uncle into the building that used to house El Hogar. He tried to ignore the way this felt like a betrayal to the girl he'd loved all those years ago, but his stomach turned just the same.

The feeling only got worse as he followed Tío Luís and the development team around the building listening to their vision and plans. Evidence from the rushed departure of the staff and members was everywhere. Office chairs still sat behind the desks that used to house computers. There were old board games stacked on the shelves of the game room and Tupperware in the kitchen. The most gutting were the posters that still decorated the walls in the small bedrooms used by homeless teens.

The scene made Saint feel legitimately nauseous.

This was wrong. He couldn't do it. He couldn't be a part of it.

Saint eyed the team from the developer, Raven Realty. They were huddled together at the other end of the room taking in the old multipurpose space. The original plan was to make a movie theater that tenants could sign up to use, but now they were discussing the possibility of creating a separate mail room with large, locked drop boxes for each unit to help prevent package theft. He left them to that discussion while he turned to have a very different one with his uncle.

But at the sight of his tío leaning heavily against the wall, he froze.

Tío Luís had his eyes closed and was practically panting. His face was pale and the tiniest sheen of sweat glossed over his forehead.

He slid closer. "Are you okay, Tío?" he asked in a quiet voice.

Tío Luís immediately straightened and opened his eyes. "I'm fine."

That was clearly a lie, so Saint didn't bother with a response. At Saint's prolonged look, his tío finally cut the shit. "I'm a little dizzy," he whispered. "It happens sometimes when I get really tired, but I'll be okay. I just need some coffee."

That was more bullshit. Saint thought about how he'd witnessed Tío Luís mainlining coffee over the last few days when usually he'd only drink a cup a day. The coffee hadn't really affected his apparent exhaustion at all, which meant it wasn't just lack of sleep. It was something else. "This is from the RA," Saint said. "You have fatigue and you're dizzy because you're trying to push through it."

Tío Luís sighed. "What other choice do I have? Things have to get done and if I don't do them, then who will?"

Saint knew then that he wasn't going to back out. It felt awful betraying his neighborhood, but the only time he'd ever felt worse about his choices was when he'd gotten the call that his wife had died. His infant daughter was in Child Protective Services, and he'd failed them. He wasn't going to fail his family again, no matter how dirty he had to get.

And he felt like he was mired in shit when he finally exited the building only to run smack into Lola, who stood on the sidewalk holding a sign that said Gentrifiers Get Out.

The shock, then the instant disappointment on her face was a punch to his already rolling gut.

"I can't believe you'd do this," she said to him.

Because he was already feeling awful, he reacted with defensiveness. "Of course you'd assume the worst. You don't even know what I'm doing here."

"I know exactly what you're doing here, because this—" she pointed to the woman next to her "—is the director of El Hogar and she was informed that the scavengers who just kicked a bunch of displaced teens out of their home would be here today showing around the sellouts they hired to destroy it. Simple deduction tells me you're either the scavenger or the sellout. Either way it's not a good look."

"Look, we are just trying to help the neighborhood," one of the foolishly brave members of Raven Realty's team spoke up.

Saint winced. The guy had no idea who he was talking to and what he was about to unleash.

Lola swung her attention to him. "Oh, you just want to help the neighborhood? Okay, Mr. Raven Realty, why don't you tell me how much of your five million dollars in gross profit is making its way to this neighborhood? Because I haven't seen it. Have you, Yara?"

The woman next to her shook her head. "Nope."

Lola continued. "But maybe instead you're providing some sort of service like feeding the hungry?" She paused as if in thought. "Then again Miss Tammy over here, she heads up one of the neighborhood's biggest food programs, she was just telling us how they're going to have to close at least one branch for lack of resources, so I don't think any of your help has made it there."

"No check for us," an older woman called out from the back.

"Hmm." Lola scratched her chin. "I know. You must be funding the programs that support the plethora of mental health services required in serving low-income and highly trauma-impacted neighborhoods."

"Where are all those programs at, because I haven't seen them," a teen said from Lola's left.

"Come to think of it, Ruby. I haven't either." She snapped her fingers as if she'd just gotten a great idea. "I got it. You're going to help this neighborhood because this about-to-be reno-vated building is going to provide free housing to the unhoused."

She took in the team's deadpan faces. "No?" She handed off her sign and then crossed her arms. "Then I fail to see how forc-ing out a program that did all of those things, in order to build yet another set of condos that are too expensive for the true resi-dents of this neighborhood to rent, is helping this neighborhood.

Maybe you can explain it to me, Mr. Raven Realty, because the math isn't mathing."

The small crowd around her began to cheer and clap, but they quickly transitioned to chanting, "If we get no housing, you get no peace,"

"Fuera, fuera, fuera," and "Ravens are scavengers!"

The anger in the air was palpable and all of Saint's instincts were telling him that things could get bad quickly. He thought about his dizzy uncle and the clueless members of the team. He thought about the community members who were completely justified in their anger. He tried to think of a way to get Lola to back down. Even for a second so he could talk to her.

But his thoughts wouldn't focus on any one thing. They kept spinning and swirling. Then the sound of shouting protesters morphed in his mind into explosions in desert streets, the sounds of bullets hitting flesh, and wails of pain. His heart began trying to break out of his chest, his lungs refusing to take in or let out air. There was a loud buzzing in his ears, even worse than the stupid boom box the crew blasted at work sites. He needed to get out. He needed to make sure his people were safe.

"Get back in the building," he barked at Tío Luís. "And take them with you." He didn't pause to see if he listened. He knew his uncle would.

Then, without thinking, he latched on to Lola's arm and began tugging her down the street.

"Hey," she shouted. "Let me go! Get your hands off me."

Saint wanted to listen. He really did. He knew he was acting irrationally, but he couldn't stop. He needed to get them both away from the powder keg set to explode at any minute. He needed to get them both to safety.

Finally, he got them around the side of the building to the narrow alley that separated the building from the shop next door. He pulled them behind the large dumpster and backed Lola into the corner. Saint placed himself in front of her, covering her body with his. His forearms rested against the bricks, his hands bracketing either side of her head. He stayed quiet. Listening.

"Saint?" she asked after a minute. "Saint, are you okay?"

He dropped his head. His forehead hovered over the top of her head. He took a deep breath through his nose. He got a huge whiff of something fruity and spicy. Lola. He did it again, inhaling her scent. "Canela," he whispered. "You still smell like cinnamon."

Lola tried her best to calm her racing heart. "It's my body wash," she whispered back despite her nerves still clamoring.

She'd never gone so quickly from angry to worried.

At first she'd thought Saint was pulling her away to yell at her or something, but then she'd seen the sweat on his forehead and the way his hand shook where it was latched on to her upper arm. And she'd remembered that he was a veteran.

Lola was all too familiar with trauma triggers. Although she doubted theirs were the same. She paused. Actually, they were probably more similar than she could imagine.

"Lola!" Yara yelled down the alley, causing Saint's entire body to go rigid.

Instinctively, foolishly, Lola put a hand on his chest. "Saint," she tried again. "Everything is okay. We are both okay."

She felt his deep inhale when his chest pressed against hers and his exhale when his breath coasted through her hair and along her face.

He leaned in briefly before using his forearms to push himself back. He spun on his heels and put his head in both hands.

Once again, Lola let instinct rule over common sense and placed both hands on his back. When he didn't react violently, she started rubbing soothing circles.

"Lola!" Yara's voice came again.

"I'm fine," Lola called back. "We're just talking." She had no idea why she lied, but she knew she didn't want Yara to come investigate.

"You sure you're good?" Yara asked.

"Positive. I'll be back in a moment, but let's pack it up. I think we made our point for now."

"Okay, mi general." Lola could practically hear the smart-ass salute in Yara's voice.

The silence in the alley grew heavier.

"I don't want to be a part of this," Saint eventually said. He dropped his hands and turned to face her. "I hate all of this as much as you do, but I can't do anything about it."

So they were going to ignore his freak-out and stick to the problem at hand. Fine. She could do that. For now. "You can adhere to your principles and not take part in it."

Saint shook his head. "My tío Luís is sick. It's chronic."

Lola paused.

"He hasn't even started treatment and his medical bills are out of control. His medications are going to cost a fortune, his insurance is shit, and he doesn't qualify for any programs."

"Well, fuck." How could she tell him to stick to his principles now? He was doing just that. Saint Vega did whatever he had to do for his family. He always had.

"This job goes against everything the company usually stands for, and I know it makes us sellouts, but renovating kitchens and sprucing up neighborhood businesses for free doesn't get him the treatment he needs."

Lola took a deep breath and let it out as she leaned against the wall. "God, this country's health care system is the fucking worst."

Saint nodded.

"I'm sorry your uncle is dealing with this, but, Saint, this is still wrong."

"I know. I know it is and I know saying that the developer was going to find someone to do the job anyway makes me sound like a dick, but it's true. There was no stopping this. Not when the owners were sneaking around to find the highest bidder."

"But city planning—"

"City planning isn't going to help, Lola. Their hands are tied just as much as ours."

"I know that, Saint, but I won't just give up. There are ten kids standing outside on that street who still need a safe place to sleep, food in their stomachs, help with their homework, and proof that their lives matter just as they are."

"Let me help," he said.

"Help how? You just said that there is no stopping this."

"There is no stopping the renovation of this building," Saint reiterated. "Not at this point, but there has to be another building out there. One that will suit all of El Hogar's needs."

"There are probably plenty that could work," Lola said, "but they're all too expensive to rent now. The ones that the non-profit can afford would need too much work and would take too much time. These kids are in crisis now. We can't wait for a miracle." They'd already been dispersed among other shelters.

"It won't take a miracle. It will just take the two of us being on the same team." His eyes pleaded for her to understand and to accept his help.

She understood that he felt guilty. He was a good guy. He always had been. None of that meant anything. His guilt wasn't going to get these kids back into a safe place with people they knew they could trust. "I won't let this just be a way for you to assuage your guilt about selling out," she said. "These kids deserve better."

"They do deserve better. Just like Rosie deserved better than to be hurt by Ms. Kirkland's need to bolster her own vanity. I'm trusting you to help make the situation better for her. I don't think it's too much to ask in return for you to trust in my genuine desire to help solve this problem."

It wasn't his desire to help that she questioned. It was her own ability to maintain objectivity around him. She'd already let him pull her away from her purpose. Quite literally. But she couldn't deny that he was a good ally to have. She'd learned a lot of things about Saint and the Vega family from Yara. His uncle, Rico, was the alderman and his cousin was entrenched in another nonprofit that focused on housing and community planning. Not to mention that the mayor was a frequent visitor to his sister's new restaurant.

If Saint could get the rest of his family on board, they had a chance to provide something great for these kids. All she had to do was focus on the possibilities and not on how weak in her stupid knees he made her. She could do that. If there was one thing Lola was good at, it was searching out her own weaknesses and destroying them.

"Fine," Lola told him. "I'll let you help find El Hogar a new home."

7

Lola placed her king on top of the queen. "I win," she said for the third time in a row.

Benny grunted. "I'm going to the bathroom. I'll be back."

Lola laughed at his disgruntled face. "You are such a sore loser," she told him as she collected the cards on the table.

"I have arthritis in my hands." He held them out for her as if she couldn't see the gnarled knuckles on her own. His hands were courtesy of his many years as a mechanic at various factories in the area. "It's not fair, because I can't move as fast as you." Except a few days ago she'd seen him fix an old-school radio with nothing but his hands and a screwdriver, so that didn't exactly jibe.

She lined up all of the cards and then cut the deck. "Benny, you're the one who suggested we play Speed. I was fine playing one of the other games." She started to shuffle the cards. "While you're in there try to come up with more reasons you keep losing," she teased.

The bathroom door slammed shut and she could hear him grumbling.

Benny had always been like that. He hated when things didn't go the way he wanted and was likely to complain, make excuses, pout, or point fingers. Her father was the same way, which made it very easy to see why the two were never really close. In fact, there were many years when they hadn't talked at all.

Benny had moved back to Puerto Rico after his divorce and his only son—just seventeen at the time—had refused to go with him despite Benny being the only parent interested in fulfilling the role. Her father, already involved in the local gang by then, had decided to couch hop with his "brothers" until he turned eighteen and got his own place. From then on the communication between the two had been nil until Iván, her older brother, had been born. Something about being a father of a son had prompted her dad to reach out to Benny. They'd maintained only sporadic contact during Lola's early childhood, until a year after Lola's mom left.

She'd never known what exactly had happened, but one day, when Lola was about six or seven, Benny had shown up on their front porch with his bags in hand. Her dad hadn't been thrilled—telling them to call him Benny because he didn't deserve to be called abuelo. He'd lived with them for a bit before it became clear that the two men could not cohabitate. Benny got his own apartment a few blocks from their place and would take her and Iván there as much as they wanted. Iván was already firmly under their dad's thumb and hadn't gone often. Lola had gone as much as her father let her, which was a lot since he usually didn't care about what she did or didn't do so long as she wasn't making him look bad.

It was during the time that she spent with Benny that she'd finally begun to see a light out of the tunnel. She'd seen that there was a world out there in which she didn't have to play the perfect daughter. Benny had taught Lola all about her namesake, Lolita Lebrón, who by some was considered a terrorist and by others a hero. Lolita had been ready to be killed for her belief that

Puerto Rico deserved to be free. When she'd led gun-brandishing members of her organization into the House of Representatives and shot at the ceiling while shouting, "Viva Puerto Rico libre," she thought for sure she would be killed. She hadn't been. She'd been arrested and sentenced to fifty-six years in prison. She hadn't let that stop her. After serving twenty-five years, she was pardoned, but she continued to fight fiercely for the liberation of her homeland. Her presence in the movement continued all throughout her life and her impact continued after her death.

Benny's teachings hadn't stopped with Lolita or even with Puerto Rican independence. It made stops all throughout the US, Latin America, and other countries in the world. He'd taught Lola to question what others said and to dig for the truth. He'd made it clear that he expected her to fight for what was right for herself and for others. But he'd also made Lola believe that she was as fierce and as capable as her namesake. He'd given Lola a purpose when she'd felt like the only path available was to be her father's pawn.

It made it all the more ironic that Benny was still a willing pawn in her father's games, even after all these years. He answered her dad's calls no matter what time they came in, he sent him money whenever he asked, he visited at least once a month even though he had no car to get there and back. It made Lola angry, but it also allowed him to also visit Iván—something she'd wanted to do for almost twenty years.

The landline started ringing as she finished setting up a new game and Lola jumped up to answer it. There was no name on the caller ID and Lola was excited. She hoped it was a call from her brother in prison. She was desperate to talk to Iván. "Hello," she said as soon as the call connected.

She expected there to be an operator or at least one of those automated voices. What she was not expecting to hear was a loud throaty but garbled growl that sounded like a mix of animal sounds.

"What the fuck?" Lola said out loud.

The line went dead.

The bathroom door opened and Benny shuffled out.

"Benny, why did Chewbacca just call you on your house phone?"

"Again?" Benny let out a growl of his own, but his was decidedly human and full of annoyance. "I don't know how he did it, but that is definitely Papo Vega's fault."

"He's still pranking you? I'm going to go talk to Maria right now."

"No!" Benny shouted.

"Why not?"

"Because I already got him back."

"Benny."

"What? He deserves it."

"You're going to get yourself kicked out," Lola warned.

"I didn't do anything that would hurt him. Besides, Papo Vega is a lot of things, but he's no llorón. He won't tell on me. He'll just try to get me back."

Lola shook her head and decided to leave it alone for now. She had more important things to discuss with her grandfather. "I only answered because I thought it was Iván."

Something in her tone must have tipped him off, because the look he gave her was overflowing with suspicion.

"When was the last time you talked to Iván?" She finished dealing out his final card.

Benny picked up his cards and examined them seemingly nonchalantly, but his grip was a bit too tight. "He called me last week."

"And did you ask him about adding me to his list of approved contacts?"

He was purposefully not meeting her eyes. "We didn't talk for long. It was only a few minutes."

She knew exactly what that meant. Iván had said no. Again. She tossed her cards on the table. "Carajo, why won't he let me visit him or at least talk to him on the phone?" She tried to keep the hurt out of her tone, but couldn't. "Doesn't he want to talk to me?" Growing up it had felt like it was the two of them against the world. Even as Iván had gotten pulled further and further into her father's world of drugs, guns, and violence, he'd never changed how he treated her—like the most treasured person in his life. She didn't understand why he wouldn't want to communicate with her, now that he finally could.

"Of course he wants to see you," Benny said, placing his own cards on the table. "He doesn't want you to see him. Not like that."

"I don't care about any of that," Lola argued. "It's not like him being in prison is a surprise and it's not like it would even be the first time I've visited a prison." She'd done some volunteering and outreach back in Cali. "He could at least talk to me on the phone."

"You know it doesn't work like that. If he adds you to his list of approved contacts then you're approved for everything: calls, letters, and visits. He's not ready for that. Give him time to get used to the idea," Benny advised.

Lola sighed. "Fine." She thought twenty years was more than enough time, but she was willing to wait a bit more.

They were quiet for a moment, staring at the abandoned game in front of them.

"Are you going to ask me about your dad?" Benny eventually asked.

Lola did her best not to scoff. "Absolutely not," she replied. She didn't have to ask about him to know what he was up to. He was undoubtedly doing the same thing in prison that he did on the streets, playing power games and ruining lives.

"He's not happy to hear that you're back," Benny supplied.

Lola ignored the sting. "Of course he isn't." She tried for a breezy tone but didn't quite make it. "The day I disappeared was probably the best day of his life."

"Don't say that," Benny barked at her. "Tu papá será lo que quieras, pero siempre te ha amado a su modo."

The scoff she'd fought back before burst out before she could stop it. "Right. His deep love for me was why he treated me like trash and belittled me whenever he could."

"He was trying to protect you," he told her in Spanish. "He knew his life was no place for a girl and that you'd need to be strong to survive, even on the outskirts. He was preparing you."

She hated that so many people used that excuse to justify the trauma they inflicted on their children. "Oh, so he decided to fuck me up completely before the world could do it. Sound logic."

"I'm not saying it was right. I'm just saying that he's not the monster you want him to be. He's upset that you're back because he's worried about you. He knows that he can't do anything to protect you, because he's in there."

"He didn't do anything to protect me when he was out here!" Lola slapped a hand on the table. "Do you know what he did the first time one of his guys tried to corner me and shove his tongue down my throat?" She didn't wait for Benny to answer. "He made Iván and the others take him out and get him laid, then he told me to stop dressing like a whore. I was wearing knee-length shorts and a tank top. Oh, and I was thirteen." She remembered the moment clearly because it was in that moment the last bit of trust she had in him died.

"That's not how it happened, Lola. They didn't take him out to reward him with a good time. They took him out and beat him within an inch of his life. They broke his ribs, his hands, his jaw, one of his legs, and they fractured his skull. He was in a medically induced coma for weeks. You never wondered why he and the rest of them stayed far away from you after that? Your papi made it clear that whoever put hands on his daughter would pay, even his own men."

Lola couldn't take it anymore. She shot to her feet. "Even if that's true, he didn't do any of that for me, Benny. He did it to bolster his own power." She placed two hands on the table and leaned forward. "He had to do something because not doing so would've made him look like his own men didn't fear or respect him enough. I was something that he owned and no one was allowed to touch his things without his permission. That was the only thing he cared about. Not looking weak."

"You always assume the worst in everyone, Lola."

Lola closed her eyes and shook her head. She couldn't have heard that right. "Benny, I learned that from you!" She dragged her hands through her hair. "You know what, I can't with this right now." She stepped aside and tucked the chair under the table. "I have too much other shit going on to sit here and listen to you make excuses for the man who ruined all of our lives. I know he's your son and you love him no matter what, but I can't listen to this. I gotta go."

"No seas así, Lolita."

She backed up. "I'll be back tomorrow for Bingo."

Benny huffed. "Fine."

Lola spun on her heels and left. She kept her head down and moved as fast as her legs could take her without breaking into a run, rage seeping out of her. She'd almost made it into the main hallway when she bumped into a body. Luckily she'd been honing her reflexes for years, so she was able to steady herself and the other person before they both fell. "I'm so sorry," she cried and winced at the clear frustration in her voice.

"¿Adónde vas tan apurada, niña?"

Her head snapped up. Oh great. She'd basically just tackled

none other than Papo Vega. "I'm sorry," she said again. "I wasn't watching where I was going."

He stared at her for a moment, examining her face much like his grandson did. "I think I hurt something in my hip," he said after too long a pause.

Oh god. She'd just physically maimed the beloved patriarch of the Vega family. "I am so so sorry, Señor Vega. Let me get a nurse."

"No, no," he said quickly. "I'll be fine. Just walk me back to my room."

Lola nodded manically. "Yes. Sure. Claro." She immediately moved to put an arm around his shoulder. "Lean on me."

He let her take a small amount of his slight weight.

Lola heard a loud crinkle and looked down.

There was a yellow chip bag peeking out of his pocket. She was about to ask him if he should be eating chips, but reminded herself it was none of her business what someone else's grandpa ate.

Instead she started forward and they began a slow shuffle toward Papo's apartment.

"You want to tell me what had you rushing down the hall like you were running from the devil?" he asked in Spanish.

She wanted to tell him "not really" but figured that he deserved to know considering she'd just bulldozed him. "I was upset."

He sucked his teeth. "I could see that, but why?"

"I got into it with Benny."

"So you *were* running from the devil." He started laughing like he'd just made the wittiest joke in the world.

"Don't call my grandpa the devil," she demanded. She expected to hear something rude back, but when she looked at him Papo Vega was smiling.

He was so weird.

They finally made it to the door of his small apartment and Lola was about to let him go when he said, "Walk me in please."

She did as requested and walked past his small kitchen and over to the tiny living room where two large recliners faced the TV, which was playing old episodes of *El chavo del ocho*. Lola helped him sit.

He flopped into the chair with a sigh of relief. "Gracias, mija."

"Are you sure you don't want me to get a nurse?"

Papo Vega wiggled around in his seat and pulled the yellow bag out of his pocket. He wiggled some more before pulling a can of Coke out of the other one. "No. I have everything I need right here." He placed both in his lap. Then he started laughing again.

Okay...

He opened the bag and shoved a handful of Funyuns in his mouth. "Can you get my remote to work? It's been acting weird all day." He handed it to her and went back to eating chips.

Lola pointed it toward the TV and hit the power button. Nothing happened. She tried a bunch of other buttons with the same result. She looked at the front and discovered a piece of black tape covering the sensor. Benny's revenge. She had just pulled the tape off when the door to the apartment swung open.

"Abuelo, how many times do I have to tell you to stop leaving the door unlocked?" a man's voice called.

She turned in time to see a guy in a Chicago PD sweater walk in followed by a man in glasses, a guy who looked like a GQ model, and finally Saint.

They all paused at the sight of Lola standing there.

"Who are you?" the cop asked.

Lola tried not to bristle at his tone.

Before Lola could answer, from behind them a high-pitched voice said, "Can you big ol' gorillas move?"

Saint's body jerked forward as a beautiful woman pushed her

way through Saint and the *GQ* model before pausing next to Saint, her shoulder touching his arm. Her curls were escaping their high ponytail and her deep tan skin was perfectly smooth and luminous. Her big, light brown eyes were filled with surprise and welcome. "Hi," she said with a big warm smile that lit up her entire face. Holy shit. She was incandescent, like looking directly at the sun.

Lola wondered if she was finally meeting Rosie's mom. The thought made her stomach clench. She frowned. There was no reason the thought of this gorgeous Instagram model being Rosie's should cause her body to do anything. There was definitely no reason for it to make her irrationally angry.

At Lola's expression, the other woman's face changed too, becoming confused. "Are you a new nurse?"

"No," both she and Saint said at the same time.

Everyone's heads swung between the two of them.

"I'm Lola. My grandpa lives here too," Lola explained.

"What are you doing here, Lola?" Saint asked, ignoring the look he was getting from the woman at his side.

Right. Now she had to tell him that she'd hurt his grandpa. This was going to suck. She opened her mouth, but Papo Vega beat her to it.

"She was helping me get back to my room," he said. "¿Y qué ustedes ya no saludan?"

A chorus of "Bendiciones, Abuelo" rang through the room.

Papo Vega just smiled and shoved another chip in his mouth.

"Hey, where did you get that from," the woman cried at the same time the cop asked, "Why did you need help getting back to your room?"

"Because I got lost on my way back from Doña Concepcion's room." He took a swig of Coke.

"Give me that." The woman rushed forward and yanked the soda out of his hand along with the bag of chips. "And stop begging at her door like a stray dog. I bring you plenty of snacks. Ones you're actually allowed to eat."

Papo Vega let out a burp. "If you're talking about that rabbit food you left after stealing my pork rinds, I threw that in the garbage where it belongs." He seemed inordinately proud of himself for that. Preening like a beauty queen.

Saint stepped forward until he was standing next to Lola, close enough for her to feel his body heat but not enough for her shoulder to touch his arm.

She fought the urge to close that space and then look at the Insta-model like, *See. I know him too.*

Not like the woman would've noticed. Her attention was only on Papo Vega. "It's low-fat granola and homemade curry kale chips."

The cop and glasses guys made the same face of disgust while the *GQ* model said, "Eww. Why would you do that to him? Isn't it bad enough that G.I. Joe over here has him in solitary confinement?" He waved a hand carelessly in Saint's direction.

As Lola expected, Saint's face revealed almost nothing; only a slight tightening around his mouth gave away his annoyance at being called G.I. Joe.

"He's in trouble because he almost put someone in the hospital, Leo," the woman replied. She walked into the kitchen with the confiscated snacks. "What should we have done?" She began pouring the soda into the sink. "Thrown him a party?" She put the can on the counter and then looked at the mess all over the tiny kitchen. "What in the world did you do in here, Abu? It's like you pulled everything out of the cabinets and fridge."

Papo Vega, who had settled back in his chair and had been cackling at whatever El Chavo del Ocho and Quico were up to, grumbled, "Ay, qué mucho tú jode," causing three of the other men in the room to chuckle.

"I wouldn't have to be annoying, if you'd listen for once," she said.

It sounded so much like conversations she'd had with Benny that Lola felt an instant connection to the other woman. Then something clicked in her head.

"These are your siblings," she whispered in an aside to Saint.

He gave her a funny look and nodded. "You went to school with the twins," he whispered back.

Right. Cristian and Eduardo Vega. They'd been sophomores when she and Saint dated. The youngest two, whose names she couldn't remember, had still been in middle school. Lola felt like an idiot for not seeing it sooner and then she felt like more of an idiot for the relief that flooded her system. Finding out this gorgeous woman was Saint's little sister and not his partner should not loosen all the tension in her body.

"You'd still be annoying, Kamilah," the *GQ* model responded. "You were born that way."

"And you were born an ass, Leo," she replied sweetly.

For some reason that set Papo Vega off and he started laughing again. He laughed and laughed until it was clear he couldn't breathe and he had tears streaming down his face.

The rest of them stood there looking at each other in confusion.

"Abuelo, are you high?" the cop twin, Cristian, suddenly asked.

Papo Vega's eyes rounded. "What?"

"I said, 'Are you high right now?'"

"Me? High? At my age? How dare you?" He tried for stern and offended then ruined it by giggling like a little kid.

For a moment everyone else was silent. Most likely cataloging mentally like Lola was. *Red eyes, check. Munchies, check. Laughing at anything, check.*

Lola's mouth dropped open.

Both Kamilah and Leo shouted, "Oh my god, you are," at the same time. But where her tone was incredulous, his was giddy.

At Lola's side Saint dropped his head and shook it while pinching the bridge of his nose.

"I can't believe you," Kamilah said to her grandfather. "What in the world would possess you to get high?"

"My hips were hurting and I couldn't find my pills."

"So you got high instead?"

"It's perfectly legal now and it's natural." The twin in the glasses, Eduardo, finally spoke. "Who knows what shit is in those pills."

"You probably do, nerd," Kamilah snipped. "And that's not the point."

Cristian stepped up in front of his grandpa and squatted down. "Where did you get weed, Abuelo?"

"Killian," Papo Vega replied.

The name caused everyone in the room to pause. Lola looked around in confusion.

After a moment Kamilah spoke. "When Killian got really bad, Liam bought him gummies for the pain." Her voice was quiet and full of suppressed misery.

Lola remembered Maria mentioning Papo Vega losing his best friend. That must have been Killian.

Leo put an arm around Kamilah and from the other side, Eduardo slipped a hand into hers and squeezed.

Lola was surprised. Until that moment, these siblings had seemed like they barely tolerated each other. Then again, what did Lola know about siblings? She had one brother who was six years older than her and who didn't even want to see her.

"How many gummies did you eat, Abuelo?" Cristian asked.

"Liam told Killian to only take one, but that stuff never works for me, so I took two."

"Oh my god," Kamilah whispered. She looked like she was going to be sick.

"But shh. Don't tell your sister," he said, holding his finger to his lips. "Kamilah will throw a fit."

Beside him, Kamilah threw her hands in the air. "I'm standing right here."

Papo Vega swung his gaze to Kamilah, shocked to see her there. "Ojitos, when did you get here?" He leaned forward. "Hey, can you do me a favor? Can you make me some tostones? I'm starving."

Leo began laughing.

Kamilah just stared at her grandfather as if she couldn't believe her eyes.

Papo Vega continued, "I haven't done marijuana in a long time. I forgot how hungry it makes you." He paused for a split second and his eyes lit up like he'd just had the greatest idea known to man. "Hey, do you know what we should eat?" He didn't wait for anyone to answer. "Fried chicken." He slapped his hand on his leg. "Ojitos, you should make some. With mashed potatoes and gravy. And some corn. Oh, and cookies. You know the peanut butter ones with the chocolate kiss on top? Or the ones with the jelly in the middle. I know! You should make quesitos con guayaba."

"This is fucking amazing." Leo began cracking up.

The other two brothers started laughing as well, which set off Papo Vega. Soon the four of them were like the audience at a stand-up comedy show.

"It's not funny," Kamilah snarled.

Lola had to bite her lip because it was kind of funny. She risked a glance at Saint and found he had his hand covering his mouth in a suspicious fashion.

He turned his head and met her gaze. His eyes were full of amusement. He tilted his head toward the door.

Lola nodded.

Saint turned on his heel and started for the door and she followed.

"Hey, where are you going?" Kamilah called to him. "You're the one who told us that we were coming tonight to play games with Abuelo and keep him company."

"Game night is obviously canceled," Saint replied. "And you don't need me."

"Oh, si claro, déjame sola con estos payasos," she scoffed. "Because I'll handle this. I handle everything."

"You sound like Mami right now," Saint told her.

Kamilah gasped in outrage. "That is the worst thing anyone has ever said to me."

"With your personality? That can't be true," Cristian said, causing the other three to laugh again.

Saint put his hand on the door handle and pulled it open.

"Princesita, you need to chill out," Leo told his sister.

They stepped into the hallway right as Papo Vega asked, "Do you want one of my gummies?"

The sound of him and the remaining three Vega brothers laughing uproariously was cut off as Saint closed the door. He led her down the hall and around the corner before he stopped, rested his back against the wall, and covered his face with both hands. His shoulders started to shake. A snort escaped, which was more than enough to set Lola off.

She too began laughing, but she didn't try to hide her amusement behind her hands.

Saint's head turned in her direction just enough for him to look at her out of the corner of his eye.

Lola could see the tears of hilarity he struggled to not release, which made her laugh even harder.

They stood there for a long while, laughing together. Like in the old days.

8

Saint took his first deep breath in minutes and used his shirt collar to wipe at his eyes. Never in his life did he ever think he'd stumble upon the scene he'd just witnessed. He couldn't believe his eighty-one-year-old grandpa had gotten stoned. Yet at the same time, he very much could believe it. If there was any senior of his acquaintance that he could see doing it, it was Abuelo.

Next to him Lola let out one of those deep sighs you let out after laughing hard for a long time. "Is it weird that this actually makes me like your grandpa a little bit?"

He froze for a moment. Shocked that anyone who'd met Abuelo Papo wouldn't like him. Then he remembered the circumstances in which they'd met and Benny's overall animosity toward his grandpa. "Abuelo has always been a character. With age he's only gotten more…" He trailed off, unable to think of the right word.

"Animated? Extra?" Lola supplied.

Saint nodded. That worked. "He's been more reckless lately. Unhinged almost."

"Because of his friend that died? The one whose edibles he ate."

"Killian," Saint replied, ignoring the pang he felt at the mention of his abuelo's best friend. While Saint had never had the type of relationship Kamilah had had with Killian, he'd still viewed the man as family. In many ways he was more of a great-uncle than Abuelo's actual brothers who lived spread out around the US and had only visited Chicago a handful of times. Saint grieved the man's loss just like the rest of the family did. "Don't get me wrong. The two of them together caused plenty of problems, but Killian was the anchor that moored Abuelo's chaotic energy. Without him Abuelo is just bouncing around like a racquetball."

"Living in the same apartment must be really hard for him," Lola mused. "It's probably very lonely." The look on her face was full of empathy and concern.

That was what Saint had always liked about Lola. She was so quick to respond to the suffering of others even if she didn't like them. Even when they were younger she had an understanding about the world that most people would never reach. He wished he'd listened to her more instead of discounting the things she said as negativity and cynicism, but he couldn't change the past. He could only try to do better. He'd do so by listening to her now and supporting her. "We need to talk," he said. It had been less than a week since they'd decided to work together to find a new home for El Hogar, and they needed to make a plan.

She seemed to hesitate, but then she nodded. "We're long overdue for this conversation I guess." She looked around. "But not in the hall. Let's go somewhere else."

Now it was Saint's turn to hesitate, but he decided to follow her lead.

They made their way out of Casa del Sol and down the street. They'd just passed Clínica Luna Nueva when Lola stopped. She sat on a long stone bench and motioned for him to do the same.

Saint sat next to her, close enough to feel her heat but not so close that she'd feel like he was crowding her. Ever since their encounter in the alley all he could think about was touching Lola, holding her.

"I'm still mad at you," she eventually said. "And I'm not talking about the fact that you are destroying El Hogar for profit."

Saint whipped his head around to look at her, but she wasn't looking at him. She was staring ahead. Was she still upset about him enlisting?

"The armed forces are nothing but a way for the US to force their white evangelical viewpoints on Brown countries while they steal their wealth and culture. And they use poor and mostly Brown bodies to do it! Why is it that these recruiters visit poor Brown neighborhoods like ours? You don't see them in Wilmette high schools brainwashing their youth into thinking that this is the only way they will be successful. No, those kids are expected to go to four-year universities, probably go postgrad, and eventually run our capitalist society. Meanwhile they are over here telling us, 'Yeah just sacrifice your bodies and brains and turn into a murder bot for us and if you survive then we will let you go to school and get out of the hood.' It's bullshit. It's a freaking con!"

"It's about protecting our country. The people that live here and the freedoms we have."

Lola's jaw actually dropped. "You can't possibly be that stupid."

At the look on his face she at least tried to soften her words. "I'm sorry. I shouldn't have said that it's just…that's so naive. It's—"

He turned back and interrupted whatever backpedaling she was about to do. "You know what, Lola. It may seem stupid to you, but to me it's about my family. My abuelo served. He sacrificed. He didn't do it for some corrupt government. He did it for his family. To give us a better future than what was possible for him otherwise. I respect him for that and I'm going to honor that."

"That's a fairy tale, Saint."

"Well, you know what? At least he did things the right way and he made sure we did too."

"What is that supposed to mean?"

"It means that none of my family members are in jail."

Lola glared at him. "And there it is," she said. "You think you are better than me. Well, fuck you, Santiago Vega Junior. You aren't better than me. You're nothing but an ignorant little boy playing superheroes. You want to go be Capitán America? Go ahead."

She'd stormed away from him in a righteous rage and Saint had let her because he'd been pissed off too.

Now Saint could only look back on that moment and shake his head. He *had* been an ignorant little boy playing superhero. He'd learned quickly that the only value he held for Uncle Sam was his ability to kill efficiently. He wasn't a person. He was a weapon. It wasn't until his little girl was in his arms that he remembered he was a person. He was a man with hopes and dreams. None of them included not being there to raise her.

"I should've listened to you about enlisting. It was..." He paused. What could he say? That it was absolute hell. Mind-fucking, soul-crushing hell. He knew saying that would only lead to questions. He didn't want to talk about that, so instead he said, "Intense."

Lola let out what could only be described as a huff slash growl. "I can't believe that after all of this time, you still think that it was about you enlisting."

It wasn't? How could that be? "We never argued about anything before that." They'd been blissfully in love. Wrapped up in each other emotionally, mentally, physically. They'd spent almost every free moment they had together. It had made her disappearance even harder.

"True, but you know what else?" She turned in her seat to look at him. "You never once invited me to your house. You never introduced me to any member of your family. We only met up at my place, El Centro when your family or friends weren't there, or somewhere around the neighborhood where no one would see us."

Saint was confused about her accusatory tone. "I wanted to spend time with you, Lola. And I didn't want to share."

She shook her head. "You didn't want anyone you knew to know we were together."

Saint fought back the urge to become defensive, because in a way it was true. He hadn't wanted his family to know about his relationship with Lola.

"You were embarrassed of me," she whispered into the evening air.

Saint was shocked. "What?"

"I was the fat, loudmouthed, bisexual girl who was always in trouble with the office and who's gangbanging father and brother were on trial for murder and you didn't want anyone to know that you were dating me. I was your dirty secret. Worse, I was the tool that you used to make yourself feel good."

His mouth hung open. He closed it then opened it again to say something. Anything. Nothing came out, so he sat there flapping his mouth like a fish.

"You would bring me home-cooked meals because Benny and I mostly ate takeout. You gave me positive attention, because I usually only received apathy or scorn. You told me I was pretty and desirable, because everyone else called me unattractive. But you didn't actually do any of those things for me. You did them for you. To prove to yourself that you were a good person."

Now he was getting mad. "I did those things because I loved you, Lola. When you love someone you want to make sure they are safe and happy."

She shook her head again. "You didn't love me, Saint. If you had, you wouldn't have kept me on the sidelines of your life, which, by the way, is the real reason I was so upset about you enlisting. To me you were everything. My life revolved around you. But to you I didn't even factor into your plans. I couldn't even get an invite to dinner!" She paused and took a deep breath.

"I didn't want my family to know about us because they were already trying their best to keep me here. They were just as against me enlisting as you were. Probably more. If they would've known about us, they would've tried to use you to manipulate me into staying. It would've made everything that much more difficult."

"For you," she exclaimed. "It would've made things more difficult for you. Plus, you never mentioned any of that to me. You never really talked to me. You listened, but you barely shared."

She had a point. There was a lot he hadn't shared with her. With anyone really.

"Shit," she continued. "It's almost twenty years later and I just had to use deductive reasoning to figure out who your siblings are, because you didn't even introduce me to them now!"

"You introduced yourself! You did everything yourself. You want to talk about keeping someone on the sidelines. You treated me like your distraction. Like your audience. Sure you talked to me about stuff, but after you'd already done or handled it. You wouldn't let me actually take part. I did all that other stuff because it was all you'd allow me to do."

"I didn't need you to save me, Saint! That's what you don't get. I wasn't looking for someone to swoop in and save the day. I just wanted someone to want me exactly as I was without caring what anyone else would think or say." She turned until she was facing forward again. Not looking at him. "You made me feel bad about myself when I was already struggling to find value in who I was. That is why I'm mad at you."

Saint turned in his seat and stared into the distance like she did. He sat with her words. He tried to take his feelings completely out of the equation, to put himself in Lola's shoes. He could see exactly why she'd arrived at the conclusions she'd come to. His private nature had kept him from sharing his thoughts, plans, goals, motivations, etc. Because of that, Lola had second-guessed the sincerity of his feelings. That was one hundred percent on him. "I'm sorry."

"You aren't going to tell me that you never wanted to hurt me, that you loved me, and wanted to be with me?" She still wasn't looking at him.

"Do you want to hear any of that?" he asked. "You'd be the first one to tell me that intentions don't matter when you hurt someone. Only the pain inflicted matters."

She nodded. "That's true." She paused. "But it might be nice to hear anyway."

He turned in his seat to face her. "Then look at me."

She didn't move.

"Look at me, Canela," he murmured.

She turned to face him, their knees touching. "What?"

He stared into her eyes, those beautiful eyes that had knocked him off-kilter from the moment he'd first seen them. "I was never embarrassed to be seen with you. You were the smartest, bravest, most beautiful, and most badass girl I'd ever met. You still are. The fact that you wanted to be with me made me proud as hell. I wanted to shout it from the rooftops and I should have. I've broken bones. I've been shot and stabbed. I've fallen through ceilings only to crash to the ground. But the fact that you ever doubted how absolutely amazing you are because of me hurts more than any of that. It guts me, but my pain doesn't matter. Yours does. I'm so sorry my actions caused it."

She took a deep breath and released it. "Thank you. I didn't realize how much I needed to hear that."

They stayed like that for a while, just looking at one another.

"Everything makes so much more sense now," Saint eventually said. "I never understood why you were so upset. I thought you saw me as weak and stupid. It made me angry. It made me want to prove you wrong."

"No, Saint, I thought you were the strongest person I knew and I admired your confidence in who you were and what you wanted."

The night before he'd had to ship out for basic training, he'd gone to Lola. They hadn't talked about their fight; they'd just spent the night in each other's arms doing their best to share their emotions physically. The following morning, the sun had hardly begun its ascent when they'd said their goodbyes. They'd both been in tears and Saint could feel her pulling away. He'd begged her to wait for him. She'd promised they would talk when he got back. Instead, she'd disappeared. "Imagine how different things would've been if we would've gotten to have that conversation when I came back from basic training."

"Imagine how different things would've been if we'd just talked about our feelings before you even left."

True.

Nothing would've prevented him from leaving, but at least they wouldn't have caused each other so much pain. "Lola," he said after a moment of silence.

"Yes?"

"What was in the letter?"

She sighed. "Does it matter?"

That wasn't what he wanted to hear. It made him think the contents weren't good. "Did you tell me everything you just said now?"

She shook her head. "I told you that my mom had come for me, but that I didn't know where we were going. I said that I was sorry for going back on my word, but that I didn't think there was anything to talk about anyway, because we clearly wanted different things. I told you that it would be the last you heard from me, because I needed to let you go. I wished you the best and then I said goodbye."

He'd suspected as much, but hearing it from her mouth made it real. It also made him mad. He'd deserved more than that, no matter what she thought of him at the time. "You never had any intention of talking when we got back," he said. "You just agreed so I would stop begging. You were already done with me when I left. The moment I didn't back down and decide to stay, I was discarded from your life."

She didn't disagree with him.

"Right." He stood.

"Saint," she began.

"No," he cut her off. He didn't think he could handle any more painful revelations at the moment. "I get it. You were protecting yourself. You have every right to do so."

"I know but—"

"Look, Lola, I know I made mistakes, especially with us. But I'm hoping that we can leave that in the past. We are in different places now. I'd like for us to be friends, and I do want to help with El Hogar."

"Friends," she murmured.

He couldn't tell if she thought it was a good or bad thing.

"I'd like that," she finally said. "If you're sure that you can leave everything in the past."

"I can," he said, even though deep down he wasn't sure he could.

9

Lola leaned against the back of the wooden bench and lifted her face to the waning sunlight. She tried to let the heat release the tension in her back and neck, but it didn't work. Her mind was still on the news she'd received earlier that day. Another trial. This time for murder.

All this time she thought Iván was going to get out soon—he'd only been sentenced to a few years for theft and drug possession—but it turned out the police had never stopped investigating her dad or brother. They wanted to make an example out of them, to put them away for life, and they'd found the way to do it. Lola didn't really care about her dad going away for life, good riddance to him, but Iván?

She cared a lot about her older brother going to prison for life. He was only twenty-three years old and unlike her father, he wasn't a ruthless criminal. He was stuck. He always had been. Their father had groomed his son to take his place in that world since her brother was a preteen. And Iván had let him because as long as all of Papi's focus was on Iván, none of it would fall on her. Iván had done his very best to keep her safe from their father's dark moods and cruel words. Lola loved him for it.

She loved her brother so much that just the thought of him paying for their father's sins broke her heart. She closed her eyes and took deep *breaths for a long minute, but it still didn't work. She felt a tear slip out the corner of her eye and down her cheek.*

"What's wrong, Canela?" asked the voice she'd quickly come to adore more than any other sound in the world. "Why are you crying?" A strong arm wrapped around her shoulder, pulling her into a hard chest.

"I'm not crying," she retorted even as she felt more moisture trail down her cheeks. "I don't cry."

"Okay," Saint soothed. "You're not crying." Hands cupped her face and wiped the tears off her cheeks.

Lola opened her eyes and met the gaze of her own personal saint. His deep brown eyes looked lighter in the sunlight, but the warmth in them was the same warmth she always felt whenever he looked at her. She felt her heart pick up pace. She still couldn't believe that this guy was her boyfriend. Her boyfriend! She, who could count on one hand the number of males she trusted and not even fill that hand.

"I'm glad you aren't crying," he said. "It's your birthday and nothing is more important than you today."

If only he knew that birthdays were never a big deal in the León household, not since her mom disappeared. Her dad had forced her to have a quince, but that was more about him flaunting his money and his power. It hadn't been about Lola at all. She'd done it, but she might as well have been a Barbie her dad was playing with. It meant nothing to her. Lola shrugged. "It really isn't a big deal," she told Saint.

"Your birthday is a big deal to me," Saint argued. "It's the day I get to celebrate the fact that you're on this earth."

Seriously, who was this kid? Since the moment they met, he'd surprised her with the things he said. He was so sweet and considerate. Borderline cheesy, but Lola liked it. She felt oddly safe with him, which was crazy because, of everyone in her life, he had the most power to hurt her.

"Is that why you brought me here?" She gestured to the park and the Buckingham Fountain in front of them.

He nodded. "I thought we could have a picnic." He grabbed the big backpack next to him and set it on his lap. "I brought you a tripleta sandwich and some yuca frita." He pulled a big paper bag out. "There's also a Kola Champagne in there." He tried to hand it to her, but Lola made no move to take it.

Lola just stared at the bag in his hands and fought back more tears. He was the sweetest. He was always doing nice things for her and trying to take care of her. No one had ever done that for her before. Sure Iván had done his best to keep her safe and Benny provided all of the necessities, but no one had ever gone out of their way just to make her happy.

God, she loved him so much and she had no idea how to show him.

Saint shook the bag at her. "Are you not hungry?"

Lola reached for the bag. "Is that even a question? I'm always hungry. Especially if it's from your abuela."

Saint smiled and took a spot next to her on the ground. "My sister made this actually, but it was under Abuela's eagle eye, so it's as if Abuela made it."

"Your sister made me food?" Lola tried to keep the hope out of her voice, but couldn't really. She was anxiously awaiting the day that Saint told her he had told his family about them and wanted her to come meet them. So far she'd met his brothers, Cristian and Eddie, but that was only because they went to the same school and had come across her and Saint talking in the hall. Other than that she didn't think any of the rest of his family even knew of her existence. Unless Saint had finally told them.

He looked away and she knew that she'd gotten her hopes up for nothing. "Actually she made me a lunch to take with me, but I asked her to include more because I was really hungry."

Lola brushed off her disappointment. Really what else could she expect. Of course he was going to be careful about introducing their relationship to his upright and successful family. Two-thirds of her male family members were literal criminals. Her mom, well, better not to think of her.

Instead she smiled at Saint. "Well, I'm always up for leftovers from your house whether from your grandma, sister, mom, heck even your dad." She unwrapped the steak, roasted pork, and ham sandwich, passed him half, and took a huge bite. She moaned at the taste of the triple meat along with the creamy tang of the mayo-ketchup and the crunch of the shoestring potatoes. "Oh my god, this is good," she said around another full bite.

He smiled at her and reached a hand up to cradle her face. A slow swipe of his thumb from the side of her mouth along her bottom lip made her swallow hard. He lifted his thumb to show her the smudge of mayo-ketchup before popping it in his own mouth and sucking it off.

Lola felt her face flame and not because she was embarrassed. Everything he did seemed perfectly designed to make her fall deeper under his spell.

Lola cleared her throat and dug in the bag for a piece of fried cassava and tossed it in her mouth before she could do something stupid like blurt out, I want to have sex with you tonight, in the middle of a public park surrounded by strangers.

They sat in silence for a few minutes while they ate, but the entire time she could feel his gaze on her. He did that a lot. Stared at her as if he were trying to figure something out. She didn't know what he was thinking when he did that, but she could practically see the thoughts zooming from one spot to another in his head.

Unable to take another bite, Lola wrapped the rest of the sandwich back up and slipped it into the bag. She pulled out the Kola Champagne and popped it open. After taking a few sips, she passed it to him. He took a few drinks of the cream-like soda and passed it back.

She rested her head on his shoulder while he continued eating. "What made you decide to bring me here?" she asked after a while of just sitting and staring at the fountain.

"I heard they do a water and light show at night."

"Like the Bellagio in Las Vegas?"

He smiled. "I doubt it will be anything like that, but I thought it could be cool to see."

"So we're staying here until nighttime?" Not that night was that far off. The sun was already setting.

"Is there a problem with that? Does Benny have something planned for you?" He looked worried.

Lola shook her head. "He told me happy birthday, made me pancakes, and gave me my present this morning. He picked up an overnight shift, so I'm on my own tonight."

Saint relaxed against the bench. "I have you to myself all night if I want?"

Lola shivered at the barely suppressed excitement in his voice. She thought of her plans for the night and shivered more. They'd done a lot of making out and touching in the last few weeks and Saint said that he was perfectly content with that, but Lola was ready for more. She'd tell him so after the water show.

Later that night she almost changed her mind.

They lay on her bed kissing and touching, but Lola couldn't turn off the voice in her head enough to enjoy herself. She kept thinking about what she'd look like in the sexy lingerie she was wearing under her clothes. She'd gone to buy something special for the night, but it hadn't worked out the way she wanted. The look on the college-aged Victoria's Secret employee's face when she told Lola that the bra she wanted didn't come in the band size Lola needed and that they were out of the matching panties in extra large was seared in her brain. The girl had been thin, slim-hipped, and busty in the right way. She'd looked at Lola with barely veiled pity. Embarrassed beyond belief, Lola had dropped everything on the table and rushed out of the store.

She'd ended up buying a bra and panties from the plus-size women's section of a department store in the same mall. The bra was black satin, but that was undoubtedly the only sexy thing about it. It had thick straps like a tank top, a wide band with five eyelets, an underwire so thick she didn't think the Hulk could bend it, and the material had this kind of floral print design that reminded Lola of old lady curtains.

Great, she thought to herself. When Saint takes off your shirt he's going to think of his abuela's curtains. She thought about her full coverage high-waisted underwear—the only pair they had in her size *that weren't cotton or shapewear.* Then when he sees the matching panties he's just going to think of his abuela.

She felt her eyes fill with moisture. God, she hated her body. She hated that she didn't have the trim curves of the other girls in school who walked around looking like mini JLos. Sure Lola had ass for days, but it was accompanied by wide hips, belly fat, back rolls, and dimply thighs. What was she even thinking? She couldn't show herself to Saint.

It took her a second to even realize that Saint was no longer kissing her neck. He was looking at her in alarm. "What's wrong? Did I hurt you? Am I moving too fast? We can stop."

Of course he'd say that. He was the sweetest boyfriend ever and he treated her like she was special. She loved him so much and she just didn't understand how he could feel the same way about her. How could he when he was the perfect guy with the perfect looks and the perfect family? Meanwhile, she was a weirdo.

"How can you love me?" she choked out. "Look at me. Look at my life. An ugly mess." She didn't know if she was referring to herself or her life. Maybe both.

"Canela," he murmured.

She loved when he called her cinnamon. He said it was because she was sweet and spicy, she knew it was because of her freckles.

"You know me better than anyone else in my life and you don't judge me when I'm not perfect," he told her while brushing his knuckles over her cheek. "You like me better when I'm not. You're smarter than anyone I know and brave in the face of any problem. You are funny and sweet. Everything about you is beautiful. How can I not love you?"

Overwhelmed, Lola couldn't speak. She just kissed him and kissed him. When he pulled her shirt off, she let him. When he put his mouth and hands on her, she let go completely. She gave every part of herself to him without shame. She let him show her that his love was deep and true. Afterward, she had no regrets.

"Hello! Lola! Are you listening to me?" her mom's voice called over the phone. "I asked how tonight's Krav class went."

Lola shook herself mentally. Lately, she'd been spacing during a lot of her conversations. It was like the talk with Saint a week earlier had unleashed all types of memories that she hadn't allowed herself to think about in years. She found them popping into her mind at the most random of times. "Fine," she responded.

Her mom must've gotten sick of Lola's distracted one-word answers because she cut to the chase. "Why did you agree to let him help if you're just going to stress about it?" her mom asked. She was the only person who knew about Lola's failed relationship with Saint.

"I'm not stressing about him," Lola lied.

Her mom obviously knew it since she responded with a very dubious, "Mmm-hmm."

"I'm not!" Another lie. She was definitely stressing about Saint's participation in the mission to find El Hogar a new building. She couldn't help but think that this was a terrible idea for many reasons, the first of which being that it required him to work with the El Hogar staff and volunteers, who hated him. Well, *hate* was a strong word, but they for sure were not in the Saint fan club.

"You do remember that I was the one who listened to you cry your eyes out after we left Chicago right?"

Lola did remember. It had been impossible for Lola to hide her heartbreak during their weeklong journey to the West Coast. At first Lola had given her mom the silent treatment. She'd just sat in the passenger seat crying and watching unfamiliar places pass her by. When she'd started talking it was only to make her mom the recipient of her horrible mood.

Her mom hadn't reacted to her shitty attitude.

Eventually, Lola got sick of not getting the reaction she wanted and had chilled out. It was then that her mom had shocked her by saying, "When I left, I cried every day for a year. I missed you and your brother so much it felt like my chest was caving in. This is going to sound crazy, but I even missed your dad." Lola had scoffed at that, but her mom had just said, "I loved him. I know it makes no sense, he's not a good or nice man, but sometimes we love what's not good for us." She'd paused and given Lola a loaded look. "I think you know exactly what I mean." That had been the moment their relationship had begun to change.

Back in the present day, Lola repositioned the phone on her shoulder. "It's not like that, Mom." She reached for the basket of freshly made popcorn on the table in front of her. "It's just that everyone at El Hogar is more likely to tell him to fuck off than listen to him or accept his help and I can't blame them. I'd do the same thing. I probably should do the same thing." She shoved a handful in her mouth and chewed.

"But you won't because it's Saint and despite everything you trust him."

"In this at least," Lola replied around a mouthful of popcorn.

Her mom hated it when she talked with food in her mouth. Case in point her next question was, "What are you eating that is so good you need to talk to me with your mouth full?"

"The bar we're meeting at has a popcorn machine running all the time." It had been Lola's idea to have the first meeting between Yara and Saint take place in a public spot. She hoped that would keep everyone, namely Yara, on their best behavior.

Her mom made a noise of doubt. "A bar? Do you think that's a good idea?"

Lola didn't think any of this was a good idea, but she knew better than to say that to her mother. It would just start another sales pitch about how Lola wouldn't have to deal with any of this if she moved back to San Diego.

The door to the restaurant swung open and Saint stepped in. He was wearing green pants, a beige crew neck sweater, and cognac boots—all together a pretty normal outfit. Yet Lola's body reacted like he'd walked in dressed in a loincloth.

Their eyes met and the corner of his mouth curled up just the tiniest bit. Lola just about slid out her chair. Damn, was he fine as fuck. Too damn fine for his *and her* own good.

"I gotta go, Mom. Saint just walked in." They said their goodbyes and Lola had just hung up when he reached the table.

He leaned down to kiss her on the cheek in greeting and Lola inhaled deeply through her nose without even thinking. There was no doubt in her mind that she was attracted to Saint, but it had been much easier for her to keep it under control when she'd still been mad and hurt by the past. Now that they'd talked about things, a lot of that past hurt and anger was gone. She hadn't realized how much it had been protecting her until it was gone. She felt vulnerable now.

"I thought I was the only one who showed up to things early," he said, reaching over to grab some popcorn. He popped a few kernels in his mouth.

"Tonight is wing night and I've learned that this place gets crazy busy, so I figured I should get here early to make sure we had a table." And also she was nervous as hell about how this would go and getting there early helped her center herself. "Why are you early?" She reached for more popcorn.

Saint shrugged. "I like to be prepared when entering enemy territory."

Lola waited to see if he'd expound on that loaded statement. When he didn't, she swallowed and asked, "Is that who we are, your enemies?"

"Not *my* enemies, but I know that I'm yours." He looked down at the table and for a split second his shoulders dropped.

Unable to ignore the urge to comfort him, she reached over and put a hand over his. "You're not my enemy, Saint."

He flipped his hand over and grabbed hers. "And what about the rest of them?"

She grimaced. "Well…that's a little bit harder."

"I figured." He nodded, intertwining their fingers.

Lola stared at their hands. His big tanned hand with its small scars and fresh scratches swallowed her pale, freckled one with its chipped purple polish.

"We probably shouldn't be doing this, right?" Saint asked, his gaze also on their hands.

They for sure shouldn't be holding hands, but Lola wasn't about to let go. "We're friends now and friends can hold hands sometimes."

His look said that he clearly didn't believe her, but he also didn't let her hand go.

She cleared her throat. "Back to the issue at hand. I think once Yara knows that you're doing it because your tío needs the money for medical reasons, she will chill out a lot."

He cleared his throat. "Actually, we can't tell anyone about that. He doesn't want anyone to know yet and I already broke my word by telling you."

She could hear the guilt in his voice. Saint was the kind of guy who took keeping his word very seriously and she couldn't help but feel a bit flattered that he'd broken it because he didn't want her, specifically, to think badly of him. "I hope you know that not telling them is going to make this much harder. Everyone at El Hogar considers you a traitor to the neighborhood."

"I know." He paused. "But I can handle it."

Warmth spread through her at his willingness to face animosity from all of her friends just to keep his word to his uncle. She watched her thumb brush over his as if soothing away hurt yet to come.

"Hey." Yara's voice cut into Lola's thoughts.

Lola's head shot up. She yanked her hand out of Saint's and shoved it under the table. It was one thing to hold his hand when it was just the two of them; it was another thing to do it in front of people. "Hey," she squeaked way too brightly. "How's it going?"

"I'm as well as could be under the circumstances," Yara responded with a significant look at the man sitting next to Lola.

This was going to be a shit show.

"Umm. Have a seat," Lola said even though Yara was already doing so. Lola had chosen the spot at the head of the table to feel in charge, but—with Saint on one side of the table and Yara on the other—she simply felt caught in the middle.

After Lola provided introductions, a tense silence settled over the table. Fortunately, the server appeared almost immediately with water. Unfortunately, the server was Mariana who also had Saint on their shit list. "Hey. I didn't know you worked here," Lola said.

Mariana smiled. "I'm always here when I'm not at El Hogar." Their face turned solemn. "I mean when I *wasn't* at El Hogar. Can't be there if it doesn't exist anymore." At that they gave Saint a dirty look.

He looked down at his hands.

Things were off to a great start. "Look," Lola began. "It's not Saint's fault that the owners decided to sell the building to some scavengers on the down-low. That was done before he was even remotely involved in this."

"True," Mariana agreed.

"Hmm," was all Yara said.

Lola knew there was more forthcoming, but at least she was letting them get drinks first.

"Are you all here for wings—" Mariana motioned to the list of wing flavors "—or did you want menus?"

"Wings for sure," Lola and Yara said at the same time, causing the other woman to let out her first smile of the night.

Mariana pulled a pen and pad out of their apron. "Great, do you know which ones and how many?"

"We didn't get to that yet," Lola admitted. "What do you suggest?"

Mariana shrugged. "Depends on how much spice you like."

"I'm half Mexican. I love spicy," Lola said. "My Puerto Rican half rebels by giving me acid reflux, but I keep eating it anyway."

"Nonsense," Yara said. "I'm one hundred percent Puerto Rican and you already know that I like 'em hot."

Lola laughed. "Fair enough." She turned to Saint. "What about you?"

Before he could even open his mouth Yara was answering for him. "I don't think he's at our level."

Saint raised one eyebrow. "Meaning?"

Yara lifted a shoulder. "No offense, but you don't look like you can handle the heat." It was clear from her tone that Yara wasn't solely referring to chicken wings.

"I can handle heat just fine," he retorted.

"Really? Is that why you're letting Lola do all your talking for you?"

"Yara," Lola admonished.

"What?" Yara asked. "I'm just wondering why we should trust him when he can't even speak up for himself."

"Not to mention he already stabbed us in the back," Mariana added.

Saint sat forward. "You want to see me handle the heat? Fine." He turned to Mariana. "I want an order of the hottest wings on the menu." He looked at Yara. "As I eat them you can grill me on my intentions."

"That's not nec—" Lola began, but Yara cut her off.

"No. He wants all the heat. Let him." She turned to Mariana. "Don't you have a wing challenge?"

They nodded. "But it's insane. They're made with Carolina Reaper peppers. There's no way."

"I'll do it," said the idiot next to her.

Annoyed by this whole thing Lola decided to prove a point. "Yara is doing it too."

"What?" the woman in question yelped.

Lola expected her to see how dumb this was and back down, but then Saint had to go and open his normally silent mouth.

"Don't tell me that you can dish out the heat but not take it," he taunted.

"Oh, we are doing this," Yara declared.

"If I eat more wings than you, I get to help find El Hogar a new home with no questions asked and no comments about my involvement in the Raven Realty project."

"And if I eat more than you, you find another way to assuage your guilt for selling out the neighbors that have supported your family for decades."

"Fine."

"Fine."

Lola rolled her eyes. "This is incredibly stupid. I hope you both realize that."

Lola looked to Mariana, who simply shrugged.

"I really want to see what happens." They wrote something on their pad then looked at Lola. "Are you taking part, or do you want something else?"

"There is no way in hell I'm eating a Carolina Reaper hot wing. You can put me down for regular buffalo wings and a bunch of bread and milk for these two."

"Oh, we have everything needed to help someone after they try the challenge and if not, there's always 911."

"Well, that's comforting," Lola muttered.

Once Mariana walked away a stilted silence fell over the table again.

"Right. Since it appears that we aren't going to be productive until you two do this, Yara, I've been meaning to touch base with you about Ruby. Did you get a chance to talk to her school?"

Yara nodded. "I made sure to talk to the principals and social workers at all the kids' schools after the shelter closed and have been in communication almost daily to make sure they are still showing up and doing what they need to do. But I made it a point to talk to Ruby's school about the situation with that kid in chemistry."

"Let me guess, they pretended to not know about it and said they'd look into it."

"Of course. I told them to make sure they did because they didn't want me showing up there and causing a scene. I talked to Ruby too and told her to let me know if they follow through and if the kid keeps touching her. I know his momma and will handle it myself if need be."

That was what Lola loved about Yara. Yara knew better than most how the teens in the shelter could get looked over and disregarded and she was willing to step in and be their guard dragon if the situation arose. That was why Lola couldn't really be annoyed with her despite this whole pissing contest with Saint. Yara was doing what she did best—looking after the people she cared about.

Since El Hogar had closed, a few of the kids had risked returning home. Some were staying with friends. Others had to find shelters outside of Humboldt Park. It broke Lola's heart to hear—it was as if a family had been separated. El Hogar was unlike anywhere else in that they really created a safe and welcoming community for the residents. It wasn't just a place where they could survive, but where they could thrive. All because Yara made it clear to anyone who stepped in the building that those kids came first and she would not tolerate anyone behaving differently.

Mariana came back shortly with a large pitcher of ice water, two huge glasses of milk, a basket of bread, and Lola's regular wings with a side of ranch and veggies. "I'll be right back with the other wings." When they came back moments later, they were wearing a pair of latex gloves and a mask over their face as they carried a basket of wings to the table. "I have a pair of gloves for y'all too." They put the basket in the middle of the table then pulled the gloves out of their pocket and placed them in front of the basket.

Dear God. The spice was so strong that Lola could smell it in the air. She had to blink her eyes because they wanted to water. Lola glanced between Saint and Yara. They both looked like they were regretting their challenge. Then they made eye contact and suddenly the determination was back. Lola watched with growing incredulity as they both put on the gloves. She couldn't believe they were about to do this.

Next to the table Mariana held their phone up, obviously getting ready to record this shit show. They also must've told the other people in the bar what was about to go down, because other people had completely stopped eating, drinking, and talking to watch. Many of them also had phones in their hands.

"Alright, y'all. These are the Hellfire wings made with Carolina Reapers, which have 2.2 million Scoville units."

"I don't know what any of that means," Saint grumbled.

"That means it's the hottest pepper in the world, bro!" someone yelled from the crowd.

While neither contestant said a word, Lola clearly read the *fuck* off both of their facial expressions. She waited for them to back down, but of course neither did.

"Ladies first," Saint said.

Yara rolled her eyes at him, but reached into the basket and pulled out a drum.

Saint reached in and pulled out a flat.

"On the count of three," Mariana yelled. Together everyone counted. As soon as they said three, Saint and Yara brought the wings to their mouths. Where Yara took a bite, Saint shoved the whole wing in his mouth and pulled out the two bones.

There was a quiet moment when neither reacted and Lola thought, *Maybe it's not that bad.* Then both of their faces changed. Their eyes bugged out of their heads.

"Oh fuck no," Yara yelled with her mouth full. She shook her head back and forth like a dog whipping around a toy.

Saint's face scrunched and he began blinking while he chewed. Then he let loose a few coughs.

"Swallow it," Mariana said.

"Holy fuck," Yara cried. She too began coughing. Her eyes were streaming with tears.

Saint's face was bright red and his leg was bouncing up and down. He made a noise unlike anything Lola had ever heard. It was like a wheezy groan. "Why?" he asked.

Lola wasn't sure if he was asking why it was so hot or why he agreed to do it in the first place. It didn't matter. The answer was the same. "I don't know."

Unable to take any more, Yara spit out what was in her mouth. "Fuck that." She yanked off the gloves, reached for the milk, and started chugging it.

Lola looked at Saint. He had his eyes squeezed closed, but his cheeks were still wet. His nose was running, but he was still chewing.

"You've got this, Saint," Lola coached. "She spit out her bite. All you have to do is swallow what's in your mouth and you win."

He shook his head.

"Come on, you can do this."

He shook his head some more.

"This is fucking evil," Yara wheezed. She grabbed a slice of bread, stuck out her tongue, and held the bread to it.

Lola turned her attention back to Saint.

He was rocking back and forth and his fists were clenched tight on top of the table.

Around them the crowd was screaming. "Swallow! Swallow! Swallow!"

Lola knew that if he quit, he'd be so disappointed in himself. She knew him better than almost anyone. Saint didn't do failure, so she decided to give him more of a push. She reached over and grabbed both sides of his face. "Look at me!"

He opened his eyes. They were bloodshot and swollen.

"Saint, you are a soldier. You went to war. You saw and did shit most people can't even imagine. This is nothing compared to that. Swallow the fucking chicken."

With a grimace that looked like he was ingesting razor blades, Saint swallowed. He immediately started coughing like he was choking.

The entire bar erupted in cheers, but Lola's focus was on Saint so intently that she still heard him wheeze, "Help," in between coughs.

"Okay. Okay." Lola grabbed the glass of milk and held it up to his mouth. "Here drink this."

He began drinking, long deep swallows of milk. The glass was empty in thirty seconds. "More," he demanded.

Someone passed Lola another glass and she snatched it up before holding it up for him. "Here."

He ripped off the gloves, letting them fall to the floor, and then grabbed the glass from her. That milk was also gone in a moment. "Oh fuck," he rasped, before letting out a few more coughs.

As if by magic two dishes of vanilla ice cream appeared in front of Saint and Yara. Saint was too busy wiping his face to notice, so Lola grabbed it.

"I had them bring y'all some ice cream," Mariana said. "Some people say it helps."

Lola scooped up a huge dollop. "Open," she told Saint.

He did and she shoved the ice cream in his mouth. She fed him a few more scoops.

"Better?" she asked.

"A little," he answered.

"I'm light-headed and nauseous," Yara said from the other side of the table.

"I feel like my insides are on fire," Saint told her.

"That's because you swallowed when you should've spit," Yara informed him.

There was a beat of silence and then Lola couldn't control herself anymore. She started laughing. Mariana joined in as if they were only waiting for someone else to start. As soon as Yara realized what she'd said, she too began laughing. Saint looked like he was in too much pain to laugh, but he at least cracked a smile and shook his head at their immaturity.

"I'll remember that for next time," he said, causing the rest of them to laugh even harder.

Mariana slapped him on the back. Yara passed him a piece of bread.

And just like that Saint was accepted into the fold.

10

Abuelo Papo eyed the dominoes on the table in front of him, the dominoes in his hands, and then the ones in Saint's hands. He looked at their opponents. With a smirk he took one of his remaining dominoes, placed it face down on the table next to him, and sent it spinning.

"What does that mean?" Rosie asked from her spot on Abuelo's knee. It had been a little over three weeks since Lola had taken over Rosie's class, and the little girl still refused to talk at school, though Saint thought she seemed a little less miserable when he dropped her off each day.

"That's the ficha I'm going to win with," Abuelo answered. A bold claim considering he'd been forced to pass on his last turn.

"How do you know that? You don't know what dominoes the other players have."

"Mamita, I learned long ago not to ask him how he does that," Saint said.

"I'll tell you," Abuelo told Rosie. "It's because I'm a—"

"Liar," Benny said from Abuelo's left.

Benny's teammate, Don Javier, laughed.

Meanwhile Saint fought his grimace. He didn't know what had compelled Lola's grandpa to challenge Abuelo to a game of dominó in the first place, but the four of them had been playing long enough for them to have learned that Abuelo Papo was uncommonly good. This was their third match and the other team had only managed to beat Saint and Abuelo once. That was mostly due to Abuelo's skills. Saint's jobs were to defend his partner and try to curb his trash-talking to Lola's grandpa. He was only good at one of those jobs as was evidenced by the next words out of Abuelo's mouth.

"It's not a lie. I will win with this ficha."

"Like the little girl just said. There is no way for you to know that."

"My name is Rosie," his daughter said to Benny with a smile.

Saint was shocked when the grumpy old man smiled back at her.

But Benny's smile fell quickly when his abuelo said, "I know I'm going to win with this one because you suck at dominó." Abuelo confidently placed the deuce-six domino down at the right end of the layout making both ends a six. "Dale, Benito. Pasa," he taunted.

Benny, the next player up, glared at Abuelo. "You don't know if I can go or not," he said in Spanish.

"I sure do," Abuelo replied. "You don't have any sixes, so pass already."

Benny grunted and knocked on the table. "Paso."

Okay. Now that he passed, Saint was up. Saint examined the layout. In his hand he had three dominoes and two of them had a six. He had the six-four and six-five. He knew his abuelo was up to something, but he wasn't sure what so he agonized over which domino to play. He quickly counted the number of dominoes for each in the layout. There were four dominoes in there that included a five, meaning there were only three more five dominoes left. Saint had two of them in his land, leaving one unaccounted for. There were also three four dominoes left (one being the double-four) including the one in his hand. He looked to Don Javier. The man only had two dominoes in his hand. Saint knew the chances of Don Javier having a four were greater, but that wasn't the only problem. The problem was making sure his next move didn't ruin whatever plans Abuelo had. If he chose wrong, it could lose them the game since Abuelo also had three dominoes (including the one he'd placed to the side). Praying he did the right thing, Saint played the six-five domino.

At his side Don Javier cursed softly and knocked on the table. "Paso."

Abuelo laughed and played the six-one domino on the other side of the layout. "Pasa de nuevo, Benito, que tú no tienes na'."

Saint had no idea how his grandpa knew that Benny didn't have any one dominoes, but when the man did indeed pass Saint wasn't surprised.

Since Saint also didn't have a one, he was forced to open the other side of the layout. He played his five-deuce.

Saint almost cursed when Don Javier played the deuce-one, but then Abuelo started laughing. He took the domino in his hand and placed it down. It was the double-one.

Benny and Don Javier groaned loudly.

"You don't have to say anything. I know you all pass," Abuelo said. Then with grand ceremony he picked up the domino he'd placed aside and put it down. The one-four domino. "¿Saben lo que se llama eso?" Abuelo asked without waiting for an answer. "¡A eso se dice capicú, puñeta!" He crowed loudly.

"Abuelo," Saint scolded his use of foul language in front of Rosie, who was taking everything in while clapping wildly.

It hardly mattered though because Abuelo was more focused on Benny, who pushed his chair back and stood up.

"That's not capicú!" he protested. "There's a double!"

"So? It's not the one I won with, so it doesn't matter. Ganamos el premio," he said in reference to the hundred point reward given to the winning team when a player won in one of two special ways: one being when the final domino played could go on either end of the layout (like Abuelo had done) or when the player won the hand with the double-zero (a play called chuchazo).

"Yes, it does," Benny argued. "It would've been capicú if one side had a four and the other a one, but what you did doesn't count. You cheater!"

At that Abuelo Papo, who'd clearly been having a great time, got mad. He slid Rosie off his lap and stood. "Cheater? How dare you! It's not my fault you are a loser! You want to know why you lost? Because you were so busy thinking about yourself that you kept screwing over your partner and falling into all of my setups."

Benny's face was turning an ugly shade of red. He was about to lose it completely.

Saint was pretty sure he was about to have to break up an old man fight if he didn't do something quickly.

Imagine his surprise when his daughter was the one who defused the situation.

"You're not being nice," she said clearly and firmly. "Calling someone a cheater just because you didn't win is not nice."

"Yeah," Abuelo Papo said.

But Saint's daughter wasn't done. She turned to her great-grandfather and said, "You shouldn't make other people feel bad when they don't win. You need to be a good sport and not call people names."

Both men stood there looking down at Rosie at a loss for words.

Abuelo Papo looked up and met Saint's eyes. He gave him an incredulous look.

Saint raised palms in a slight shrug. What could he say? Every word out of her mouth was the truth.

"You both should apologize," Rosie told them.

"That's going too far," Abuelo said and at the same time Benny said, "I'm not apologizing to him."

Apparently his little girl was on a roll, because she scolded them some more. "If you don't apologize then everyone will know that you don't know how to play nicely. People won't want to play with either one of you anymore. Then what will you do? You won't have any friends to play with."

"He's not my friend," Abuelo argued. "He's the thief who stole all of my left shoes and put them in the donation bin."

"Only after you replaced all the pictures in my living room with pictures of Walter Mercado," Benny accused.

Abuelo smirked. "I was only trying to show you 'mucho mucho amor.'" He made a circle around his heart with one hand, kissed his fingers, and then lifted it toward Benny just like the famous astrologist used to do.

Saint closed his eyes and rubbed them with the heel of his hand before rubbing the rest of his face. Maria had mentioned the ongoing prank war, but Saint hadn't really believed it. "Abuelo, you're going to get yourself kicked out."

"I didn't take anything. I just put the Walter Mercado pictures in front of his other pictures."

"You two are being bullies and it's not good to be a bully," Rosie told them.

"You tell them, Rosie," came the voice Saint least expected to hear at the moment.

Rosie clearly didn't expect it either, because when she heard Lola's voice she swung her head in Saint's direction and looked over his shoulder in horror. Everything about her expression screamed *busted*.

Poor thing. She'd been caught talking by the one person she didn't want to know how well-spoken she was.

Luckily, Lola didn't make a big deal out of it. Instead she turned her attention to her grandfather. "Is this really how bad you've gotten, Benny, so bad that you need to be reprimanded by a four-year-old?"

Benny scowled. "No."

Lola scoffed. "Then prove it." She crossed her arms over her chest. "Apologize to them all for ruining their game."

"I didn't ruin anything. He did."

"I did not," Abuelo protested.

"You did." Saint spoke up. "You were talking trash to them both the entire time."

"That's how you play!"

"You did it to mess with Benny," Saint told him. "When you saw him getting upset, you did it even more instead of backing off."

"Because he only wanted to play to try to make me look like a fool, but I made him look like one."

"I'm no fool! You are!" Benny yelled.

Lola shook her head. "I take it neither one of you is going to apologize for your behavior."

"Yo no hice na,'" both grandfathers claimed simultaneously then glared at one another for reading their mind.

"In that case, I'm leaving," Lola said.

"But you just got here," Benny said.

"I know and it's a shame I have to go," she told him. "But I don't hang out with meanies."

Without thinking Saint said, "Rosie and I are nice and we don't hang out with mean people either. Can we tag along with you, Lola?"

Lola looked at him with a small smile pulling at the corner of her mouth.

God she was beautiful. Saint kept waiting to get used to it, but every time he saw her the feeling of awe just grew.

"Are you asking me to hang out, Saint Vega?"

"I am."

"You can't go with him," Benny said.

Lola simply gave her grandfather a look that said, *you thought.* Then she turned back to Saint. "I'd love to spend time with you and Rosie. Maybe some time without distractions will let these two reflect on their behavior." With that she spun around and started making her way out of the common area.

Saint held out his hand for Rosie, who rushed up to grab it. "I'll see you on Sunday for your weekly outing," he told his abuelo, expecting some sort of protest for him leaving earlier than usual.

Instead, his abuelo just stared at Saint as if trying to puzzle something out. After a moment he seemed to shake it off. "Adios, mi amor," he said to Rosie and blew her a kiss. To Saint he said, "I'll see you soon," before walking away.

Something about his tone put Saint on edge, but Saint brushed it off. He was about to go spend time with Lola and Rosie. He was going to need all of his focus in order to get through it, especially considering how slowly Rosie had begun walking and how tense her little body was. He paused just outside the door, while Lola continued down the hall, clearly giving them space.

"I know you probably don't want to go somewhere with Miss León," Saint said to his daughter, who nodded immediately. "But," he continued, "Abuelo Papo and Señor Benny need to learn their lesson about treating everyone kindly. If we back out now and leave Miss León by herself, is that kind?"

Rosie shook her head.

"So what do you think we should do?"

Rosie sighed the most world-weary sigh. "We need to go with her, because *you* said we would." Her tone was distinctly put out.

"I also said that she and I used to be friends. Do you remember?"

"Yes."

He slowed them both to a stop in the hallway before they reached the front lobby. "Well, I asked her to join us because I'd like to be her friend again," he said to Rosie. "What do you think about that?"

His daughter stayed quiet for a minute. "I guess it's okay because you don't have any friends," she observed.

"I have friends," he told her, a bit offended.

"I never see you play with them," she said.

"Tití Kamilah is my friend and so are your other tías and tíos. Your wela and welo. The primas Alex, Gabi, and Avery. The primos Teo, Everett, and Ricky."

"Those aren't friends. They're our family."

"Your family and your friends can be the same people. Look at you with Liliana-Mei and Carlos-Li," he said, referring to his brother Eddie's kids. Rosie spent time with them every week and sometimes multiple times a week. She loved every second of it.

"But you need to have other friends too."

She had a point. "So do you, but how are you going to get them if you don't talk at school?"

"I have a friend at school," she retorted smugly.

"Who?"

"Trevor."

Saint's immediate thought was *Who the hell is Trevor?* Then he remembered that these were kids. He needed to get his shit together. He checked himself. His daughter was allowed to make any kind of friends as long as they treated her nicely and didn't try to get her to do bad things.

"Well, that's good. I'm glad you have a friend at school."

She perked up. "Papi, now you'll have a friend at my school too."

He hoped that was true. He really did want to stay true to his word and be Lola's friend, inappropriate hand holding aside. "So you're okay with going to hang out with Miss León now?"

Rosie nodded.

"Are you going to talk to her?"

"We'll see."

Saint knew that was all he could ask for, so he didn't push. He walked them both into the lobby where Lola was waiting by the door.

She was scrolling through something on her phone and frowning in concentration.

"Everything okay?" Saint asked as he and Rosie walked up to her.

Lola looked up and the sunlight streaming through a narrow skylight in the ceiling caressed her face. It made the freckles on the bridge of her nose and her cheeks stand out even more and her eyes lighten to the shade of a copper penny.

Saint was hard-pressed not to continue walking until he'd backed her up against the door and kissed every one of those freckles before nibbling on her plush bottom lip. He'd meant it when he said he wanted to be friends, but he couldn't stop dreaming about her, thinking nonstop about whether she'd taste as sweet and spicy as she smelled. It was becoming a real problem. His right hand and wrist were beginning to cramp from overuse.

"Everything's fine," she told him, pulling his thoughts out of the gutter just enough for him to remember where he was and who was standing at his side. "I'm just looking at a commercial realty website for the center."

"Oh? I thought that we were waiting until Yara had her budget meeting with Mrs. Fonseca." Saint still wasn't sure how they'd managed to pull themselves together enough to have any kind of conversation after the fiasco that was the hot-wing challenge two days ago, but they did manage to agree that they needed to know what their budget was before looking at any properties.

"I know, but afterward I thought it was a good idea to see

what's out there and how much it's going for before Yara goes in there, just in case she has to negotiate."

"Smart." Saint pushed open the door and motioned for Lola to proceed him out. Rosie followed her and he stepped out last.

He watched Lola's round hips roll in her light jeans as she strutted down the walkway in black, high-heeled combat boots. High-waisted jeans usually reminded him of the stuff his mom wore when he was a kid, but he wasn't thinking about any of that at the moment. He was thinking about the amazing things they did for Lola's ass and thighs. Saint had never considered himself an ass man or a man of any specific body part really, but with Lola it was different. With Lola he was obsessed with everything from the way her skintight black turtleneck hugged her breasts to the way her cheeks wiggled with every step. He remembered a rap song that said, "I hate to see her go, but I love to watch her leave," and that was exactly how he felt. He could watch Lola walk forever as long as she came back in the end.

"To be honest though, I don't really know what I'm looking at. It's hard to picture any of these places as a community center."

They stopped at the edge of the small parking lot. "I can help you go through them if you want."

"Would you? I have some potential properties that I think could work. I printed them out, but they're at my apartment," she said, apologetically.

"I don't have a problem going to your apartment unless you do."

"I'm fine." She looked down at Rosie. "Is that okay with you, Rosie?"

His daughter gave a regal nod, but otherwise looked uninterested.

Lola looked back at him. "It's close enough to walk. Come with me." Then she held out a hand for his daughter to hold.

Rosie reached up to grab Lola's hand, leaving Saint shocked.

He'd assumed his daughter would rush to him and hide behind his legs as she'd done at school, but no. She obviously felt at least somewhat comfortable with Lola. His spirits rose and he went to hold his daughter's other hand as they walked down the street.

Lola turned her head to look at him, her eyes full of amusement and mischief. "I've been meaning to ask you how you're feeling after the other night."

Ugh. He did not want to talk about that. That damn chicken wing had put him through hell. His stomach still wasn't back to normal, and he wasn't one hundred percent sure, but he had the suspicion that he'd seared all of his taste buds. He grunted at her, sure she'd catch on to the fact that they were not going to talk about his stupidity.

She laughed. "Rosie, has your daddy ever talked to you about peer pressure and how it sometimes makes us do things we shouldn't do?" she asked in a wry tone.

Rosie nodded her head.

"Hmm. Interesting," Lola murmured. "Looks like someone should practice what they preach."

"Quiet, you," Saint grumbled, causing Lola to laugh again. He couldn't help the smile that crept along his face in response. He liked making Lola laugh, even if she was laughing at him and not with him.

They walked along in silence for a few moments but, out of the corner of his eye, Saint watched Lola give Rosie multiple considering looks. Finally, she asked, "Rosie, can I tell you something I haven't really told anyone?"

Rosie's head snapped up and she stopped in the middle of the sidewalk to give Lola her full attention. He was not surprised. His daughter loved bochinche.

Lola smiled. "I'll take that as a yes." She leaned in and lowered her voice as if imparting a secret. "When I was little, a bit older than you actually, I used to not talk either."

Rosie's eyes grew wide. So did Saint's. She'd told him a long time ago that she'd been a quiet kid, but he'd never believed her. Not outspoken Lola.

"It's true. For a long time I didn't talk in school and a lot of the time I was quiet at home too." She began walking again, forcing them to follow.

Rosie's eyes swung to Saint and he could tell that she was dying to ask why. He felt similarly, so he asked for both of them.

"Well," Lola answered. "There were things in my life that I couldn't control and that made me feel really nervous. When I was around people or situations that made me feel like that, I would stop talking. It was my brain's way of protecting me."

They paused at the corner and looked both ways before crossing onto a more residential side street.

Rosie's hand squeezed his as she urged him to ask more. "Rosie and I would love to know what helped you."

Lola smiled at him. "When I was in second grade, my teacher helped me by having me see the school psychologist. I found out that this actually happens to a lot of kids. It's something called 'selective mutism.'" She looked down at Rosie, who was still watching her with wide eyes. "That means that kids who can speak perfectly fine in most situations go silent or mute when they're around something that makes their brains nervous."

"How did you start talking again?" Saint asked. This time without any prompting from Rosie.

"Most kids would begin to see a therapist, but I kept visiting the school psychologist." Lola led them across another street. "She was so nice that she spent her free time learning everything she could about selective mutism to help me." They approached a small apartment building and Lola stopped in front of it. She turned to face them as she began digging in her purse. "Eventually I learned that new situations and people aren't so scary. I gained confidence in my ability to handle different situations."

She pulled out a set of keys. "Once I realized that by expressing my thoughts and needs, I could make some of those situations better, I started talking…and I kept talking." She put the key in the lock and opened the front door.

Rosie followed closely at Lola's heels, but Saint didn't move. He couldn't. He was too busy trying to process everything Lola had just said. His brain wouldn't settle on any one thought. He was thinking about how bad he felt for young Lola, knowing the type of life she had at home that made her feel anxious and unsafe. At the same time he was thinking about Rosie. What could possibly be happening in her life that was making her feel unsafe? Was someone doing something to her? Was it him? Was he not loving enough? Why did she feel like she couldn't tell him what was going on? Did she not feel safe with him?

Lola stood at the door watching him like she could see the panicked thoughts rushing around in his head. She gave him a look of calm support. "That was so long ago, I'd almost forgotten about it, but do you know why I shared that with you, Rosie?" Rosie shook her head, but Lola didn't notice. She was still looking at him. "I think you might be like me. I think you may need some help with something that is making your brain anxious too. That thing might be school, but it might be something you don't even know about. Sometimes our brains just work that way. It's not because of anything bad."

Saint took a deep breath. Then he took another. Lola was right. There was no reason to spiral. He didn't even know if that was what was happening with Rosie. She could just be very very shy. She could just not be comfortable in that class or school. There were tons of reasons she could be quiet and even if she had selective mutism it didn't mean it was the result of some terrible trauma. "Whatever it is, mi amor, I will find a way to help you."

His little girl slid her hand out of Lola's and put it in his. She squeezed and smiled at him, her eyes full of love and trust. Then she tugged him along as she followed Lola into the building and up the stairs.

They came to a stop at a door on the second floor. Lola turned to them. "Be forewarned that my apartment is tiny and a mess. I haven't really finished unpacking yet and there's still stuff I need to move into my storage unit in the basement."

"We are the last people to judge you for being messy." Saint wiggled Rosie's hand as he looked down at her. "Right, Little Miss Piggy?"

She made a face at him, which he interpreted to mean, *Daaad!*

"My kind of people." Lola opened the door. "Welcome." She motioned for them to precede her into the apartment.

The first word that popped into Saint's head upon entering Lola's apartment was not *messy*. It was *colorful*. Sure the walls were a basic white and the floors a neutral mid-tone wood, but they were hardly noticeable due to the plethora of colorful rugs and bright art covering almost every inch of the small open space. Walking into Lola's apartment reminded him of walking into some of the marketplaces in Afghanistan, a rainbow of colors and plethora of textures.

"This is the world's smallest coat closet." Lola pointed to their left. "Next to that is the bathroom. Also tiny in case you're wondering." She held up her arm like one of the models on *The Price Is Right*. "But otherwise, yeah. This is my humble abode."

Directly to their right was the kitchen, which consisted of a small range with a microwave above it, a mini dishwasher, a smaller-than-average fridge, and minimal cabinets. Lola had bought a narrow kitchen cart she was using as an island.

Next to that was the living space where a small TV stand held up a medium-size TV and a bunch of folksy-looking knick-knacks and pictures. In front of it was a large colorful rug with an intricate design beneath a small ottoman that was being used as a coffee table, and a mustard yellow velvet couch covered in about fifty throw pillows and a white fur blanket.

A few feet along the wall from the TV stand, next to a huge window, stood a large dresser with a mirror above it. That made Saint suspect that Lola's bed was across from it on the other side of the room although he couldn't tell because in the way stood a set of three huge bookshelves that almost reached the ceiling. Again, every shelf was full of color from the books to the plants and the pictures.

Rosie stood in front of the wall next to the bookshelves looking at the gallery of artwork Lola had displayed. Saint walked over to join her. "Did you make these?" he asked, astonished by the different styles.

Lola came up alongside him. "No, that's all stuff I've picked up from different art shows, markets, street fairs, and stuff like that. Although, some I did get during my travels. Most of these are from Indigenous artists from the areas I bought them in. There's a lot from Mexico, because, well, I was in California and it was easier to take trips there. I have some from Puerto Rico too, including a few Taíno pieces, but I for sure want to get more."

"I don't remember you being this into art," Saint said while studying a canvas painting of a woman and a jaguar.

"I wasn't, but my mom is. She'd take me to all these different galleries and shows. We'd talk to the artists and listen to lectures. I realized how these people took these painful personal memories or these terrible things that happen in the world and turned them all into something beautiful. I thought to myself, isn't that what I'm trying to do? Create beautiful change from human suffering." Her mouth quirked to the side in a self-conscious expression that Saint found adorable. "I mean, I can't create beautiful art to save my life, but I can definitely appreciate it." She lifted a hand and softly brushed the tips of her fingers along a framed photo collage of Lolita Lebrón and snippets from news articles about her. At the top it said, "There is no victory without pain."

Now Saint understood. This is where she came to recharge, to inspire herself, to remind herself of her mission when she was worn out and tired. This was her safe space, her inner sanctum, and she'd invited him and his daughter inside. He would make sure that she didn't regret her welcome.

11

Lola pulled up to the address Saint had given her yesterday afternoon after they'd spent some time narrowing down potential buildings based on location and price alone. They now had to take closer looks at the places they kept and decide if they would work for everything El Hogar needed. Hence why she was at his house on a Saturday evening.

Saint and Rosie's house was on a street that fell right on the border of Humboldt Park and West Humboldt Park. It was clear that the gentrification hitting the rest of the area hadn't quite made it to this neighborhood. The number of fixer-upper homes still vastly outnumbered the newly renovated ones that probably cost more than she'd made in the last ten years. However, Saint and Rosie's home didn't fit into either category.

It was a big redbrick two-flat whose exterior showed age even though it was still a beauty. With its off-center covered porch, light brick accents, and decorative wrought iron gate it reminded Lola of an Old Hollywood starlet aging gracefully while still throwing out her flirtatious charm. The house wasn't the nicest on the street or even the biggest, but somehow it had more presence. It simply drew your eye. Kind of like its owner.

Saint stood on the front porch. He looked so damn good in his long-sleeved shirt and jeans. He took a few steps down and motioned for Lola to open her window.

"Parking out here is impossible," he told her. "Pull around the back and park in the driveway. I'll meet you back there."

Lola followed his direction and pulled around to the alley. She slowed when she saw him step out next to a two-car garage. He motioned for her to pull into the space next to it and she did.

"My cousins came home unexpectedly," he said when she opened her door to get out.

"You live with your cousins?" she asked.

"They live upstairs," he replied. "But they're in their early twenties and still in school, so they frequently show up in my house begging for food when they're hungry and to use my Wi-Fi when they forget to pay their bill."

Lola smiled in nostalgia. "The college years. Good times."

"I've been trying to get rid of them, but they decided it's movie night which usually means they're too broke to entertain themselves."

Lola got the distinct impression that Saint did not want his cousins to know about her. She tried to ignore the pang that caused. "Should I go?"

He gave her an alert look. "Do you want to go?"

"I mean, it seems like you're busy." Lola fiddled with her keys. "I don't want to impose."

He grabbed her hand. "I want you here, Lola. It's just that my cousin Alex is my tío Luís's youngest and she doesn't know about anything going on."

"You mean about his diagnosis?"

He nodded. "Or about the Raven Realty job, she'd have a fit."

Lola's relief that he did want her around battled with her

annoyance at having to keep a secret. Lola didn't like secrets and lies. She preferred to be up-front. "Well, we just won't talk about it, but I think we can still talk about El Hogar without mentioning any of that."

"So you'll stay? Every twenty minutes Rosie's been asking when you'd get here."

"Using your adorable daughter to reel me in. That's playing dirty."

He was completely unrepentant as he smirked. "I'll do whatever it takes to make you stay." He tugged softly on the hand he held and Lola followed.

She didn't say anything else as he led her through the small backyard featuring a set of four patio chairs and a small ash-filled firepit. The lawn was sprinkled with toys: a basketball, Hula-Hoop, unicorn helmet, some superhero figurines, a monster truck, a princess tiara, and there was a magic wand sticking out the top of a sandcastle that had been built in the small sand table.

Lola eyed the open bag of salt and shovel leaning against the house next to the back door. It was almost spring break for heaven's sake. However, they were in the Midwest. If things got crazy enough, it could snow in May or June.

Saint opened the back door and motioned for Lola to enter.

She stepped over the threshold and her jaw dropped. "Oh my god." The apartment was beautiful. She could tell that it had just been recently renovated. There were sparkling new appliances in the kitchen and an open floor plan where she could see from the back door all the way to the big bay windows at the front of the house, but it still held tons of old charm. There was large built-in cabinetry on either side of the window in the dining room. Separating the living and dining areas was an archway with two decorated columns that matched the original wooden beams and baseboards. "I hope whoever renovated this place gets a job on HGTV, because this is amazing."

"I did it," Saint said from behind her.

"You did this?" Lola wished she could've dialed back the incredulity, but she simply couldn't.

He did a head tilt, shoulder raise, pursed lips thing that she figured was his version of a shrug. "My cousins helped."

"The cousins that live upstairs?"

"I figured since they helped me renovate the place, the least I could do is let them live here."

Lola got the distinct feeling that when he said he let them live there he also meant for free, because that was what Saint did. He took care of his family.

The sounds of talking filtered into the kitchen area from one of the rooms on the right. She could make out the low, soft tones of a man's voice and two higher tones, but it was the peal of delighted girlish laughter that stopped her in her tracks. Was that Rosie? Lola didn't think she'd ever heard the little girl laugh before. It was so cute.

The man's voice rumbled. "You know, Av. I'm not sure you can rock the hot pink like I can. Right, Rosie? It looks better on me."

A giggle.

"Stop hating, Teo," a woman's voice responded. "This color was made for my skin tone. Rosie knows what she's doing."

More giggles from Rosie.

Lola couldn't help herself; she went toward the sound.

"I don't know about that. She told me this color would look good and now I'm a frog," another voice stated.

"But a cute frog," Rosie said. "Kind of."

"Why, you little punk!"

There was a scuffle and the girlish giggles exploded into a frenzy of squeals and laughter.

Lola reached the door and found a young guy, who looked a bit like Zac Efron, lounging on a princess-pink bed while wearing a large floppy hat with hot pink flowers sticking out of it. Next to him sat a beautiful girl with light brown skin. She had a hot pink feather boa on and a crown on her head. They were both watching the small woman in what looked like a green towel poncho tickling Rosie as the little girl laughed and kicked.

"Mi amor, Miss León is here," Saint said from behind Lola.

Everyone's head whipped toward Saint, and Lola found herself being scrutinized by four pairs of light eyes.

Lola cleared her throat. "I think at this point it's fine to call me Lola. I mean, she's seen my art collection, so I'd say we're friends now."

Rosie smiled at her, but didn't say anything. She wiggled around until the woman who'd been tickling her sat back and Rosie was free. She hopped up and rushed to grab Lola's hand.

Lola pasted a smile on her face. "Hi, Rosie, I'm happy to see you."

The little girl pulled her into the room toward the other occupants. She gestured at Lola as if saying, *Tadah.*

Lola figured that was her signal to introduce herself. "Hey. I'm Lola. Rosie's substitute teacher."

The woman sitting on the floor gave Rosie an odd look before looking at Lola. "So she really doesn't talk at school, huh?" she asked Lola as she stood up.

"Not yet, but we understand each other just fine. Right, Rosie?"

Rosie nodded.

The woman held out a hand. "I'm Alex, Rosie's favorite second cousin."

"Umm excuse me," the other woman said, standing up. "That honor goes to me." She held out her hand to Lola. "I'm Avery."

"Y'all are both liars," the guy said, sitting up and scooching to the edge of the bed. "I've been Rosie's favorite since I bought her that American Girl doll that looks just like her." He looked at Lola. "I'm Matteo."

"It's nice to meet you all. Sorry for interrupting your…" Lola took a look around the room.

"We were getting ready for our fashion show." Alex gestured to her frog towel cape and the rainbow scarf she was wearing like a belt. "All designs courtesy of Rosalyn Marie Inc."

"You designed all of those outfits, Rosie?" Lola asked.

Rosie nodded with a proud smile.

"You're really good." Lola looked at Saint. "What about you? Where's your outfit?"

"According to the boss—" he pointed at Rosie "—I'm the guy that takes pictures of the models."

"That's because Rosie knows there is no way she can make you look good enough to walk the runway," Matteo said with a smart-ass smirk.

Saint gave him a blank stare. "You're wearing a child's church hat and a *Backyardigans* sheet like a dress."

Lola couldn't help but laugh. Matteo did look ridiculous. They all did, but it was cute that they didn't seem to care one bit.

"Case in point," Matteo said, "And I still look good as hell."

"Yas, hunty," Avery cheered. She lifted a hand and snapped three times.

Alex whipped a señorita fan out of her sash, flipped it open, and began waving it at Matteo like she was trying to cool him off.

Matteo began twirling and posing like he was really at a photoshoot.

Alex pulled out her phone to take pictures, following Matteo out into the kitchen where he jumped on the island counter, crossed his legs, and blew her a kiss.

"Yes. Yes. Yes," Avery began coaching. "Get it! Slay it! Work it!"

Matteo got more and more ridiculous while they all busted up laughing. Eventually he was on his back, resting on his elbows, with his chest popped out and head tipped back, one hairy leg bent coquettishly, and his socked feet pointed looking like a swimsuit model in *Sports Illustrated*.

"That's it!" Avery yelled. "That's the one."

"This is your new Grindr profile pic," Alex agreed. She looked at the picture on her phone and made a face like she was trying to hold it together. She held it up for Matteo to see while Avery peeked over his shoulder. Suddenly they were all on the floor cracking up, piled on each other like puppies. Rosie jumped on the very top of the pile and joined in the laughter.

"So those are my cousins," Saint murmured at her side. "I'd tell you that it doesn't run in the family, but you've met my abuelo. You know it does."

Lola smiled. "I love it." It was clear that these three were very close and that Saint was very fond of them. She'd always wondered what it was like to be a part of a big family. Her mother had a bunch of siblings who had kids and grandkids, but she didn't keep in contact with her family. Lola only knew of them via social media and that was only the ones who had public profiles. "I hope you know how lucky you are," she told him.

When she turned to look at him, Saint was grinning down at his pile of family members on the floor. "Yeah," he agreed. "I'm very lucky."

The group finally separated and were now just sprawled all over. Alex looked at them upside down and Lola realized she had the same eyes as Rosie, Leo, and Papo Vega. "So, now that we've officially welcomed you to the nuthouse, why don't you tell us what you're doing here."

Avery rolled onto her stomach and began kicking her feet in the air. Matteo followed suit.

"Yeah," Matteo seconded. "Because we highly doubt you're here for teacher reasons on a Saturday evening."

"Lola is letting me help her find a new building for El Hogar to replace the one that got sold," Saint told them.

At that they all shot to their feet.

"The shelter that helps the queer kids who get kicked out of their homes?" Matteo asked.

Lola tensed. She didn't think any of them would say something offensive, but you just never knew. "Yes, the building got sold out from under us without warning and now we're rushing to find a new place."

"That's such bullshit," Alex exclaimed.

"Alex, language," Saint scolded.

"My bad." She began removing her Rosalyn Marie Inc. outfit. "I just can't believe this keeps happening. It ticks me off."

"I mean, really?" Avery added. "Who does that?"

"Sells a homeless shelter for profit or kicks their kid out for being queer?" Matteo asked as he also took off his high-fashion ensemble. "Because the answer to both is assholes."

"Language," Saint reminded them.

"Have you talked to my dad about this?" Alex asked Saint, who froze.

Luckily Alex didn't seem to actually want a response, because she turned her attention to Lola. "We've been trying to help out area businesses with free or really cheap labor. This is way bigger than anything we've done yet, but I think my dad would like the idea of helping out."

Lola looked at Saint, who was staring back at her straight-faced, but Lola could see the panic in his eyes. He wanted to change the subject. "Once we have more of a plan, I'm sure Saint will talk to him about it."

"I will. Don't worry about it. You're supposed to be focusing on finishing up the school year anyway. Ds do not get degrees."

Alex narrowed her eyes at him.

Avery laughed. "Look at Saint throwing out zingers for his new lady friend." She waggled her eyebrows.

"Oh, I'm not—"

"Old lady friend," Saint interrupted her to say.

Lola's jaw dropped. Did he really just say that?

Saint seemed to realize what he'd said. "Not *old* like age old. I meant that we went to high school together."

"Y'all dated in high school?" Matteo asked.

"No," Lola said at the same time Saint said, "Yes."

Lola glowered at him. Seriously? He'd spent months keeping their relationship a secret from his family back then and now he was just telling everyone about it?

The cousins pounced on the potential gossip.

"So what is it, yes or no?"

Saint, the big dummy, finally kept his mouth shut, but it was too late. The cat was out of the bag so to speak. "We did," Lola admitted.

"For real?"

Alex leaned forward, resting her forearms on the counter. "How serious was it?"

When neither Lola nor Saint answered, three pairs of eyebrows went up.

"Oh, so it was that serious," Avery concluded.

Matteo shook his head. "And here I thought innocent, good boy, Saint was a virgin until marriage."

Much cackling ensued.

"Okay, enough," Saint demanded. "Get it together or go home."

"Noooo! Don't kick us out," Avery cried. "We want pizza."

"Yes. All we have upstairs are two packs of ramen noodles and condiments we got from takeout."

Matteo slumped over the island. "We're wasting away!"

Even Rosie rolled her eyes at the dramatics.

"Go pick a movie and behave yourselves," Saint told them. Then he looked at Rosie. "Rosie, go make sure they pick something appropriate, because they need supervision from someone more mature than they are."

A chorus of, "Rude," "Now that was just uncalled for," and "Give him a girlfriend and all of a sudden he's got jokes," followed the group to the living room.

As soon as they were out of earshot Lola turned to Saint and said, "That was all your fault, you know."

He nodded. "I had to give them something or Alex wouldn't have let the topic of El Hogar go."

"Ah." Made sense. What better way to distract from neighborhood gossip than with personal gossip about someone who was usually very private.

"Anyway, you can go ahead and join them in the living room. I'm going to order these pizzas. Anything in particular you want?"

"I'm good with anything except anchovies."

He nodded and pulled his phone out of his pocket, before turning away.

Lola stood there for a moment. She could hear and see the cousins in the living room with Rosie, but she wasn't sure she wanted to go hang out with them just yet. What if they asked more questions about her and Saint, like what they were doing with each other now? She couldn't answer that question, because she didn't know. Yes they'd said they were friends, but it didn't feel that way. It felt like less, but it also felt like more. She felt like she was on a jungle adventure and at some point she'd gotten lost but she hadn't realized it until she stumbled across a path. Now she was standing there wondering if she should follow it, scared about what would await her at the end.

Unwilling to join the rest of the group without Saint, Lola

decided to be helpful and straighten up. She collected the discarded fashion show outfits that had been left strewn across the kitchen floor, then carried the pile to Rosie's room. She sidestepped toys, books, and shoes on the floor until she reached the bed. She dropped the pile there and was getting ready to exit the room when something caught her eye.

There, on Rosie's dresser, stood four pictures of a woman who had to be Rosie's mother. She had Rosie's button nose, naturally arched eyebrows, and perfect bow-shaped mouth. She was beautiful in the way that made everyone stop and stare. What was surprising was how young she seemed. In the first picture, which was a selfie, she couldn't have been much over eighteen with her edgy bob dyed fire-engine red. In the picture of what was obviously their wedding—she was wearing a white sundress and holding wildflowers and Saint was in a special-looking uniform—she looked a bit older, her hair grown out a bit and now the color of clover honey with blond highlights. The next picture was of her cradling a large baby bump and smiling down at it. It couldn't have been taken long after the wedding photo because her hair had grown out a few inches showing rich brown roots. The final picture was of the obviously exhausted but ecstatic couple holding their newborn daughter. They both looked rumpled and a bit sweaty. Saint looked like he'd come straight from the field in a smudged white shirt, fatigue pants, and dusty boots while his wife was still gorgeous despite her frizzy ballerina bun, red-rimmed eyes, and swollen bottom lip where she'd visibly bitten it hard enough to break the skin. There wasn't much of Rosie to see as she was bundled up until only her pudgy cheeks and tiny nose showed. It hardly mattered. The love in the picture practically radiated from the frame.

Lola turned to search the rest of the room for more pictures of Rosie's elusive mother, but there were none. The rest of the pictures on the walls and nightstand featured only Rosie and Saint or Rosie and members of the Vega family. She felt her curiosity grow. It was clear that the woman loved her daughter, so where was she? What had happened to her? She was so young. It didn't seem possible that she was gone gone. Then again. Lola knew better than anyone that how things looked from the outside were hardly ever how they really were.

"The pizza should be here soon," Saint said from behind her, causing her to jump.

Lola spun around. "I'm sorry," she blurted out. "I came to drop off the things and then I noticed the pictures and…" She trailed off. What could she say? *I was jealous of the woman you loved enough to marry and have a kid with and I wanted to know if she was prettier than me?* That was immature as fuck and Lola refused to stoop to that level.

"If you want to know about her, just ask," he said.

"Where is she?"

"She's dead. Car accident. Rosie was a baby."

"I'm so sorry."

He nodded.

"You must've loved her a lot."

He was silent, then cleared his throat and looked back out toward the dining room. "Let's join everyone else. I don't trust my cousins to keep things G-rated around Rosie."

Message received. Saint would not be discussing the love he had for his dead wife with the girl he'd dated in high school.

She followed him out into the living room where they sat watching Disney+, laughing at the cousin's commentary, and eating pizza when it arrived. After the cousins had left and they'd settled Rosie in bed, they discussed all of the functions a new community center would have to serve and what types of buildings would be most likely to provide them with a base to begin. Through it all Lola felt the specter of Saint's wife hovering over her shoulder and whispering in her mind that no matter how right this all felt, Lola didn't belong there—that Lola was nothing more than an interloper.

At the end of the night when he walked her to her car, gave her a long hug and a kiss on the cheek, Lola whispered back to his wife that she wasn't there for Saint. She was there for El Hogar. Now, if only she could believe that.

12

Lola had never been Miss Popularity. She had acquaintances and people she was friendly with, but it was all very surface level. She was an intense person, she knew that, and she knew that many people didn't understand it. Most people didn't want to think deeply about things like she did and they certainly didn't want to go out of their way for other people like she was ready to do at the drop of a hat. Most people were just trying to survive and that was totally fine. But it left her feeling lonely a lot of the time, which was why she was grateful to have reconnected with Yara. Even when the woman was smirking at her like a smug asshat.

"What?" Lola huffed.

"I'm just wondering if you've noticed how breathy your voice gets every time you say his name," Yara said.

Lola would've known exactly who Yara was referring to even if they hadn't just been discussing the list of properties she and Saint had put together. Mostly because she did know that she basically sighed his name now. It was annoying and completely unlike her. "I have no idea what you're talking about."

Yara started laughing. "I wish I'd taken a video of that. Your acting is worse than a low-budget web series."

Lola couldn't argue with that. "Why are you here bothering me right before the school day starts?" she asked even though this had quickly become their semi-daily tradition. Yara would show up with coffee for them both on the days Lola didn't have morning meetings and they'd sit in Lola's classroom and talk.

"Don't try to change the subject." Yara took a sip from her rose-gold bejeweled thermos. "And don't think I didn't notice you two snuggling up in the alley at the protest and holding hands on the night we don't speak of."

Lola opened her mouth to explain what really happened at the protest, but then closed it. She didn't think Saint would want anyone knowing about his panic attack. As for the night they didn't speak of, that Yara just had just spoken of, Lola had no explanation for holding his hand at the bar beyond just the feeling that she had to. She didn't think that would help her case, so she kept quiet.

"All those sparks flying between you two."

"Sparks? What sparks? There are no sparks." She was lying through her teeth, of course. There were definitely sparks. Unwanted sparks, but sparks nonetheless. It had always been that way between them.

Yara laughed. "Next time you are going to try to act, warn me so I can pull out my phone."

"Asshat," Lola mumbled.

"Plus, I remember back in the day when you two would snuggle up all over El Centro when you thought no one was looking."

Again. Saint had always been the cautious one. If it had been up to Lola, they would've been making out all over the city. She pushed away the automatic sting she felt whenever she thought about that time.

Instead, she tried to go back and look at things through the lens Saint had given her during their talk. She believed him when he told her that he wasn't embarrassed to be seen with her like she'd originally thought. She'd seen the confusion, shock, then offense on his face when she confronted him. Realizing she hadn't been so dumb to love him back then had gone a long way in soothing old hurts she'd thought long scarred over. However, the fact remained that he'd been selfish. He'd only thought about his feelings, his convenience, his goals, his future, and his desire to save her. He hadn't thought about what she wanted, what she felt about the situation, or what her plans were. He'd just assumed that she would follow along, grateful for his love and care, like an accessory on his arm. "Well, that was a long time ago."

"You know what they say, donde hubo fuego…" Yara waggled her eyebrows at Lola.

Lola shook her head back and forth quickly. "No. Aquí no hay cenizas." Lola lifted her hand and began ticking things off with her fingers. "His grandpa tried to poison mine, his daughter won't talk to me, his uncle's company is destroying the shelter that we love, and he is in charge of that project, so I think it's safe to say that this old flame has died completely and the ashes have blown away." Not to mention the fact that he'd specifically said he wanted to be friends. Friends not lovers.

"And yet you still say his name like a dreamy teen thinking about their celebrity crush."

Lola was literally saved by the bell when it went off signaling that it was time to go pick up her class from their designated arrival spot. She hopped up. "As fun as this inquisition has been, I have to go get my babies."

"And I have to go meet with Fonseca about how we are going to fund a new shelter." Yara collected her things and together they walked toward the door. "But before I go, let me just point out that for someone claiming that the past is dead and buried, you have sure put a lot of thought into why this won't work." She sashayed out the door that led to the front of the building.

Lola scowled while locking the door behind her. Yara was way off base. She had to be, because only an idiot would entertain the idea of her and Saint getting together. It would never work between them. Saint liked to play the savior. He wanted someone he had to save and that was not her. Lola saved herself. She always had and she always would.

Instead of continuing to think about it, Lola went to the back of the school to meet her class at their lineup spot. When she arrived she saw Rosie standing at the front of the line with Kamilah.

After their encounter at the old folks home, Kamilah had begun dropping Rosie off in the mornings. They chatted a bit and were friendly. Lola liked Saint's sister. Lola had come to understand that Kamilah was the closest thing to a mother that Rosie had. She dropped her off every morning, picked her up almost every afternoon, and it was clear they had a relationship that was closer than a typical aunt and niece. For that reason alone Lola liked her. On top of that, Kamilah seemed like someone she could actually be friends with.

"Good morning, Rosie. You and your tía look too cool for school."

They matched. It was adorable. They each wore a striped shirt and jeans with a green utility jacket and sneakers. Their curly hair was down and freshly styled although Rosie sported a headband with a large off-center bow. Oh, and they both seemed to be wearing the same nude color lip gloss.

Rosie tucked herself closer to Kamilah's leg, but she smiled at Lola, which was always a win.

"Good morning," Kamilah said. She was holding a large cup of what Lola had to assume was iced coffee. She looked tired and she seemed dispirited. Lola was used to her energy bouncing off the walls like one of the kids every morning. "She picked my outfit today, as you can see." She smiled, but it was a pale comparison to the bright smile she usually flashed at everyone. She took a large pull from her straw.

"Is everything okay? You seem not yourself today."

Kamilah looked briefly taken aback, but she answered anyway. Exploded really. She hardly breathed as she said, "I'm fine. It's just running a new restaurant while planning a wedding is about as easy as I thought it would be—aka not at all easy. And my fiancé would gladly elope if it meant that he'd get out of participating in his own wedding, so he's not the most helpful. Of course, my mother would love to take over planning the whole thing, but then we'd all go poor and have to live on the streets because it would be super extra and also probably tacky. And everything would be so much better if I could just talk to my best friend, but she won't return any of my texts or calls even though I've apologized a million times. It's like she's disappeared off the earth, but all her mom will tell me is that she is off finding herself." She barked out the most insincere laugh Lola had ever heard. "But yeah. I'm totally fine." She chugged the rest of her coffee. "I wish there was whiskey in here," she muttered to herself.

Wow. Okay. That was more than Lola expected and she wasn't exactly sure how to respond. It was clear that Kamilah had needed to vent, so Lola said what she wanted people to tell her when she was venting. "That sucks. I'm sorry you're dealing with all of that."

Kamilah nodded. "Thank you." She took another drink from her cup and scowled down at it when all she sucked up was air. She let out a disappointed huff and then looked back at Lola. "Anyway, I've heard through the family grapevine that you've been hanging out with my brother and that you two have something of a history."

Oh shit. Lola couldn't read her tone or her expression, so she just nodded.

Kamilah smiled and it was a lot closer to her normal beam. "Good. He spends too much time alone or trying to wrangle us gaggle of psychos into some semblance of order. He needs someone normal in his life."

Lola winced inwardly. There was no way in hell she could be described as normal. Her life had been the very opposite of normal from the moment she was born, and she'd chosen a path that would ensure it continued that way. She was a poorly banked fire at the best of times—the tiniest bit of friction could easily get that flame roaring again. The last thing she wanted was for Saint or Rosie to get burned.

"Good morning, Miss León," an enthusiastic little voice yelled.

Grateful for the interruption, Lola turned. "Good morning, Trevor."

Trevor Wright had to be one of the coolest little kids she'd ever known. He was as sweet as a spoonful of sugar, as smart as a whip, as outgoing as a puppy, and as cute as a button. Seriously, he had the best personality and the Gymboree ad face to go along with it.

He came running to her and wrapped his arms around her hips for a big squeeze. He looked up at her with bright hazel eyes surrounded by a tawny brown face. "I'm so happy to be back at school. I missed you so much," he said with such feeling that it seemed he hadn't seen her for years, rather than the previous day.

Lola felt her heart melt. "I missed you too." She returned his hug. God, she loved this kid.

"Trevor, be careful with your new shirt please. Yesterday you came home looking like you'd played paintball with no protective gear."

If only she felt the same about his mother, Heather. Lola sighed before letting go and looking up. "Good morning, Ms. Blake," she said to the impeccably dressed and super made-up woman in front of her.

"Call me Heather. How many times do I have to tell you, dear?" She gave a tight and completely fake laugh.

Lola's jaw tightened at the condescending way the younger woman said "dear." Heather reminded Lola a lot of the parents she'd worked with at a magnet school in San Diego. They tended to forget that they weren't in expensive private schools where their money and their background talked for them.

Heather continued. "Sorry we were almost late." She held a white hand up to her chest and newly manicured nails flashed in the light.

Were those rhinestones? They were. Each claw-tipped nail featured a different design on top of a nude base color.

"Trevor spent ten minutes trying to figure out if he wanted to bring his best friend Rosie a banana, an orange, or some grapes."

He'd befriended Rosie at the beginning of the school year, before Lola had taken over the class, and worked hard to maintain their friendship despite Rosie's lack of communication.

In the time she'd been in the class, Lola got a kick out of watching Trevor maintain both parts of the conversation while Rosie just sat there. He'd just chatter away asking her questions and then answering them himself as if he'd read her response right out of her head. Rosie didn't seem to mind. She stayed close to his side when she could and played with him silently.

"Oh no, Miss León. Don't tell me you're sick. You poor thing."

Lola frowned in confusion. "No. I'm perfectly well."

Heather's green eyes looked her up and down. "Oh. You just look a bit under the weather." She motioned to Lola's face. "Eye shadows." She dug around in her purse for a second and pulled out a tube of bright red lip gloss. "Here." She handed it to Lola. "This is our newest shade. It's called Popped Cherry. I'm a little bit paler than you are, but this shade should work well enough.

At least it will distract." She cackled. "Oh, and whenever you want my help picking out concealer, just let me know. Our stuff is good enough to cover up tattoos, so your freckles would be completely gone. We got your back, girl."

The "we" referring to Heather's small makeup brand that she ran with her mom and sister. "Uh. Thanks."

The bell sounded and Lola encouraged the students and their companions to say their goodbyes for the day. Companions were welcome to follow the children into the classroom, but she wanted to foster an environment of confident independence.

As always, Rosie maintained an iron grip on her aunt despite Trevor bouncing along beside her and telling her everything that had transpired since they last saw each other seventeen hours ago. When they reached the classroom door Lola unlocked it, pushed it open, and stood to the side to let the students enter.

Everyone filed in except Rosie, who actively began trying to pull Kamilah the other way.

"Come on, Rosie. Not today please," Kamilah begged. "I have to get back to the restaurant."

Rosie pointed toward the exit and then tugged Kamilah again.

"No, mi amor. You aren't leaving. You're staying here and I'm going to work."

Rosie shook her head vehemently.

"Today is the last day before spring break and I bet you're going to be doing a bunch of fun stuff today." Kamilah looked to Lola pleadingly.

Lola took a deep breath and prayed her interference didn't cause things to escalate. "It's true. I have a bunch of fun activities planned and we have a special school-wide assembly."

Rosie was unimpressed. She pulled Kamilah's hand again.

Lola walked over and held out a hand. "Come on, Rosie. Let's go eat breakfast. Then you can help me take attendance."

Rosie eyed the hand then looked back at Kamilah.

"Go," Kamilah told her. She opened her hand and wiggled it until it popped free. "I'll see you later."

Defeated, Rosie slipped her other hand into Lola's.

Kamilah ran a hand over Rosie's head. "I love you, mamita. Be good. Learn stuff. Make friends." With that she booked it out of there as if the devil were on her tail.

Lola looked down at the little girl, who was staring at her aunt's retreating back. Her heart twisted. "I know you want to be home where you feel more comfortable, but I'm here for you, Rosie. Whatever you need."

Rosie squeezed her hand, but she also let out a sad sigh.

Lola sighed too. Let another day begin.

In what seemed like both the blink of an eye and an eternity, the day came to an end. Lola watched little Bryson get ready to go home and fought the urge to growl. She honestly didn't think she'd ever seen anyone move slower. Never mind that every day he requested to go to the bathroom at the last possible minute even though she'd try to send him earlier. She didn't know what it was about kids that made them want to make things as difficult as possible at the most inconvenient times.

"Bryson buddy, the bell already rang. The parents and other grown-ups are waiting for us outside. I really need you to hurry please." She eyed the rest of the students in line to make sure they all stayed put and kept their hands and feet to themselves.

"Okay." He continued to move at the same pace. Actually, he began to move slower. It was like watching a sloth pack up a backpack and put on a jacket. After it wandered around the room for five minutes, of course.

Lola just happened to meet eyes with Rosie, who rolled her eyes and shook her head like a mini-adult. To keep from laughing, Lola turned back to Bryson. "How about I help you and we put the rest on as we walk to the back?"

"Okay."

Lola wrangled his arms into his jacket, grabbed his things, shoved them in his backpack, and zipped it as she walked to the door. She purposely took Bryson's hand so he couldn't fall behind. "Alright, friends, let's rock and roll." She rushed them through the hall and out the back door as fast as she could without making them run.

As soon as they hit the back playground she spotted Saint. He was wearing yet another sawdust-covered flannel and pair of worn-in jeans. It was absolute nonsense how everything she told Yara and herself that morning jumped right out of her head as soon as she saw him. It was like her hormones took over and her brain went on vacation. On cue her nipples perked right up. *Down, ladies.*

At his side stood Papo looking like an adorably old Mr. Rogers in a cable-knit sweater and slacks. Lola was glad to see him out and about. He seemed to be having an animated but one-sided conversation with Heather, who kept tossing her long blond hair and making eyes at Saint.

Saint on the other hand was barely paying attention to them. His eyes were locked on her.

As her students began giving her one-armed hugs and fist bumps before running off to their parents, Lola kept her feet moving toward Saint. Rosie kept pace with her as did Trevor, but she hardly paid them attention. She was focused on how Saint took in her leopard print pencil skirt, white blouse, and mustard yellow blazer. His eyes caressed every curve in a very not-friend way before settling on her face.

"Miss León," he said when she reached him.

"Mr. Vega." She bit her lip and his eyes focused there.

"Good afternoon, Miss León," Heather cut in.

Lola shook herself mentally and looked at the woman who was eyeing them both. She noticed that both Rosie and Trevor were standing a few feet away showing Papo the abstract art projects they got to take home that day.

"Good afternoon, Ms. Blake. How was your day?"

"Oh, you know, just slaying and being a boss babe."

Lola cringed inwardly.

She turned to Saint. "I own my own business. With that and taking care of my son and working out every day, it's a lot, but then you know that, being a single dad and all."

Saint nodded.

She turned to Lola. "You are so lucky that you don't have to worry about all that."

Lola almost rolled her eyes. She didn't understand why parents felt the need to say things like this to nonparents. As if it was only random chance that prevented Lola from having a kid and not conscious and deliberate decision-making. It was annoying.

But the woman wasn't done yet. No, the shark was still circling the waters. "You get to keep spending your money on cute outfits like the one you're wearing today." Then she went in for the kill. "It's so brave of you to wear bold patterns and colors like that. Go off, sis."

Of course. "Brave" because fat women should only wear black to trick people into thinking they're smaller than they are, while bold colors and patterns were only for thin women. *Insert eye roll.* She couldn't even start on the "sis" thing. Lola opened her mouth, but Saint spoke first.

"You know, a few moments ago, in front of my grandfather and a group of other parents, you asked me what I find attractive in a woman. I didn't answer then because the question seemed inappropriate, but I'm going to answer now. I think the most attractive woman is one who is so confident in herself, physically, mentally, professionally, that she doesn't see other women as competition. She doesn't feel threatened by their success, so she doesn't feel the need to attack them with rude, snide, passive-aggressive comments. I like a woman who empowers, protects, and cheers on other women. But mostly, I find self-awareness and human decency attractive." Then he completely dismissed her. "Have a good evening, Trevor's mom."

The woman's head swung between them, face red and blotchy. She stood there staring at Lola as if waiting for her to jump in and defend her.

When Lola stayed silent, because really what was there to say after that set down, the woman got even more upset.

"I'm going to report this incident to the principal," she threatened. She stalked off to where Dolores was standing by the other set of back doors talking to some parents.

"What does she think the principal is going to do to you?" Lola asked, shaking her head at the lack of logic.

"I'm not sure. I think she just felt a quite strong urge to talk to the manager." He emphasized the "uite" part of *quite*.

Lola laughed.

He turned to her and smiled. "By the way, I think you look good today." He accompanied that with a lick of his lips and another look up and down her body.

Lola's pussy swooned. Stupid lady parts.

Stop that right now.

"That's inappropriate, Mr. Vega."

"Oh, I thought friends could compliment each other. Sorry."

She heard the unsaid "not sorry" in his tone and did roll her eyes then. "I have an after school meeting, but I'll be ready to check out some more places after."

Papo came strolling forward with Rosie.

"Text me when you're ready."

"Okay." Lola turned away then remembered something and turned back. "Rosie's report card is in her backpack. It's going to freak you out, but don't worry. It's because I could only grade the things I had data for."

Before he could say anything she spun on her heels and rushed back into the building. She hated walking into meetings after they already started.

Luckily Dolores was also running late. They met up at the door to the library.

"Am I in trouble?" she asked the woman with a smirk.

The principal snorted and rolled her eyes. "Absolutely not." She paused. "Unless you don't share with me where you got that skirt."

"I'll send you the link," she said, striding into the room.

13

"Vez. This is why you need a wife."

Saint cut a look at Rosie to make sure she still had on her princess headphones and was fully engrossed in the show she was watching on his phone, while she devoured her M&M's cookie sundae, before he shot his abuelo a serious scowl. Usually that was enough to get anyone bothering him to stop talking. Abuelo was one of the very few people immune to its power.

"A wife wouldn't let you spoil her with video games and ice cream after the report card she got," he continued.

"I already told you that Lola could only give Rosie grades for the standards she had data on. Everything else had to be marked minimal because it was from before Lola was there. Plus, this was your idea," Saint reminded him.

"Well, I'm her favorite abuelo, so it's my job to give her ice cream even when she brings home bad grades. You're her dad. You're the one who is supposed to stop me."

Saint snorted. Yeah right. There was no force on earth that could stop Abuelo from doing anything. "I'm serious," Abuelo continued. "She needs a mother, and you need a wife."

Saint fought the urge to growl at his grandfather and tell him to mind his own business, like he would to anyone else who dared say something so completely asinine to him. "She has a mother and I have a wife," he said instead.

"She had a mother and you had a wife," Abuelo corrected, straightforward but not unkindly. He took in Saint's pained expression and his face softened. "It's been almost five years."

Saint stirred his rapidly melting Turtles sundae and watched the fudge and caramel swirl into the vanilla soup in his bowl. "Four years, one month, and fifteen days," he murmured. When there was no response he looked up.

Abuelo sat back with his eyebrows high on his forehead. They stared at each other for a few seconds. "I know your pain, mijo," Abuelo eventually said after a quick glance at Rosie. "I know exactly what it's like to lose the woman you love too soon…" He trailed off, his mind no doubt drifting to Abuela Rosa Luz, the woman he'd loved from the moment they met to the moment she closed her eyes for the last time.

That was the problem. Saint hadn't gotten the chance to grow to love his wife. His knowledge of the exact time that had passed since her death didn't stem from an abundance of love, but an abundance of guilt. Maybe if their relationship had been founded on love instead of responsibility and sensibility, maybe if he had tried harder to create even a friendship with her, maybe if he hadn't been so blinded by his own self-importance…maybe, maybe, maybe. But the fact was that he hadn't done anything right regarding his wife and because of that his daughter didn't have a mother. Because of that he was constantly floundering, trying desperately to make it up to Rosie but always falling short.

He looked over at her just when she happened to glance up at him. Everything about her face, from the deep bow of her top lip to the soulful eyes that were almost too big for her tawny brown face, was a carbon copy of her mother. Saint felt a pang in his chest. He loved this little girl so much, more than he ever thought himself capable of loving anyone, and she wouldn't talk at school because she had undiagnosed anxiety. Something he'd completely missed the signs of.

He ignored the spark of anger that always flared when he thought about how unfair it was for him to be doing this alone. Then the guilt was back stronger than ever because Robyn had probably felt the same when she'd been alone taking care of newborn Rosie and Saint had been off fighting a war he no longer even believed in. If he'd been home with his wife and infant daughter he would've seen how worn out Robyn was. He would've intervened and she wouldn't have wrapped her car around a tree after falling asleep at the wheel. But knowing that and vehemently wishing it hadn't happened were two completely different things.

In the end the result was the same: he was now Rosie's sole parent and it was his responsibility to raise her to be happy, healthy, and well prepared for the world she'd find herself in. Too bad he had no idea how to do that.

"Saint, you're too young to go the rest of your life trying to do everything alone. Being alone is exhausting."

"I'm not alone," Saint said.

Abuelo nodded. "Of course you have us and we do what we can, but it's not the same as having a partner, someone whose strengths make up for your weaknesses, someone who understands you, supports you, and completes you in a way that no one else can."

Saint could only shake his head. He absolutely did not want that. For as long as he could remember he'd been an outcast in his own family: quiet, serious, and taciturn when everyone else was loud, vibrant, and fun-loving. God knew he loved his family and would do anything for them and they would do the same for him, but sometimes he just didn't get them and he knew they felt the same about him. However, he didn't want their understanding. He didn't want them to know him, truly know him, because then they'd see through the facade. They'd know he wasn't the strong, steady, and dutiful war hero they thought he was.

"No one else is raising Rosie but me and we are doing just fine." He collected their trash, scooped his little girl into his arms, and tried his damnedest to ignore the way his declaration tasted like the ash of a lie on his tongue. Thank god his grandfather for once didn't push harder.

They walked through the doors of the ice cream shop and Saint lowered Rosie to her feet, but she immediately grabbed on to his hand. He gave hers a light squeeze and she used all the strength in her little hand to squeeze back. It was a game they played. It never failed to make his heart melt like his sundae. "Are you ready to go visit Wela and Welo, mamita?"

"Why can't I go look at old buildings with you and Miss León?"

"Because your abuelos are leaving tomorrow, they'll be gone for a while, and they want to spend time with you before they leave." Saint would be forever grateful to the twins, Eddie and Cristian, for planning a last-minute cruise for their families and buying Mami and Papi tickets to go along. Even better, the cruise left from Puerto Rico, so his parents had decided to spend some extra time there with Mami's family. Saint really felt this was what his parents needed to finally cut the cord to El Coquí. Once they began having adventures, he knew they wouldn't stop. "Plus, I need you to babysit Abuelo Papo," he added while ignoring the snort behind him. "He gets himself in trouble when you aren't there to remind him of the difference between right and wrong."

She nodded at him as if that made complete sense. Sadly, it sort of did. "Okay. I'll make sure Abuelo Papo behaves and doesn't make Welo mad."

"It's a father's right to make his kids mad after all the times they made him mad," Abuelo Papo declared. "It's called the circle of life."

"That sounds more like the circle of pettiness," Saint told him.

"Yeah? Tell me that same thing again after this one goes through puberty."

Saint shuddered and almost crossed himself. He was not looking forward to the teenage years. "Hurry up please. I don't want to be late." His truck was only a few feet away.

Abuelo purposefully began shuffling his feet. "I'm still waiting for you to tell me what happened with you two after high school." At Saint's alert look in his direction Abuelo laughed. "You think I didn't know there was something going on back then? You were smiling nonstop for no reason."

His abuelo was good at using his over-the-top personality as a distraction for just how observant he really was. It didn't surprise Saint at all to find out that Abuelo had known there was something going on with Saint back then.

"I knew you were in love, I just didn't know with whom until your abuela showed me the letter she'd found on the doorstep."

Saint stopped walking. "You have the letter from Lola?"

Abuelo shook his head. "Your abuela and I thought it best if we got rid of it."

Saint looked down to his daughter, who was watching them with wide eyes. "Get in the truck and buckle yourself in, okay?" He hit the button on his keys to unlock the door.

Once Rosie had closed the car door behind her, Saint turned on his grandpa. "I can't believe you," he said in a quiet but stern voice. He wanted Abuelo to know that it was not okay. "You had no right to read a letter addressed to me, you certainly had no right to get rid of it, and you definitely should have told me about it before now."

Abuelo nodded, looking ashamed. "You're right. I'm sorry.

It wasn't my place. I'm sure saying that I was trying to help isn't enough."

"Help how? Do you have any idea what I went through because I didn't get that letter?"

"I do now, but at the time I was trying to protect you. I knew from experience how hard it was to serve. I knew that it would only get worse, but you'd made your choice. You were already gone and she was saying goodbye, not see you later." He paused, his eyes earnest. "I just didn't want to make it harder for you."

Saint could understand Abuelo's desire to protect him, especially given the message in the letter. That first year away had been the most difficult of his life and, if he were honest with himself, he didn't know that getting the letter would've made it easier. Sure he would've known that Lola was safe, but he also would've known that she didn't want to see him again, that he'd ruined their chance at happily-ever-after and couldn't fix it.

"I forgive you," he told Abuelo, because at this point what else was there to do about it.

Abuelo brightened up. "Good. Now let's talk about what's happening with her now."

"I'm not talking about that with you."

"Why? You think I don't see what's going on here, the real reason you want to help with El Hogar so damn bad?"

"I'm doing it because it's the right thing to do."

Abuelo snorted. "Don't try to lie to me. Más sabe el diablo por viejo que diablo."

Fine. He wasn't pulling one over on Abuelo, but that didn't mean that he had to talk to him about it. Especially since Saint himself didn't know what was going on between him and Lola. He knew that he definitely still had feelings for her, more flirty than friendly feelings considering that he couldn't ever stop himself from checking her out. There was attraction between them, there probably always would be, but that didn't mean they could have a relationship. She'd made it clear time and time again that she had her own path and she wasn't going to veer from it for anyone. It hurt, but it was best for him to get it through his head that they both had their own priorities and being in a relationship wasn't it. It was why he needed to focus on being friends only, no matter how hard it was to remember when they were together. "Just get in the car, Lucifer."

"What in the ever-living hell is that thing?" Lola asked in his ear. Most likely so that Ronnie, the Realtor, couldn't hear from where he stood in the middle of the room.

Saint looked at the small, square, covered pit in the floor. "I think it's some sort of draining system from when this was a slaughterhouse," Saint replied, although he couldn't be sure.

"Nah. That's a murder hole," said Lola.

"A what?"

"A murder hole. You know. Where murderers dump the dismembered body parts of the people they just murdered."

Saint bit the inside of his lip to keep from laughing. He'd known the run-down building, which had been everything from an old slaughterhouse to a car shop to an underground boxing gym, would be a hard sell for Lola, but it was surprisingly affordable. Well, more like unsurprisingly affordable because the place was a dump. "Besides the murder hole, what do you think?"

She leaned close again. "I think that I'm almost positive my dad used to move drugs out of here back in the day."

"Seriously?"

Lola nodded her head and pointed to the mural that covered the entirety of a wall at the far end of the open space. "My brother's friend Berto painted that mural. I remember watching him do it while Iván and I were waiting for my dad, who was in the back talking to the owner. My dad came out a while later with a smug look on his face and busted knuckles. I always knew what that meant. He'd just made a deal with someone who didn't want to be making deals with him."

It always amazed him how Lola could just say these things. He loved that she wouldn't allow her father's actions to make her feel shame. Even when she'd been treated like nothing more than his daughter by others, she never lost her sense of self. She was not Rafael León's daughter. She was Lola León and his sins did not reflect her character. "I thought you mostly stayed with Benny back then," Saint said.

"I did, but as soon as Benny would get on my dad's case about his lifestyle and choices, my dad wouldn't let me go. I'd stay at the house with him and his crew. Then he'd forget about it or he'd get a new girl who didn't want his kids around and I'd be allowed to go again."

"Was it a relief when you stayed with Benny for good?"

She nodded emphatically. "I mean I was still upset about Iván going to prison, but I was so glad to be with Benny and not have to worry about going back. Obviously, he's not the easiest person to live with and Benny has never been the affectionate type, but he taught me so much and always encouraged me to learn more, dig deeper, and think for myself. He taught me to speak up and do something when I saw something that was wrong. He's a lot of the reason that I am who I am."

"I can relate to that. It may not seem like it, but my abuelo Papo is a large part of me being who I am," Saint shared.

"I remember. You became a soldier because he was one."

"It was more than that though. I wanted to be like him. I know he seems reckless and carefree now, but he's not." He tried to think of how to explain it in a way that she could understand. "When I was in second grade the twins started kindergarten. My parents would send the three of us to the bus stop and tell me that I was in charge. It was right on the corner, so it's not like it was far, but I felt so grown. Anyway, the twins would always play around while we waited for the school bus. I'd have to basically chase them down the street and wrestle them onto the bus every morning. One day I got sick of them always playing around and running off, so when the bus came I got on without them. I figured that they'd miss the bus and then our parents would have to take them. They'd get in trouble and learn to stop playing around. But when the bus left without them, they decided to walk to school instead of telling our parents what they'd done. I was sitting in class feeling smug when I got called to the office because my parents were there."

Saint remembered walking down the hall planning everything he was going to say. When he reached the office, he saw his mom standing there crying with Kamilah on her hip and Leo holding her hand on the other side. Papi was yelling at the poor staff about them losing his sons while Abuelo Papo tried to calm him down. "The twins had never made it to school and no one knew where they were." They'd asked him where the twins were and he'd said that he didn't know. Then they'd told him to confirm that the twins had gotten on the bus. He'd thought about lying, but couldn't. "I will never forget the looks on my parents' faces when I told them that I got on the bus without them because they were playing hide-and-seek. They were so disappointed. They didn't even yell at me. They just turned away and told the principal to call the police." Saint had sat in the office with Mila, Leo, and Abuelo Papo while his parents, school staff, and police officers went to look for his brothers. "While we sat there my abuelo asked me why I would do that. I tried my best to explain myself and he listened to me. When I was done he told me that he understood my frustration then he said something I've never forgotten, 'Junior, in this life we all have responsibilities. Duties. My duty as your abuelo is to protect the family and make sure they have everything they need to be happy. Your duty as the big brother is to protect and lead your little brothers and sister because they're not ready to do it themselves. Fulfilling our duties is hard, but it's the most important thing we can do, because it keeps people safe and helps them be happy.'" Saint realized that he felt bad because he'd failed at his duty. He'd vowed to never do that again. "I saw a completely different side of my abuelo that day. After that I paid more attention and I noticed that he did take his duty seriously. He was always the first one there whenever one of us needed help; he still is. He will do whatever is necessary to make sure we have what we need even if that comes as a detriment to himself. He does it all with a smile on his face and without making you feel bad about it."

Lola smiled at him. "I can see that. He loves helping and so do you."

"It's not very different from what Benny taught you. When we see a need, we should do what we can."

"True. It's weird that we both went on to serve others, just in completely different ways."

Saint didn't think it was weird at all. He thought it made them a good pair.

She took another look around the building before saying, "I think we can both agree that this one isn't it." She started for the door.

He watched her walk through the open space and couldn't help but notice the damn leopard print skirt that hugged her hips and ass in a way that made him unable to look away. She hypnotized him like a watch on a chain.

He was not surprised by the actions of Trevor's mom earlier that afternoon—he honestly couldn't remember her name even though she'd tried to pass him her name and number. The way Lola worked that skirt, the whole outfit really, was enough to make any woman envious. Lola looked lush and soft in a way that made him want to nestle into her body, but the way she carried herself let him know straight off that she was strong, capable, and she knew the power she held. She was an immortal warrior queen walking amongst mere mortals.

"Show me the next place on your list," he told her.

The next place was more promising. It was an old doctor's office that had been purchased by a company hoping to make it into a boardinghouse, but the project was stopped halfway through. It shared a building with what had once been a beautiful theater, but had fallen into disrepair.

Ronnie, the Realtor, opened the front doors and let them in. "I'll let you two walk around and check it out. I'll wait out here." The door closed behind him.

Lola looked at Saint. "This place is haunted."

He gave her a look.

"Seriously," she said. "I've watched enough ghost hunting shows to know that when the person who is supposed to be giving you the tour doesn't even want to go inside, that place is hella haunted."

"You watch ghost hunting shows?"

"Yes. Why do you say it like that?" she asked, raising a challenging eyebrow.

Saint shook his head. "Those shows are nonsense."

Lola laughed. "Okay, I will agree that most of them are overly produced bullshit, but you can't knock ghost hunting shows until you watch *Ghost Adventures*. These guys actually do their research, try to debunk things while they investigate, and they really care about respecting the people and places they visit. I mean they do say 'dude' and 'bro' every three seconds, but they are legit and fun."

Because she looked so adorably animated, Saint refrained from telling her that there was no such thing as legit when it came to ghost hunting. Instead he started examining the old lobby space around them. "This place would probably be the easiest to renovate," he told Lola. "It already has small rooms with plumbing in each one as well as offices. It has a huge space that used to be the lab, one that was radiology, and another that was the pharmacy. All those spots are completely empty now and can easily be made into a kitchen, a computer lab, and a multipurpose room."

Lola poked her head around the doorjamb leading into a hallway and then pulled it back quickly. "Do you think the ghosts are from patients or do you think they moseyed over from the abandoned theater?" She turned to face him and bit her juicy bottom lip. "I'd almost rather have patient ghosts. Imagine how dramatic theatrical ghosts would be."

Saint smiled to himself. He found this superstitious side of Lola delightfully surprising—it was such a contrast from her usual no-nonsense persona. It made her more human, more approachable. "Did you listen to anything I said?"

"Of course I did and I agree with you. This place would be awesome. I'm just wondering how easy the ghosts would be to get rid of. We can't have ghosts wandering around scaring already traumatized kids."

"You know," Saint pretended to muse, "all you need to do is mention property values and you'll sound just like the Raven Realty people discussing the locals."

Lola gasped. "You're right! I'm trying to gentrify their home and kick them out!" She put a hand to her chest. "I'm just like those vultures."

"I don't know about all that, but you should definitely apologize." He was one hundred percent teasing, but Lola replied like he wasn't.

"Are you crazy? You don't talk directly to spirits unless you want to open yourself up to a connection that they can use to hitch a ride."

He snorted. "You cannot honestly tell me that you believe in that stuff. It's ridiculous."

"Christians believe that a divine being impregnated a teenager with a magical miracle man who would then be tortured and killed only to resurrect three days later, all of which somehow means that every single person who believes in him can be forgiven for the shitty things they do, but I'm ridiculous for believing that our energy doesn't always completely disappear when we die?"

Well, when she put it like that. "Touché. Although, personally, I'm more of a most-of-the-Bible-is-metaphorical type believer."

"To each their own," Lola said, opening a door and peeking her head in.

Saint had to laugh. She was so damn cute. "So these ghosts, can they see us?"

She shrugged. "I guess it depends on if it's intelligent—they can see and interact—or residual, just sort of there, haunting."

"Let's hope any ghosts here are residual ones, then."

"Why?"

"Because I don't want them to see me do this." Saint reached for her and pulled her into his arms. He lowered his head and then he stopped, his mouth millimeters from hers. He stared into her gorgeous molten penny eyes. "I want to kiss you so bad," he confessed. "I want to do more than kiss you. I want to drop to my knees, strip you out of that skirt, and worship you. But we agreed to be friends and I don't want to ruin that, so if I am. Stop me. Tell me to let you go. I—"

"Saint, shut up and kiss me already."

He didn't need to be told twice. Saint didn't just touch his lips to hers. He tilted his head and sealed their lips together. He bent a bit, so he could wrap his arms around her and lift her until her mouth was almost level with his and she was balancing on the tips of her toes. He twisted his head, worked his tongue, changing positions over and over until Lola was clinging to him like she'd fall if he let go. He pulled back and gave her mouth one more smacking kiss, then another. Finally, he nuzzled her nose with his own. "How was that?" he whispered against her mouth.

"It almost made me wish some intelligent spirits were here, so they could confirm that it was as good as I thought."

A rumbling laugh escaped his mouth. "You don't need them. I can tell you that it was definitely that good." He straightened and let her go, although all he wanted to do was pull her tighter against himself. "Let's go talk to Ronnie about getting a one percent discount per ghost and we can pick Rosie up before heading back to my house to make a plan."

She nodded and stepped back, but Saint just couldn't forgo contact completely, so he grabbed her hand and interlocked their fingers, his proclaimed desire for mere friendship clearly in the rearview mirror.

Shortly thereafter, they were back at Saint's place, all engaged in different things, but still together. There was a sense of belonging with Lola here that made him equal parts nervous and excited.

Saint looked down at Rosie. She was lying across the couch with her head on the throw pillow in his lap. She was smiling about whatever was happening in the princess movie she was watching while he looked at the blueprints for the supposedly haunted building on his computer. She laughed and then looked up at him to see if he thought it was funny too. Saint smiled even though he had no idea what had just happened. Then put his hand in her hair and started twisting a curl around his finger. She'd always loved that. Sometimes it was the only way she could fall asleep. She smiled at him and then snuggled closer. *Love you, Papi* she mouthed at him.

"Love you too, baby." And oh boy did he love this little girl. From the moment he'd heard her heartbeat he'd known that he'd do absolutely anything for her. He was beginning to feel the same way about the woman sitting nearby.

Saint looked over at Lola. She'd lost her shoes and blazer at the door and was curled up on the chair in the corner with her laptop, a notebook in her lap, and a pencil in her mouth as she typed. She was obviously deep in concentration, staring intently at the screen with a little frown between her brows. She scrolled down to read something. Then she plucked her pencil from between her lips and scribbled something down. She turned back to the laptop, scrolled down on the trackpad a few times, scribbled something else down in her notebook, and then went back to typing on her laptop. Back and forth she went. Her head and hands constantly in motion. Her silky hair had started to fall out of the loose messy bun she had put it in and her lipstick had worn off long ago. Because the pencil was no longer in her mouth, she began to chew on her bottom lip. Saint wanted to offer to do it for her, but of course he wouldn't. Not with Rosie right there.

Things were complicated enough between them. Saint wouldn't confuse the situation more until he was certain Rosie could handle it.

She had an appointment with the therapist in a few days. Maybe once she was actually diagnosed and receiving care he could mention it to her therapist and see what they said.

Until then, anything more serious than a few stolen kisses was off-limits.

14

There were plenty of other things Lola could be doing on a Sunday night before a week off work, but here she was at the senior center helping old people pick out costumes to wear before they got on the tiny stage to sing karaoke. Honestly, there was nowhere else she'd rather be. Not when she got to spend quality time with Benny and Saint, Rosie, and Papo. Leo Vega was there too.

"Traigo yerba santa pa' la garganta…"

Lola watched Doña Olga shake her hips to the music as she sang the popular Celia Cruz song with more energy than skill. At least the woman had stage presence. She had everyone in the audience singing along.

Even Lola couldn't hold back. She might not sing, EVER, but she would dance. So she grabbed on to either side of the black and bright floral skirt of her long, button up maxi-dress and swung them back and forth as she cha-cha'd by herself.

"Wepa! Dale, muchacha!" she heard Papo Vega say from her right. She turned her head and found him smiling at her and giving her two thumbs-up from where he stood with Saint and Rosie.

Lola smiled back, winked at him, and then completed a spin before going right back into her cha-cha.

"I didn't know you two were so friendly," Benny said in Spanish.

Lola looked at her grandpa but didn't stop dancing. "Why do you sound so upset about that? Am I supposed to hate him irrationally just because you do?"

"My hate for him is not irrational," he grumbled. "He sewed all of my underwear together last week. It took me an hour to get it undone."

"And what did you do to him first?"

Benny smiled. "Dumped out his hand sanitizer and put clear glue from the art room in the bottle."

Lola rolled her eyes. These two were loving this game way too much. She wondered if either of them realized that. "You still won't tell me the rational reason for your hate."

"He's a traitor to his people, but everyone acts like he's the greatest thing ever."

"A traitor to his people?" Lola asked, only momentarily puzzled before it made sense. When Benny was a baby his father had been severely wounded when Puerto Rico's Insular Police, under direct military command from the US-appointed governor, opened fire on peaceful protesters. The Ponce Massacre. After that, Benny's father became an active member of the Partido Nacionalista de Puerto Rico. He viewed members of the police force and anyone who served in the military as traitors to Puerto Ricans, the punishing hand of the government that was actively oppressing the people. He'd raised Benny with that same philosophy. "You don't like him because he's an army vet," she concluded.

Benny didn't respond, but he didn't need to.

She knew she was right, just as she knew that there was more to it than that.

Everyone acts like he's the greatest thing ever.

"Who thought Papo Vega was great?"

He growled. "Todo el condenado mundo." He affected a high, womanly voice as he continued in Spanish, "'How talented.' 'Look at those beautiful eyes.' 'I love his voice.'"

Aha. Lola knew that Papo had been part of a popular band, but there had to be a specific woman Benny was thinking of. There was only one person it could be. "Benny, was Abuela Manuela a fan of Papo Vega?"

"A fan?" he scoffed. "If he'd given her a chance she would've been a groupie. She told me so herself."

Lola had never met her abuela Mani. She and Benny had separated when her dad was still a kid. She'd moved to New York City with a friend, and she'd died shortly before Lola was born. For everything she'd been told by Benny and her father, the woman had been cold and selfish. She hadn't wanted a family and had resented her husband and son. Lola knew better than to take those claims at face value considering the sources. However, Lola couldn't deny that talking about sleeping with another man to her husband, especially when it was clearly not something he was okay with, was inconsiderate at best and purposefully hurtful at worst. "I'm sorry she did that to you, Benny."

He waved her off, clearly embarrassed to have told her so much. "That's in the past. No me importa."

That was obviously a lie. He still cared about the past enough to let it make him hate Papo Vega in the present, so much so that he was making both men miserable. "You know none of that is Papo's fault, right?"

He glared at her. "I didn't say anything to you when you dated that girl who was 'just friends' with her ex and I didn't say 'I told you so' when she dumped you for him, so don't say anything to me about my relationship with my wife." He stalked off.

Lola watched him go and realized that she could've been more careful with how she broached the topic. If it was something he could move past easily, Benny would've done so already. "He didn't have to bring up Jessica like that," she grumbled to herself.

"That didn't look good," Saint's voice said in her ear. "Are you two fighting?"

"As always, Benny wants me to mind my business although he has no trouble being all up in mine."

"Yeah, I heard what he said about your ex, Jessica is it?"

"Are you fishing for information about my past lovers?"

Saint grimaced. "I wish you wouldn't use the word 'lovers,' but yeah. I guess I am."

"And do you think that's fair since you've made it clear that you don't want to discuss your wife?"

Before he could say anything, Papo Vega wandered up to them. "Saint, ask her to dance with you."

Lola's heart skipped a beat. She would love to dance with Saint. Anything to get close to him. They hadn't been alone together since their haunted real estate tour, and Lola understood that anything physical was off-limits in front of Rosie, but dancing seemed like a perfectly acceptable loophole.

"This is karaoke not a dance," he replied, dashing her hopes.

Papo Vega shook his head. "Tan serio." He looked at Lola and held out a hand. "Since my grandson is clueless, do you want to dance with me?"

Lola couldn't help but smile and say yes, even though she felt a bit like a traitor after her conversation with Benny.

The next singer began and Lola scrunched her nose at the song. "Mi Libertad." She could never hear Frankie Ruiz's song about how much he desires his freedom from prison and all the things he wishes he could do without thinking of her brother.

She would just picture Iván sitting in his cell missing his life and regretting his choices. It was painful.

"This can't be a favorite song of yours," Papo Vega said as he led her through the salsa steps. "Who do you think of? Your dad? Brother?"

"My brother," she replied and then, because he was Papo Vega and he was magical, she shared more. "He's now been in there longer than he was ever free, and he had nothing to do with the killings. He's just unlucky enough to be Rafael León's son."

"That's sad," he agreed.

"Yeah. So much wasted potential and all because my dad wanted to control everything."

"Do you know that I know your dad?"

"Everyone knows my dad. He's infamous."

He shook his head. "Not know of him. Know him personally."

"Really?"

"When I was in Los Rumberos, he used to come to El Coquí with his mother to see our shows. I introduced him to my boys even though he was a few years older. They played together. I liked him. He was a natural leader. He talked to my boys about important stuff like how the education system was failing them and played a big part in keeping Black and Brown people poor. He was probably only twelve or thirteen. I used to think, 'Wow. That boy is going places.' I was so sad when I saw him going down the wrong path. Talk about wasted potential."

She understood what Papo Vega was trying to do. He was trying to remind her that her father was just a man, a highly flawed man, but a man nonetheless. Like her brother, he'd been made into what he was. If they'd been talking about anyone else, Lola would be able to accept that. She dealt with "troubled youth" all the time and could easily separate the action from the person. But when it came to her father, she couldn't be objective.

He'd done too much. Ruined too many lives, including hers and Benny's. "My dad was never going to follow anyone's rules but his own," Lola said. "Benny ensured that when he drilled it into all of our heads that the rules of this country were designed to keep us subjugated and we have to be willing to break the rules in order to create new ones that are fair for all. Unfortunately, my father is too selfish to want equality for all. He just wants power for himself."

"If you tell him that I said this I will deny it, but I always admired your abuelo. He fought against the system no matter what. I don't even know how many jobs he lost because he was always pissing off the management. I didn't fight back. I wanted safety and stability for my family, so I gave in. I played the game even though I knew it was fixed against me."

"Sometimes all we can do is survive," Lola told him, taking a page out of her old therapist's book.

"You probably don't want to hear this." Papo Vega spun her around and then pulled her back into the steps. "But you remind me of your father. You are smart and passionate, a natural leader. You have a fire in you that draws people in. They want to be near you to warm their hands on your flames."

"If you are trying to flirt with me, Papo Vega, comparing me to my dad and then a fireplace is not the way."

He laughed. "Call me Papo. And me flirt? I leave that to the young ones like my grandsons." He shot a look at Saint, which made her do the same.

Saint was staring at her with a look in his eyes that made her light up like the fire Papo Vega accused her of being.

Lola tore her eyes away and brought her attention back to the old man in front of her who wiggled his eyebrows at her roguishly. She laughed. "Is comparing me to my father supposed to be some sort of revenge for trying to get you kicked out and almost tackling you in the hall?"

"No! Why would you think that?"

"I don't know, but they say revenge is a dish best served cold."

"That may be true, but passion is best served hot." He twirled her out and then back in. "And I wasn't trying to offend you, you know," he said. "I told you all of that because I wanted you to know that, like the young version of your father, I admire those qualities and I like you."

Lola flushed with pleasure at the praise. "I like you too… Papo."

"Good." The song drew to a close. Papo let her go and stepped back. "Now it's my turn to sing. I picked this song for you. Don't waste it." He pushed her in the direction of Saint. "Go serve my grandson something hot. He's been in the cold for too long."

Lola looked back at Saint. He was still staring at her with desire. Reminding herself that she was a badass bitch, Lola grabbed the proverbial bull by the horns. She strutted over to Saint, adding extra sway to her hips. Without speaking a word, she grabbed his hand and pulled him out the side door and around the corner to a darkened hallway. As the sounds of a famous bolero began, she stepped close to Saint and drew his arms around her.

Papo's strong and still beautiful voice began to sing, "Bésame. Bésame mucho."

She wrapped her arms around Saint's neck.

He released a rough exhale and pulled her closer. Then he started to sway with her.

"I don't think we ever danced with each other," she said after a moment.

"That's because you wouldn't go to prom with me," he responded. "Something about refusing to uphold society's patriarchal views that women were only worth effort if they are dressed up like purchasable dolls."

She looked up at him. "I stand by that."

He smiled down at her. Then his face became somber. "It's not that I don't want to talk about her."

Lola knew exactly whom he was referring to and she almost told him to stop. She didn't want to think about his wife. She just wanted to enjoy being in his arms. However, she wanted to know, so she let him continue.

"Robyn and I didn't have a normal relationship."

"What does *that* mean?"

"We met at a bar near the base. We had a one-night stand. Right before I was due back, she found me and told me she was pregnant. She'd grown up in the system and she didn't have anyone. No family. No friends. She had a part-time job as a waitress. That was it. We both were willing to do whatever was necessary for our child and Robyn needed medical insurance, so we got married and I left to continue my tour. Then, before I could even really get to know Robyn, she was gone. That's why I don't talk about her. If I open that door, then Rosie would start to ask questions. She'd want to know more and I can't answer those questions because I don't know." He shook his head at himself. "How do I tell my daughter that I can't tell her about her mom because I never even knew her outside of a few letters she sent me, most of which were about the pregnancy. I won't lie to my kid. Rosie deserves better. Robyn deserved better."

Lola's heart squeezed. "You deserve better too, Saint." She could see Saint doing all of that. He had such a thing for helping, for doing things correctly and honestly. She could see that his loveless marriage was more of a sore spot for him than it probably would be for Rosie. "Don't put that kind of pressure on yourself. Rosie will eventually need to be told the truth, but don't think it's somehow going to scar her or ruin her life. Kids tend to understand more than people give them credit for and they are more resilient than they seem. She'll probably be disappointed, but she'll understand."

In the distance the song ended and another began, but Lola paid it no mind. She continued swaying with Saint.

"I'm terrified that I'll ruin her. That I'll do something the wrong way or say something I shouldn't have and mess her up. She's obviously already dealing with something because she feels so much anxiety about it that she won't talk in school. I didn't even know. I mean I knew she wouldn't talk, but I would've never connected it to anxiety if it weren't for you. I shouldn't be trusted with her. I'm going to fail her."

She could feel his heart beating frantically where her cheek was resting on his chest. The hands at the small of her back began to clench. His breathing was agitated even though he was trying to take deep breaths.

Lola rose onto her tiptoes and wrapped her arms around his neck. "Is this okay?"

He nodded and pulled her closer.

She pressed a kiss to his cheek.

He turned his head and caught at her lips with his. It was a deep but quick kiss. Then he buried his nose in her hair and inhaled deeply. He exhaled and she felt it all along her scalp. The hairs on the back of her neck and arms rose in prickly pleasure. "Keep doing that."

He did and after a few moments his body relaxed. She prayed what she said next wouldn't cause him to panic again, but it needed to be said. "Saint, did you know that anxiety is more likely to be hereditary the younger someone is when they start to display symptoms?"

"Do you think her mo— Oh. You're suggesting I have anxiety."

She tightened her arms. "Please don't be mad, but yes, I am."

"I'm not mad," Saint assured her, returning her squeeze. "Most people can't live through what I've lived through, done the things I've done, and not be messed up."

Lola was certain he'd had symptoms of anxiety before he joined the army, but she didn't say so. She was just happy that he wasn't mad at her for essentially sticking her nose where it didn't belong.

"I know I need to talk to someone. There's just so much to do that I push it off. I'll get to it when there's time."

"Make time," she told him. "It will help you, which will also help Rosie."

"You're right. I already found her a therapist who specializes in selective mutism. I'll see if that clinic has someone who can see me or if they can refer me to someone."

"I think that's an excellent idea."

"It would probably help her feel more comfortable with the process if she knows that I'm doing it too."

Lola smiled at him. "I'm so proud of you," she told him.

He gave her a look of disbelief.

She doubled down. "I am. You're strong, selfless, kind, hardworking, and you've never been led around by your ego. You're not one of those people who has to flaunt what you do. If anything you'd prefer it if no one noticed, but I notice, Saint. I see you and the amazing person you are."

He began to shake his head in denial, but Lola didn't let him. She put her hands on both sides of his face and pulled his mouth to hers. My god she loved kissing this man. His lips were soft and luxuriant, his tongue sweet. He backed them up against a door and she felt all the hard planes of his body against hers. "Did I mention sexy as hell?" She slid a hand down his back and grabbed a handful of taut ass cheek.

He paid her back in kind. "Lola," he whispered. "Canela." He groaned and dove back into her mouth.

She used her free hand to clutch at his hair and raised her leg to hook it on his hip.

He used his grip on her ass to lift her up. Her toes barely

brushed the floor, but it didn't matter because Saint anchored her with his hips and Lola whimpered at the feel of him between her thighs, hot and hard. She was just about to open the door behind her and drag him into the room when she heard someone exclaim.

"Oh shit!"

She and Saint sprang away from each other. They turned in unison.

Leo Vega stood in the doorway holding Rosie's hand with one hand and covering her eyes with the other. He wore an expression of extreme shock, but it didn't last long. His lips curled into a wry smile causing his eyes to crinkle just the tiniest bit at the corners. He raised one single eyebrow.

Objectively, Leo was probably the most handsome of the Vega brothers. He looked like he'd walked right off the set of a telenovela and had the kind of presence that demanded attention. He oozed charisma and sex appeal. The problem was that he clearly knew it and thus, he was obnoxious. Especially when he opened his mouth.

"Damn, bro. I didn't know you had it in you. You animal."

"Language, Leo," Saint barked.

"Really? She just saw you with your tongue in her teacher's mouth and her hand on your ass in the middle of the hallway at an old folks home, but my language is too much?"

"Leo," he growled.

Leo removed his hand from Rosie's eyes, bent down, and scooped her into his arms. "Rosie, mama, have you heard of the birds and the bees? It might be time for you to learn where babies come from."

Saint growled again and Leo smirked, obviously enjoying pushing his brother's buttons.

Alright. Enough was enough. "Rosie already knows that babies come from the bodies of their mother if they're a mammal.

Otherwise they come from eggs that the mother laid. We talked about that in science. Guess what, Leo, preschoolers handled the topic with more maturity than you, a grown man. How sad is that?"

Leo stayed quiet for a moment, eyeing Lola. Then a huge smile appeared on his face, a genuine smile devoid of snark. "I like you, Lola León. I give you full permission to make out with my brother in dark corridors. Maybe it will help him lighten up." He began to walk toward them. "Now, if you'll excuse us. This little girl who knows where babies come from has to go tinkle in the potty. Her incredibly mature words not mine."

Lola barked out a laugh. "Fair enough."

Saint shook his head and chuckled to himself as he watched them disappear down the hall. "I really thought he'd grow out of being an annoying punk."

"Some people just are how they are." She tried to decide if she should broach the topic, but then she went for it. She was Lola León after all. "What do you think we should tell Rosie about what she saw?" She was asking Saint to define what was going on between them as much for herself as for Rosie.

"I think I'll just wait to see if she asks me about it. If she does, I'll tell her that we really like each other and leave it at that."

Lola felt a pang of disappointment although she was hard-pressed to figure out why. His plan made sense and it was the truth. They did really like each other. They always had. That was sort of the problem. How could she keep things in perspective, when all she could think about was how much they liked each other? "I should get back in there. Who knows what our grandfathers have done in our absence."

Saint stared at her, his dark brown eyes taking in everything about her and most likely reading her mind too. "Do you regret it?"

"Regret what? Kissing you?"

He nodded.

"No. Absolutely not. Saint, if there is one thing about this whole situation that I know, it's that I want you. You do it for me. Always have."

He took a step closer to her and then seemed to stop himself. His eyes burned as he held her gaze. "I've wanted you since I was seventeen. Regardless of time or distance. I wanted you even when you were on the other side of the country and I was on the other side of the world. That's my truth."

"I used to lie in bed and think of you. I'd touch myself at the memories."

He took another step toward her. "Don't tell me that. Not here. Not now. Not when I can't do anything about it. I'm hanging on by a thread, Canela."

Lava rushed through her veins. "I am too." She took a deep breath and tried to calm herself. "But you're right. Now is not the time or place."

"Go," he told her. "Go help viejitos pick out silly outfits to sing songs in. Go before I don't let you."

Lola chanced one more glance into Saint's eyes, now overflowing with the same fire Papo Vega had referenced earlier, then booked it out of there as fast as she could.

15

When Abuelo Papo had guilt-tripped him into volunteering at Casa del Sol's monthly karaoke night, Saint couldn't imagine anywhere he'd hate being more (besides back in battle). But that was before he'd seen Lola walk in wearing a badass leather jacket with a pretty flower dress that had buttons all down the front, a pair of gold hoops, and brightly painted lips. From that moment all he'd thought about was unbuttoning that dress and smearing that lipstick. After doing one of those things in the hall, he found it even more difficult to concentrate.

She'd told him that she wanted him. Saint wanted to strut like a peacock. He wanted to announce that fact on the microphone. Then he wanted to drag her off to somewhere private and show her how much that—no, how much she—meant to him.

Abuelo walked up to stand next to him. "Esa cara de bobo que tienes me dice que mi canción funcionó." He nudged Saint with his elbow and waggled his eyebrows. "Se besaron mucho, ¿verdad?"

Saint couldn't take offense because he was sure he was sporting a stupid face. However, he would not be telling his grandpa about the hot kiss they shared nor would he mention getting caught by Leo and Rosie. The last thing Abuelo Papo needed was more encouragement. "Aren't you supposed to be working?"

Abuelo waved a hand. "Leo's fine as the MC. He has Rosie helping him now."

"I think you're confused. He was helping you, not the other way around."

"But he loves being the center of attention."

"Again. I think you're confusing the two of you." Although, Abuelo and Leo were similar in ways that were scary to contemplate. Dear lord, Leo would probably be worse than Abuelo when he was old. Saint almost crossed himself to ward off the possibility.

"Fine, I'll go relieve him from his duty, but only because you begged me to."

Saint didn't respond to that nonsense. He just kept filling the little paper bags in front of him with popcorn.

Moments later Leo was at his side. "Can any of these old people sing something recorded after 1970 for the love of god? This is boring as hell."

"How did he talk you into this?"

Leo scoffed. "How do you think? Guilt." He grabbed a bag of popcorn and tossed some in his mouth. "He reminded me that I had to leave early the last time I visited."

Leo was many things, but he would never brush off Abuelo. "What happened?"

"I was working. I'd just stopped in quickly while we were on our way back to the station." He tossed a kernel in the air and then caught it in his mouth. "Then we got a call. There was this huge incident at the old theater on Augusta."

"The one attached to the old clinic?"

Leo nodded.

"Lola and I were just there last week. We thought the clinic could be a good spot to use for a new El Hogar, but it's too expensive even with all of the damage. We're trying to think of ways to raise money, but in the past the organization has done everything you can think of and barely received anything for it."

"How does El Vecindario keep opening all of these different departments or whatever, if they have no money?"

Saint had asked Yara that same question. "They get government funds, grants, and stuff like that, but the money is only to be used for certain things, so it's not like they can just move it around. Sometimes even the donations they get come with caveats of where they can be used." Saint shook his head. "You'd think people would be willing to donate to El Hogar since it provides so many services for unhoused kids, but they don't."

"Because most of the kids are gay and our freaking community is still homophobic as fuck." Leo shook his head. "Hypocrites."

Abuelo Papo's voice blared through the space. "And now I have a special song that I picked out for one of our amazing volunteers. Lola, get up here!"

Saint swung his head to the other side of the room where Lola was frantically shaking her finger in a negative.

"Don't be shy. You'll like this song. I promise."

"I can't sing," she called.

"Everyone can sing, some just sound better than others," Abuelo argued. "Ven." She didn't move so he got the audience involved. "Lo-la. Lo-la. Lo-la." He chanted.

More and more people jumped in until the whole room was chanting. Even Rosie was clapping in time from her spot at the side of the stage.

Lola threw up her hands in defeat and stomped over to the stage. "I warned you all," she said. "You're going to regret it." When no one rushed up to take the microphone from her, she sighed. "I probably don't even know the song."

"It's from one of your favorite movies."

"How do you know that?"

"Your abuelo told me." He motioned to Rosie, who hit a button on the stereo system in front of her.

The title of the song and original artist appeared on the screen behind Lola. "'Pelo Suelto' by Gloria Trevi."

Saint remembered the song vaguely from when his tía Carmen used to play it on repeat at family functions.

A rhythmic stomping sound started and the lyrics popped up. Lola began to sing, "A mi me gusta andar de pelo suelto."

"Did you know this was from a movie?" Leo asked.

"No." Saint watched as Lola started to get into it, stomping her foot and shaking her shoulders to the beat.

It was immediately clear to him why Lola liked the song. While it was literally about the singer liking to wear her hair down and loose, in context it was more the singer's declaration of who she was and promising to be herself no matter what anyone said. It was an in-your-face anthem and the perfect fit for Lola.

Leo grimaced once Lola hit the chorus where the style changed from speaking to the beat, almost like rap, to actual singing. "She wasn't lying about not being able to sing."

His observation was on point. Lola couldn't seem to hit a single note correctly. However, Saint wasn't going to give his brother an inch, because he'd take a hundred miles. "She's doing great." Lola was clearly having a moment up there.

She fully embraced the experience, swinging her hair and singing about how she was going to be however she wanted to be and she wasn't going to be afraid of anyone. The audience was right there with her, clapping along and cheering. She strutted up to Rosie and shook her hair in her face. Rosie started laughing and parroted Lola's movement as she danced along. It was the cutest fucking thing Saint had ever seen.

"Rosie likes her," Leo said with some surprise.

"She does." Saint didn't take his eyes off the stage.

"But she won't talk around her."

Saint shrugged. "I don't know why. I don't think Rosie even knows why, but she talks about Lola all the time and asks about her. She's even told me that Lola is the best teacher."

"Well, I guess it's good that you're both obsessed with her, because if it was only you, there'd be a big problem."

Saint tore his eyes away. "I'm not obsessed. We're spending a lot of time together because we are trying to find a place to set up a new El Hogar."

"Oh, did you expect to find it in her throat or up the back of her dress?"

"You're not as funny as you think you are."

"Now I *know* you're lying. I'm hilarious. You're just mad that I'm calling bullshit."

Saint didn't respond.

"Look, bro. I don't care how you want to dress up whatever it is you're doing with her. All I know is that for the first time since you came back, you seem, I don't know, alive. Lord knows you've been a serious stick-in-the-mud since you were born, but ever since Robyn died and you came back to take care of Rosie, it's like you've been a zombie or something, just going through the motions. I like seeing you alive, and if it's because of her, you have my full support…even if her singing reminds me when the cats in the alley behind El Coquí are in heat."

Saint barked out a laugh. "It's not that bad."

"It is."

It was. And Leo was right about him too, as much as Saint hated to admit it. It wasn't that he'd simply been going through the motions. It was that everything had changed so quickly and in such an unexpected way. Then everything just kept right on changing and he'd never been able to catch up. The only way to get through it had been to just keep going even as he felt himself falling farther and farther behind. It had taken Lola completely knocking him off track for him to stop, look around, and realize that he was nowhere near where he wanted to be. Lola who never faltered in her path, who could look at something, see what was wrong, know how to fix it, and work doggedly until the task was completed.

Working with her pointed him in the direction of the shore, so that he could finally stop simply treading water. He was going to help create a new home for the kids in his neighborhood who needed it most. He'd help Lola create a place they could go to be safe, eat, sleep, learn, grow, and just have fun. Somewhere they could have a positive experience no matter what they'd experienced before. Lola was giving Saint a sense of purpose and he was so glad she had decided to come home.

16

The front door to Saint's house swung open revealing Rosie in a black dress covered in daisies and a leather jacket. She had little combat boots on her feet and thick tights on her legs. Her curly hair was down but with a severe part on the right, with the left side held back by a twist. There was no missing the similarity to Lola's look a few days earlier at karaoke night.

Lola's heart melted.

"Look at you, girlie. You look awesome."

Rosie smiled, grabbed Lola's hand, and pulled her into the house.

Lola looked around but didn't see Saint. She did hear a shower running in the distance. "Is your dad still getting ready?" she asked, having learned to ask Rosie yes or no questions.

Rosie nodded. She pulled Lola over to the couch and pointed at it.

Lola sat. "I'm really excited about today," she shared. "Have you ever been to Navy Pier?"

Another nod. Then Rosie turned away and headed to the kitchen.

Lola heard the refrigerator door open and close.

She returned a moment later with a juice box, which she handed to Lola along with the remote. "Oh. Thank you, Rosie. You are such a good hostess."

She smiled. She motioned for Lola to stay there, pointed to the TV, then spun on her heels and raced to her room.

Apparently, she was supposed to entertain herself while the Vegas finished getting ready. Not wanting to offend Rosie, Lola turned on the TV and opened the juice box as directed. On the screen some distinguished-sounding British man was narrating a scene of sea otters frolicking in the water. Lola had barely begun to pay attention when a door opened somewhere in the house and heavy footsteps approached.

Saint entered carrying a pair of black, white, and gray Nikes that almost perfectly matched her black, white, gray, and purple ones. He had on a black hoodie with thin white cursive lettering and black jeans, but it was the hat that did her in. It was a simple all black baseball cap, but she hadn't seen Saint in a hat since they were teens and fuck did he look good in it.

He stopped short upon seeing her sitting on the couch. "You're here."

Lola swallowed the drool in her mouth. "Yep."

"Where's Rosie?" He took a seat at an island stool and pulled on a shoe. His bicep filled the arm of his sweater.

Lola stared. "Uh." She tried to pull herself together. "She went to her room."

He slipped his other shoe on, tied it, then stood up. When he adjusted his sweater to make sure it lay how he wanted, Lola almost groaned. This was not good. It was as if every single thing he did was designed to make her wet.

He knocked on Rosie's door. "Nena, come on. It's time to go. What are you doing?" Of course, there was no answer, but there was a lot of sound coming from the room.

The door swung open, and Rosie stepped out in a brand-new outfit. This one featured tattered jeans, a graphic T-shirt, and a flannel wrapped around her waist. Almost an exact replica of Lola's except, where she was wearing an old Tupac concert T-shirt she'd found at a resale shop, Rosie was wearing a Disney Princess shirt.

She held a mound of hair ties, a brush, and a container of gel in her hands, which she promptly held out to Saint.

He grunted in annoyance. "Why did you— What do you think you're doing? It took me forty-five minutes to get your hair exactly how you wanted it. We aren't going through that again."

A mulish expression, almost exactly like the one her father made, appeared on Rosie's face. She pushed the hair ties into his hands. He was going to redo her hairstyle whether he wanted to or not.

Saint shot Lola an apologetic look then his gaze traveled over her outfit and took in the sleek low bun at the back of her head. All annoyance fled from his face, chased away by warmth. "Let me guess," he said to Rosie. "You want me to put your hair in a bun."

She nodded so fast she reminded Lola of a martini in a tumbler.

He sighed. "Get me the thin brush and the spray bottle too."

Rosie was off like a shot.

"Am I about to watch you do your daughter's hair?"

"I'm sorry. I know we're running late, but she will have an attitude all day if I don't fix it."

"It's not that," Lola said. "I just don't think I can handle it. I might burst into flames. Horny flames."

"Really?" he asked, drawing out the word, the corner of his mouth quirking upward.

Before Lola could answer Rosie was back. She tossed the things at Saint and then climbed onto the kitchen stool. She sat

facing Lola with Saint standing behind her. She drew her finger down the middle of her head indicating where she wanted
her hair parted.

Lola bit back a smile.

"I know." Saint removed the barrettes holding her twist in and
then unraveled it. He sprayed her entire head with a cloudy solution from the spray bottle, probably something that would help
moisturize Rosie's very curly hair. Then he finger combed it.

Lola watched his fingers work, mesmerized. "Who taught
you how to do that?" she asked, her voice breathy.

"When Kamilah was little she and my mom used to fight
about her hair every morning. Kamilah would wiggle around,
my mom would yell at her, she'd say that it hurt, then my mom
would call her tender headed or bop her on the head with the
brush, and the cycle would repeat. It took forever, they hated
every second of the process, and it put us all in a bad mood."
Once he had the tangles out, he used the thin end of a tiny brush
to make a center part. Then he began using the bristle brush to
pull her hair to the nape of her neck where he wrapped a big
hand around it. "My abuela tried to step in, but she had straight
fine hair, so she had no idea what to do. After she got a roller
brush stuck in Kamilah's hair and they had to cut it out, she was
fired from the job."

Rosie opened the gel and held it up to him.

He put some in his hand and smoothed it onto her hair before picking the brush back up and smoothing everything down.
"One morning, I just couldn't take it anymore. I told my mom
that if she taught me, I'd do Kamilah's hair." When he slid the
hair tie off his wrist to loop it around the low ponytail, Lola just
about slid off the couch.

The curl of his lips told her that he for sure caught on to that.

"It took me a while and there were some tears, Kamilah's and
mine—" Saint twisted the thick ponytail into a smooth rope

and coiled it around until there was a perfect bun "—but eventually I figured it out." He held out a hand and Rosie passed him another hair tie, which he used to secure the bun. "I did Kamilah's hair every day until she was in the second grade and wanted to do her own."

Calm it down, Lola. He's not talking dirty in your ear. He's doing a child's hair while talking about doing another child's hair. It should not have her this worked up. "That is the cutest thing I ever heard. You had to be what, eleven?"

Saint was smoothing down some flyaways as he answered. "I was nine or ten when I started and around twelve when I stopped. It was stressful at the time, but now I'm grateful for the practice because this little one," he said, giving Rosie a quick tickle, "is a lot more demanding than her tití ever was."

"Was doing little girls' hair like riding a bike and you just hopped right back on?"

He laughed. "God no, the women in my family and their friends took it upon themselves to give me refresher courses and more advanced training." He grabbed the gel and picked up the tiny dual-sided comb/bristle brush. Then he did the most diabolical thing anyone had ever done to her. He began to lay Rosie's edges like a pro.

As someone who was always fighting with her wispy baby hairs, Lola was both turned on by and jealous of Saint's ease at creating curves and swirls along Rosie's forehead, temple, and ears. But she was mostly turned on. Something about watching his big hands and thick fingers, slick with gel, work with dexterity and skill.

You're a pervert. Cut it out. "Can I use your bathroom before we go?"

The smile on Saint's face grew. He knew exactly what he was doing to her. "Sure. Let me show you where it is."

Lola popped off the couch. "No worries. I'll find it."

Saint didn't respond. He picked up a towel from the counter and began wiping his hands. "Rosie, you're all done. Go put your shoes on so we can leave."

Rosie hopped off the stool and went into her room right as Lola passed by Saint. He grabbed her arm and walked her to a door right off the kitchen. "The bathroom is right here. Ignore any mess. This is mostly Rosie's bathroom." His words were normal, but his tone was not. It was rough and gravelly, filled with need.

Lola fisted the front of his hoodie, pulled him into the bathroom with her, and jumped him, slamming their mouths together.

He pushed the door closed behind them and leaned into the kiss. His hands slammed onto the counter next to her hips. "Fuck," he groaned in between kisses. "Lo que me haces."

Lola was about to hop onto the counter and wrap her legs around his waist when he suddenly pulled away. "We can't. Rosie is probably done putting on her shoes already."

Lola panted. "You're right. Go, before she comes looking."

Seemingly unable to help himself, Saint leaned in for one more kiss and Lola held still to make sure she didn't wrap herself around him like a vine. He backed up and cracked the door open. "Good. She's still in her room." He slid out the door and winked at her before he closed it.

Lola slumped against the mirror behind her. She closed her eyes, tilted her head back and just breathed for a moment. Shit, that man was potent. After a few more calming breaths, Lola slid off the counter, did her business, and washed her hands. When she exited the bathroom, Saint and Rosie stood in the kitchen by the back door. Lola couldn't help but notice Rosie's purple Nikes.

"You ready to go?" Saint asked.

"Yep, all good." Within moments they were in the car and

on their way. "I can't wait to see how everything at Navy Pier has changed," she told them both.

"It's different. There's tons to do."

Lola turned in her seat to look at Rosie. "You know, Rosie. This isn't the first time your dad has taken me to Navy Pier."

Rosie just stared back at her, patiently waiting for Lola to continue the story.

"We took the bus there once and I got your dad to eat a Chicago-style hot dog. You know, the ones with tomatoes and pickles and peppers on them."

Rosie's nose scrunched and she grimaced in disgust.

"Don't make that Mr. Yuck face, they're good." She poked Saint in the bicep. "Tell her. Tell her how good they are."

Saint shook his head and looked at his daughter through the rearview mirror. "It was nasty," he told her. "I hated it."

Rosie laughed.

"You traitor! If it was so gross then why did you eat the whole thing?"

"I only ate it because I wanted to impress you, Lola."

She went warm at the words. "Well, I don't care what you say. Chicago dogs are delicious and I can't wait to eat one." She tried to keep the affront in her tone, but she was too pleased by his admission of wanting to impress her.

"You have fun with that," Saint said. "Rosie and I are going to eat bacon cheeseburgers. Right, Rosie?"

Rosie nodded.

"Your loss."

"Wow, the Centennial Wheel looks way bigger up close," Lola said. She eyed the two-hundred-foot-tall ride like it was a monster.

Saint put a hand on her shoulder and gave it a comforting

squeeze. "You don't have to go," he told her for the fifth time. "I know you're scared of heights."

"I'm not," Lola said. "I used to be scared, but I knew I had to do something about it if I wanted to travel. So, I tried some exposure therapy."

"In what way?"

"I hiked and sat at cliff edges. When I traveled on a plane, I kept the window shade up and forced myself to stare out of it. When I got more comfortable with that, I went zip-lining and then bungee jumping."

He was not surprised by that at all. Lola was not the type of person to accept in herself anything that she considered a weakness. If she had a problem, she'd beat it into submission. "And it worked, you're no longer scared of heights?"

"They still aren't my favorite. They never will be." She looked down at Rosie, who was looking at Lola like she was the coolest person she'd ever met. "But I try my best to never let my fears stop me from doing something I want to do."

The line moved forward and suddenly it was their turn.

Before he could ask about the seating arrangement, Rosie dove into the cart, pulling Lola behind her. Clearly, his daughter was not afraid of heights since she wiggled right up to the opposite window of the gondola. Lola sat next to her. Saint sat between Lola and an empty spot while a group of four—two adults and two older kids—sat across from them talking to each other.

As soon as they started moving, Lola tensed. Their gondola was barely off the ground when her leg started bouncing. She turned her head to whisper to him, "How long does this ride take again?"

"I think like ten to fifteen minutes," he whispered back.

"Fuck my life," Lola exclaimed.

Silence from the other side of the gondola.

Lola seemed to realize that she'd said that out loud. Her cheeks reddened. "Sorry," she said to the family across from them and to Rosie. In her lap, her hands were wringing.

Saint reached over, separated her hands, and interlocked his fingers with hers.

She clamped on immediately, squeezing until his bones creaked.

He rubbed his thumb back and forth in a soothing motion.

Rosie watched with a look of concern and guilt on her face. The poor thing felt bad because she'd been the one who wanted to go on the Ferris wheel. It was her favorite thing to do.

Saint pulled his phone out of his pocket, unlocked it and opened the camera app. "Here." He passed it to Rosie. "Take pictures of the view to show the family."

Rosie snatched the phone and bounced in her seat in excitement. The kid loved it when he let her play on his phone.

Once she was occupied, Saint leaned in and whispered in Lola's ear. "Just close your eyes and imagine we're in the car or something."

She must've really been nervous, because she didn't even make a smart-ass comment about how dumb his suggestion was. She slammed her eyes shut and leaned her head on his shoulder almost like she wanted to bury her face in his chest. She began taking deep breaths and letting them out in a practiced way.

They sat like that for the remainder of the ride and while Saint felt bad for Lola he couldn't deny that he liked being this close to her.

As soon as they started making their final descent Rosie handed him back his phone. Then she put her little hand on Lola's thigh and patted it.

He could almost hear her little voice saying, *There there. It's okay. I'm here.*

Lola's hand came up and landed on Rosie's. His daughter turned her hand around and gripped it.

Saint couldn't contain his smile. Watching the two of them interact was quickly becoming one of his favorite things. Their connection was so organic even though Rosie still hadn't said a word to Lola.

The gondola came to a stop and Lola popped up like a cork out of a champagne bottle. She was out of there as soon as the door opened. "Well, that was certainly an experience," she said once they were farther away.

"Are you okay?" Saint asked.

"I'm fine."

She didn't look fine. She looked pale and a bit sweaty.

Rosie tugged on the hem of his hoodie and pointed at the building that housed her second favorite place in Navy Pier.

"That's a good idea, Rosie," he told her. "I think a cupcake and gelato is exactly what Lola needs to feel better."

Lola squatted down in front of Rosie. "Thank you for being so sweet and thoughtful, Rosie."

His daughter let out a blinding smile.

Lola returned it. "Can I give you a hug in thanks?"

Instead of nodding, Rosie launched herself at Lola, who caught her, but also fell on her butt in the process. They both started laughing while squeezing each other.

Saint grabbed Lola under her arms and lifted her to her feet as she maintained a hold of Rosie.

"Thank you so much for this monster hug," Lola said. "This is just what I needed to feel better." She smiled over at Saint. "Although, I will still accept cupcakes and ice cream."

"Then let's go get some," Saint said, leading Lola through the crowd with a hand on the small of her back.

Meanwhile, she carried his daughter in her arms and chatted at her about her favorite flavors of gelato.

Saint wasn't sure how the day could get any better, but it did. They pigged out on dessert, played some games, rode the carousel, ate more food, and took in more attractions until the sun set. Then they went in search of a good spot to watch the fireworks.

"Rosie, are you tired?"

Saint expected Rosie to climb into his lap and snuggle up to him like she always did when she was sleepy, but she didn't. She sat on the stair beneath Lola and wiggled her little body around until she was comfortably snuggled against Lola's thigh. It wasn't exactly a surprise. Rosie had been attached to her ever since their hug earlier. But what blew his mind completely was when Rosie tipped her head up to the sky and said, "I love fireworks. They're so pretty. Do you like fireworks, Lola?"

Lola's breath caught and for a second she didn't breathe. She stared down at the little face below hers. "I love fireworks too," she choked out. "Fireworks are my all-time favorite." She tipped her head up to the sky and swallowed.

Saint watched a tear roll from the corner of Lola's eye, down the side of her face, and into her hairline as she swallowed repeatedly. He understood completely because emotion clogged his own throat. He didn't think any words out of Rosie's mouth would ever surpass the first time she called him Dada, but listening to her sweet little voice direct a question at Lola did. It was in knowing that the words meant so much to Lola that they could cause her, a woman who tended to view any emotion but angry passion as a weakness, to shed a tear of joy.

He reached over and grabbed the hand Lola wasn't currently using to rub at her heart through her chest. He squeezed and was rewarded with a hard squeeze in return. Knowing that Rosie was enthralled with the fireworks exploding in the sky, he lifted her hand to his mouth and gave it a kiss.

Lola turned her head to look at him. Her eyes were lit brighter than the fireworks raining down on them. The apples of her cheeks were rosy and her smile wider than Lake Michigan. She looked soft, happy. With him and with his daughter she was happy.

The thought made his heart pound because the feeling was wholly reciprocated. She made him happy too. Seeing how much she cared about his daughter made him happy. Seeing how much she cared for everyone in her orbit, how much she cared for the community. Lola was building relationships and creating ties that tethered her to Humboldt Park, to him. That was what he wanted, to be firmly tethered to Lola.

He leaned close enough to whisper in her ear. "Do you remember what happened the last time we were here?"

She nodded. "You told me you loved me on the carousel," she whispered back.

He stared into her eyes. "And you told me that you loved me too."

She smiled. "Then we made out until people complained loudly."

"I think we should do that again. These people seem like they need something to shake them up."

"The fireworks aren't enough?"

"There are more fireworks right here. Between you and me."

"While that's true, I'm pretty sure Rosie fell asleep against my leg and it's not in your best interest to make me choose who to snuggle with."

"It's like that, huh?"

"Sorry. She's cuter than you."

"I can't argue with that."

Lola bit her lip. "But." She stopped.

"But what?"

"Well, I was just thinking that if we took her home and tucked her into bed, then maybe we could hang out on your couch, watch Netflix or something."

"Hmm. She is a pretty deep sleeper, but sometimes she gets up in the middle of the night to use the bathroom."

Lola's expression fell.

"I have a TV in my bedroom."

"Really?"

He nodded. "I have Netflix, Discovery Plus, HBO Max…"

"Stop. You had me at 'bedroom.'"

He loved going back and forth with her, but he needed to make sure they were on the same page. "Are we doing this, Lola?"

"Taking Rosie home? Yes."

"Are we taking her home, so that I can lock us in my bedroom and have my way with you?"

She shook her head side to side.

His heart stopped.

"You're going to lock us in your room so that *I* can have my way with *you*."

"Even better."

He stood and scooped Rosie up from where she had indeed fallen asleep against Lola's leg, her head resting against Lola's thigh. He didn't blame her, he intended to do the same thing.

Once Rosie was settled on his shoulder, he reached down and grabbed Lola's hand.

She intertwined their fingers and they began the trek back to his truck.

Saint couldn't help thinking how they probably looked like any other family—mom, dad, and daughter—on their way home from a day of fun. He liked the thought too much. He needed to keep his expectations at a rational level. He knew that Lola cared about Rosie a lot and he knew that she had feelings for him, but that didn't mean that she was thinking about forever. Not like he was.

They got to the truck and buckled Rosie in. The drive back

to his place was made in silence. He didn't know if it was because they didn't want to risk waking Rosie up or if they both
just had too much on their minds. All that he cared about was
Lola's hand in his and the hot looks she kept shooting his way.

They pulled into the garage and Saint almost forgot to turn
off the truck before flinging his door open. He was on Lola's side
in a heartbeat. Before she could open the back door, he pushed
her up against it and took her mouth in a hot kiss.

Lola pulled away after a long moment. "You put her to bed.
I'll wait for you in your room."

"Okay, but you aren't allowed to take anything off," he commanded. "I want to undress you."

She huffed out a little breath full of desire. "You'd better
hurry."

Saint would hurry to get Rosie settled, but then he was going
to take his sweet time with Lola.

17

Lola stood in the middle of Saint's room trying to calm her racing heart. She felt jittery, but not from nerves. She was supercharged with lust and all he'd done was say a few provoking words and kiss her.

She took another look around the room. What had appeared bright and cozy in the daylight was nothing but varying shades of shadow in the dim lighting of the one lamp she'd turned on. It should've been cold with the monochromatic color scheme, but somehow it wasn't. Maybe it was all the plush texture. The rug was lush, the pillows plump, and the comforter bulky. Or maybe it was that the entire room smelled like Saint—fresh laundry and something with a bite. It made her feel like she did when she was young and used to hide under her covers, warm and safe.

Lola untied the flannel around her waist, sank onto the edge of the bed, and removed her shoes. She flexed and wiggled her toes while rolling her ankles in an attempt to soothe her sore feet. It had been a long day with a lot of walking, but Lola wouldn't have changed a thing about it. It would always be a favorite memory for her because it would remind Lola of the day Rosie Vega finally felt safe with her.

"I thought I said not to take anything off."

Lola looked up.

Saint leaned one shoulder against the door watching her.

"I never agreed to that," she said, raising an eyebrow as she smoldered back at him.

He straightened and stepped into the room, closing and locking the door behind him. "I thought it was an understood order." He began walking toward her. As he did, he took off his hat and tossed it onto the bench at the end of the bed.

Lola stood and met him halfway. "Oh, Saint, you should already know that I don't take orders." She pulled her shirt over her head and dropped it to the floor.

Saint sucked in a breath. "Fuck, you're beautiful."

Watching his eyes darken as his pupils dilated made her grateful that she'd worn one of her sexy bras. It didn't push her boobs up to her chin, but it was purple lace and had enough support to make her full double Ds look perky.

"It's your turn now," she told him.

"I want to touch you first."

She wanted him to touch her too, but not as much as she wanted to touch him. "Take your shirt off, Saint."

He raised an eyebrow. "Is this how it's going to go, Canela, you fighting me every step of the way?" His voice was rough but soft.

Lola shook her head. "No, because I already told you that I plan to have my way with you." She moved forward until they were practically chest to chest. She kept her eyes on his as she grabbed on to the hem of his hoodie and the shirt underneath. "So you're going to stop fighting me." She began to lift them both. "Isn't that right, Saint?"

He licked his lips. "I feel you testing me. I know you think

I'm going to balk, pull some macho shit and tell you that I'm the boss."

And if she was? She wouldn't feel bad about it. She'd had too many people try to dictate to her.

"What you don't seem to realize is that I love watching you take what you want." He leaned down until their noses touched. "You want to be in control, Canela?" He rubbed his nose against hers and then leaned even closer. "Take it." His lips brushed hers as he spoke the next challenge-infused words. "Take me." Then he leaned back and raised his arms.

Lola ripped the hoodie and shirt over his head and then stopped to admire what she'd revealed. It was clear that he took care of himself even if he wasn't shredded like a gym bro. Fuck a gym bro of any sex. In her experience they did nothing but eat bland-ass boiled chicken, exercise everything but their brain, and judge anyone who didn't fit into their very narrow standard of beauty. She guessed some people would say that Saint had a "dad bod" but those people were idiots. Saint had a Daddy Bod, which was a different thing entirely.

She placed her hands on his chest and rubbed his pecks before sliding them up into his hair. She used her grip to pull his head to hers. She did what he'd dared her to. She took. Her kiss let him know exactly who was in charge. She pillaged his mouth, bit at his succulent lips, and then soothed the sting with her tongue.

He groaned and crowded her, his hands touching everything he could reach.

She broke away and tugged on the waistband of his jeans.

He followed.

Once she had him where she wanted him, she pushed against his abs. "Sit."

He plopped down onto the edge of the bed.

"Watch." Lola reached up and loosened her hair from the bun at the back of her head.

Meanwhile, Saint's eyes roamed all over her body, making every inch of her hum.

She shook her hair out and moaned as she gave herself a quick head message.

"I can't wait to make you moan like that." His voice was deep.

Lola dropped her hands and turned her back to him but quickly looked at him over her shoulder.

His eyes were glued to her ass as she'd expected. She'd caught him staring at it with a look of stunned lust more than once. His obsession with her ass was so great that she made sure to always put on a little show for him. Lola had swished her hips more in the last few weeks than she had in her entire life. The poor guy had no idea she'd done it on purpose, but he'd enjoyed himself, so she didn't feel the need to tell him.

Lola unbuttoned her jeans, lowered the zipper, and then grabbed the waistband on either side. She began lowering her jeans, wiggling her hips a bit because they were tight but also because she liked how Saint's breathing accelerated. When she finally pushed her jeans over her hips, revealing her full cheeks and the purple lace thong that matched her bra, Saint let out a groan.

Lola smiled.

"Eres tan mala. You like this," he said, voice low and accusing. "You love torturing me."

In response Lola rose onto her tiptoes, bent in half, and pushed her jeans to her ankles.

"I need to touch you," he groaned. "Let me touch you, Canela." His tone was urgent now. "Please."

Lola shivered at the word. She liked that. Liked knowing that he wanted her so much he was willing to beg just to touch her. She finished taking her jeans off then straightened and turned to face him again. "I'm going to touch you first and if you're good, then you can touch me. Can you do that?"

He nodded.

But he shouldn't have been so confident, because Lola wasn't going to make it easy for him. Not when she was enjoying this so much. With an evil grin she reached back and unclasped her bra. It fell to the floor.

"Coño." His hands fisted the edge of the bed. "Si supieras lo que me haces."

She slunk closer until she was between his thighs. "I can see what I do to you." She leaned in until the tips of her breasts just barely brushed his chest. His body went rigid. His arms jerked as if he were going to grab her, but he stopped himself. She gave his cheek a soft kiss right at the corner of his mouth. "Good boy," she whispered.

He shivered. "Lola," he murmured.

"I get tested regularly. Everything has always come back negative." She placed her hands on his shoulders and then ran them down his torso until her fingertips touched the waistband of his jeans.

"Me too even though it's been years since I've been with anyone. I also use condoms regularly."

She lowered to her knees as she unbuttoned and unzipped him. "I just want to make sure you're okay if I use my mouth with no protection."

"Fuck yes." The words were more a puff of air than sound.

Lola absolutely loved that she'd reduced this lawfully good man to nothing but curse words and panting need and she hadn't even put her mouth on him yet. She tugged at his jeans and boxer briefs and he lifted his hips without prompting. She leaned in and kissed his lower abdomen as a reward.

He sucked in a breath.

She pulled his pants, underwear, and socks off and tossed them to the side. Starting at his big feet she massaged her way up his legs, stopping to give his calves some extra attention before moving on to his knees. She noticed a scar on his thigh. She looked up to ask him about it and was met with the sight of his hand wrapped around himself and stroking. "Hey." She gave his leg a little tap. "I said no touching."

"You told me I couldn't touch you, not myself."

"I told you to be good," she returned.

He squeezed harder and moved faster. "This is good."

"It looks good." She placed her hands over his. "Move your hand."

He did so immediately.

Lola knew how difficult that had to have been for him, but he told her he'd follow her orders so he did it. As a reward Lola grabbed him and took over where he'd left off.

He let out a rough grunt.

Then she used her mouth and he let out a steady stream of curses, dirty praise, and pleas.

Lola couldn't think of a time she'd ever felt so empowered. She had this man completely at her mercy and they were both loving every second of it.

"Lola," he panted. "I don't want to come like this. Not before I've touched you."

Lola ignored him because she absolutely wanted him to come like this. She wanted to know that she'd done this to him.

"Lola." His voice was all dark warning.

She kept right on going.

Saint's patience snapped. "It's my turn now." He used the hand in her hair to roughly but not painfully pull her away. Before she could protest he kissed her just as roughly, using the extreme heat between them to forge their mouths together. He lifted her to her feet with that same grip, stood, and switched their positions. She was sitting on the edge of the bed and he released her mouth to drop to his knees in front of her. "You think torture is fun, do you?" He put one big hand on her chest and pushed her down until she was flat on her back. He grabbed her panties and yanked them down her legs. "Let's see if you feel the same way in a minute." Then he spread her legs wide and put his mouth on her.

Lola almost laughed thinking he was too hungry to torture her, but boy was she wrong. It went on forever. He'd bring her right to the brink and then back off. She tried demands, curses, dirty words, everything she could think of and still he played with her. "Saint, please. I can't take any more. Please," she begged again and again.

It seemed like *please* really was the magic word, because Saint said, "Okay. I'll let you come, but you have to be quiet. Can you do that?"

"Yes. Yes I can," Lola practically wailed. "I promise I can, but please."

He moaned. "I love it when you beg me like that, all sweet and needy."

"Please," she whined again.

"Good girl," Saint murmured against her flesh and then dove back in. This time he didn't play with her. He applied himself to the task with gusto.

Within moments Lola was on the edge. "That's it. Right there." A swirl of the tongue and a pump of two fingers and Lola was launched right over the edge. "Yes," she hissed, doing her best to stay quiet. "Así. Así, mi amor."

He stopped and she almost screamed because, even though she'd just climaxed, she wanted more.

"What did you just say?"

Why was he asking questions at a time like this? She lifted her head to look down her body at him. "What?"

His hair was a complete mess and so was his face. "You said, 'mi amor.'"

She froze. Her ardor instantly cooled. Had she really said that?

Saint wiped his face against her thigh then lifted himself to his feet. He leaned over until his hands were on either side of her torso and he could look into her eyes. "Did you mean it?"

Lola had no idea what to say. She knew that she had strong feelings for him. Feelings that were similar to the ones she'd had at sixteen but stronger—fuller and deeper. She didn't look at him through the lens of hero worship as she had then. Lola knew him now as he actually was, flawed but determined to be better. She knew he was as stubborn as he was caring and that although he had this insane need to fix everyone's problems, it stemmed from his desire to help and from a love he felt for people in general. She knew that she hated leaving him after they'd toured a building or worked on a plan. She wanted to stay with him all the time, which was scary, because she was a person who liked her space. But did any of that equal love? How the fuck would she know? The only people she'd ever loved had been family and look how well that had gone for her.

"I don't know," she whispered, because she couldn't be anything but honest with him. She tried to ignore the disappointment that showed in his eyes before he dropped them to her chest, but she couldn't. It made her defensive. "Do you love me?" she asked, expecting him to say the same thing as her.

"I've loved you since I was seventeen, Lola. I loved the girl you were and I love the woman you are now."

"How do you know?"

"I know because since the moment I met you every version of my future has had you in it. When you were gone it nearly drove me out of my mind because I kept picturing a future with you even when it was impossible."

"Even when you married someone else?"

"As shitty as it makes me, yes, even then."

Lola didn't think it was shitty of him. He'd said that they'd both entered into the marriage because of responsibility and necessity, not love. "As long as you both knew the score and you never led her to believe anything else, it's not shitty." She lifted her head and kissed him on the mouth.

He returned her kiss. After a moment he lay on the bed next to her. He pulled her close and despite everything Lola snuggled into his arms. "It's okay for you to not be sure if you love me or not, Lola."

"Are you sure, because you looked at me like I'd punted your puppy off a bridge like in *Anchorman*."

His lips curved. "I promise you, no glass case of emotion here. All I need to know right now is that you want to be with me. Everything else we can work on."

"Of course I want to be with you, Saint. I've never wanted anyone more. Look, I've been with other men and women since I left. I even dated a few people long-term. But here's the truth: I never actually took anyone else seriously, because no one compared to you."

His dark eyes lit with an inner fire. "You have no idea what it does to me to hear you say that."

"I think I know exactly what it does to you." She wiggled against the hard length poking her hip.

He groaned. "Mmm. That happens every time I'm around you, but hearing how much you want me just makes it more eager."

"Feeling you makes me eager."

Saint rolled onto his back and pulled her with him. "You promised to have your way with me and yet all you've done so far is drive me out of my mind."

Lola sat up, straddling his hips. His thickness felt delicious between her legs, so she rocked against it, making him groan.

"Hey, when I say I'm going to do something, I do it," she said with another swivel of her hips.

"Good." He stretched his upper body to the side, reached into the top drawer of the nightstand and pulled out a condom. He tossed it to her but she wasn't ready so it bounced off her left boob and onto his stomach. "Then do me."

"Oh, I plan to," she said, rolling her hips more firmly and reaching for the foil package. She used her teeth to open it then slid it down his length, protecting them both.

"Do it. Ride me."

Lola lowered herself onto him slowly, relishing the tight stretch. It was so good. She rolled her hips and bit her lip.

"So good." He huffed out a breath when she rose up and slammed down again. He gripped her ass in both hands, but he didn't try to direct her movements. He just held on.

Because his hands were otherwise occupied Lola touched her own breasts, palming and lifting them, flicking and squeezing her nipples. She moaned low in her throat and threw her head back, working her hips in small tight circles.

"Oh, Canela, look at you. Do you have any idea how beautiful you are like this, riding my dick, playing with your tits, and taking your pleasure?" He raised his head to lave the nipple she had pinched between her fingers. "Magnificent."

She loved his voice. She loved the dirty and worshipful words coming out of him. She wanted to respond in kind, but she refused to have her thoughtless words ruin the moment again. Instead she just moaned, hissed, panted, cursed, and blasphemed.

Lola felt like she was the one in a glass case of emotion but hers was one of pleasure and it just kept filling.

"That's it," he urged her on. "Así. Cógelo."

The pleasure built and built, causing cracks to appear all along the sides. Suddenly the pressure became too much. The glass case exploded. A pleasure so good it was painful rained down on her in shards that dug into every part of her body. She shook and jerked and was almost too far gone to realize that he'd also found release.

She slumped forward onto Saint's chest then tried to roll off, cognizant of her size, but he didn't let her.

"Stay right where you are," he told her. "Don't you dare move."

She kissed his chest. "Does this mean you're the boss now?"

"Yes. But don't worry. I have no problem sharing the position."

They went back and forth, taking turns being in control. After round four, in which Saint had put her on her hands and knees and made them both come so hard they shouted and then froze to see if they'd woken Rosie up, they both lay on their backs exhausted.

"I've been dying to ask you about your tattoos," Saint said, running a finger along her clavicle where it said "si se puede" in calligraphy. That one was pretty self-explanatory, a popular rallying cry for Latine people protesting for their rights.

"Well, did you know that 'si se puede' began with Dolores Huerta, a labor leader, civil rights activist, cofounder of the National Farm Workers Association, and all-around badass woman?"

"I did, but I love hearing you talk about it."

She turned her arm to show him her wrist. "These overlapping triangles represent my bisexuality."

"I sort of figured that when I saw the pink, purple, and blue," Saint said. He lifted her arm and placed a kiss on the line art silhouette of a woman with a raised fist. Below it was the word *Empower* with a fist as the *P*, the woman symbol as the *O*, and the equal sign as the last *E*. "This one I also get. It's your social justice warrior."

"If you already understand, then why ask?"

"Because this is the first time I've seen this one fully." He motioned to the colorful half sleeve that took up her right arm from shoulder to elbow. "And I had no idea the one on your back even existed."

"I'll tell you all about my tattoos as long as you tell me about the scar on your thigh."

He grimaced. "I thought you hadn't noticed that."

"Are you serious? I notice everything about you."

"You're not doing a very good job of getting me to believe that you don't love me."

"I never said that I didn't. I said that I'm not sure and don't try to distract me from the scar."

"You first," he replied.

Lola lifted her arm and looked at the depiction of a beautiful woman's head. One half of her face was painted in the Taíno style with a headband covered in Puerto Rican imagery and a Flor de Maga in her hair while the other half wore a feather headdress engraved with Mexican imagery and face paint that reflected the Aztec culture. "This is supposed to represent the two parts of me." She showed her arm off to Saint. "Half Puerto Rican and half Mexican."

He rolled them so he was on his back and Lola was half on top of him. He pulled her close and nuzzled her neck. "And all beautiful, badass, warrior woman."

She liked that. She'd never thought of it like that before, but she could see it and she liked it. "Thank you."

"My pleasure." He lifted his hand and traced his fingers along the tattoo on her shoulder blade.

Lola shivered.

His voice deepened. "Tell me about this one."

She ignored the way his voice made her wet and focused on answering his question. "It's the outline of a lioness head because my last name is León." The lines were relatively simple and there wasn't much detail to it besides the eyes, which looked almost real.

"Yes, what's the story behind the style? It almost looks unfinished."

"It's not finished," she said.

"Is it new?"

She shook her head. "It's the first tattoo I got actually."

"Why isn't it done, Lola?"

"Because I realized that I would just have the one lioness." She swallowed. "Lions are supposed to live in prides. It didn't seem right to have her alone without pride mates."

He was quiet for a long time. "This is how you really see yourself—a lonely lioness, incomplete because she doesn't have a pride."

She nodded against his chest. "A one woman pride."

He squeezed her tight. "I think today has made it clear that Rosie idolizes you and I already told you how I feel about you. You're not alone anymore."

She wanted to believe that, but even as she basked in his love she couldn't let go completely. "Now you go," she told him. "How did you get that scar."

Saint shifted in his spot, obviously uncomfortable talking about it. "I got hurt on one of my missions as a Green Beret."

"Oh my god," she whispered. Of course, she'd assumed as much, but hearing it brought back into the forefront of her mind that he'd been to war.

"But the mission was still considered a success."

"I don't give a fuck about the mission, Saint. I care that you were injured."

"It wasn't bad. Just a few cracked ribs."

He thought cracked ribs weren't bad? Lola opened her mouth to inform him otherwise, but then he said something worse.

"And I was technically impaled, which is where the scar comes from, but it wasn't that bad."

"Stop saying it wasn't that bad. Impalement is bad!"

"It missed everything vital and I walked away from it. Other people didn't walk away."

That gave her pause. She guessed that when you look at it that way having broken ribs and being impaled with something seems way better. Still it wasn't good. "Tell me the whole story," she said. She'd been reluctant to mention or discuss his time at war mostly because they had never seen eye to eye and she didn't want to fight with him, but it seemed important now for her to open that door. If they were going to be together they needed to be able to talk about it.

"I can't say much, but we were tasked with retrieving a hostage. We'd done recon and had a solid plan, but..." He paused, thinking.

"Plans are wont to go off course."

"Exactly. There was an explosion. I went through the floor and landed on some kind of rod. Two of my unit and the hostage landed next to me. There was an older woman on the floor too. They were all in worse shape than I was. I still don't really know how I was able to do it, but I got them all out and was able to hide them safely until we were found."

"The rest of the unit?"

"Gone."

"Oh, Saint. I'm so sorry."

"Can you believe that they gave me a Silver Star Medal for that? I did what I was trained to do, but they treated me like some sort of hero."

Lola thought he was definitely a hero. He's saved himself, two of his fellow soldiers, and two civilians.

"I let it go to my head." His tone held so much embarrassment and shame. "I strutted around the base like a fucking peacock. Men were dead and I was celebrating myself at a bar and having a one-night stand in a fucking bathroom."

"That's when you met Robyn?" she asked.

He nodded. He fell silent.

"You want to know the worst part?" he asked.

"Tell me."

"Before the mission, I was counting down the days until I could be done. I'd decided not to volunteer for another tour. It'd finally been clear to me that I'd been wrong about everything and you'd been right all those years ago. I'd been fed a load of bullshit. I'd swallowed it down and said thank you.

"But the worst thing was that after I got that medal, I opened my mouth for another spoonful of shit. Like one of your pre-school students, I was swayed by a fucking sparkly star."

"Saint, of course you did. It validated everything you'd gone through, every choice you'd made. It gave everything a meaning. That's a completely natural reaction."

"Maybe."

"Let me tell you one thing. I know what I said when we were young made you feel like I'd never accept your decision, that I thought you were a puppet."

"You were right."

"No, I wasn't. I have my own thoughts about the war, about the military in general, but I will never devalue your bravery. It takes bravery to fight for what you believe in and it takes even more to be willing to lose your life for it." She paused. "It takes even more bravery to question those beliefs honestly and be willing to make changes when you realize they aren't what you thought."

"What changes have I made though?" he asked. "I'm still playing by all of the rules. I'm not like you. You're willing to burn it all to the ground if that means things will get rebuilt better."

"It's not my place to tell you if you're doing enough, Saint. All I can say is that I'm here to support you and I think you are brave, noble, and good in bed."

He flipped her onto her back in the space of a second. "Good in bed, hmm?" He nuzzled her neck, placing kisses under her jaw.

She moaned. "Yes. Good as fuck."

"Let's see if I can be even better. Evaluate me, please, Ms. León."

Lola thought of reminding him that it was her turn to be in charge, but decided against it. Saint was just too good at making her body sing. "I like your growth mindset, Mr. Vega," she said instead. "Let's see if you can score distinguished in every domain."

He did.

18

Lola watched the sunlight streaming through her window play lovingly among the planes and dips of Saint's torso. She untucked her hand from under her cheek and let her fingers do the same. She felt more than heard the rumble of pleasure he released.

"I like taking afternoon naps with you," he said, his voice rough.

Lola smiled, her cheek bunching up where it was smushed against his peck. "I don't know that we did enough sleeping to call this a nap."

He ran his hand down the skin of her back and palmed her naked ass. "It was your idea to take advantage of Rosie's afternoon with Kamilah."

That was true. The moment she heard that Kamilah would be picking up Rosie for a spa day before her engagement party later, Lola had told Saint to get his ass to her place ASAP. He'd arrived twenty minutes later. Two minutes after that they'd been in bed ripping each other's clothes off.

In the two weeks since their trip to Navy Pier, they hadn't gotten to do much but sneak kisses when Rosie wasn't looking.

They both thought it was best to keep things strictly friendly around the little girl as they didn't want to send the wrong message. Plus, Rosie had been talking to Lola more and more each time they saw each other outside of the classroom (Rosie still hadn't spoken at school), and Lola was not about to risk the newfound trust Rosie had given her. Even if it was difficult as hell to keep her hands off Saint when they were all together.

Speaking of hands and Saint, his had slipped between her thighs. She sighed. "It was for sure one of my better ideas," she said in response to his previous comment.

"I have a few good ideas I think you'll like," he said, pulling her mouth to his.

Lola's hands had just begun their own exploration when her phone started ringing from the charging plate on her nightstand. "Ignore it," she said between kisses.

"Another great plan."

Whoever was calling her didn't agree, because the moment it stopped ringing it started up again.

Growling in annoyance, Lola looked over to see who it was. It was Yara. Lola tensed. Yara didn't call Lola. She texted. More to the point, Yara especially didn't call Lola in the middle of the afternoon on a Saturday. "I have to take this," she said, unease pooling in her stomach.

The moment she answered the call Yara began talking. "I'm sorry to call you on a weekend, but this couldn't wait."

Lola sat up. "What happened?"

"It's Marcus and Ruby."

"Tell me everything," she demanded, climbing off Saint and sitting at the edge of the bed.

Behind her he sat up as well, alert and ready, but she didn't pay him any attention; she was focused on what Yara was saying.

"They had told us that they were staying with a friend while everything with El Hogar gets sorted out, but what they failed to mention was that this friend lived in a tent city."

Lola's heart lurched. She felt like a failure. She should've had something set up already.

"Last night the place was raided by angry residents trying to force them all out. The police were called to deescalate the situation."

Fuck. De-escalation was almost never what ended up happening when the police showed up. Lola reached for the sheet on her bed and tugged it free. She stood up and wrapped it around herself.

"Ruby live streamed the whole thing."

The tone of her voice told Lola all she needed to know. It was bad. Lola plopped down on her couch in her sheet toga. "Is Marcus—" Lola's throat spasmed, preventing her from asking, but Yara knew anyway.

"He's alive. A little roughed up, but alive."

"Where is he now?" Lola could hear Saint moving around in her little bedroom area, but she maintained focus on her conversation.

"Mariana picked them up," she responded. "They're both at their place." She paused. "I watched the video. It's disgusting, Lola. I mean all the -isms and -obics. Someone called Marcus the f-slur. The video is dark and Ruby was moving around a lot, but, Lola…it looked like someone in a uniform."

Lola's Mexican and Puerto Rican came out simultaneously. "Pinches cabrones. Saramambiches," she snarled. "They aren't going to get away with this. We aren't going to let them."

"We're already mobilizing."

"Good." Lola's mind started whirling with tasks. "The media needs to be contacted. We need to demand any dash- and body-cam footage of the incident be released. We already know how that's going to go, so get in touch with other local groups, so we can all make that demand together."

Saint walked around the couch wearing nothing but a pair of unbuttoned jeans and, for the first time ever, Lola couldn't care less. He sat on the tiny ottoman that served as her coffee table and just watched her, his expression tense and concerned.

She held up a finger to him. "Make sure Ruby downloads the live video to her phone, so that it's saved in case the platforms take it down. Maybe even have her share it, so multiple people have it and she won't have to look at it again if she doesn't want to." She exhaled roughly. "God, those poor kids." She shook her head. Tears formed in her eyes.

Saint reached over and grabbed her hand, weaving their fingers together. Lola immediately felt more centered. She rubbed her thumb over his in thanks.

"Do you think the therapist that used to help out at El Hogar would do an emergency session with them?" Lola asked.

"That's a great idea. I'll call her as soon as we hang up."

"Once there's a meeting time and place, let me know and I'll be there."

"Okay. I'll add you to our chat group, so you stay updated. I'm sure everyone will want to meet ASAP."

"Whenever it is, I'll be there."

After they said their goodbyes and hung up, Lola collapsed backward onto the couch. She stared at her aging ceiling. The white paint had long ago started to turn an extremely pale yellow. There were thin cracks leading her eye to the dusty ceiling fan. She tried to remember if she'd cleaned it when she moved in a few months ago. She doubted it. By the looks of it, it had been a long while since the thing was cleaned. That was just her life, she guessed.

She didn't have the time or the energy to sit there and examine little things like that. She was too busy trying to just make it by. Her life was an endless cycle of checking tasks off a never-ending to-do list. At the top of her list was to find those kids a safe place to stay. So far she'd failed them.

"I take it there's a problem with some of the kids from El Hogar."

"Two of the kids were staying in a tent city. They got harassed by neighbors and roughed up by the police, who were supposed to be de-escalating the situation."

Saint shook his head. "What is wrong with people?"

"They suck."

"Do you need to head over there?"

Lola lifted her head to eye him. "It's your sister's engagement party."

"I know, but if you need to be with Yara—"

Did he not want her around his family? Sure, she'd been around Papo Vega plenty, and she'd seen Kamilah and Leo in passing, but this was a family party, and bringing her would be a declaration. All of Lola's old insecurities reared back up.

"Saint, do you not want me to meet the rest of your family?" She was thinking specifically of his parents who had been on a prolonged vacation in Puerto Rico until two days ago. It was one thing to meet his youngest siblings and cousins, but it was quite another to meet his parents.

His head tilted to the side like he couldn't have heard her right. "What?"

"Are you embarrassed to introduce me to your parents because of my family?"

"Absolutely not. Why would you even think that?"

"Because if anyone remembered my dad and everything he did it would be them, and—"

"Lola," he interrupted her, "I want you to meet my parents. I want to walk into my sister's restaurant with you on my arm and show you off like the queen you are. I want to tell everyone that I'm lucky enough to be with you and that, if they're equally lucky, you can be a part of their lives too. Then I want you to work your Lola magic and have them all eating out of the palm of your hand, because more than anything, I want them to love you as much as I do."

Lola blinked quickly. "Dear lord." She fanned her face. "For someone who's known for stony silence, you sure do have a smooth tongue."

His lips curled. "You like my tongue."

"Stop! Enough! You're going to make me melt into a pool of horniness and then we'll be late."

He stood up and pulled her to her feet. "I know how we can take care of that and save time. We'll just shower together."

Lola snorted. "My shower is barely big enough for me. There's no way we'll both fit."

"Trust me. I have it all figured out."

Lola looked around the crowded main hall of Kane Distillery and cursed Saint for following his twin brothers out of the room without first introducing her around.

Suddenly she heard, "Her name was Lola. She was a karaoke girl. Whipping all her hair, and her dress cut up to there."

Lola spun to find Leo walking toward her. She rolled her eyes at his teasing.

He stopped before her. "You look beautiful."

Lola leaned in and kissed Leo on the cheek. "Thank you. You look handsome."

"Keep it in your pants, León. I'm not trying to get on my brother's bad side. He's killed before."

"Hey." Lola smacked him on the arm with her clutch, probably harder than she should have considering they barely knew each other. "That wasn't some video game he played from his living room couch while eating cheese puffs and releasing noxious gas out of both ends. It was real life, his life, and he lives with those memories every day. The last thing he needs is for you to throw it around like it's a joke."

Leo stared at her like he couldn't believe that she'd just said that to him. Or maybe he couldn't believe that she'd whacked him.

"Wow, I don't think I've ever seen Leo speechless. Have you?"

Lola turned to face the voice and found herself looking up at a blue-eyed giant. Okay. He wasn't a giant, but he was certainly one of the tallest men there. He was at least six-four and as wide as a Cadillac. He was handsome too, in a Superman retired to become a sexy lumberjack kind of way. He looked like he could split a log with his bare hands like that GIF of Chris Evans.

Said large sexy man was currently looking down at Kamilah, making it obvious who he'd asked the question of. His eyes held a pinch of amusement, an underlay of lust, and a wealth of love. This was obviously the fiancé.

"I've never met anyone with that power," Kamilah replied. "Not even Sofi could cow Leo." She looked gorgeous in a deep green, V-neck, lace midi dress that belled out into an asymmetrical fishtail hem at the knee. In the past Lola would've been jealous of the way it flattered Kamilah's tight curves and only seemed to highlight how flat her stomach was.

Now Lola loved her own curves even if they were more ample and squishy. Her body might not be the kind that had traditionally graced fitness magazine covers, but it was strong despite everything she'd put it through. Lola did yoga almost every day in addition to her Krav Maga classes. She was healthy despite what "helpful" strangers might imply, projecting their own phobias onto her. Those people could suck it. Besides, being "healthy" didn't determine whether or not her size was justifiable. No one determined her worth, but her. She was fat and she was sexy. She was also rocking the shit out of her own formfitting dress.

Lola León, you are a bad bitch in every sense of the word, she reminded herself.

"Miss León, welcome to my engagement party: the sequel." Kamilah laughed, then paused. "Although I guess I should call you Lola now. It would be weird to keep calling you Miss León since you're dating my brother. Don't think I don't want to hear all about that by the way. Well, not *all* about it, if you catch my drift. There are things about her brothers that a little sister just doesn't need to know."

Kamilah's big fiancé leaned down and sealed his mouth with hers. After a second he lifted his head.

Kamilah sighed. "I was rambling wasn't I?"

He smiled. "A bit."

"Thanks for that."

"My pleasure," he replied in such a way that made it clear it really was.

Kamilah looked back at Lola. "This is Liam, by the way. My fiancé, if that somehow wasn't clear."

Liam shook his head at Kamilah then turned to Lola and held out a hand. "Liam Kane."

Lola shook it. "Lola León."

"I know. Rosie has been talking about you all day."

Lola's mouth stretched into a wide smile at the thought of Rosie gushing about her to the people she loved. "Where is she?" She searched the huge room for the little girl.

"She's probably on the restaurant side playing with all of her cousins."

"Where's Saint?" Kamilah asked.

"The twins needed his help with something."

The relaxed and happy look on Kamilah's face changed instantly to one of anxiety. "What do you mean? What could they need help with? Did they say? What are they planning?"

Lola simply blinked at the bombardment. "Uh…"

Liam wrapped an arm around her. "It's okay. It's probably nothing."

"You don't understand my brothers. They're definitely up to something. The twins like to act like they're above it all, but they are demons and Leo, don't get me started on him."

Lola hadn't even noticed that Leo had seemingly disappeared after Kamilah started talking.

Liam nodded along, "Yes, but Saint is with them."

Kamilah released a long breath and pressed a hand to her chest as if calming her racing heart. "You're right. They're with Saint. He'd kick their asses to Milwaukee and back before he'd let them mess with me today." She paused. "But I'm going to go find them, just in case. Con permiso." She took off and Liam followed.

Lola observed them. It was interesting. It was as if there was an invisible rope connecting them that wouldn't let them get farther than a couple feet away from each other, but it also allowed energy to flow between them both, vitalizing them.

"Who is Mila going to find?" Saint asked in her ear from behind.

Lola spun and found him standing there with two drinks in his hand. "Oh, she's going to find you."

"Me?" He passed her one of the drinks in his hand. "This is a special drink Liam's friend came up with using the whiskey Liam created for Kamilah."

"That's so cute," Lola said as she accepted the glass. "And she's looking for you because I mentioned that your brothers asked you to help with something and she sort of freaked out." She took a sip of the drink in her hand. It was delicious, the bite of whiskey perfectly balanced with sweet mango and passionfruit juice, the tartness of lemon juice, and just a hint of bitterness. "She's a bit high-strung, huh?"

"Kamilah is Kamilah, but she's probably even more nervous about today. This is technically their second engagement party."

"Oh, that's why she called it 'Engagement Party: the sequel.'"

"More like Engagement Party: Take Two. Let's just say that the last one did not end well, and Leo unknowingly played a part in that."

Lola grimaced. "Damn. Do you want to go find her and assure her that you all aren't planning some elaborate prank to ruin her day?"

Saint shrugged. "She'll figure it out. Besides, it will distract her from the fact that someone else is about to bring the drama to her party." His eyes were on something behind her.

Lola followed his gaze to a duo of women standing where the distillery opened to the parking through a set of garage doors. They were both beautiful in an untouchable way, like movie stars or something. One was older, although it was difficult to tell how much since she was so well put together. She eyed the group as if preparing for battle. The younger woman looked more excited. She was smiling widely, the whiteness of her teeth almost blinding.

"Eva? Flaca?" a voice asked from the crowd.

At her side Saint stiffened. Actually, it seemed like everyone in the room stopped and tensed. Lola had never seen a party full of Latinos go silent.

The woman's head swiveled in the direction of the voice. "Hello, Luís."

Lola recognized Saint's uncle when he pushed his way through the crowd to stand in front of them.

The man didn't stop. He didn't say anything else. He walked right up to the younger woman and wrapped her in a hug. The younger woman returned the embrace with a strong hug of her own. She buried her face in his neck.

"That's my cousin, Evalisse," Saint murmured to her. "She's a Broadway actress. And that's my tía Carmen, her manager."

Okay. That explained who the women were, but it hardly explained why everyone was staring at the scene as if they were all standing on a nuclear bomb and those two held the activation codes.

A tall thin young woman appeared out of the crowd. Carmen looked at her. "Gabi," she said as she leaned in for the perfunctory cheek kiss.

"Mami," the woman replied. "It's good to see you."

Carmen nodded. Then she looked beyond her daughter. "And Alex?"

Gabi tried to seem breezy, but even from across the room Lola could tell she was even more uncomfortable. "Oh, she's around here somewhere. She probably hasn't heard you are here yet."

For the first time Carmen's impassive face cracked. A flicker of pain was there and gone in a second. "Right. I'm sure I'll see her in a second."

The most uncomfortable silence in the history of the world followed. There were at least forty people in the room and not one made a sound.

Then Papo Vega's words filled the space. "What is wrong with you all?" he asked in Spanish. The crowd parted and he made his way toward the women. "Stop acting like Carmen and Eva are zombies who will infect you and eat your brains. They're family, even if they did leave us for New York." He reached the small group. He held his arms open to his daughter and she stepped into them. After a tight squeeze he leaned back and held her face in his hands. She was taller than him in her heels, but Papo pulled her head down and kissed her on the forehead. "Welcome home, mi amor."

At the patriarch's words the family finally reacted. They

swarmed forward and soon the women were engulfed in a wave of family members embracing and welcoming them.

Saint didn't move. He stood scanning the crowd. "I should find Alex," he said.

She didn't miss that he'd said *I* and not *we*, but she really didn't want to stand there by herself. "Do you want me to go with you or stay here?"

He grabbed her hand. "You can come with me." He led them through the crowd and through the doors that led to the restaurant where a bunch of young kids, including Rosie, were running around while the older ones sat slumped in booths showing each other stuff on their phones. Saint met eyes with a handsome boy who looked to be around fourteen or fifteen. The boy pointed to the hallway that led to the bathrooms.

Saint tugged them in that direction and sure enough there was Alex. She leaned against the wall, double fisting the strong whiskey drinks. Next to her stood Avery, who also had two drinks in her hands.

"What's up?" Alex asked them with very practiced nonchalance.

"Are you okay?" Saint asked.

Alex shrugged. "Yeah. Why wouldn't I be?" She took a deep drink out of one glass and then the other.

Saint paused. "You know who just got here, right?"

"Of course."

Avery chimed in. "The audible gasps drowned out La India screaming about not wanting to see someone ever again."

Alex snorted. "The irony."

The men's bathroom door opened and Matteo appeared.

Avery passed him one of the drinks in her hand.

"Hey," he told Saint and Lola with a nod. "You came to check on Alex?"

Alex sucked her teeth. "I don't know why everyone is worried about me. So my mom randomly showed up today after vowing not to step foot back in Chicago when she stormed out after Abuela's funeral *twelve years ago*, leaving my dad and seeing Gabi and me maybe once a year when she could squeeze in a few days for us to visit her and Eva in New York. Why would I be upset?" She drained the drink in her right hand and then the one in her left.

Saint took both glasses from her with one hand and set them on a ledge. "Take it easy with those."

Alex took Saint's drink from his hand and started in on it. "No can do, primo. I plan to get plastered, so these two have a valid reason to take me home early." The thick strap of her blue wide-leg jumpsuit slipped off her shoulder and Avery pushed it back up. "Because I'm not sticking around here to watch everyone roll out the red carpet for them after talking hella shit about the situation this whole time."

Lola was thrown off. She never would've expected there to be so much drama in the Vega family. From the outside they looked like such a close-knit group. Then again, one thing didn't have to negate the other.

Avery's phone buzzed. She pulled it out and read the text quickly. "Okay, Monica got the chisme."

"Of course," Matteo said. "There's nothing your sister loves more than being in on all the good bochinche."

"Facts," Avery agreed. Her phone buzzed again. She read the text then gave Alex a look of concern. "According to what your mom told my mom, with Monica standing right there, Eva's got a huge secret project that's going to be based out of Chicago. It looks like they're here for a while, prima."

"Fuck," Alex and Saint said at the same time.

19

Saint took another sip from his drink. As nonchalantly as possible, he asked the woman next to him, "Are you ready to meet my parents now?"

Lola spun around on her heels to face him. "Umm. Do you think it's a good time? I mean with your aunt and cousin surprising everyone..."

The truth was that he'd very strategically picked this party to introduce Lola to his parents, because they'd be in a good mood and more likely to think before they spoke, but they'd also be distracted enough to not interrogate Lola like the FBI. However, now, thanks to his tía's propensity to make a grand entrance or exit, he could tell that both of his parents were agitated.

Papi was standing around stern-faced while Mami had taken on the personality of a hummingbird, flitting around from group to group laughing a bit too loudly and moving her hands around more wildly than normal. The situation wasn't ideal.

"My parents are not the patient type. If we don't go to them, they'll come to us and they'll be annoyed that they had to seek us out first."

At Lola's wide-eyed look, Saint mentally face-palmed. He should not have told her that. He could tell that she was nervous and he had not helped. *Get your shit together, Vega*, he scolded himself like he would've done to one of his men.

He reached a hand up under her hair and gave her a mini neck massage. "Just be yourself. They respect honesty more than anything." He slid his hand down to the small of her back and gave a little nudge of encouragement. "Come on."

His parents were standing in a small group with Abuelo Papo and Tío Rico. As Saint neared with Lola, he could begin to distinguish their voices from everyone else's.

"It's a damn shame," Tío Rico said.

Tío Rico was technically the oldest brother by about ten minutes, and he never let Papi forget it. Despite looking almost identical, the twin brothers were otherwise very different. Papi was low-key and pretty blue-collar. He preferred to keep his head down and get things done, like his mother. Ricardo Vega II, named after his father, had inherited his father's larger-than-life personality and easy charm along with his name. What he hadn't gotten from his father was his musical talent, so once it was clear Rico wouldn't be schmoozing the community with a microphone and a song, he began to do it with a mic and a speech. His uncle was the quintessential local politician but with one big difference: he actually cared about his community enough to put its needs before his own ego. Which was why Tío kept getting elected alderman.

"That's what happens when two people get married without knowing what the other one wants," Papi said from the other side of Tío Rico. "Anyone who knows Carmen knows that she was never going to be happy being a stay-at-home mom. She was always ambitious and selfish."

"No le digas egoísta a tu hermana," Abuelo scolded.

"She was. She never did anything to help anyone, because

everyone would do everything for her and she would do for herself."

"She was little, Santos," Tío Rico argued.

"She's four years younger than us, Rico, not fourteen. She could've had more responsibilities, but because she was Papi's little estrellita, she didn't have to do anything but rehearse."

Abuelo Papo bristled in irritation. "What was I supposed to do, shit all over her dreams like you two did to Kamilah?"

"Papi," Tío Rico intoned. That was too fresh a wound to poke at. His parents and Kamilah were still rebuilding their relationship and they didn't need anyone making comments about it.

His father, always ready to go toe to toe with Abuelo Papo, didn't back down. "All I'm saying is that she was raised to think that what she wanted was more important than what anyone else needed and that became more than clear when she used Eva to make her own dream come true and left her other daughters with their father como si fueran confeti de desfile, lo que sobra."

Saint winced. Thank god Alex wasn't around to hear Papi call her leftover parade confetti. Deciding that now was as good a time as any to interrupt, Saint cleared his throat. "Con permiso," he said, bringing himself and Lola closer. "We just wanted to say hi."

Abuelo Papo's eyes lit up on seeing Lola standing at his side. "Lolita!" he exclaimed. "¡Que alegría verte!" He came forward and pulled Lola into a hug and kiss.

Lola smiled. "Hi, Don Papo. It's nice to see you too."

"Nada de eso 'Don Papo.' Call me Papo. Don is for old men."

Tío Rico laughed. "Then I guess you should just call me Rico." He held out a hand and Lola shook it. "Good to see you again, Miss León."

Saint hadn't known that they'd met before, but he couldn't say he was surprised considering his uncle's job and Lola's habit of bumping heads with authority figures.

"Please, call me Lola," she told him with a smile, leaving Saint to believe that their previous run-in had at least been amicable.

Saint looked at his parents, who were watching him with considering expressions. He knew that they were both aware of Lola's place in his life. Rosie had brought her up multiple times in their FaceTime conversations while his parents had been away and they'd both tried to subtly pry information out of him. It was one thing for them to know of her and another for them to meet her. He swallowed. "Mami, Papi, I want to introduce you both to Lola León."

His papi was the first one to move. He held out a hand. "Nice to meet you. I'm Santiago Vega Senior."

Lola reached out to shake it.

Mami took a different approach. She drew Lola into a half hug and cheek kiss. "Mucho gusto. Yo soy Valeria."

"So," Papi began as soon as Lola and Mami finished their embrace, "I hear you're a Humboldt Park native. How does it feel to be back?"

Saint released a breath of relief. His dad had at least started with something easy.

"I love it," Lola answered. "I've always wanted to come back and am happy I was able to finally make the move."

"You're here to take care of your abuelo, right?" That was Mami, who viewed caretaking as one of the most important roles one could provide for their loved ones.

Lola nodded. "Yes. Benny was lonely here all by himself and created a bit of mischief as a result."

Papi gave Abuelo Papo a significant look. "We know how that goes."

"Por favor," Abuelo scoffed. "Si yo soy un angelito."

They all had a laugh at that.

"Papi, you are about as angelic as one of the fallen," Tío Rico said.

Abuelo shrugged. "They were still angels."

Papi ignored Abuelo's nonsense and continued talking to Lola. "It must be hard, it being just the two of you."

Lola seemed to bristle at that. "Well, I mean, both of my parents are still alive and I have my brother."

"Right, but your mom lives far away, no?" At her nod, Papi continued. "And you dad and brother…" He paused, obviously trying to think of a polite way to discuss them. "Well, it's not like they're around."

"No, they are both in prison," Lola said in her straight-forward way. "But Benny talks to them on the phone and he visits them as well."

"You don't visit them?" Mami asked.

Lola shrugged. "Prisoners only receive letters, calls, or visits from people they've approved, so I haven't had any contact with them since before I left. But my brother has finally added me to his list of approved contacts. I should be able to see him soon."

That was the first Saint had heard about Lola visiting her brother, but he did his best not to react to the news. He did not like the idea of Lola walking into a prison. Just the idea of her being surrounded by criminals was enough to cause his heart to race. Forget the fact that her family had probably made a bunch more enemies while inside.

In her small purse, Lola's phone began to ring. Since he knew for a fact that she'd put it on Do Not Disturb with only two exceptions, he knew it was either Casa del Sol or Yara. He had a strong feeling it was the latter.

"I'm sorry," Lola said to his parents while digging in her purse. "I've been waiting for this call. There's an emergency situation with El Hogar that I've been waiting to get more information on."

Sure enough, he saw Yara's name and picture on the phone

when Lola pulled it out. She shot him a look. "Go ahead," he told her.

"Are you sure?" Lola asked.

"Of course," Saint replied. He knew that if Yara was calling it was because Lola was needed and he knew that being there for the kids was more important than chitchatting with his family. There would be time for Lola to get to know them.

She looked at his parents. "It was nice to meet you both. Hopefully we can talk more soon." She turned to Abuelo and Tío Rico. "It was nice to see you."

The elders said goodbye and wished her well.

Saint put a hand on Lola's arm to prevent her from scurrying away. "I'll walk you out." He linked their hands and started making their way to the distillery doors.

"Damn it," Lola said as soon as they were outside. "I was hoping to talk to your parents about more than my incarcerated family members before getting called away."

"Don't worry about it," Saint told her. "We'll set something up with them for another time. Just go do what you've got to do."

Lola gave him a big grateful smile. "You're the best." She went up on her toes to give him a quick kiss. "I'm glad we thought to bring my car. Are you sure you'll be able to get home?"

Saint nodded. "I have over thirty family members here. Rosie and I will be fine." He gave her another quick kiss. "Keep me updated, okay?"

Lola started walking backward. "Of course." She blew him a kiss, spun around, and hurried to the front of the building where she'd parked.

Saint sighed and made his way back inside. When he reached his parents it was to see that the small group had been joined by none other than Tío Luís and Eva.

He hadn't seen his tío for over a week. They were hardly ever in the office at the same time now that Saint was on-site at the Raven Realty project. Saint examined him closely, trying to see if he was showing any signs of his RA flaring up, but his uncle was beaming. It was clear by his megawatt smile and the way he kept using the arm around her shoulder to squeeze Eva into his side that he was ecstatic to have his oldest daughter there.

"Saint, mira quién llegó," he said as soon as he saw Saint approaching.

Eva smiled, her teeth practically blinding him. "Saint, it's good to see you. I'm glad you're safe and home."

Saint gave her a hug. "I'm glad you're home too." He had been on tour when she'd left for New York twelve years earlier, so it had been weird to come home on leave to find her and Tía Carmen gone, and even stranger to be seeing her again now for the first time in over a decade.

"Tell them about your secret project," Tío Luis urged her.

"If I tell everyone then it will no longer be a secret and I can get sued," Eva said with a playful smile.

"You should tell your mom that because she's already telling people about it. By the time she's done, the whole neighborhood will know," Mami said.

Saint had never attended one of Eva's shows, but she had to be a great actress, because she didn't even blink at the snark in Mami's tone. "She's just excited for me. Working with Chord Bailón is a big deal."

Saint frowned. Where did he know that name from?

"Chord Bailón?" his cousin Lucy said in an overly loud voice as she joined the group with her wife, Liza. "As in the sexiest member of the Barrio Brothers?"

"The sexiest *living* member maybe," Liza added, "but everyone knows Erik was the sexiest."

Oh right. Now Saint remembered who they were. In the early 2000s they'd been one of the hottest boy bands until one of their members died tragically. After that they'd broken up and the remaining members had either gone solo or disappeared.

"I shouldn't have said anything," Eva said. "His involvement is a total secret. Please, please don't say anything to anyone outside of the family. If word gets out, he may change his mind about basing the show here."

"Of course, we'll keep it in the family, prima. That's what we do." Lucy turned to him. "Hey, I ran into your new girlfriend outside. She said something about a housing emergency and a possible protest."

"What?" Tío Rico exclaimed.

Everyone looked at Saint.

He cleared his throat. "Well, since El Hogar closed they've done their best to keep up with the displaced teens, but it turns out that two of them were staying in a tent city. There was an altercation with neighbors and police last night."

Tío Luís's head dropped while everyone else had varying looks of anger, disgust, and concern.

"Fuck," his tío Rico hissed. "This is going to be a headache. Are you sure she mentioned a protest?" he asked Lucy.

She nodded.

"And she's leading it?"

Another nod.

"Fuck."

Saint jumped in then. "Why does it matter if she's leading the protest? Isn't the reason for the protest more important?"

Tío gave him a pitying look. "I take it you don't know your girlfriend's history."

Saint straightened his spine. "If this is about her dad—"

"No. Of course, it isn't. This is about her. When she came into my office with the director of the community center a few weeks ago, I looked into her. She has a record."

"What kind of record?" Papi asked.

"She has a tendency to instigate rowdiness at protests. She was arrested multiple times at demonstrations back in California."

Saint shook his head in disbelief although a large part of him questioned why. He knew Lola. He knew she was more likely to beg forgiveness than ask permission. Actually, with her fiery attitude, she was most likely to give the middle finger and keep doing what she was doing.

"She's a violent criminal just like her father and brother?" Mami looked at Saint. "And you have her spending time with my granddaughter?"

"She's nothing like them," Saint argued.

"Really?" Papi asked. "Because I knew her father before he was the Puerto Rican Al Capone. He started his lawbreaking during the riot. He was thirteen or fourteen. He and her grandfather were there for every meeting, march, and protest, but Rafa didn't think things were moving fast enough. All of a sudden, he was hanging around the gangbangers talking about taking back the neighborhood. From there he just got worse."

Saint didn't have to ask what riot. Everyone knew which one. In the summer of 1977, there was a two-day riot in the neighborhood after a confrontation with police led to the deaths of two young Puerto Rican men. Buildings were burned, people were panicked, many injured, and some dead. His uncle had said that the riot and its aftermath was what made him want to be a local politician.

"Lola is not her father," he told Papi. "She cares about people. She wants to help those kids and would never put anyone in danger." He did his best to ignore the part of him that wondered if that was true.

20

Lola sat at the island reading the email she'd received from Yara for the third time. She kept getting distracted by the sight of Saint's back. She couldn't help it. He was just built so spectacularly. He was wearing a T-shirt, but she could still see the muscles flex as he dipped down to open the oven and pull out a pan covered in thick slices of toasted bread.

He caught her staring when he suddenly turned to grab some minced garlic from the island in front of her. He smiled. "Don't start that," he murmured. He placed the garlic in a pan with melted butter then turned it off.

"It's your fault." Lola bit her bottom lip. "You can't invite me over for breakfast and then open the door looking like that and make fresh Texas toast and expect me not to want to jump your bones."

He licked his lips, eyes gone hazy with lust. He pulled a silicone basting brush out of a drawer and used it to give the butter garlic a mix. "You need to stop." He brushed the mixture over the toasted bread. "Rosie is about to call for me at any second."

Now that he mentioned it, the sound of the girl playing in the tub with her dolls had gotten pretty quiet.

"Papi, I'm ready to come out now!"

Lola smiled at how well he knew his daughter. "How much water do you think is on the floor?"

"Enough to make me happy that I tiled the floor instead of just refinishing the old wood one."

"Go get her ready," she said. "I'll guard the toast and bacon with my life."

"I'll be right back. Then I'll make the scrambled eggs."

She waved him off. "Go. Then maybe I can focus on this email from Yara."

His pause was brief, but Lola noticed the shadow of worry that passed over his face. "Is it a work thing?"

She shook her head. "We're finalizing the plan for the protest."

It had been no surprise to her when the incident at the tent city two and a half weeks ago had almost gotten buried. She'd been a part of enough causes to know that the first instinct of a community is always to brush something under the rug. It took the rug getting ripped out of the house, into the air, and beat until the dirt fell out for most people to even admit that it was dirty. Lola was more than willing to be the one standing there holding the stick. She'd thought Saint understood that about her, but lately she wasn't sure.

For the last few days he'd been making these comments about how fast things had moved, how well the organizations worked together after years of collaboration, implying she was sticking her nose where it didn't belong.

Case in point, he averted his eyes now and said, "Yara has always been so good at organizing these things. She really knows how to do it right."

She'd been brushing his comments off, knowing how much

of a worrier he was, but she was annoyed. "I get it, Saint. You think my involvement is unnecessary."

He looked at her then. "What?"

"It's fairly obvious you don't want me to be a part of this. You aren't very subtle."

"That's not it."

"Then what is it, Saint, because I'm sick of these little leading comments you keep making. I'm not Hansel or Gretel to be following breadcrumbs through the woods, so just tell me."

"I know this is important and I want to support you in the cause, you know I do. I just don't know why you have to be out on the front lines."

"Why wouldn't I be?"

"Because it's dangerous."

"Saint, do you remember what you told me when we used to argue about you enlisting?" He didn't answer, probably because they'd argued about it so much that he couldn't pinpoint a specific thing. Lola could. It was what he told her when she realized that she was never going to change his mind. "You told me, 'I believe in this fight. I believe that this needs to be done. If I could be there making it happen but I don't, I wouldn't respect myself anymore.' Do you remember now?"

He nodded.

"That's how I feel. I believe in this, and I know that I need to be there regardless of what may happen. Unless you can tell me why it's okay for you to put yourself on the front lines for a cause you believe in but not me, I don't think there is any more to say about it."

"Papi!" Rosie called from the bathroom for the second time.

He gave Lola a look but didn't say another word. He went to get his daughter ready for the day.

When he came back, Rosie in tow, they ate breakfast together and talked about other things. She could've almost forgotten about the conversation if he hadn't stepped in it again right after they finished eating.

"Rosie and I want to take you to the movies for your birthday. The one she suggested starts in an hour."

"Sadly, I can't. I have to go pick up Benny. We're going to see Iván today."

"What?"

She didn't like his tone, as if she'd blindsided him. "I told you he finally put me on his approved contacts list."

"You did. I guess I just didn't think you'd be going there. I thought you'd do a virtual visit."

"I haven't seen him for almost two decades. Of course, I want to see him in person."

Saint sent Rosie to play in her room. As soon as the little girl was gone he leaned forward and murmured, "It's prison, Lola."

"And?"

"What if something happens?"

"Like what?"

"I don't know. A fight or something."

"I'm sure they have procedures in place to handle that."

"I still don't think it's a good idea. What if you see someone you don't want to? You said they had a lot of enemies. I bet that at this point most of those enemies are either occupying cells next to them or dead."

"Are you really trying to get me to not visit my brother?"

He shook his head and for a second she thought he was doing it to her, but it became clear he was shaking it at himself. "You're right. I'm sorry. Of course, you're going to see him as soon as you can and you'd want to do it in person. You both deserve to have that."

"Yes. We do."

As she stood at the back door a few minutes later Saint pulled her in. "I'm sorry," he said again. "I was out of line. Do you forgive me?"

"Yes," she said instantly, because what else was she going to do? Say no and leave mad at him for something he already admitted was wrong? She cared about him too much for that.

Besides, she wasn't really mad at him. She was mad at herself because for the briefest moment she'd considered giving in to what he wanted.

"Are you ready?" Benny asked her as he stared at the doors to the visitation room.

Lola nodded then took a deep breath and tried to find her inner peace. It had been a struggle to get to where she currently was. From having Benny beg Iván to add her to his list of approved contacts to arriving at the prison and initially being denied access because her clothes were "inappropriate." She'd been wearing a pair of black pants and a billowy top. She's worn the outfit to work multiple times and had never once been looked at askance, but because her pants fit her curves and her top showed the barest hint of cleavage she'd been turned away. She'd had to leave and search out the nearest clothing store to find a new outfit. It had been difficult considering most stores were now in full summer mode, but she'd eventually found something. She was now the proud owner of a light brown mumu that covered her from neck to ankles and made her look like a burlap sack. The thing was ugly as hell, but it was comfortable and she would be wearing it around the house frequently. *Take that, petty and power-high staff members.*

She heard a sound from the hall and her heart picked up its pace. This was it. She'd be seeing her brother soon. The door was opened and he walked in. Lola knew him instantly. Their eyes met. Iván didn't smile. He made no reaction as he was led to the table they'd been assigned. Meanwhile, Lola cataloged everything from the sprinkles of gray throughout his dark brown hair to the deep frown line permanently etched onto his face and the way he favored his right leg as he walked. It took her a second to remember that her brother was forty years old now.

As soon as he reached the table Lola shot up and wrapped her arms around him, squeezing with all of her strength. His embrace was much less intense than hers, but she heard a huff from him that sounded almost like relief. She felt moisture build in her closed eyes, but for once she didn't care. She was with her brother. She was holding him.

"That's enough," a hard voice barked. "Sit down."

Lola swung her head in the direction of the visiting room officer and glared. "I haven't been able to hug him in twenty years." Her words sounded like an explanation, but her tone said *fuck off*.

"I don't care," he returned. "I said, 'Sit down.'"

Lola opened her mouth, but Benny's low "Lola, cállate o nos van a botar" had her shutting it. She didn't want their visit to get cut short. She let Iván go and took her seat on the other side of the table even though it stuck in her craw.

"Happy birthday" were the first words out of Iván's mouth.

Her smile was full of surprised pleasure. She was surprised he remembered considering everything he dealt with on a daily basis. "Thank you." She swallowed the emotion clogging her throat. "I'm glad to spend it with you."

He scoffed. "Yeah, I'm sure you always dreamed of spending your thirty-fifth birthday in a prison."

She reached over and grabbed his hand. "I've always dreamed of spending any birthday with my only brother."

He looked down at their hands and his lips finally curled in the tiniest smile. Then he pulled his hand back. "You've been good?" he asked.

For the second time Lola found herself trying to figure out how to pack almost two decades of life into a few sentences. If she shared, would he feel bitter? She didn't want to hurt him. "Yes," she said simply.

"And Mom?"

"She's good too."

He looked at Benny. "Is she always like this?"

Benny snorted. "Esta cotorra? Usually it's trying to get her to stop talking that's difficult."

Iván shook his head at her. "If you hold back, this is going to be a really boring visit."

"There's so much I want to tell you, to talk to you about. I don't know where to begin. I don't know what you want to hear."

"Lola, I've been here for a long time and most days have been exactly the same, me sitting around thinking and wishing I were somewhere else. You aren't going to hurt my feelings by telling me that you've been able to actually go out and do things. That's what I want to hear. I want to hear that you've lived. I don't want you to sit here looking at me with pity and second-guessing every word."

She nodded. "Okay. I'll do better." Then she launched into a rundown of her life since leaving Humboldt Park. She told him about the years it had taken before she'd been able to forgive their mother, going to school and her semester studying abroad in Mexico, about shitty dates she'd gone on and was ecstatic when he laughed. She told him about the few times she'd been arrested after protests. He hadn't liked hearing that, but he did tell her that he was proud of her strength and perseverance.

"Tell him about your boyfriend," Benny said.

Lola shot a look at him. She didn't want to talk about Saint. Not after what had just happened between them. She still couldn't believe that he'd thought to tell her she shouldn't visit her brother. If she'd listened to him then she wouldn't have had this time with Iván. The thought was enough to make her mad all over again. The audacity of the man thinking that she was going to just do what he wanted because it would make him more comfortable.

Iván's eyebrows raised. "You've only been back for a few months and you already have a boyfriend?"

"More like she has the same one from before she left."

Lola's mouth dropped. She stared at her abuelo wide-eyed. "You knew about us?"

Benny rolled his eyes. "Of course I knew about you and the Vega boy. We lived in a tiny two-bedroom apartment and neither one of you were good about sneaking around." He shook his head. "I was old, but not that old."

"You're dating one of the Vega guys? I'm shocked."

"Why shocked?"

He shrugged. "I don't know. They're just so…soft."

Lola took umbrage at that. "Saint served in the military for twelve years and did multiple tours in Afghanistan. He received a medal for saving two of his fellow soldiers and two civilians."

Iván lifted both hands palms out. "Okay. My bad. Your man is a hero."

She felt her face heat. "I didn't say all that. I'm just saying, he's not soft." Although he had the ability to be soft and sweet, like when he was interacting with Rosie or when he was holding Lola in his arms. Those were the times that she liked him the most. She didn't need or want some chest thumping "alpha male" who was so emotionally stunted that he saw everything but utter dominance as a weakness that needed to be extinguished. That kind of man was too much like her father.

Lola scolded herself mentally. She'd promised not to think of her dad who was currently somewhere in the same building as her. But the curiosity proved too hard to resist. "How is he?" she asked Iván.

He didn't even have to ask who. He shrugged. "I don't see

him a lot because he's on a different block, but he's as good as someone can be in here."

She looked at Benny, who had visited with him briefly while she'd been on her outfit journey. Her father had steadfastly refused to put her on his list of approved contacts, not that she'd asked or even wanted him to. However, she still couldn't deny that the rejection had stung.

Benny gave a shrug very similar to Iván's. "He is how he is, Lola. Being here has only made him angrier. It didn't change him for the better."

"Being here doesn't change anyone for the better," Iván said. The bleakness in his tone made it clear just how much of an effort he'd been putting forth to sound normal. The fact that he did it all for her benefit made her heart squeeze.

"I'm back now," she said. "I will be here to see you as much as they let me."

Iván's expression warmed. He opened his mouth to say something and then froze. "Drop your heads," he hissed suddenly, doing exactly what he'd demanded.

"What?"

"Drop your fucking heads."

Shocked at the vehemence in his voice, Lola did as he said, but too late.

"If it isn't Little Lola León," a voice said.

Since there was no longer a point to hiding her face, Lola looked up.

The older man standing by their table looked vaguely familiar, but she didn't have to recognize him to know what was going on. Because of who she was talking to and who she was sitting with, she'd just been recognized by one of Iván or her father's enemies. Most likely a member of The Emperors.

She waited for one of the overzealous guards to bark at him to keep it moving with the same energy they'd had for anyone touching their loved ones for more than a second. No reprimand came.

"It's good to see that you've finally come home. Very good," he continued, a threat suggested in his words.

Years ago she would've been scared. Now she refused to cower in front of anyone. She stared at him, silently letting him see how unbothered she was by his presence.

He smirked. "It's good to see that at least one of you inherited your father's fire."

Her eyes narrowed at the slight to her brother.

His smirk grew.

"You have someone waiting to visit with you," was all she said.

"Yes, and I can't wait to let them know that Rafa's little girl has finally returned."

Lola snorted in derision. "Rafa hasn't given a shit about his little girl since the day she was born. I highly doubt he's going to start now."

"I don't know about that. Blood is blood after all. Enjoy the rest of your visit." With those parting words he strolled away as if he were taking a walk in the park and not through the visiting room of a prison.

As soon as he was gone Iván stood up. "This visit is over," he said.

"We still have twenty minutes left."

He shook his head. "Don't come back," he told her.

"I'm not staying away because of *him*."

"That's Guillermo Hernandez. His brother was one of the guys we—"

She cut him off. "Iván, I'm not scared of him."

"You should be. He may be in here, but he still has connections. Just like Papi."

"I don't care about any of that. I care about you. *My* brother, who I'm going to visit no matter who it pisses off."

"I'm not putting *my* sister in the sights of someone who'd love nothing more than to use her to get to us."

"He's already seen me, so me staying away doesn't accomplish anything."

"I'll get word to Papi. He has some favors he can call in, but either way you need to keep your distance and be careful."

"You've been here almost twenty years because of him, Iván. When are you going to stop being his fucking puppet?"

"Lola!" Benny scolded.

Her brother reared back as if she'd slapped him. Then his face hardened. "That's what you've never understood, Lola. There is no stopping for me now, there is no new path with a moral high ground that I get to take, there's only surviving and I'm going to make sure we both do that even if I have to sell my soul to the devil." He backed away from the table. "I'm taking you off my list. Both of you." He turned to leave.

Lola shot out of her chair. "Don't do this, Iván."

"Hey! Settle down!"

Lola swung toward the guard. "Oh, now you want to say something? Where was all that little dick energy a few moments ago when I was being threatened?"

"That's it. You're done."

Lola caught sight of Iván being escorted away by another guard out of the corner of her eye. "Yeah. I am done."

Lola silently raged as she and Benny were kicked out and her privileges were suspended. It hardly mattered. Iván had made it clear that there was nothing for her here.

21

Saint watched the bubbling volcano that was Lola whirl around her apartment collecting things and placing them in her backpack. She seemed to be checking necessities off an invisible list in her head. She didn't look at him once as she continued with her mission.

He felt like she hadn't really looked at him since the day she'd gone to visit her brother. He knew he'd crossed a line. He shouldn't have tried to convince her not to go. He would never allow anyone to prevent him from seeing his family for any reason and he should've respected Lola's right to do the same. He understood he was wrong and he'd apologized. Lola said she forgave him, but she was treating him like she hadn't.

"Hey, you never told me what happened with your brother. Did you have a good time?"

Lola tossed a water bottle onto the counter with a little too much force. "It was good for a while. Then we argued and he removed me from his contact list again."

Saint felt bad for Lola, but he couldn't deny that a part of him was glad. "What did you argue about?"

"What else, my dad."

Rafael León was a looming presence in every relationship Lola had, familial or otherwise. "When your brother calms down, he'll change his mind and add you back on."

She shoved the water bottle in the side pouch of her backpack. "I doubt it, but hopefully he'll at least add Benny back on."

Saint raised his eyebrows. If Iván had removed Benny too, then things must've gotten pretty bad. He wanted to ask more questions, but Lola's short answers made it clear that she wasn't interested in talking about it. At least not with him.

Instead, he gestured to her backpack and the mound of supplies on her tiny kitchen island. "What can I do to help?" Since his fuckup he'd been doing his best to show his support even though the whole thing still had him on edge.

Saint hadn't slept deeply since the night of Kamilah's engagement party. He felt like he was in the middle of an old rickety rope bridge and the ropes were all beginning to unravel. He was just a few frayed threads away from a fatal plummet. Despite that, he was determined to show Lola that he could and would be there to support her.

To that end, Saint had dropped Rosie off to his parents at his brother Eddie's house in the suburbs. His brother had converted a large shed in the yard into a guesthouse for their parents so they no longer had to live in the apartment above El Coquí. He wanted Rosie far away from Humboldt Park while he and several of his family members attended the protest with Lola.

"I think I'm almost done," Lola replied to his previous question. She stood by her tiny kitchen counter triple-checking the supplies. It reminded Saint of how he and his fellow soldiers would recheck their supplies before heading out on a mission. "I just want to grab a few more first aid things." She turned and headed to her bathroom.

Saint stayed staring at the backpack. It had never occurred to him how much like a soldier Lola was until she'd brought it

up, but she was. Except her battles were fought at home and the
goal wasn't to create change through violence—it was to create
change through the type of awareness that cannot be ignored.
He admired her. He truly did, but he also knew firsthand what
it was like to be a soldier.

He'd seen what happened when overly zealous soldiers went
out on missions. Their passion could cloud their judgment and
people got hurt or killed as a result—themselves, fellow soldiers,
civilians and innocent bystanders. And Saint hadn't been able to
control any of it, just like he couldn't control the outcome now.

In recent years, Saint had watched news coverage of protests
gone awry all over the globe. People were waking up, taking
note, speaking out, and making moves, which was a good thing.
However, heightened emotions led a lot of people to react before
they really thought of consequences. According to the information his uncle dug up, Lola was definitely one of those people.
What he knew about her personally easily convinced him of the
validity of the claims. Lola had always been an act first, think
later type of person and, as a natural leader, she was really good
at getting others to do the same. He'd witnessed himself how
much the other staff and volunteers of El Hogar looked to her
and valued her ideas.

It was all too easy for Saint to imagine an incident getting
incited at the protest. He could picture it clearly. Some naysayer
getting mouthy and offensive and Lola coming back swinging
with her usual zeal and fire. Things would escalate and suddenly
the scene would descend into chaos. Shouts, bangs, pops, cries…
fire, violence, fear.

Suddenly, Saint felt the need to sit. He plopped down onto
Lola's couch. His legs began to bounce up and down along with
his stomach. His heart sped up and his breathing accelerated as
he struggled to take in enough air. It was both unbearably hot
and freezing at the same time, causing him to shiver and sweat in
equal measure. His eyes were wet while his mouth was dry. The

room around him seemed to blur and twirl. He closed his eyes but it didn't help with the feeling of swaying. He felt like he was on the deck of a ship getting tossed in a storm. His mouth suddenly flooded with saliva like it usually did before he threw up. He swallowed thickly and tried to rest his head between his knees, but that made the tightness in his chest squeeze and pinch. He didn't understand what was happening, he couldn't process anything, all he knew was that something was terribly wrong with him.

His entire body was rebelling at the same time.

He was dying.

He struggled and fought with his own body. His sole focus was on survival. Nothing else. He heard sounds, felt touches, saw shapes and colors, but nothing truly registered. Not until something was shoved in his hands and then lifted up to his face, covering his mouth and nose.

"Breathe," a voice commanded.

Saint tried.

He wasn't sure if he succeeded until the voice said, "That's it. Keep breathing."

That sounded like a good idea, so he did it some more. His breaths slowed—became more productive.

"Good. Now lower the bag."

When he did, Saint found that it was easier to breathe than before. He took more breaths, each one deeper than the last. His heart slowed from a rocket breaking free of gravity while shooting into space to a cheetah sprinting through the grass while on the hunt—still too fast but better than before.

He looked around into a sea of concerned faces. Lola sat next to him holding his hand while Avery and Teo looked on in mild panic. Avery had tears in her eyes. He recognized Lola's blue-haired friend, Mariana, from that hellhole bar that served those devil wings. Next to Mariana, a woman sat on the coffee table directly in front of him. She must've been the one coaching him.

His suspicions were confirmed when she put a hand on his knee and said, "Keep taking nice deep breaths. Try to slow them down even more. In and then out."

"Fuck," Saint rasped, slumping into the couch cushions and leaning his head back. He still felt jittery as if his bones were pebbles on the ground during a stampede.

"You had a panic attack, but you're okay," Lola said from his side. "Just keep breathing."

Saint closed his eyes and focused on his breathing, but he still heard the conversation happening around him.

"You think it's about the protest?" Teo asked.

"He did look freaked out when we protested outside the old El Hogar building," Mariana said.

Great. He'd thought he'd successfully hidden that from everyone. Then again, barking orders at people and dragging Lola out like there was a fire probably hadn't been as subtle as it felt at the time.

"This is obviously triggering for him," said his unnamed coach.

"What do we do with him? Take him to the hospital or something?" That was Avery, who was still audibly upset.

Saint shook his head. He didn't need the hospital. He just needed a moment to get his shit together.

"He doesn't want that," Lola said. "I think he just wants a second."

Saint squeezed her hand in thanks.

"Either way he should stay back," his coach decreed. "The last thing he needs to do is stress out at a protest."

A round of assent echoed around him. He wasn't offended. He agreed wholeheartedly. He had no business going to the protest in his condition. He rolled his head to look at Lola. He said the only words he could think at the moment. "I need you."

Lola's brow furrowed. "Of course. I'm right here next to

you." She lifted their entwined hands and kissed the back of his. "I've got you."

She didn't get it.

He tried again. "Stay here. With me."

"What?"

"Don't go to the protest. I need you to stay with me."

In the long pause that followed, their audience looked around awkwardly. Suddenly, they all got busy doing stuff in other areas of the apartment and talking loudly as if to fill the silence.

Saint heard Mariana say something about the guilt for the Raven Realty project getting to him. A distant part of his consciousness reminded him that he didn't want his cousins knowing about that, but the majority of his attention was on Lola.

Lola, who just stared at him as if he'd turned into a slimy worm right in front of her. "You want me to skip the protest I helped organize."

It was a statement not a question, but he felt compelled to answer anyway. "I have a bad feeling about this and I tried to ignore it, but I can't."

"Saint, that's the anxiety messing with you. Everything will be fine."

She didn't get it. She didn't understand. This was a bad idea. It was going to ruin everything. He couldn't explain how, but it was. He just knew it. "Please," he murmured. "Please don't go. Stay here."

Lola looked at him, indecision on her face.

"Please," he whispered a final time.

Her face changed from hesitancy to certainty. Then guilt and remorse. "I can't," she whispered back. "I want to, but I can't. I have to be there." She sounded like she was trying desperately to convince them both.

Saint did the only thing he could do at that point. He nodded his head and let her go.

22

"Stop kicking the back of my seat," Benny growled.

"Then move your seat up," Papo retorted with another push on the back of Benny's seat. "And roll up your window. I already told you that I'm cold."

"You two need to cut it out," Lola said. "I swear, I will pull this car over and you two will get out and walk."

"He started it," Benny said from the passenger seat beside her.

"I did not," Papo argued. "You did when you put glitter in my dentures case. For two days I looked like a rapper who's too poor to afford real gold teeth."

Lola watched in the rearview mirror as Papo flashed his teeth. She didn't want to be the one to tell him that he still had a bit of gold and silver glitter in the spaces between his teeth. She could only imagine how bad it had been a few days ago. She bit her inner lip to keep from smiling. She had to admit, her grandpa was holding his own. She was impressed. He never seemed like the type.

"I was just returning the glitter from the envelope that exploded as soon as I opened it," Benny said. "Also, no one wants to hear you sing every single song that comes on the radio. You aren't that good of a singer."

"Now it's obvious you're lying, because I'm an amazing singer and everyone knows it."

Lola locked eyes with Rosie in the rearview mirror. The little girl shook her head sadly, like an old woman lamenting kids nowadays. "Don't you wish we had a calming corner right about now?"

"Yes *and* a feelings chart *and* a recovery wheel," Rosie said.

Lola looked at the two men. "You hear that? A recovery wheel. That means things are as serious as they get."

"Don't look at me. Benny is the one who is petty and rude."

"Papo," Lola warned. "I will not tolerate name-calling in my car."

He huffed. "Fine. I'll just stay quiet, then."

"Por fin. Gracias a dios," Benny mumbled.

"Benny, enough," she told him. "I won't tolerate bullying either."

"I don't know why you're making us do this. You know we don't get along." Benny had a point.

"I want you two to at least try to act like the adults you are. It's not that hard to just be courteous."

"I'll behave, if he does," Papo offered.

"Fine," Benny grumbled. "I'll just pretend like he's not here."

"Benny." Lola drew out his name so he knew he was on thin ice.

"Okay. Okay. I'm done."

It had become more than clear that Benny and Papo were the ultimate frenemies. They hated being together but couldn't stay away either. Her mom liked to say, "Es mejor estar sola que mal acompañada." But Lola suspected that for Benny and Papo it was the opposite. They'd rather be in what they considered bad company than alone. She didn't blame them.

Now that Lola knew what it was like to have people, she was terrified of going back to being alone. That's why she'd suggested this family dinner at El Coquí.

She felt Saint pulling away.

She knew she shouldn't have left the way she had yesterday, but she was still unsure of what she could've done instead. Skipping the protest had not been an option. Everything had gone fine—it had been a planned peaceful protest that ended up remaining peaceful, as rare as that was. But even if it hadn't been, Lola made it a point to be on the front lines when she needed to be. How could she expect others to follow her if she wasn't willing to lead? It had been crucial for her to attend. Yara had been nervous at the scale of the event and needed Lola's support. Hell, she'd basically handed the reigns over to Lola, begging her to do all of the talking. Lola was able to keep everyone calm and focused on their message of how the gentrification of the neighborhood was causing a terrible housing crisis that was only exacerbating the social issues already present in the neighborhood. Most importantly, she was able to check in with Marcus and Ruby, who'd both hung on to her like a lifeline—making her surer than ever that she'd done the right thing.

On the other hand, she'd left Saint at her place stressed out and practically spiraling. How could she expect Saint to just be okay with the risk that involved? She was completely stumped. All she knew for sure was that she didn't want to lose Saint over this.

Her music paused as a call came in on her car's stereo system. *Speak of the devil.* She pushed the answer button on her steering wheel. "Hi, Saint, I'm pulling up to El Coquí with Benny, Papo, and Rosie."

"Hey, I'm going to be a little late. Gabi and Alex called a last-minute meeting at the office."

Oh fuck. Lola grimaced. She'd hoped that Avery and Teo had missed that comment Mariana had made about Saint being involved with Raven Realty, but it was obvious they hadn't and that they'd not only found out about the project, but shared the information with Luís's daughters. "Umm, Saint—"

"They are giving me dirty looks. I gotta go. I'll be on my way as soon as this is done." He said goodbye and hung up before she could even respond.

Lola pulled up to the parking lot and noticed that it was jam-packed. "Wow, there's never any parking here. It's always busy."

"Tití tells Papi to park in the alley when there's no parking."

"Sí. Park there," Papo said. "There's a space next to the dumpsters."

Lola figured that if Papo told her to park there, there should be no problem, so she did as directed.

Together they exited the car and walked around to the front entrance. As soon as they entered, Papo waved away the hostess. "We'll wait at the bar, Dulce."

"Sure thing, Abuelo Papo."

Lola frowned. "Is that one of your cousins?" she asked Rosie.

The little girl shook her head. "Everyone here calls him Abuelo Papo."

Ah. That made more sense.

"Ay que lindo. It's a family outing," a voice said as they reached the bar.

Lola looked up to see Leo standing behind it while Liam sat on a stool in front of him.

"Except where is Saint?" Liam asked.

"He's coming soon," Lola told them.

Rosie scrambled up the stool next to Liam and plopped down. "What's that?" She pointed to the glass in front of him.

"A new beer from my friend Dev's brewery," Liam replied, but he wasn't looking at Rosie. He was eyeing Benny. "Who's your new friend, Papo?" There was an edge to the question that Lola didn't quite understand.

"Friend?" Papo laughed. "He's not my friend. Este es un enema que no se me sale."

Benny scowled, Leo chuckled, and Liam seemed relieved.

Lola intervened before they started up again. "Papo, don't compare my grandpa to an enema."

Papo gave the most insincere apology ever. "Sorry. I'll be good now. I promise."

"I'm sure," Lola replied.

At her tone, Leo laughed. "Look at that. You figured out that Abuelo is never good. You really are one of us now."

Lola tried not to, but she couldn't help but smile at the sentiment.

Papo made a sound almost like a harrumph. "And what are you two doing? I've never seen you hang out before."

"We're not," Liam said. "We're trying to figure out what to do about Kamilah and Sofi."

Leo immediately shook his head. "No, he's trying to figure out what to do. I say good riddance."

"Who is Sofi?" Lola asked.

Papo answered before anyone else could. "Sofia has been Kamilah's best friend since middle school. They had a disagreement a while ago and Sofi hasn't talked to her since."

"Kamilah had hoped she'd come to the engagement party," Liam said. "She cried about it after everyone left." Liam's face was tense and his tone harsh. It was clear he didn't like that his fiancée was upset. "I don't know why Sofi can't just get over it already."

"Because she's a stubborn brat," Leo called from down the bar where he was pouring cola into a glass.

"Hey, Tío Leo," Rosie piped up. "Do you think she's still mad about—"

"Rosie! My favorite little person ever!" Leo suddenly yelled. "Come back here and help me make your kiddie cocktail!"

Rosie slammed her mouth shut, hopped off the stool, and raced around to the opening of the bar.

"That was subtle," Liam muttered to no one in particular.

Lola had to agree. It was clear that Leo had done something to this Sofi person that he didn't want anyone to know. She'd bring it up to Saint later. He'd know how to help.

"Hey, is she supposed to be back there?" Lola asked. "That doesn't seem legal."

Leo waved her off. "Don't worry. It's not like I'm going to have her juggling bottles like a Las Vegas showgirl."

In her pocket her phone buzzed. She pulled it out and saw a text from Saint.

Things are going down. I don't know if I'm going to make it. Eat without me.

Lola sighed. All this for nothing. "Saint isn't sure if he's going to make it. Let's get a table and order some food before it gets any later."

Papo put a hand on her shoulder. "Don't worry, nena. We will have fun without him. Just you wait."

She was surprised when she did.

Hours later, after a night of good food and better company—Papo and Benny had been almost civil once they sat at a table with the kind of food Casa del Sol would never have allowed them. Kamilah had come out to chat and make eyes at her fiancé while Leo kept everyone entertained with humorous anecdotes from the firehouse. Lola and her little crew were leaving El Coquí, walking to the far reaches of the packed parking lot, when all of Lola's instincts went on high alert. They were telling her that they should've taken Liam up on his offer to walk with them. She had an itchy prickly sensation at the back of her neck and a knot in her stomach despite the delicious food they'd just consumed. She didn't get this feeling often, but when she did, she knew to listen to it. The feeling had saved her on more than one occasion. She was just about to tell her three companions to turn around and head back to the front of the building when two shadows materialized on either side of them.

Immediately Lola pushed Rosie behind her while Papo and Benny stepped closer. They circled the girl like a herd of elephants protecting their young. The little girl let out a whimper and Lola's heart broke.

"There's no need for guns," Papo said. "We'll give you everything we have."

"Shut up," one man said.

"You. Walk." The other one used the gun in his hand to point at Lola, then toward the alley.

Everything became clear. This wasn't an armed robbery. They were there for Lola. These men were sent by Guillermo Hernandez.

I should've listened to Iván.

Lola choked down her terror and tried to think. Her mind raced. She knew better than to go with them to a different location, but if they only wanted her then maybe she could keep the others safe. She thought about the pepper spray on the key chain in her hand then quickly discounted it. Both men had guns and by the time she sprayed one then the other could shoot. There was no way she would risk Rosie, Benny, or Papo. If only she could separate them somehow. She needed to do something quickly, before Benny did. He was hot-tempered enough to make things worse for them all.

"I'll go with you," she told them. "I won't make a sound or cause any trouble, but these three stay here."

"No, mi leona," Benny exclaimed. He only called her "his lion" when he was feeling highly emotional.

"It's okay, Abuelo." She only called him that when she was emotional.

"This isn't a negotiation," the man on the right said. "You come with us quietly and without problems or we shoot one of them."

"Look, I get it. You're here for me. I'm not getting out of it and I'm not trying to, but they have nothing to do with this, so there is no reason to include them now. They are both in their eighties and she's only four."

At that they shared a quick look and that was all Lola needed to see. It was clear that neither one liked the idea of hurting a child.

"We let them go and what do they do? They run off and cause a scene. No. They're coming too."

"I bet your car is in that alley. Let's do this. We go there together, the driver gets in, one of you keeps your gun on me until I get in, you get in and then we take off. Leaving them here. By the time anything else happens we're long gone. You get exactly what you want without hurting people who don't deserve it." She used the only card she had again. "She's just a baby."

"Fine, but if any of you even breathe wrong, she's the first one I shoot."

Lola was almost positive that was a lie, but she knew with certainty that none of them were willing to call that bluff. The little hand in hers squeezed and she squeezed back. She'd get Rosie out of the situation safely if it was the last thing she did. She just needed to stall until she thought of something.

She met eyes with Benny then looked down toward Rosie and back up. He gave an infinitesimal nod. He knew she was planning something and he would be ready no matter what.

En masse they walked past the distillery and around the corner of the building. Sure enough a dark sedan with pitch-black windows and no license plates sat tucked in by the dumpster enclosure.

"Hurry up," one barked.

"I'm old," Benny barked. "This is as fast as I go." He fell a bit farther behind.

"I said to hurry the fuck up."

"Help me, nena." Benny reached for Rosie's shoulder and pretended to use it to help him walk.

The man growled but didn't say anything else.

Lola noticed Papo staring fixedly at the enclosure, but she brushed it off as him doing his best to not startle either man.

"Keep your gun on them," the first one said before walking around to the driver's side of the car.

The second man pointed the gun right at Lola, figuring she was the one to worry about. He was right. She was ready to tear him apart with her bare hands.

The moment the first man dropped the hand holding the gun to open the door, there was an explosion of movement from the dumpster enclosure as Leo Vega launched himself at the man.

Lola lifted her keys and sprayed the second man in the eyes, before he could turn his face away. At the same time Benny dropped to the ground, dragging Rosie and Papo with him and covering Rosie's body with his own. She knew that she was supposed to run away. It was the first thing she'd learned in Krav Maga and the first thing she taught her students, but she wasn't going anywhere without Rosie or the others, so her only option left was to fight.

Silently thanking her mother for making her take Krav Maga, Lola used a move she'd practiced hundreds of times to disarm the guy in front of her while he was still wailing in pain. She hit his arm to knock the gun away from anyone, but she didn't let go. She grabbed the barrel with one hand and used the other one to punch him in the throat. Because he instinctively loosened his grip to grab his injured throat, it was easier for her to rip the gun out of his hand. She tossed it behind her and then used all of her strength to kick him in the knee.

The sound of a gunshot boomed in the alley, followed immediately by a shout of pain.

Lola spun to see the other assailant running down the alley, abandoning his fallen friend. She didn't see Leo. He had to be on the other side of the car. She didn't know how it was possible for her stomach to drop when it was already in her feet, but it did.

The back door to the restaurant was thrown open and people spilled out. There was a horrified scream and shouts for someone to call 911 even though the blaring sirens were already close. Someone was yelling Leo's name over and over. For some stupid reason all Lola could think about was how Leo had just called her one of them and now because of her, he might be dead.

23

Saint looked around Gabi's transitional designed office, with its perfectly balanced mix of modern and traditional styles, and wondered yet again how he'd gotten stuck there.

It had all started when Saint had stepped out of the office bathroom and almost ran right into Gabi and Alex. Both women had been standing legs akimbo and arms crossed over their chests. If their stances hadn't told him that he was in trouble, their faces for sure had.

"We need to talk," Alex had said.

"My office. Right now," Gabi added.

"I'm supposed to meet Lola for dinner at seven," he said, trying to get out of whatever shitstorm was coming.

"You better call and let her know you'll be late, because we are handling this now."

They'd moved as a unit toward Gabi's corner office, probably to give him some privacy to make the call, but Gabi had turned at the last second. "If you aren't here in three minutes we will come find you."

Saint almost shivered. Dear lord, why was he just now noticing how scary his cousin could be.

After having yet another awkward conversation with Lola, he'd stepped into Gabi's office only to be completely blindsided by the very first question out of Alex's mouth.

"You want to explain to us why we just found out that our company is in charge of the renovation that kicked those kids out of their only homes and sparked the very protest we were at yesterday?"

Now here he was an hour and a half later and he was still nowhere near being done explaining. He'd tried to get them to understand that by helping El Hogar find a new place, they could make things right. He'd tried to tell them that he'd just been doing what their father had asked him to do, but that had opened him up to questions he couldn't answer about why. Thankfully, Tío Luís had arrived to save him from the reaming he'd been getting and had finally told his daughters about his diagnosis. Unfortunately, Eva had come with him, which added a whole other layer of tension to the situation as the sisters were still circling each other warily like a group of fencers.

"Papi, I just don't understand why you'd keep this from us," Gabi said.

Saint's phone vibrated in his pocket. It was probably Lola wondering where he was. He ignored it in the hope of not calling attention to himself.

Alex, always willing to be the blunt one, added, "You have a chronic illness that will affect your mobility and you run a construction company. How did you think this was going to go? Did you think we wouldn't notice until you were on-site using a motorized cart and one of those grabby things like a viejo at the grocery store?"

Tío Luís opened his mouth to reply, but Alex wasn't done.

His phone stopped buzzing only to start again. Lola was probably pissed and justifiably so. He slowly slid his hand into his pocket and started pulling his phone out.

"You always tell us how valuable we are to you and to Cruz and Sons, but when it came down to it you completely disregarded us. Instead, you put your faith in Saint. On top of that, you have him and everyone else hiding it from us like we are two fragile little girls who can't handle reality. Do you have any idea what a slap in the face that is? You might as well tell us to go to the kitchen and make you a sandwich."

The phone quieted right as he finally pulled it free of his pocket. Saint discreetly checked his screen. He had multiple missed calls. None of them were from Lola. They were all from Kamilah.

"Alex, I don't think he intended—" Eva began only to get cut off.

"Gabi and I are the ones here every day and we're the ones who've been here the entire time building his vision and following his plans, so we are the ones discussing the situation with our dad, not you."

"Alex, enough," Tío Luís began scolding, but Saint missed the rest because he read the latest of the flurry of texts he'd gotten.

ANSWER YOUR FUCKING PHONE!! I GOT CALLED TO EL COQUÍ!! LEO GOT SHOT!!

He exploded out of the chair, startling everyone. They asked him questions, but he was already gone. He was down the hallway, pulling up his brother's number as he went. The moment the call connected, he barked out, "Where?"

"He's at Humboldt Park Memorial. He was stopping your girlfriend and Rosie from being held at gunpoint."

Saint's heart stopped. His soul left his body. He hung up and took off running. He would never remember the frenzied drive to the hospital although he was sure that he broke many traffic laws on his way, including pulling up to the front of the building and parking in the pickup zone without giving a single fuck.

He raced into the emergency department waiting room, his eyes going immediately to Rosie. She was in Lola's lap curled up in a little ball, her face hidden as Lola smoothed a hand over her head over and over. The moment Lola saw him heading in their direction, she nudged Rosie and leaned to whisper in her ear.

Rosie's head snapped up and she looked in his direction. In a split second she was up and running to him.

He dropped to his knees and caught her, pulling her to his chest where his heart finally began beating again. His daughter wrapped her legs around him and kept pushing her face into his neck like she was trying to burrow into him. Her little body shook with the force of her sobs. Saint couldn't do anything but tighten his arms, close his eyes, and just feel her there. Words were beyond him and he was too full of rage to cry.

Someone had done this to his little girl. Someone had made her shake and tremble like this. Someone had caused her to cry so hard her tears were soaking his shirt. He would destroy them. He opened his eyes and found himself staring at a familiar pair of hips. He tilted his head up and looked at Lola.

"What happened?" he grit out.

"It all happened so fast," she said. "We were walking to my car and suddenly these guys were there. They wanted us to go with them." Her voice trembled like her body.

Saint was on his feet in a second pulling Lola into his arms too. She wrapped her arms around him and Rosie, effectively boxing her between them both. Rosie didn't seem to notice and if she did, she didn't mind.

He looked at the chair where Benny sat, then at the empty ones around them. "Where is everyone else?"

"Liam stayed at the restaurant with the police while Kamilah came with us. When we got here, Papo started having some chest pains so she had them take him back to get checked out. She's with him. No one else has gotten here yet."

Saint gulped. "Leo?"

"Leo woke up right before the ambulance arrived. He'd hit his head against the car when he fell and got knocked out."

"Cristian said he'd been shot."

"He was. In the shoulder. When they took him in the ambulance he was awake and talking, but we haven't heard anything since."

Before he could ask more questions the glass doors to the entrance opened and most of his immediate family came pouring in, his parents leading the charge, a look of desperate worry on their faces.

"Y Leo?" his mom asked, the wild look in her eyes showed him exactly what he'd looked like a few moments before. "Where is he? Where's my son?"

Saint could only shake his head. "I just got here. I don't know anything."

His mother dove in between him and Lola and pretty much snatched Rosie out of their arms. He almost said something, but he could see that Mami needed to hold Rosie in her arms to be assured she was safe, just like he had.

She started peppering Rosie's face with kisses as tears slid down her cheeks.

"Where's Kamilah?" Eddie asked. "She was with him."

"She's with Abuelo."

"What happened to Papi?" His dad looked shell-shocked.

"I guess he started having chest pains. Kamilah took him back so he could get checked out. That's all we know so far."

Eddie hustled Mami and Papi over to the nearest chairs and got them to sit. Moments later more family showed up and they had to answer the same questions over again. They passed Rosie around, kissing her head, embracing her, and thanking god she was okay. Saint never took his eyes off her, which was how he knew that through it all she didn't say a word.

Eventually they all settled into a tense silence.

After what felt like forever but had probably only been a few minutes, his dad threw his hands up in the air. "¡Puñeta! ¿Es que nadie aquí nos puede decir nada?"

Mami rubbed his arm distractedly.

The door to the treatment area of the emergency department opened and Kamilah walked out still in her chef whites. Everyone stood and rushed over, talking at the same time.

Kamilah had to raise her naturally loud voice to be heard. "Abuelo is fine. They say they are pretty sure it was just the adrenaline, but they are going to run all of the tests anyway. I'm sorry I didn't answer any calls. I think I left my phone in the ambulance. I can't find it."

Mami grabbed her hand. "Y Leo?"

Kamilah shook her head and shrugged in helplessness. "I tried to get information, but they wouldn't tell me anything. They just keep saying that they're treating him."

"I just don't understand," Eddie said. "If it was a robbery, why try to take them?"

"Because it wasn't a robbery," Cristian's voice said from behind them. They turned to see him standing there in his police uniform. Liam followed behind and bypassed them all to go to Kamilah, who had picked up Rosie and was rocking them both.

At his side Lola's body went as still as a statue.

A terrible thought popped into his head, but he brushed it off. There was no way. There was no way this had to do with Rafael León and thus Lola. There was no way she'd know it and not tell him so immediately.

"What do you mean it wasn't a robbery?" Tío Rico asked.

"It was an attempted kidnapping."

Kamilah gasped and tightened her hold on Rosie. "You mean." She stopped and looked down at Saint's daughter.

"No," Liam said, brushing a hand over Kamilah's head. "They were after someone else." He lifted his eyes and looked right at Lola.

Saint didn't think it was possible for her to go even more stiff.

"My partner called me," Cristian said. "They got one of the perps to talk. He said their orders were to get Lola at any cost."

He couldn't even imagine what they'd wanted her for. And to say that they were to take her by any means necessary. His daughter was with her. Rosie could've been hurt. She could've been killed.

Saint felt sick. This was all his fault. He should've never let her out of his sight. He shouldn't have let her get so close to Lola, not when he knew that the past could come for her at any time.

"Saint," Lola murmured at his side. "I'm sorry. I would never have put anyone in danger on purpose, especially not Rosie. You know that, right?" She squeezed his hand.

Saint turned to look at her. The woman he loved. The woman he'd welcomed back into his life with open arms. "Did you know they were still after you?"

"What?"

"You told me that your brother had revoked your privileges. This was why, wasn't it? Because you were still in danger and he was trying to protect you."

The guilt was written all over her face. "When I saw Guillermo Hernandez, he made some vague threats, but I didn't think—"

He shook his head in disbelief. "You didn't think that one of the most dangerous gang members the neighborhood has ever seen had the means to make good on his threat? You didn't think to tell me about this threat so I could be forewarned? You didn't think before you went wandering all around the neighborhood yesterday protesting with a bunch of innocent people including your friends and my family? You didn't think before you took *my daughter* out in public with you with only two old men as escorts?" he scoffed. "Of course you didn't think, because you're Lola León and you don't have to think. You just act because you already know everything, and whoever doesn't like it can fuck off. Right? Isn't that how you work?"

"That's not fair," she said.

"Fair? When you hid this from me and now I don't even know if my brother is alive right now?"

"I have never once hidden who I am or what I'm about from you. You have known that since we were teenagers."

"So now it's my fault that you lied to me, because I should've known better?"

"That's not what I—"

"You're right. I should've known better. It's like the story of the scorpion and the frog and I'm the gullible frog who put you on my back."

"And here we go. Super Saint is back thinking that if I'd told him about a threat, he would have been there to save me," Lola barked. "I don't know how many times I have to tell you that I don't fucking need you to save me."

"I'm not trying to save you, Lola. All I wanted was to be your partner, but you are so closed off it's impossible. You refuse to give even an inch. Everything is your way or no way. You're self-centered."

"I'm self-centered? How do you figure? I live my life fighting for the rights of others."

"I wonder why you really do it, Lola. Do you really feel that strongly about these causes, or is it you trying to prove that you aren't like your dad? Reckless, stubborn, power hungry, and selfish."

Lola sucked in a quiet breath. It was the only indication she gave that she was hurt. Her face looked carved from stone. "You told me that you loved me, but you lied. If you really loved me, you wouldn't constantly be trying to fix me." She shook her head. "If I am reckless and stubborn, it's only because I'm fighting for people and ideas I believe in. I am who I am. I'm not changing for anyone. Not even you."

With that she turned her back on him and walked out. Benny shot him a hateful look before he followed.

Saint plopped into the nearest chair and dropped his head into his hands. He'd failed yet again.

24

"Thank you for coming in on Memorial Day," Mrs. Fonseca told her. "I'm sorry our meeting on Friday got canceled. There was an incident I had to handle."

"Not a problem." Lola fought the urge to fidget in her seat. If the first time she'd been in here felt like stepping into the past, it was even more so now when Lola knew she was in trouble.

"I know this is your personal time, so I'm going to keep this as brief as possible." She met Lola's gaze. "I'm retiring this year."

"Congrats, you deserve it," Lola said, only mildly surprised. Fonseca had had a long career at the center, and she did deserve to retire after her many years of service to the community. She paused. "But that's not why I'm here, is it?"

Mrs. Fonseca linked her fingers together on top of her desk. "I'd hoped to put your name forward as my potential replacement, but I can't, in good faith, do that now."

Lola swallowed. She'd figured something like this was coming, but it hurt all the same. "Can I ask what made you change your mind?"

"There is no doubt about your passion and your qualifications, Lola. I understand that the circumstances weren't completely in your control. However, none of that changes the fact that your presence here has caused a clusterfuck of epic proportions and your continued presence could put our members and staff in danger."

"I get it. I'm a liability." Wasn't that basically what Saint had told her? All she did was put the people around her in danger with her history and her reckless actions. She wondered how much of that was valid. The truth was that even knowing there were people out to get her, she still wanted to stay. Maybe she was reckless. Selfish.

"I'm sorry, Lola."

Lola shook her head. "Don't be. You have this organization and everyone in it to think about and I was only thinking about me." She paused, waiting for Mrs. Fonseca to deny her selfishness. When she didn't, Lola knew it was true. "Look, I don't want parents to be even more scared to send their kids to school and I don't want to cause the staff more stress, so I think it's probably best if I remove myself from the long-term sub position and you find someone else to cover for the next few weeks."

"I think that is a sensible plan and I appreciate your consideration."

"Can I at least leave the kids a message? I don't want to just disappear like the last teacher."

"Of course, Lola, and if there is anything I can do to help you, let me know. I want to help you."

Lola thanked her because she knew Mrs. Fonseca was earnest in her desire to help, but Lola couldn't see herself getting a position anywhere at the moment. Not when her story, name, and picture were plastered all over the local news.

Lola walked to her classroom—no, the classroom she'd been serving. She thought of taking all of the items she'd purchased, but that didn't feel right. It felt like inflicting an unnecessary wound on the students, who'd already been through so much. Instead, she packed up any personal items she'd brought, recorded a video message for the kids in which she tried not to cry, and then left.

She had just made it to her apartment when her phone started ringing in her purse. She dumped everything on her couch and reached into her purse to find her phone. Lola figured it was Yara calling, but the number on her screen was Benny's apartment phone.

"Hola, Benny."

There was a long pause on the other end and lots of throat clearing.

"Benny?"

"Me llamaron de la prisión." Another long pause that had her holding her breath. "Murió tu papá."

Lola gave her head a shake as if dislodging something from her ear. She didn't know why she did that, since she knew she'd heard him clearly. Maybe it was because while she'd heard the words, "The prison called. Your dad died," she just couldn't understand them.

"What happened?"

"I don't know. They couldn't tell me anything. There's an investigation."

Lola was numb. She searched her heart for grief, but she honestly didn't know if she would ever feel it. Her father was gone, and she was sad that he had never lived a life worth living and she'd always regret the opportunities and potential he'd wasted, but grief was something different. Grief was what she could feel practically seeping through the phone. Her heart hurt for Benny. Her grandfather had loved his son, despite everything. "I'm so sorry for your loss, Benny."

"*Our* loss, Lola," he corrected.

Lola disagreed. She had lost her father years ago, probably before she was even born. In a lot of ways she'd already mourned that person, that relationship.

"He was a terrible parent and in many ways he was a bad man, but he was still as much your father as he was my son," Benny continued, his voice breaking on the word *son*.

It was then that Lola felt her eyes water.

"Mi niño bello," he choked out the words.

"Give me a few minutes. I'll be there as soon as possible, okay?"

It was a testament to how much pain he was in that he didn't even try to argue with her. "Okay. I'll see you soon. Te quiero mucho, mi leona."

"Y yo más, Abuelo." She hung up.

Saint sat in the uncomfortable plastic chair and stared at his brooding brother. He remembered so clearly the day his parents had finally brought Leo home a week after he'd been born. Saint had been with his grandparents, trying to help keep the two-year-old twins entertained when his parents had arrived. His papi came in first, carrying in all of the stuff from the hospital and the car seat. Then his mami had arrived looking tired, but happy. It was nice to see her that way after she'd been so sad before. In her arms was a wiggly bundle of blankets. She'd sat on the couch and called her boys over to meet their little brother, Leonardo. The twins had taken one look at him and left instantly to inspect the things their papi had brought in, which were way more interesting than the baby.

Saint sat next to his mom asking a ton of questions which she answered patiently. Leo had been at the hospital to finish growing a little more because he'd left her belly before he was ready. He'd had to sit under special lights so his skin wouldn't be yellow, get special medicine to make his blood stronger, and wear a special mask to help him breathe until his lungs got stronger. Saint told her that his brother was still too small. To which his dad replied, "He's tiny, but he's already tons of trouble." His abuela told Papi not to say that, because he'd give the baby bad luck.

Abuelo smiled at the awake and wailing baby and said, "It's too late. Some people are simply born too spicy and Leonardo is one of them."

Through the years his baby brother had certainly lived up to the prediction of being too spicy and troublesome. But nothing had prepared any of them for Leo to be once again in the hospital fighting for his life for a week.

When they'd first been told that Leo had been shot in the shoulder, Saint had hoped it wouldn't be serious. There are no vital organs there. But after listening to the many specialists and surgeons treating his brother, his family had learned the hard way that the shoulder contains the subclavian artery, which feeds to the brachial artery (the main artery of the arm) as well as the brachial plexus, the large network of nerves that control arm function.

The bullet that had struck his brother had broken his clavicle and damaged both the subclavian artery and the brachial plexus. The first week had been one of no sleep, frequent prayer, and constant worry that the emergency surgery Leo had undergone hadn't fully stopped the bleeding or he would get an infection. Then they'd spent week two learning about the surgeries still in Leo's future that would hopefully correct the nerve damage and allow him full function of his shoulder and arm. All that to say that Leo was still in trouble and would be for a while still.

And it was Saint's fault. He'd failed yet again to protect his family when they needed it most.

Leo's raspy voice pulled him out of his thoughts before they could spiral. "Stop staring at me like that." He skewered Saint with a glare. "Why are you still here anyway? I thought I told you to go mope somewhere else."

"I'm not moping," he lied. "Besides, if I leave, then Mami comes. Is that really what you want?"

"Point taken," he said with a stretch of his neck. Suddenly

he froze, even his breath, and his face went stark white. He was in pain.

Saint grit his teeth and fisted his hands. He hated seeing his brother like this, but he already knew better than to tell Leo to push the little button that would release additional morphine into the IV in his arm. His brother was being stubborn about using pain medication. "Not using the medicine they give you is preventing you from resting completely, you know."

"Being in the fucking hospital is preventing me from resting completely. They're in here bothering me every ten minutes."

Saint didn't reply to that because it was true if only a little hyperbolic.

As if to prove Leo's point, there was a knock on the door before it slid open and the nurse, a very familiar, middle-aged Afro-Latina, came in. "Leo, I'm here with your next dose of medication," Sofi's mother announced. Sofi's mom had been a trauma nurse for as long as they'd known her, so it hadn't been too much of a shock when she'd first come in to announce she was going to be one of Leo's nurses. They all knew that she was competent and a badass, so they were glad she'd been assigned to Leo. She was just the kind of nurse he needed.

"When do I get to leave?" Leo asked her irritably.

Just like her daughter, Alicia Santana was quick-witted. "When the doctors are sure that your artery won't reopen and cause you to bleed out," she replied, without missing a beat.

He harrumphed at that.

"Have you not slept?" she asked. "Are you hungry?"

"I'm not a crabby little kid," he responded, sounding like exactly that.

Alicia just gave him a look before going back to typing something in his chart on the computer that sat atop a rolling cart.

Leo scowled. "How come your daughter hasn't come to bother me?"

"Because I'm here to do it for her," Alicia said breezily while still typing.

Leo scoffed. "As if she'd ever let someone else have the pleasure of annoying the shit out of me for fun."

Alicia finished typing, clicked out of the program, and took a small cup over to Leo. "Sofi is not coming," she told him in a very clear and strong tone. "She is busy living her own life." She held out the cup with the pills.

Leo took out the two pills. "What life?" he sneered. "Sofi's life is boring as hell without me."

Saint frowned. He knew that Sofi and Leo frequently entertained each other in the form of constant bickering, but something about the way Leo phrased that gave him pause. Why would he specifically be the one who made her life interesting? If anything that honor would go to Kamilah, Sofi's actual friend. Saint looked closely at Leo but all he could tell was that he was annoyed and in pain. He was just trying to get a rise out of anyone and everyone. At least that was typical Leo behavior.

But Alicia didn't fall for it. She rolled her eyes as Leo placed the pills in his mouth. "I'll be sure to tell her you said that." She lifted his large cup of water from the bedside tray table and held the straw up to his mouth. Once Leo swallowed the pills she put the cup down and backed away. "Use the pain medication," she told him. "They gave it to you for a reason."

"I don't need it," Leo said.

It was her turn to scoff. "Not using it doesn't make you any stronger you know. Don't be an idiot. Use it."

"Your bedside manner is excellent. I can't wait to leave you a stellar review on your comment card."

"And I can't wait for you to sleep for longer than a half hour so you aren't an annoying little shit anymore."

"Now I see where your daughter gets it from."

"Yep. And I taught her to never suffer fools, especially foolish men who don't know what's good for them." She gave him a look that Saint couldn't interpret, but Leo seemed to, because he finally shut his mouth. "Take the meds and take a nap," she repeated before leaving.

Muttering to himself about bossy and annoying Santana women, Leo finally hit the button to release morphine into his system.

Saint let loose a quiet sigh of relief.

They sat in silence for a moment before Saint couldn't hold it in anymore. "Leo, I owe you two things."

"A sponge bath from a hot nurse who isn't Sofi's dragon of a mother and the fifty bucks I won for being right about the number of times Kamilah would cry?"

Saint shook his head. "First, I have to thank you. Rosie is my everything. She's the reason I live and breathe."

Leo scowled at him. "What are you doing right now?" he asked gruffly, although it was clear he knew the answer.

"Without you, things could've gone way differently. I cannot tell you how grateful I am to you. You saved her. You saved them all."

"Stop it," Leo growled, his eyes growing wet.

But Saint couldn't stop. "Which leads me to my second thing. I'm sorry," he choked out, his own eyes wet. "I should've been there. It's my duty to be there. To keep you all safe and I failed. At every single turn I failed and now you're paying the price."

"Shut up!" his brother yelled, startling him into silence. "You're not my boss and you're not my babysitter. I'm a grown fucking man and I make my own choices. I choose to put my life on the line for others every time I gear up and walk into a burning building, but I don't see you getting all upset over that. To be honest, that night I had made the choice to act even before I knew who it was, because I would've intervened for anyone in danger. So don't make it sound like I'm some sidekick that was forced to act because the superhero wasn't there, and don't use the consequences of my choice to beat yourself up. You can fuck all the way off with that shit."

Saint sat there.

"I mean fuck. First Kamilah. Now you. What is with this family's obsession with being martyrs?"

"You're right. I'm giving myself more importance than I really have."

"You are and don't even start on the 'If I hadn't gotten involved with Lola then none of this would've happened,' because you don't know that either. The world is chaos and we don't know what will set off anything."

"Are you really using the butterfly effect to win this argument?"

"No." He smiled. "Because I already won it with my sidekick slash superhero comment."

He had. But it was nice to see him smile even if it was only a flash of one. "Can I still tell you that I love you, you annoying little shit, or is that not allowed either?"

He grimaced. "I love you too," he mumbled under his breath. A moment later he spoke again using his normal voice. "When are you going to bring my favorite little person to see me?"

It was Saint's turn to grimace. "I don't think it's a good idea until you look a little better. Seeing you like this with all these machines might scare her even more."

He settled back into the pillows. "How is she?"

"Not good. She's pretty much stopped talking completely. She sleeps in my bed every night and wakes up crying multiple times. I've had to start using the bathroom with the door cracked while also talking or singing and I have to take ninety-second showers while she's sleeping, because she wants to be with me at all times. The only way I got her to leave my side today was to physically hand her off to Liam."

"Liam?" Leo's voice was smoothing out, signaling the beginnings of the drug's effects.

"Yeah. She clings to him like Saran Wrap whenever I'm not around. I think his size makes her feel safe."

Leo yawned. "And he's basically mute too."

"Inappropriate."

"You're right. Sorry."

"Anyway, Rosie's going to therapy twice a week, so hopefully we see some improvements soon."

"I hope so, because I'm not trying to listen to you sing 'Mary Had a Little Lamb' every time you have to take a shit." Leo blinked multiple times in a row.

It had been decided that upon his release from the hospital, Leo was going to stay with Saint since he couldn't stay alone and he refused to stay with anyone else who had the space for him. Saint couldn't exactly say he was looking forward to it. Leo had already proven himself to be a horrible patient, but he wanted to be the one to take care of him regardless. Maybe then this ball of guilt in his gut (justified or not) would dissolve.

"I'll leave any singing to you," he told his brother. He was surprised when his words seemed to cause Leo to pause. Singing had always come naturally to Leo. It had always been something he just did, singing since before he could even talk. All the worries the doctors had about Leo's underdeveloped lungs were a nonissue as soon as he'd begun belting out notes while listening to the boleros their abuela liked.

Before Saint could ask him what was going on, Leo said the one thing that could distract him. "Lola came to visit me yesterday," he forced out around another yawn.

"What? Why?"

"Because apparently you both have delusions of grandeur and like to think that you're responsible for the actions of others."

She'd come to apologize to his brother. "What did she say?"

"She said she was sorry that I was caught in the cross fire because she didn't take the threat seriously."

"You told her something similar to what you said to me?" He hoped Leo had least used more metaphors and fewer *fuck off*s.

"I told her that they would've come for her regardless and I'm just glad I was there to help her distract one guy while she took down the other."

"Wait. What?"

Leo looked at him in confusion. "Has no one told you?"

"Told me what?"

"Bro, your girl is like an action movie character. After I jumped at the first guy, she disarmed the other guy and beat his ass in the space of a minute. If she hadn't been so careful because of Rosie and the viejos being around, she probably could've taken both dudes out by herself." He took in Saint's face. "If you don't believe me, watch the video."

"There's a video?"

"Of course there's a video. Our building has at least three cameras back there, more if you include the Ring ones at the doors. Ask Cristian. I'm sure they pulled them for the investigation." Then Leo closed his eyes and finally fell asleep.

He wanted to, but he failed to see what difference it would make. His relationship with Lola was done either way. She simply didn't love him. She cared deeply about him—that he didn't deny at all. He knew that she cared deeply about Rosie too and even the other members of his family. Lola cared about many people and the many things that affected them, but that was as far as she was willing to go.

He couldn't blame her, not really. All her life she'd had to count on herself to fulfill her emotional needs, so that's what she did. She didn't trust anyone else to love and support her and that mistrust caused her to keep everyone at a distance.

It was like having a neighbor who was super friendly when he ran into them outside. They waved at him and stopped to chat.

They would talk, laugh, and share stories. They would even offer help with his car or advice about his garden. He invited them over to his house for cookouts or to watch the game, and they came and enjoyed themselves. He could almost think he and his neighbor were friends except they never once invited him into their house. In fact, all of the windows were blocked with thick curtains, they had security cameras all over the place, and their fence was six feet high with a hidden gate. As if once they entered their home, everything and everyone else ceased to exist.

That's what loving Lola León was like. She was never going to let him into her inner sanctum no matter how much he wanted to be there and tried to prove that he was worth the risk.

Their relationship was doomed from that point alone, but then there was the fact that Lola was fearless to the point of being reckless. She was so used to taking care of herself that when she factored consequences she only factored in ones she thought she could handle. She didn't make adjustments for the people around her who would be affected simply because she didn't account for them. It wouldn't be fair to say that they were nonentities, but they fell below everything else on her list of priorities.

Saint couldn't afford to not make the people around him priorities. He was a father, an older brother, a son, grandson, nephew, and cousin. He had a lot of people in his life who his actions affected. He was beginning to understand that he wasn't responsible for them all, but that hardly meant he could discount them completely. This was why he'd begun going to therapy, because he wanted to be a better man for them. One who wasn't constantly terrified of failure. He couldn't be with someone who refused to give an inch even if it meant allaying some of his fears.

He hated to admit it, but his abuelo Papo had been right. Saint needed someone who was going to be his partner and unfortunately Lola was too used to being a one-woman pride.

25

"I've been thinking about coming back," Lola threw out there just to see her mother's reaction.

Her mother was disappointed, as per usual. On the screen of her laptop she simply made a hmm sound and continued pruning her basil plant.

"Did you hear what I said?"

"Yes, Lola. I'm not that old yet."

At fifty-eight, her mom wasn't old at all. Because she took care of her skin, drank a gallon of water every day, had been mostly vegetarian for years, and exercised every morning, her mom could pass for someone much younger.

Lola couldn't even count the number of times they'd been asked if they were sisters. Many people commented on how alike they looked but always felt the need to specify that they were talking about their facial features as if Lola wouldn't know her much bigger body was different from that of her slim mother's. They were even more rude when they found out that they were in fact mother and daughter. They'd look between the two of them as if they just couldn't understand how her tiny mother had birthed such a large human. It made Lola want to stomp around and say, *I am an ogre!* Shrek style. *Judgmental Idiots.*

"You don't seem very excited by the idea," Lola couldn't help but point out.

Her mom finally gave the camera her full attention. "That's because I know you aren't really coming back."

"Why wouldn't I? It's not like I have anything here. I'm unemployed, single, I have exactly one friend who I haven't talked to in days because she actually has a life. Benny has told me multiple times that I'm annoying and to stop stalking him, so our relationship obviously worked better when I was on the other side of the country, and the one time I talked to Iván on the phone after dad died he made it clear that he still doesn't want me to visit him. It sounds to me like it's time for me to cut my losses." It wasn't even like she'd done the one thing she'd been determined to do, namely find a new El Hogar for the kids. Ruby and Marcus were staying with a cousin who'd stepped up after seeing them on the news, but it had been made clear that it wasn't a permanent situation. They still needed a real home. But the one building that could work was still too expensive for them to bid on even though it was in foreclosure. It was only a matter of time before some other scavenger, like Raven Realty, swooped in and snatched it up. Even if they did manage to buy it, they still didn't have the money to renovate. Lola was failing at life in a way she'd never experienced before and she couldn't help but think that this was a sign. "I made a mistake coming back to Humboldt Park."

Her mom didn't seem to agree, because she gave Lola the same pursed-lipped, raised-eyebrows look she always did when she felt like Lola was being extra. "You didn't. And I know you aren't coming back, because you have always wanted to be in Chicago. From the moment I dragged you out of there, you vowed to return. You may have lived here for longer, but San Diego was never home to you. It was just the incubator that kept you safe and allowed you to grow until you were ready to return to Humboldt Park." She tried to hide it, but the regret in her voice was noticeable. She'd always hoped Lola would want to stay in San Diego with her. Her mom loved it there, not that Lola blamed her. San Diego was gorgeous, the people were mostly chill, there was tons to do, and it had everything great California had to offer. It just wasn't home.

Plus, no matter that they'd spent years rebuilding their relationship, Lola and her mom didn't see eye to eye on many things and therefore there was always a distance between them. If Lola was honest, she knew that she was the one who kept that distance in place. They were just too different. Her mother was passive to the point of being a complete pushover and Lola couldn't stand it. They used to argue about things constantly, and by that she meant Lola would argue at her mom, who would just nod along. That would get under Lola's skin even more and cause her to argue harder. The circle went round and round until Lola would want to scream, "Stick up for yourself, dammit. Feel strongly about something for once!" She knew she wasn't being fair, her mother had been conditioned to react that way by years of abuse, but she just couldn't understand her continued passivity. Their relationship had actually improved a bit when Lola moved back to Chicago.

God, what did it say about her that all of her relationships worked better when she was far away?

"Mom, I'm sorry. All you've ever tried to do was keep me safe and make up for the shitty childhood I had and all I did was be a difficult pain in the ass."

Her mom shook her head. "Lola, you brought back good grades, spent most of your time volunteering, and I didn't even have to worry about you getting pregnant by accident because you dated only women in college. Anything else was minor."

"You've bailed me out of jail multiple times."

"That was because you were fighting for what's right."

"But—"

"Lola, I know we don't usually agree on how to do things, but I have always been proud of you. You're a force to be reckoned with and we need more women like you."

But am I too much?

It was a question that had played in her head since the night at the hospital. Saint had basically called her self-centered and unyielding. He'd told her that she didn't take anyone else's needs, wants, or feelings into account when it came to her decision-making and she would not give quarter even when faced with evidence that she should.

The truth was that she feared he was correct. Lola honestly wasn't sure that happiness was ever a goal she strived for. It didn't factor into her mission. Having been born into a world of constant combat, it seemed like her destiny was to always be fighting. She had been forged in battle. She had the tools and the training that others did not. Therefore it was her responsibility to use them for the greater good. It was her purpose. But what if it wasn't? What if there had been another path this entire time and she'd ignored it.

Did she even want to take that path? Was she so unsatisfied with the path she was on? What would happen to the people she was trying to help if she veered from this path?

Her mother's voice pulled her from her thoughts. "Lola, your phone is ringing."

"What?"

"Your phone."

It was Casa del Sol. "Fuck." She picked it up.

"Hi, Lola, it's Teresa. I'm one of the secretaries at Casa del Sol. I'm calling because we have an issue with your grandfather. He's perfectly fine," she rushed to say, "but we need you to come in."

"What did he do?" she asked, but she knew. One of them had finally gone too far in the prank war.

"He got into a fight with another resident."

Papo Vega. "Shit. Okay. I'm on my way." She hung up and looked to her mom, who just waved her off.

"Go," she said. "We'll talk later."

They said their goodbyes and Lola rushed out, uncaring that she was wearing nothing but a pair of sweatpants and a crop top with no bra.

She arrived at Casa del Sol and was shown immediately into a familiar conference room. It was empty so she sat to wait.

A moment later the door opened again and two people were shown in, but it was not the two troublemakers she'd expected. It was Saint and Rosie.

Upon seeing Lola sitting in the chair, Saint froze, but Rosie did not. She dropped her dad's hand and raced around the table so she could jump into Lola's waiting arms. She wrapped her arms around Lola's neck and squeezed with all the strength in her little arms.

Lola pulled her close and hugged her back. She hadn't realized until that moment just how much she'd missed the weight of Rosie's tiny body in her arms or the smell of her hair in her nose. She felt her eyes well, so she closed them. She pressed a kiss onto the side of Rosie's head and rocked them back and forth. "Hi, sweetheart. I've missed you too."

"Are you okay?" Her little voice came out muffled.

Lola leaned her head back and Rosie raised hers. She met Rosie's eyes and stared into them. The poor thing. She'd been worried about Lola. "I'm okay, amor. Those bad guys are both in jail."

"What about the other one, the one who sent them?"

Lola shouldn't have been surprised at the amount of information Rosie had gleaned from the conversations she overheard.

Kids were a lot smarter than people gave them credit for. "He's going to leave me alone now."

"How can that be?" The voice wasn't Rosie's but Saint's.

Steeling herself against the sight of him, Lola turned her head.

He'd sat across from her and was leaning forward with his arms resting on the table. He looked just as gorgeous as ever with those dark eyes and lush lips. But there were dark circles under his eyes, frown lines on his forehead, and an aura of stress pouring off him.

"He's lost interest in me." She looked down at the table. "My dad died, so there is no one to torture by hurting me."

"I'm sorry about your dad," his voice was low and soft, genuine.

"We didn't have a relationship so…" She trailed off.

"Sometimes that doesn't matter."

He was right. It didn't. Benny had been talking about her dad a lot lately. Telling stories Lola had never cared to hear before. It had given her a completely different side of her dad to consider. Like too many others he'd been a young man, full of promise, who'd been failed by society at every turn. At first he'd let the bitterness and anger cloud his judgment. Then he'd begun to get a taste of success and the power that had previously been denied to him and the means of obtaining it no longer mattered. Why would he adhere to or uphold a system that did nothing for him? It was a thought Lola had many times about her own life and the battles she chose to fight.

Once she was able to make that connection between his journey and that of so many other youths, including herself, she was able to look at it without the lens of her own trauma. She began to truly mourn his death because it meant that there was no hope for redemption for him or for their relationship. That loss of opportunity was what really hurt. She'd never get to talk to him and tell him that while she understood how he'd ended up where he did, his actions had hurt her. The possibility that he would reflect, own up to his failures, and apologize to her was now gone forever. It would be a wound that she continued to carry.

"How's Leo?" she asked, wanting to be done with the topic of her father.

"He's getting stronger. They're hoping to be able to do more work on his nerves soon."

The door opened and their grandfathers entered together which was weird enough. Even more odd was that neither one looked like he'd been fighting. Add to that the fact that Maria wasn't with them and Lola was instantly suspicious.

Saint must've been too, because he asked, "What's going on?"

Instead of answering, Papo looked at Rosie and said, "Teresa has an *Encanto* coloring book and some M&M's at her desk and she said she'd share with you. Why don't you go sit with her?"

Rosie was off Lola's lap and gone in a flash, and Lola thought she saw a look of shock on Saint's face.

Papo closed the door behind her. Both he and Benny sat.

"What is this?" Lola asked.

"An intervention," Benny said. "You two are being stupid and we are sick of it."

"And just when did you decide this?" Lola asked. "You two don't even like each other."

Papo shrugged. "He's not that bad for a miserable bully who doesn't know how to play dominó or let go of the past."

Benny shot Papo a dirty look then said in Spanish, "And I decided that, for your sake," he looked at Lola, "I can tolerate this insufferable and ignorant fool who tries too hard y siempre anda más perdido que un juey bizco."

Lola raised an eyebrow. "For me?"

Benny nodded. "Because you want to be with him." He pointed at Saint.

It was Lola's turn to shoot a dirty look. Who said she wanted to be with Saint? He was a judgmental asshat who thought he was better than her.

"I didn't think you liked me," Saint said to Benny.

"I didn't at first," Benny replied. "I thought you were only slightly less insufferable than your grandfather. Then I met your little girl and I decided anyone who was raising a kid like that couldn't be all bad. Plus, you make Lola happy. At least you did until you acted like an asshole and hurt her."

"Benny," Papo interjected. "We agreed to be nice."

Benny grumbled something and crossed his arms.

"At least for now," Papo continued. Then he looked down at the table and them. "Now, let's discuss all the mistakes you have both made in detail."

Lola groaned while Saint huffed out an angry breath like a bull.

Papo smiled. "Just kidding."

"But in a real sense we are not," Benny interjected.

"You both have the same problem," Papo said. "You both think you need to control everything and freak out when you can't."

"That's not true," Lola protested. At least it wasn't true about her.

Benny snorted. "Lola, nothing was ever stable for you growing up and you had no control of that. But you wrestled that control away the moment you could and since then you've had it in a choke hold. You won't give it up even for a second because you are terrified it will send you right back into chaos."

"Saint," Papo said. "From too young an age, we put you in control of things you had no business being in control of. We made you feel like everything and everyone was your responsibility and because you accepted it, we didn't examine what we were really doing to you. We were putting too much pressure on you and setting you up for failure, because, the fact is, no one can maintain control always."

"Things are going to go wrong and people are not ours to control," Benny added.

"Not even god tries to control people," Papo told them.

"We get it, we both have control issues," Saint said.

Papo nodded. "Sí, and those issues are preventing either of you from being a good partner to the other."

Benny looked to Saint. "I was…" he paused and corrected himself "…I am a lot like you. I have very firm beliefs about what is right and what is wrong and I fight to uphold those beliefs. I also think there is a right and wrong way to do things and look down on anyone who doesn't do things the way I think they should. My expectations are high, usually too high, and when people don't meet them I judge them for it, even if I don't mean to. Even worse, I expect the most from myself and beat myself up when I fail to uphold my own standards."

"I'm not like that," Saint protested, but there was uncertainty in his voice.

Benny ignored him. "Do you know what that constant judgment and pressure for perfection got me?"

Saint shook his head.

"Unhappiness. I chased my wife away, I ensured my son would resent me and keep me on the sidelines of his life, I made it so that anyone I could've called a friend rejected me, and my grandchildren didn't trust me to provide them with help and protection. I spent most of my life with only myself as company and I am my own bully. It's miserable."

"Oh, Benny," Lola whispered.

"Don't end up like me," Benny told Saint.

Saint dropped his head and stared at the table.

Lola wondered what was going through his head.

"And you." Papo was looking at Lola.

She sat rigid in her seat, sure that she was about to hear some harsh truths she wasn't ready for. Over the course of the last ten days she'd been doing a lot of thinking. She wondered about the truth in Saint's claim that everything she did was her attempt to prove she wasn't like her father. She was terrified that he was right and that Papo was about to prove it to her. She wanted to cover her ears and shout out *la, la, la!*

"You are a strong woman, una luchadora, like Joan of Arc. You fight for the people who are being treated unfairly by the people in power and you are good at it, but beware that you don't end up a martyr. No one has said that you have to sacrifice *everything* for the cause and not everything is a battle you must win. It's okay to compromise sometimes and you are allowed to take things for yourself. It doesn't mean you have lost and it doesn't take away from your devotion. It means you value the people in your life and are willing to do what you have to for them to be happy and for you to be happy too. Don't sacrifice your happiness."

Lola was stunned. Was that really what she was doing, sacrificing the things that made her happy in order to continue fighting without compromise? She was. She felt so strongly about the importance of what she was fighting for that she was purposefully forgetting that she was also important. She thought about what she would tell anyone who was doing what she was doing. She'd tell them that self-care wasn't selfish and that no one could pour from an empty cup. She'd remind them that they needed to enjoy life and appreciate the little wins. She'd remind them that it was okay to ask for and accept help. Yet here she was ignoring her own advice.

She felt like the biggest hypocrite.

Again, Lola asked herself what was more important to her. Did she want to be the selfless warrior her community needed or did she want to be happy? She stopped that thought in its tracks.

Why couldn't she do both? What was preventing her from being happy and continuing the work she loved?

The fact that what made her happy was Saint and Rosie, but the work she did made him unhappy.

It wasn't that he didn't support the causes or feel the same way about them as she did. Lola knew he understood the importance and he wanted to support her. The problem was that her way of doing things caused him to have literal panic attacks. It wasn't fair to put him through that just as it wasn't fair to expect Lola to give up fighting just to make him comfortable. They were at the same impasse. Lola knew there was a solution somewhere. She just needed some time to figure it out, because she was done feeling guilty for wanting to be happy. She was going to fight for her happiness and Saint and Rosie were key parts of that. She was no longer complete without them.

26

Saint was still sitting with his own revelation. He was a judgmental and delusional dick. His entire life he'd sat in this supposed knowledge that he was stronger, smarter, and more capable than others which was why they needed him. He'd honestly thought they needed his protection, his advice, his guidance in order to live their best life. When they proved that they didn't, he was offended by it. Who did that? Entitled assholes, that's who.

That was exactly what he'd done to Lola. He'd told her he wanted to support her, he'd told her that he loved her, he'd practically begged her to let him in. Then he'd spent the whole time judging how she did things, acting like he knew better than her, and trying to get her to do what he wanted. Of course she had kept things to herself and hadn't let him totally in. He'd proven that he couldn't be trusted with the most vulnerable parts of her.

He thought about what Benny had said. *I spent most of my life with only myself as company and I am my own bully. It's miserable.* Saint understood that all too well. How was it that he could have this inflated sense of importance, but be so insecure at the same time? His thoughts about himself were harsher than anything anyone had ever said to his face yet he thought he was the one who was going to fix everyone else's life. *Make it make sense.*

Here he'd been telling her that she didn't know how to be a partner, but neither did he.

He looked over at Lola. She was looking back.

God, she was so beautiful. Just seeing her molten penny eyes and that spray of cinnamon across her nose and cheeks made him feel centered. Until that moment, he'd been like this spinning-top toy that Rosie had where the players use rip cords to launch the top and send it spinning. He'd been spinning wildly until he locked eyes with Lola and realized what he had to do.

He wanted to apologize to her right then and there, promise to do better, and ask her to give him another chance. But he'd learned that apologies were worthless without actions to back them up. He had to prove that he could be the partner she needed and that he could be trusted with her heart and the rest of her soft spots. He knew exactly what to do, but he'd need some help to do it.

Saint shot out of his chair. "I'll be back."

He didn't miss the frown on Lola's face. He knew if he opened his mouth again, he'd word vomit everything in his head before it was time. He held her gaze for another moment, praying that she understood what he was saying. *Soon.*

Then he turned and strode out of the room. He left Rosie at the front desk and stepped out of the front door. As soon as it closed behind him, he picked up his phone. The moment the person on the other side answered he said, "Hey, it's Saint. Can we talk? I need your help."

"You need my help?" Eva sounded both surprised and suspicious.

"Yes, you're the only one who can help me."

"I'll do my best. What's up?"

"I know you aren't supposed to talk about the secret project, but I have a question for you."

"Okay…"

"This guy you're working for, is he in charge of everything?"

"Yes. He's the main investor, the writer, the lead, everything. I mean, he has people to help, but the buck stops with him."

"And he wants to keep this completely under wraps?"

"Yes."

"How do you think he would feel about owning the building you do the production in?"

"What?"

Saint rushed to explain. "There's a building in the neighborhood that has a small theater on one side and an old clinic on the other. The clinic is a perfect base for a new shelter for unhoused teens, but it's too expensive for the community center to buy and renovate the building. If your guy bought it and rented the other space to El Vecindario then we could fix it for the shelter. He could restore the theater at the same time under the guise of it being for the community center, but really it's so that he doesn't have to risk anyone finding out about his production."

There was nothing but silence on the other side of the line.

"This guy, isn't he from Chicago?" Saint continued.

"He is."

"You don't think he'd want to do something for his hometown?"

She sighed. "I honestly don't know, Saint. I've known him for a while, but I still don't really know him, you know what I mean? He's very private."

"I get it. I need to get the final okay anyway, but would you be willing to just reach out to him, see if he'd be up to meeting with us? Tell him that if he wants us to, we'll sign NDAs."

"Okay. I have a meeting with him later this week, so let me

know ASAP if you want me to broach the subject. I'll tell you what he says."

"Thank you so much, Eva. You have no idea how much I appreciate it."

"I've heard that this is what family is for, so I figured I might as well give it a try."

They said their goodbyes and Saint hung up. He spun on his heel and rushed back into the building.

"Papi, what are you doing?" Rosie asked around a mouthful of candy. She was sitting on Teresa's lap with a colored pencil in hand. Saint was still surprised by the change that had overcome his daughter the minute she'd been back in Lola's presence. It was as if the lingering fear and uncertainty had fallen right off. As if she'd just needed Lola to tell her that everything was okay. The obvious love between them made Saint even more determined to do what he needed to.

"I'm being the kind of man I want to be, by keeping my promises."

He practically ran down the short hall to the conference room. He threw open the door and was instantly relieved to see Lola still sitting there.

"What was that about?" Abuelo Papo asked.

Saint didn't take his eyes from Lola. "I have an idea for El Hogar."

She narrowed her eyes at him.

"I'm not trying to be the hero, I promise. I just wanted to talk to Eva to see if it was even a possibility before I told you and let you decide if we move forward. The ball is in your court."

She still looked suspicious. "What's your idea?"

Saint filled her in on everything he discussed with Eva. When he stopped talking, Lola just sat there.

He was moments from losing all hope.

Finally she opened her mouth. "I mean we'd definitely need

to run this past Yara, who'd need to talk to Fonseca and I'm sure we'll need a more formal plan with actual terms and stuff, but I think it could work."

"Well, Eva has a meeting with him later this week, so, if we want her to talk to him about it, we better get working."

"Why are you doing this, Saint?" she asked. It was clear from her tone that his answer would determine whether or not she gave him the chance to help.

"Because I said I would help you and I want to follow through, but this time there are no strings attached. As a matter of fact, after setting everything up with Eva, I'll remove myself from the equation completely. This will be all you. Well, you and Yara." He held his breath, willing her to tell him that she didn't want that, she wanted him to do this with her.

Lola was once again quiet for a long stretch. "I should call Yara. If she agrees, I'll let you know. Anything else we can discuss after."

Saint's shoulder dropped. "Yeah. Right. Okay. Just let me know."

She stood. "I will." Then she left.

There was a beat of silence before Benny spoke in Spanish. "You realize that at no point did you tell her how you feel, right?"

Fuck.

27

Lola swung the door open to the small conference room in El Centro that she, Yara, and Saint had been using for the last week. "Why aren't you ready to go?" she asked Yara as she burst in. "We're supposed to meet them there in thirty minutes!"

Standing on the other side of the table wearing a cute but totally casual denim jumpsuit and colorful headscarf, Yara did not look ready for a business meeting with a former pop star. Lola looked down at her own outfit, which consisted of black high-waisted trousers, a strapless bustier-type top, and a white blazer. She'd second-guessed herself a million times before determining that it was businessy enough, but here Yara was looking like 2002 JLo. "You look good, as always, but that is not the vibe we discussed."

"Hunnie, I create the vibe not follow it," Yara said. She motioned to the table. "Have a seat for a second."

"We don't have a second," Lola exclaimed. "We gotta go."

"We have enough time for this. Trust me." She motioned to the table again, before sitting on the opposite side.

With an impatient huff, Lola plopped down. "What's up?"

"I don't know how to say this, so I'm just going to jump in."

Lola's stomach dropped. Did anything good ever come after the words, "I don't know how to say this"? She doubted it.

"Fonseca offered me the position of director and I accepted it. Starting next month I'll be the director of El Vecindario."

Lola squealed. "Oh my god, Yara! That's amazing!" She hopped up and rushed around the table where Yara met her and they hugged. "Congratulations. I'm so happy for you. I can't imagine a better person for the job."

"Are you sure? I know Fonseca had been hoping to put you there."

Lola immediately shook her head. "No. I've been gone too long. I need to pay my dues and reconnect with this neighborhood before I'm anywhere near ready for something like that. You have dedicated your life to this place. You deserve this."

Yara beamed at her. "Have I told you yet how happy I am that you're back?"

"Not today."

"Well, I am."

"Me too."

Yara waved her hands. "Anyway, back to what I was saying."

"There's more?"

"Duh." Yara pulled out the chair and sat back down.

Instead of going back to the other side of the table, Lola took the chair next to her.

"As you can imagine, this means that I'll no longer be the director of El Hogar."

Oh right. There was no way Yara would be able to do both. She often wondered how Fonseca was able to have enough time for one position. "I think Mariana would be a great replacement," Lola suggested. "They are so passionate about the shelter."

"I was actually thinking of someone else."

"Who? Brittany? I don't think she'd want to leave teach— Did you just roll your eyes at me?"

"I did and I'm going to do it again. Watch." Yara gave her a magnificent and prolonged eye roll.

"That's mean and unnecessary."

"What's unnecessary is you completely missing the point here." At Lola's continued silence and confused expression Yara scoffed. "I mean you, mensa."

"Me?" Lola asked. "But I'm too dangerous. My past—"

"Your past is just that, your past. I respect Fonseca's decision to put distance between you and the center. There clearly was a target on your back, and that could have endangered our members. But things have changed since your father died, and anyway, do you know how many of the kids we serve come from the same background as you do? Should we turn them away because of their parents' choices?"

"Absolutely not."

"Then why would I do that to you?" Yara reached over and grabbed Lola's hand. "I have plans for El Vecindario and to accomplish them, I need people on my team that I can trust. I trust you with every fiber of my being and I know that you are the best person to take over my role. That's why I'm making you go to this meeting without me."

Anything warm and fluffy Lola had been feeling at Yara's praise flew straight out the window. "What? I can't go to this meeting alone."

"You won't be alone. Saint will be there."

"But he's only coming because his cousin is the one who organized this and he wants to be available to answer any renovation questions. He already said that we are the ones in charge."

Lola still wasn't sure how she felt about this change of his. Of course, she loved the fact that he'd finally realized that he didn't always know best and he was working on being supportive. However, she didn't know where exactly they stood. Were they just working together for the sake of El Hogar? Were they friends? Did he still have any feelings for her? In the last two weeks he had given her exactly zero hints.

"*You* are the one in charge," Yara countered. "I have every faith that you will kill this meeting. You'll Krav Maga the shit out of this."

"But—"

"No buts," Yara told her firmly. "As the new director of El Hogar, this is on you now."

"I haven't accepted the position," Lola pointed out.

Yara snorted. "Don't make me roll my eyes at you again. We both know that you'll take the job."

Lola fought the urge to grumble that Yara didn't know her like that. Mostly because Yara did in fact know her like that. Lola was totally taking the job. There was really nothing else she could envision herself doing.

"Besides," Yara continued. "I've had a huge crush on Chord Bailón since forever. I know I would make an ass out of myself and probably jeopardize my relationship, so really you're saving my pride and my marriage by going without me."

It was Lola's turn to roll her eyes. "Yeah. I'm such a great friend."

Yara smiled. "You truly are." She clapped her hands loudly. "Now get out of here, before you're late and make our organization look bad."

Lola popped out of the chair with a look at her friend. "I can't stand you." She grabbed the folders off the table and turned to leave.

Yara smacked her on the ass. "Love you too, Boo Boo."

"That's sexual harassment," Lola called as she rushed out the door.

"Sue me!" Yara yelled back.

Lola practically ran to her car, not an easy task in four-inch heels, and raced to the theater where she was meeting the rest of the group. Luckily there was a parking lot attached to the property, so Lola didn't have to try to find a space along the busy street. She pulled up next to Saint's truck and a black SUV with tinted windows. Shit. Everyone else was already there.

She threw her car in Park and jumped out. She sped to the front of the building, yanked open the huge, heavy, gilded front door, and stopped at the sight of the two men standing in the old but still opulent lobby.

Her attention should have gone to the rich, famous, and incredibly good-looking man she was supposed to shmooze. Instead it locked onto the person it always did whenever he was in her vicinity.

Saint stood tall and impossibly sexy in a pair of navy blue pants, a white-and-blue-striped button up with the sleeves rolled up, and a cognac belt and shoes. He looked like the cool guy at the office that everyone else drooled over. She kind of wanted to ask him to bend her over a desk.

Of course, there was no desk in this scenario. Only a big dilapidated building that she was going to try to bamboozle a hermit millionaire into buying for her.

"Lola!" Rosie called, appearing from one of the side hallways and running toward her.

Alex followed behind her.

Rosie threw her arms around Lola's hips and squeezed as much as she could even though her tiny arms barely spanned the width.

"Hey you," Lola said, giving the little girl a one-armed hug. "I didn't expect to see you here." She was a bit shocked that Saint had brought her considering the state of the building.

"Prima Alex was supposed to watch me, but since she told Papi that there was no way she was staying behind he had to bring me too."

"Well, you know I'm always happy to spend time with you. Just make sure you stay close to us and are careful where you walk."

Rosie slipped her little hand into Lola's as if it were the most natural thing in the world. "I know. Papi already told me." She turned her attention to the group standing at the base of the grand staircase.

Right. Time to get this show on the road. Lola walked over to them. "Hello. Sorry I'm a bit late. A situation arose at the community center and my colleague Yara couldn't make it."

"No problem. You're right on time."

Lola would've immediately recognized Chord Bailón even if she hadn't already known it was him. He looked so similar to his younger self except now he had facial hair and was buffer than his teenage counterpart. Same dark eyes, same deep dimples, and ridiculously straight white teeth. The main difference was in his aura. Where before he'd had this goofy, fun-loving, and camera ready persona, everything about him now screamed "leave me alone." Which was exactly why she was glad that both of her hands were occupied, leaving her unable to shake his. Not that he'd held one out to her. Nope. His hands were firmly in the pockets of his tattered jeans.

Lola quickly took in the rest of his very casual outfit. "I don't know why, but I suddenly feel overdressed," she blurted like an idiot then winced. *Way to make a good first impression.*

"You look great," Alex told her. "Most people dress up when they have a business meeting." She gave a very brief but significant look in the pop star's direction.

Saint elbowed her in the side and gave her a "shut it" look.

Lola was sure the man thought he was being inconspicuous, but he was not.

"We can't all pull off baggy overalls, dusty work boots, and messy buns," came Chord Bailón's very dry rejoinder.

"One of the many perks of working for my money," Alex tossed back without hesitation.

Saint jumped in. "Alex, there's an ice cream place down the street. Why don't you take Rosie there and get her a scoop? I don't really want her wandering around here with us."

Alex either didn't catch on to the command or ignored it completely. "I don't know, Saint. As one of the Cruzes in Cruz and Sons, I think I should be here to discuss the potential renovation."

"Cruz and Sons, but with all daughters," Chord Bailón mused aloud as he eyed Alex.

Lola didn't know how she managed it, being barely tall enough to reach the man's shoulder, but Alex raised her chin and looked down her nose at him. "Seems my big sister has been a real Chatty Cathy."

"Alex, I agree with Saint," Lola cut in. "Rosie shouldn't be in here with us. We know which areas are safe to walk on, but the main concern is the air quality and the masks I brought are too big for her face."

"Fine," Alex said, finally grasping that she'd be more helpful where she couldn't antagonize the man they were trying to woo. "Come on, Rosie." She held out her hand to the little girl. "Choosing ice cream over work seems like the perfect way to spend the day."

Rosie grabbed on to Alex's hand and they turned to leave.

"Get her a miniscoop," Saint said.

"Nope," Alex replied over her shoulder. "You asked me to take her, so now everything else falls under my jurisdiction and we're about to eat our weight in sundaes. Right, Rosie?"

Of course the newly five-year-old was one hundred percent down with that plan and vigorously nodded.

The doors closed behind them and the three of them let out audible sighs of relief. Lola knew why she and Saint were relieved, but she wondered about Chord Bailón. She didn't get to muse for long though, because Saint jumped in.

"I'm sorry about that. My cousin is dedicated to her father's company and can be a bit intense."

Chord Bailón turned his attention from the door and placed it on her. "You represent the community center, correct?"

Lola couldn't help the butterflies she felt in her stomach. He had such a strong presence that she doubted there was a human alive who wouldn't react to it. She gulped. "Yes."

"You'd like to use the other side of this building for a homeless shelter for teens."

Lola nodded and then jumped into her pitch. "El Vecindario has served the community for nearly—"

Chord Bailón cut her off. "What about the noise?"

Lola blinked, confused. "I'm sorry?"

"If this side becomes a functional theater, there will be noise late at night. I'm not going to curb the normal operations of a theater to accommodate these kids' bedtime."

Really? That's what he was thinking? She couldn't help but think that this was a huge mistake. Her thoughts must've been clear on her face, because Saint jumped it.

"We will obviously take soundproofing into consideration during renovation. We've already talked about having the bedrooms at the far side of the building with the lesser used rooms for both the theater and shelter in the middle." Saint motioned to the stairs. "Should we take a look around, so we can tell you a bit more about our plans?"

He shook his head. "I toured the building yesterday. It needs a lot of work, which we both know will cost an exorbitant amount of money."

Lola felt her hopes dashing. He wasn't going to do this. He was too cold and unfeeling. He was going to turn them down flat. "I understand, Mr. Bailón—"

"Why are you doing this?" he asked.

Lola's irritation spiked. This man had but one more time to interrupt her before she gave him a piece of her mind, superstar millionaire or not. "These kids deserve a safe place. Not just a place to sleep, but to be their true selves and be surrounded by people who will accept them and build them up. I will do whatever it takes to provide that for them."

He didn't react to her at all. He simply turned his attention to Saint. "What about you? You work for the contractor not the community center, why are you doing this?"

Lola winced inwardly. She didn't think Chord Bailón was going to feel moved by Saint's desire to make up for the Raven Realty project.

The side of Saint's lip curled. "Love," he said. "I gave it up seventeen years ago to fight for a country that doesn't love me or those I care about. It left me disillusioned, lonely, and unable to feel hope. Then Lola showed back up." He looked at her with such raw emotion on his face that she couldn't help reaching over and gripping his hand.

He squeezed her hand. "I have watched her pour her love into everyone around her over and over again. She's done that for the teens and staff at El Hogar, she's done it for my daughter, and she's done it for me. She considers everyone in this neighborhood a loved one and she will go above and beyond for them. She made me open my eyes and look beyond myself and my family." He looked back at Chord Bailón. "You want to know why I'm here, it's because of her. She inspires me to be a better human being, the type who doesn't just show up in times of need, but every day."

Lola's heart lit up like a shooting star. So many people only saw her as a difficult troublemaker. Someone who was never happy and always trying to rock the boat. To know that Saint, of all people, understood her motivations and was inspired by her...

well, it touched a place inside her that no one ever had. Saint had always been able to reach her like no one else. He knew her better than just about anyone, the good and the bad. She loved that he'd never shied away from either. "Saint," she whispered, emotion making her throat tight.

Saint looked ready to pull her into his arms, but a loud throat clearing brought them both back to reality. Right. There was a musical superstar standing next to them waiting for them to explain why he should spend his money on their project. She'd forgotten about him.

They turned to look at Chord Bailón, who stood next to them with his phone in his hand. He looked as serious and as distant as he had the whole time.

She wondered what the hell had happened to him that not even witnessing two people bare their hearts could break his stoicism.

"When I begin a project, I give it my all," he said. "I need to know that those involved are in it for the right reasons and will do the same." He waved his phone around. "I just texted my lawyers. They're going to put in an offer for the building and draw up a rental agreement for the community center."

Lola was shocked. "Wait. What? You're going to do it? You'll buy the building and rent part of it to El Vecindario?"

For the first time his emotionless facade cracked and his lips quirked the tiniest bit. "You may be the only person I've ever met who is more intense than I am, and I mean that in the best way possible."

She could only stare, dumbfounded. "Uh. Thanks."

"We'll be in touch," he told them before shoving his phone in his pocket and swaggering away, no handshake or goodbye.

The moment he was out the front door, Lola spun to face Saint. "We did it!" she exclaimed.

"We did." He let out a laugh of disbelief.

He turned to her. "I love you, Lola León, and I want to be with you, but I want you to know for sure that I'm going to support you in everything that you do. I will never again make you choose between being with me or doing what you need to do. Your goals are now my goals. Your fights are my fights. I will be at your side on the frontlines."

She shook her head not in disagreement but in amazement that he was willing to do this for her. "Saint, I want to be with you too, but I don't want you to always be afraid for me and I don't want you to put your own mental health at risk to be at my side. I will never stop fighting for what I believe in, but I know now that I don't have to lead the charge in the field, ready and willing to burn everything to the ground. There are other ways to fight and I want to try them."

"Lola, I know how much being out there means to you and I can't tell you that I won't worry, but I'm working on it. I've started therapy and I plan to keep going."

"I love that, but I need to show you that I'm willing to be a true partner to you too and that means compromise. I'm going to work on strategically dismantling oppressive systems without a battering ram and flamethrower."

"Unless you really have to."

"Unless we both agree that I really have to. Together."

"Together. I love the sound of that."

For the first time in a very long time, Lola felt hope. She might just get everything that she never thought she could have but always secretly wanted. She smiled at Saint and he smiled back, a huge unguarded smile that raised the apples of his cheeks and caused his eyes to crinkle in the corners. She hadn't seen that smile since they were teens and in that moment she realized just how much everything had weighed on him. Her eyes began to water. She never again wanted him to carry such a heavy burden alone. "I love you, Saint. You are completely selfless and brave and I am in constant awe of the way you love the people in your life without limits."

There was a second of quiet happiness and relief between them, before Lola launched herself at Saint, unable to hold back anymore.

He caught her as if he'd been waiting for it and in moments they were wrapped around each other as tight as they could be. Saint's arms banded around her back and clenched.

Pain, like scraping sunburn and poking a bruise, shot across her back. Lola hissed at the soreness.

Saint immediately released her. "What happened? Did I hurt you?"

"It's okay," she soothed. "My back is just a bit sore."

"Did you get hurt? How?"

Lola figured it would be better just to show him, so she slipped her arm out of her blazer and turned as it slid down to reveal her surprise. She knew the second he saw what caused her tenderness, because the silence became weighted and heady.

A finger brushed over her new tattoo as soft as a butterfly wing. Lola shivered but this time it was in pleasure.

"You finished the tattoo."

"I did."

"Tell me about it."

Lola pictured it in her head. The previously incomplete lioness was now fully fleshed out to the point that she looked ready to jump off Lola's shoulder blade, but that wasn't all. "I think the roses speak for themselves." Colorful roses of various sizes encircled the lioness's head from ear to ear, making it look like she was peeking out of a rosebush.

"Rosie," he whispered.

She nodded.

"And the sun?"

Golden yellow lines spread up and out like a sunset haloing the lioness's head. "It's not technically a sun."

"It's not?"

"It was really hard to find a way to represent you, Saint. Thankfully, I remembered when we met. You told me Santiago actually means Saint James, the patron Saint of Spain. You were very proud of that for some reason."

Saint groaned in embarrassment. "I was such a dork."

Lola laughed, "Yeah, but a cute dork."

He groaned again. "Finish telling me about your tattoo." Another brush of fingers.

"Well, I figured there had to be a symbol or something to represent 'Santiago' and I discovered his emblem is a scallop shell."

"A scallop shell? Really? It's not something cool like a snake?"

"Sorry. I'm pretty sure that's Saint Patrick. He's the one who scared all of the snakes out of Ireland."

"Hmm, so how did a shell become a sun?"

"That's the stylized shell used to represent the Camino de Santiago. Remember you also told me about the route used by believers to make the pilgrimage to the Cathedral of Santiago de Compostela in Galicia?"

"Why do I find this long explanation so fucking sexy?"

"Because, as we've previously discussed, you're a dork."

"Probably." He turned her to face him, his brown eyes warm. "Now tell me why you added roses and a saint's emblem to your tattoo. I know you didn't do it for me."

He was partially right. Lola had gotten it for the same reason she got her other tattoos, because it meant something so important to her that she needed to express it somehow. Even if it was just for herself. However, she also hoped that he'd see it and understand the true meaning behind it. "You know why," she murmured.

"Tell me anyway."

"Because you and Rosie make me feel whole, not alone. With you two, I have a real pride, a family."

He rewarded her honesty with a kiss that was somehow deeper and more intense than all the rest. It zinged all over her body until it landed securely in her heart, spreading a sweet warmth to all her limbs, like slipping into a bath. It surrounded her surely as his arms did.

"I love you both so much." She spoke against his lips. "I love Rosie and I love you. You're my very own patron saint."

"That's blasphemy," he said, but he smiled against her mouth.

"Ask me if I care."

"Of course you don't. You're Lola León. You make your own rules."

"Damn straight." Lola marveled that this man knew her so well, loved her so well, and he was hers to keep.

EPILOGUE

"Oww! ¡Coño! That hurts."

"Do it again anyway."

Papo Vega looked up from the half-completed coloring page featuring a picture of the "Be Our Guest" scene from *Beauty and the Beast*. He examined his grandsons.

Leo was currently growling at Saint, who was leading him through one of his many shoulder exercises. "This is fucking bullshit. This is supposed to make me feel better, not worse."

"Watch your language around my daughter," Saint said with more patience than Leo probably deserved at that point.

Rosie's head popped up at the mention of her and she gave her uncle a pitying look.

Leo had been staying with Saint and Rosie ever since his release from the hospital and it was clear that everyone was ready for him to go home. His funny and lighthearted grandson had been replaced with a bitter and angry asshole, for lack of a better word. He was difficult to be around and snarled at everyone like the beast he was beginning to resemble. Everyone was letting him get away with it too, because he'd been shot. More so because he'd been shot protecting the family (although Papo still hated to call that asshat, Benny, family).

But what the family couldn't see was that Leo didn't want to be babied or treated like a hero. That was why, the more they ignored his behavior, the worse it became.

That was also why Papo refused to tiptoe around him. "When are you going to shave your face and cut your hair?" he asked Leo. "You look like a werewolf who got stuck in the middle of changing."

"Better than looking like the Crypt-Keeper from *Tales from the Crypt*," Leo shot back.

"How dare you? I still have all of my hair."

"*That's* your problem with what he just called you?" Saint shook his head.

"Who's the Crypt-Keeper?" Rosie asked.

"Don't worry about it," Saint told her before anyone else could chime in.

"Yeah, I'll show you later," Leo said.

Saint gave him a death glare and Leo glared right back.

"You must really want the other side of your clavicle broken," said a voice from behind them all.

Everyone turned just as Lola stepped fully into the kitchen and pushed the door closed behind her. Even though she moved quickly the humid air had rushed in reminding Papo that it was the hot and muggy beginnings of summer, which also probably contributed to Leo's mood.

"Saint isn't going to break my other shoulder. He's my over-protective big brother."

"I meant me," Lola said. Sashaying up to Papo and giving him a kiss on the cheek while never taking her eyes off Leo. "Show Rosie anything *Tales from the Crypt* related and I'll be the one breaking your other shoulder."

Okay, so maybe not everyone tiptoed around Leo.

"Saint, you're going to let her talk to me like that? I'm your baby brother."

Saint scoffed. "As if I *let* her do anything."

Lola placed a quick kiss on Saint's mouth. "Good answer."

Papo was happy that Saint had someone like Lola in his corner. She was everything that he needed and he was the same for her. They both needed a partner who wouldn't be plowed over by their strong personalities and stubborn streaks. It wasn't that they brought the best out of each other, but they had the ability to take those best parts and laser focus them into building something lasting together. And the way they both loved Rosie. No stranger would ever look at the relationship between Lola and Rosie and think, "evil stepmother." If anything, Lola was a mama bear and treated the little girl as if she were her flesh and blood.

It had only been a few weeks, but every day Rosie got better and so did Saint. They were less anxious and more flexible when it came to changes. Lola's mother, Xiomara, was on her way for a prolonged visit and instead of freaking out about where the woman was going to stay, Saint had nonchalantly told Lola to move in with him and let her mother stay in her apartment, a suggestion that just a few weeks ago would've had him second-guessing everything.

They were really building their little family unit and Papo was so glad to have played a part in pushing them together. Sure, his plan this time around was a lot more subtle than outright blackmail, but these two were warriors. If he would've pushed too hard, they would've fought back with everything they had. No, getting these two together required skill, finesse, and strategy, like guerrilla warfare.

"Abuelo Papo?"

"Sí, mi Rosita?"

"Why is Tío Leo in such a bad mood all the time? He used to be more fun."

"Well, he's going through a lot right now. He's never liked sitting around for a long time, but he has to because he's still recovering from his surgery. That also means that he's in a lot of pain, which can make people crabby. Plus, they told him that he probably won't be able to be a firefighter anymore and he loved his job. Can you see now why he'd be in a bad mood and not fun?"

Rosie used the purple crayon to color in the wall. "I think he misses Tití Sofi."

"Tití Sofi?" Now what on earth could Sofi have to do with Leo's mood? Usually all they did was fight constantly.

"Yes." She paused in picking up a crayon. "Can I tell you my secret and you won't tell?"

Papo's curiosity instantly peaked. "Of course, mi Rosita. You know how good I am at keeping secrets. I never told your papi about the cookies, did I?"

"That's because you ate more than me." She colored in a spoon.

That was true, but he still wanted to know. "Tell me or the next time you come to visit me I won't give you any of my secret stash of Hot Cheetos."

"Fine." She let out an annoyed huff, sounding just like her dad. "A lot of days ago me and Tío saw Tití Sofi with a guy at Starbucks. Tío said a lot of bad words. He was in a really bad mood." Rosie picked up another crayon and started to color in a dancing plate. "After she kissed the man goodbye, Tío Leo went up to her and they argued." She colored in another plate. "He told her that he couldn't believe she was on a date with someone else. She told him that she was done with all of us Vegas and told him not to call her anymore." She switched out crayons. "Then he bought some Starbucks and told me that if I kept everything a secret he'd buy me something else too. We went to the store and he got me this coloring book, but he was still in a bad mood."

Papo picked up a blue crayon to color in the frosting on a cake, but he didn't pay too much attention to what he was doing. He kept thinking about what Rosie had just revealed. Leo and Sofia. Sofia and Leo. Papo thought back to all the times they'd swiped and snapped at each other. He'd said that he couldn't believe she was dating *someone else*. She'd told him not to call her *anymore*. Suddenly he saw their constant fighting not as passive-aggressive play, but as a distraction tactic, like a magician who used exaggerated hand gestures with one hand to distract the audience from what his other hand was doing. Hmm. His lips curled into the smile. It looked like he had his next project. He just had to find her first.

★ ★ ★ ★ ★

ACKNOWLEDGMENTS

In all my years working toward being a published author, I never stopped to think about how completely nerve-wracking writing the acknowledgments would be. I don't know that I have sufficient words to express my gratitude to everyone who helped make my dream a reality, but I will try my very best.

To my phenomenal agent, Patrice Caldwell, thank you for emailing me at 3:00 a.m. to tell me how much you loved my story. You have been this book's most fierce champion from the very beginning. I'm eternally grateful for you and your badassery. I can't wait to see what else we accomplish together.

I'm grateful for Pouya, Katherine, Joanna, Meredith, and the entire New Leaf team for being in my corner and being as excited about my career as I am. New Leaf has been my dream agency since I first started exploring the possibility of becoming an author and I still can't believe that I get to be a leaf!

I also give immense thanks to my editor, April Osborn, for gently and gracefully guiding me through the publication of my debut novel. I love that I can completely entrust my characters and stories to you knowing that you will make them the best versions of themselves.

Additional thanks go to the marvelous team at MIRA and Harlequin—Ashley MacDonald in marketing; Justine Sha in publicity; Lindsey Reeder and Abi Sivanesan in digital marketing/social media; Alexandra Niit, cover art director extraordinaire; and everyone else who helped this book reach its full potential.

I must thank my amazingly talented cover artist, Andressa Meissner, for creating a gorgeous cover that completely reflects my story and is so special that I cried tears of joy when I saw it.

My journey to getting this book published has been years in the making and it would not have happened without the kind, supportive, and special people I've met along the way.

To my Here Comes Trouble crew—Mai-Ling, Marlena, Becka, and Amanda—thank you for being there drinking mojitos with me from the very beginning and for making me feel capable whenever I doubt myself.

To my WI crew: The Lizzes, Lorelie, Carla, Carrie, Jen, Tricia, and Molly. Thank you all for making me feel welcome always. A special thank-you to Liz Lincoln for always answering my chaotic texts, letting me vent, and just being the kind of friend who drops off awesome cross-stiches and waffles when I'm having a rough time.

Mil gracias to my amiga hermanas in my LatinxRom crew—Alexis, Priscilla, Mia, Adriana, Sabrina, Angelina, Liana, Diana, and Zoraida—for taking me under your wing, celebrating my milestones as if they are your own, being my biggest cheerleaders, and answering all my dumb questions.

To all the friends I made through Twitter (Denise, Taj, Stacey, Lisa, etc.) thanks for the words and GIFs of encouragement and celebration.

A very, very special thank-you to Author Mentor Match for hooking me up with the greatest mentor ever, Brittany Kelley. Brittany, having you as a mentor has been one of the greatest things to happen to me. You helped me trust in myself and my voice when I was really doubting my abilities. This book would not be what it is without your support and guidance.

And, of course, I would not be here without my family and friends.

Marsh, you know at this point you are more than my best friend. You are my ride or die. Point. Blank. Period.

To my titis, tíos, and many cousins, this book would not exist without you all simply because I wouldn't have any stories to tell. You have all surrounded me with love and laughter for my entire life, which is exactly what inspired this story. But don't go looking for yourselves in the characters because the inspiration doesn't go that far. LOL.

Annie and Marcos, you both inspire me every day to never give up, to keep trying no matter how hard things get. Thank you both for providing me with the opportunity to be the Cool Titi to my loves Ezmi, Isaiah, Israel, and Xavier.

Mom, through your example, you taught me to be strong, resilient, hardworking, forgiving, and caring. I am always in awe of you and so grateful to call you my mother.

To my abuela, who will never get to read this, everything I am is because of you. I love you and miss you with all my heart. Para Siempre.

Finally, I thank you, the reader. Thank you for picking up my book and giving it a chance. I'm so incredibly lucky to share my characters and stories with you. I hope this story was exactly what you needed it to be, whether that be a reflection of yourself and culture, a few hours of entertainment, or anything in between.